It Came from the Trailer Park

Three Ravens Publishing
Chickamauga, GA USA

It Came From The Trailer Park
Is a collective work of contributing authors and Published by Three Ravens
Publishing
threeravenspublishing@gmail.com
P.O. Box 851 Chickamauga, Ga 30707
https://www.threeravenspublishing.com
Copyright © 2021 by Three Ravens Publishing

Publishers Note: This is a collective work of fiction. Names, characters, places, and incidents are a product of the author's imagination. Locales and public names are sometimes used for atmospheric purposes. Any resemblance to actual people, living or dead, or to businesses, companies, events, institutions, or locales is completely coincidental.

Table of Contents

Introduction

"The dread of something after death..."
(Shakespeare, 1609)

Will was on to us. We dread it, alright. But how we love to look.

Just one peep won't hurt. Will it? And Death, Medusa in our mirror, stares us back with unblinking eyes, unflinching gaze, and like Dickens' Ghost of Christmas Present before the midnight fire, Death whispers, "Come closer and know me better."

So, like wary old Scrooge, we take one step. A careful step, mind you. Then another, perhaps a little less careful. Just beyond that door, Death is smiling. The shade of our non-being, the very shadow of our non-existence smiles, extending what might, in some nightmare, pass for a hand. "Come closer. Yes. Yesss! Room for one more."

Oh God, why do we play with dead things? Why do we peek at accidents, poke at roadkill, Google the macabre? I know why: Rehearsal. We're playing the part we know we must play; dancing with the inevitable partner; trying the shroud for size. It's fun. It's comforting. It's truth.

Show me a person who can't face death now and I'll show you a person who won't face death then. Not that death will care (or even notice) whether you face it flat-footed or screaming like a virgin in a cheap horror movie. Still, it's better to play, eh? Better to get used to the idea. That's why you've come to this cadaverous collection, isn't it? You wish to play.

I've killed a lot of people. In movies, I mean, and on television. Would you be surprised to learn that people like to die? Onscreen, that is. Take the word of a guy who does death for a living, everyone wants to die. Repeatedly! I've never met a person who doesn't say, after we've filmed their death scene, "Should we do it one more time? I think I could die better."

Rehearsal.

Close your eyes. Right now. I'll wait. Good. Now, imagine a coffin before you. Nice wood, soft satin, eh? Feel it. The coffin is empty. The room in which the coffin lies is empty. It's just you and the coffin. Go ahead, take a glance 'round to be sure. Yep, you're alone. The coffin empty. The room empty. Go on. No one will ever know.

Lie down.

Comfortable, isn't it? Stretch out your feet. Settle in. Fold your arms. A smile. "This is fun!" See, I told you. Yes. Yesss. Rest there for a moment, just one more moment. In a minute or so you'll climb out all goosebumps and grins, thrilled at your little dark play adventure, and –

SLAM! The lid! BANG! BANG! BANG! BANG! BANG! BANG! Now the solid sound of nails into wood. Now the screeching sound of *your* nails into wood, clawing at the lid in the dark in the coffin in the room in this, the moment you realize, alas, too late I fear, that your time is...now. A childhood rhyme comes dusting down from the attic of old things, and, against your will, lands upon your tongue. It wriggles the ancient words in a dry scream: "The worms go in, the worms go out, the worms...the worms...the worms..." The scream is silent. The box is moving. Soon you will not be.

"Cut!" Relax, my child. It's only a rehearsal - for now.

Enjoy pawing through these putrid pages. Dive into the soft tissue of these ignominious imaginations. No one will know. Feel the material, eh? Don't be afraid to touch the slimy, wet, dead things in here. Your fingers may, after all, find something quite familiar.

Bill Oberst Jr.
Los Angeles, CA
Halloween, 2021

Bill Oberst Jr. is an Emmy Award-winning actor and the recipient of the inaugural Lon Chaney Award For Excellence In Horror Cinema, presented by the Chaney family. His website is https://www.billoberst.com

It Came from the Trailer Park

Eye of the Beholder

By: Mel Todd

" A dim, here are the reports you wanted," the attack coordinator began. "The aerial scouts have finished their reports and our shamans have isolated areas that have abundant supplies of water, wood, and plants to harvest. There are some animals, and the indigenous species is not as prevalent in this area as others."

Shalus looked up from the data of how many had died of starvation this month, pushing platinum tendrils of hair out of his face. He sighed at the numbers and the lack of options. "Is there any information as to the edibility of the plants?"

"The samples returned by the aerials vary. Some were lacking most nutrients, the few pieces of what look like tree fruit or tree seeds, have a tolerable taste, but little that we need. However, there were three plants that taste like the food of the gods and our shamans say if we can come back with seeds, it would grow here."

"That is wonderful news." Shalus frowned. "And the indigenous?"

His coordinator wrung his long triple jointed fingers. "Dangerous in groups. They have weapons that can kill, but our scouts are faster and deadlier than they will ever be. If we attacked directly, they might win; if we raid; they will never have a chance."

"Which means more of our people will die, as will theirs," Shalus frowned.

"Our people are already dying, and we have seen how warlike they are. We have no choice. Their world is so rich, even losing a few thousand of their people will barely be noticed. Their technology is more advanced in flight and weapons, but they seem to have no knowledge of world portals and their data methods are rudimentary." The coordinator set down chips of data. "Here is another overview."

Shalus closed his eyes but nodded. "Send out the *helihe* and *tsnick*. I want fear and destruction sowed. Get the indigenous species to flee the area. If they are killed, and the *tsnick* or *helihe* don't eat them, bring back their bodies. We can study them and see if we can learn anything."

"As you order Adim." The coordinator bowed twice and backed out of the office. Shalus rubbed the bridge of his nose and hoped the scouts could clear out the area fast. Kill the current populace or scare them; it didn't matter to him. He just needed to be able to send in raiding parties to collect as much as they could and too many of his 'raiders' were men who had never fought an organized battle. Their crops had started failing, then famine followed by floods had swept through his region leaving his people desperate. Desperate people didn't really care about anything except survival.

On the other side of the compound the scoutmaster opened the pens where the *helihe* and *tsnick* were held. "Out, you have your keep to earn." He cracked the long whip he always carried. It cracked across the backs of the beasts that slinked out of the two sets of pens. They swirled around each other snarling and yipping as the whip cut through fur.

"You know the orders. Go in, kill, scare, get them to leave that area. Anything you kill you are free to eat. Make sure you do, there won't be any food here for you. Count yourself lucky. If you do well, maybe we won't eat your children."

Pairs of beasts lifted furred and whiskered heads, watching him, eyes dark with hate. "Or die on that strange planet, I don't care. You know the price if you don't come back," he snarled, the whip cracking at the pen that held their cubs.

Shoulders hunched, they nodded as one and turned to look at the portal forming. At the command, they flowed through, silent furred hulks breathing in air that didn't reek of despair.

Cam stretched to her full six foot-two height; bucket of blackberries lifted high in the air. "I shore love my berry sog, but the pickin's a chore," she muttered in a soft southern drawl. Her wheat blond hair was drenched with sweat in the Georgia summer, but either she picked the berries, or the animals did. And she wanted something sweet.

"Another hour 'bout do it I wager." Cam tilted her face to the sun but only held it for a moment. She had chores and studying to do.

A deep growling whine from the nearby kudzu had her setting down her bucket and pulling out the 1911 strapped to her hip. She had extra bullets in her overalls, but the 1911 served to scare away most predators, be they on two legs or four.

"Hello?" She called out, sharp blue eyes scanning the area. Another whine that for all the world sounded like a cry for help.

Moving over to the kudzu, she knelt down expecting to see maybe a fox or worse case a coyote injured under the green leaves. While bears were occasionally seen up here in the foothills of the Blue Ridge Mountains, she'd never had any of them do more than wander across her front yard. And if someone was poaching bears, then not killing them, she'd be having a talk with them.

"I ain't gonna hurtcha. I might be able to help." She spent her life patching up her brother and other animals. It was the reason she was studying to get her vet tech certification. Nothing better she could think of than working with animals. Much better than people.

With the 1911 ready, safety off, in her right hand she pulled away the draping kudzu with her left and froze.

"Holy smokes, what in God's name are you?" She breathed out the words as she stared into two sets of beautiful purple eyes. "I ain't never seen nothing like you. Ya hurt dahling?"

A soft mewl of agreement, and Cam felt her heart tumble. She had never fallen in love, she'd never even had a date. Men didn't like girls like her. They liked girls like Suzy Mae, her cousin. Or at least that's what her good for nothin' brother Bobby Joe liked to remind her.

"Well come on out dahling, I'll see what I can do." She flipped the safety on and backed up, never taking her eyes off the impossible creature.

Cam knew, as the creature emerged chewing on a kudzu leaf with apparent pleasure, that she'd never fall in love more than she just had. As the Georgia sun struck the beast, Cam didn't know whether to sing with joy—she had a passable singing voice—or cry with rage.

The size of a large tiger, it had four eyes, each a rich purple. Two faced forward and two were on the sides of its head. Tall, tufted ears with antenna waving on each side. Built like a mix between a cat and a dog, the structure reminded her more of the pictures of some of the big animals from the Natural History Museum. Its fur was the color of dusk, not gray but not black a blue gray brown that she'd never see outside of the sky. It had a muzzle like a cat but the claws, the very big and scary claws, remained extended as it crawled out.

But all of that paled at the lash marks across its back. Cam had seen enough damage from animal attacks and human, to recognize a weapon versus a claw. And these had been made by a weapon. Even worse maggots had grabbed on to the exposed flesh and were gobbling away.

"Oh dahling, I can help. But it will hurt. Ain't much I can do 'bout that," she said looking at the creature. "Ah don't know whatcha are, but ain't no one need to suffer like that."

The creature gave her a long hard look, then closed its eyes and sunk claws into the ground.

"Huh, well whaddya know." Cam stared at the creature and those claws. Wild animals weren't good about pain, and they sure as heck didn't understand people. But this wasn't any animal she'd ever seen. "Fuck it. Ain't letting no creature walk around with maggots on it."

She pulled off her pack and dug out her first aid kit. While it wasn't one made for animals, it would have to do. Something this big, it had to weigh upwards of a hunnert pounds wasn't something she could carry home to treat.

"You're so beautiful you know that? You escape from a zoo or a lab somewhere?" Cam kept up her soothing chatter as she flicked off the maggots with her knife. The creature just lay there, not purring, but calmer than Cam would have ever expected from a wild animal. Even one she'd never seen nor heard of before. But then she'd only gotten her Associates degree before she had to quit, so she figured there was a lot of stuff in this world she didn't know about. But she knew this creature was hurting.

"Okay, this is going to sound funny, but I don't got no way to stitch you up, and nothing to make it not hurt." She checked the wound again. Deep but not actively bleeding. "So, I'm use some glue to close you up. It's gonna sting like the devil, so don't go hurting me none, kay?"

The creature, it wasn't a cat nor a wolf, so she couldn't come up with a better word, looked at her over its shoulder and nodded before burying its face in the kudzu it was gnawing on.

"Ah swear you almost understand me. Dangedist thang." She refused to think about a predator eating kudzu. Though she did worry about it having an upset stomach. "Okay, dahling, hold on." Cam had her superglue out and after she carefully cleaned each wound, she pulled them together and held them until the glue set. It took a while, but the creature only whined a few times, then kept busy gnawing on the kudzu.

When she finished, you could see the marring, but it looked like a warp in the fur pattern, not a possibly life-threatening injury.

"Well, there you go. Now I wish I could convince you to take it easy and definitely no licking." It stopped from where it had been about to lick the area and hunched down. "You wouldn't like the taste nohow." The shadows had gotten long, and Cam stood stretching her back. "I've got to get going. Wish I knew where you belonged, but for now be careful you hear?" It nodded again sitting on its haunches.

"Well, I never." Cam just grinned. She grabbed her bucket of berries and slowly started backing out, never taking her eyes off the creature. There was being insane, treating a wounded wild animal, and being stupid. Turning your back on a wounded wild animal qualified as stupid. She glanced behind her once, when she swirled her head back to look at the mysterious creature it had disappeared. Cam stood there for a long time, then headed home, quiet and listening for anything about to pounce.

She spent the next two days studying and trying to find that creature on the net. But while she was getting high eighty's on the practice exam, she couldn't find nothing on the beauty she treated. Lost in thoughts about how strange the creature's physiology had been, the noise of two sets of tires driving up pulled her out of her musing.

"Jesus bless, I don't need this today," she muttered and stood out on the porch of her daddy's house watching her uninvited visitors. When her parents died, they left the two-room log cabin in the foothills of the Blue Ridge Mountains to her. They left her brother the house in the city and most of the money. Cam didn't hold it against them. No one thinks they'll die when their kids are barely out of high school. But she got the house her daddy's ma grew up in, and it suited her just fine. Bobby Joe got the house and the fancy college degree. Too bad that boy wanted her to be just like the bimbos he dated, or worse like Suzy Mae. That tweren't ne'er going to happen. Her cousin didn't have the common sense that God gave a squirrel, but she had a figure that made an hourglass blush. Cam knew she didn't have any figure besides that of a rectangle, but she was pretty certain she had more common sense than most men. Something that she was sure would be proved again today.

With a feeling of doom, she watched her brother and Reverend get out of their cars. The two men nodded at each other as they made their way up her paved drive.

Cam set herself at the top of the steps, blocking the way up. If she was lucky, they'd say their piece and leave before she got too annoyed.

"Afternoon," she said, her voice loud in the quiet afternoon.

"Now Camilla, aren't you going to invite us up for tea?" the reverend coaxed, his too big smile, and sparkling eyes as always giving her the heebies.

"Really, Cam. That ain't how a lady's supposed to treat guests," Bobby chided and Cam narrowed her eyes.

"No, but I figured shooting you with rock salt cause you're trespassing might be a bit extreme, this ain't a bad compromise." She crossed her arms. She'd bet three dollars Bobby Jo was here to try to get her to sell the property, and the reverend was here to get donations for his latest pet project.

"Camilla Jones, that isn't any way to treat a servant of the lord. Your ma would be mighty sorrowful about your actions," Reverend Aaron Hayworth protested. "I'm just here looking for time or donations to our mission to Kenya. We sure could use a strong woman like you to help with the fair we're organizing."

"My ma would have held her tongue like any good Christian woman, and she'd have helped until her feet hurt so bad Pa would be massaging them for hours. Pa however would have kicked you off the property. You know he didn't hold with missions, saying you should be ministering to the people here first. Sides, you just want me to come and do the grunt labor that the rest of the congregation has weaseled out of." She didn't move from her stance leaning across the entrance to her porch. If either of them sat down, they'd be here for hours. And she needed to study, darn it.

"Cam, that ain't no way to talk to a man doing God's work. It's just more proof that living out here by yourself like, is making you-"

"I swear to Jesus Bobby Jo, if you say uppity, I'm coming off this porch and testing some of my hog-tying techniques on you." Cam straightened up, narrowing her eyes and taking one step down.

Bobby held up his hands and took a step back. "I'm just saying you might want to be a little sweeter. Look at Suzy Mae. She's got fellas asking her out every night."

Cam's temper flared. She wanted her certification, to get a good job, and not be a single mom in a double wide like half her family. "She shore does," her accent got thicker when her dander went up. "She's got them after her like she's a bitch in heat, and she's about as picky. Now unless you got some reason to be here, both ya, git." She knew she should calm down, but right now she was really thinking about grabbing that double-ought and peppering their asses with rock salt.

"Cam, I'm just trying to look out for you. I got a great offer for this old place. Enough that you could get out of this dump and live closer to the city. And you would haven't to risk this place falling down around you."

"See, Camilla? Bobby Joe's a good brother to you."

Cam felt her blood boil. She'd reshingled the roof by herself. The porch was brand new, and she'd built it. The path to the house was paved with stones she'd dug out of the river herself. All the plumbing was updated, and she loved this one-bedroom cabin.

"I think you boys ought to take yourselves out of here. 'Fraid my patience is darn well spent."

"Now, Camilla Jones—" the reverend said at the same time as Bobby Joe started speaking.

"Cam, it's better for you-"

A loud growl came from the azaleas she had planted along the creek bank. The bushes shook like something huge was in there.

"Bear!" Bobby yelped and went scurrying back to his shiny Escalade while the reverend went whiter than her night shift and backed up to his town car. Both men slammed the doors as something huge and furry peeked out.

"I'll call animal control," yelled the reverend as both men peeled out, leaving dust in their wake.

"Crap, I don't need no bear sniffing around here. I can't afford to be buying new doors cause the bear decides he wants my fish." Cam took two steps backwards and grabbed her 30-06, not the double-ought that held nothing but rock salt.

The cars disappeared down her gravel road. Cam hoped they both got dings on their paint jobs before she shifted her attention to the bush, rifle ready to snap up. There weren't a lot of bears in this area, but it could happen, though not when there was so much food available in the woods. As soon as the motor of the car faded, the rustling increased, and Cam got her rifle ready.

A familiar fuzzy, four-eyed, purple creature stuck its head out of the bush and looked at her.

"Well, I'll be. How did you find me dahling?" She lowered the gun and watched the impossible creature come out. The wounds on its back were still sealed. It slowly moved up to the steps and whined a bit.

"Ah still don't know whatcha are, but you're awfully smart. What are you doing here? Besides rescuing me?"

The creature, she needed to give it a name, really. She'd think on that. But it whined at her and gazed at the gully. The gully flooded in the winter, and dried in the summer, but it acted as an impromptu wall on one side, so she never much minded it. From that gully came another thing.

"Oh my," was all Cam could manage. Where her purple tiger was sleek and almost elegant, this was like a mini rhino with fur and fangs. It reminded her of a drawing she'd see in some of the more fanciful ideas of hell. This would make a good hellhound, except for the damn bear trap on one bleeding swollen foot.

"Daymn Ben Jenkins and his traps. That man never picks them up, and we ain't had no bear attacks in years. But at this rate there's going to a man wearing his traps if this keeps up. Now you just wait here." She shook her finger at both animals, then trotted over to her garage. It wasn't even big enough to hold a compact car much less her truck, though she daydreamed about a motorcycle. But it was organized and had every tool she'd claimed from the house and whatever had been left up here.

"There," she said, grabbing a crowbar and a pair of gloves. A minute later she was standing about two feet from the creature, admiring it. Ugly as hell, but she could see it would be strong and fast, though it didn't follow any of the rules her veterinary books talked about. She also stopped inside the house and got her pet med kit. Maybe it would let her help before running off. On the off chance it might let her brush it, that fur needed brushing in the worst way, she grabbed a brush. Some of the local dogs would come over just to let her brush them. She swore as soon as she was through with school, she'd get a dog and a cat.

The two creatures were where she had left them, the purple tiger standing guard over the hulking rhino-dog. Cam shook her head. She'd have to see if she could get pics, but first she needed to get that trap off its paw.

Cam knelt next to the rhino-dog and looked at it. "This may hurt, so please don't go biting off my head or arm or anything, kay?" She swore the purple-tiger snorted, but it just watched the area around them. There weren't many bird or squirrel sounds, which didn't surprise her. Part of her wanted to run and hide from these two. They looked scary and dangerous, but she'd never been able to resist an animal in pain. She tugged the gloves on and using the crowbar to brace one side she pushed down on the other grunting.

"That man doesn't take care of nothing he owns, darn thing is rusty as can be." She got it clear of the beast's paws. "Okay, pull your paw out now," she murmured, all too aware of its teeth and their proximity to her neck, but she didn't realize just how close they were until she'd closed the trap and sat back.

Cam looked up into a mouth full of fangs and molars and felt her desire to deck the creature flood up. "Ya might want to step back a bit; you're too close." Mostly she was talking to herself, trying to remember it was just an animal and didn't understand how humans viewed large amounts of teeth. To her amazement the beast huffed and hobbled back two steps.

A shaky breath escaped her. "Thanks. Now you want me to look at that?"

The rhino-dog looked at her purple tiger which nodded. The beast sat on its hind haunches, exposing that it was very male and held the injured paw out to Cam.

"Well, I'll be. You two shore are smart. Let's take a look see." She grabbed the med kit, then his paw. To her relief, it didn't look like the bones were broken. The skin was bruised under the fur, and it probably hurt like the dickens, but it wasn't broken. She stared at her med kit thinking. "I'm going to wrap it in this ace bandage. It'll give you some support but should fall off in a day or two or your teeth can pull it off no issue." Cam glanced at them, but they just looked at her, the paw still hanging in midair. "Huh, something else, I tell ya."

With brisk but gentle movements, she wrapped the paw then looked at his coat. It was longer and heavier than the tiger's fur. She was pretty sure it was reddish brown, maybe like an Irish Setter, but it had so much filth coating it. She saw ribs on both of them. Seeing ribs on animals meant they were underfed, especially through coats like that.

"Tell ya what, I got some offal from a few rabbits I shot that I ain't disposed of yet. You can eat that. and I can brush the two of you out, see if there's any then else a worrying you?" Two sets of ears perked up, one long and pointy with tufts, the other round and thick like satellite dishes. Cam laughed with sheer joy and headed back in. There wasn't anything in the world she liked as much as animals. They didn't put hands where hands weren't invited, and they never criticized her about why she wasn't what they thought she should be.

A minute later she was out with a bowl of offal. In theory she was going to make some gravy from it, but she'd been avoiding the messy cleaning up and processing of it to study. Then Bobby Joe, and Reverend, so this was as good a use for it as any.

"Ain't much, but it might help. Kinda funny you chewing on that kudzu, stuff is edible I guess, but definitely not my first choice." Cam set it between them, and it was gone in two bites, one each.

"Sorry kiddos, that's all I got, but I can try to keep extra around." She settled herself down on the bottom step, legs spread and brush ready. There might also have been the shovel she's used to dig up potatoes that morning within arm's reach. "So, who's first?"

The words had barely left her lips before Rhino's body was between her legs almost squirming. She had to go up one step because he was big enough his back was at her head level on the first step.

"Anxious, are ya?" She grinned and started off slowly, and the beast moaned. Cam froze; it sounded like a fancy musical instrument you'd hear in a concert where you had champagne, not beer. He turned and looked at her, his eyes the amber of a tiger. It was such an obvious don't stop she giggled and began to groom him with enthusiasm. He sang to her the entire time. It was like having her own concert, with music she'd ne'er imagined.

His coat was a rich brown red with dark mottling to it, almost as if he had natural camouflage in the patterns. It explained why he'd disappeared into the bushes. "Oh yes, you're a good boy. But come on, Rhino. It's Twilight's turn now."

Both animals looked at her, and she shrugged. "I like My Little Pony, you're Purple, hence Twilight. And you look like somewhere in your ancestry there was a rhino. So, unless you want to tell me your names, you're stuck with those. Now come on, be a good boy and let Twilight in."

Rhino sang, the mournful sound, but moved and flomped on the grass rolling, messing up all her work. Cam just laughed, typical animals. Get them groomed and pretty and all they wanted to do is roll around.

Twilight moved between her legs and set a massive head on her leg, eyes closing. "Darned if I can figure out what you are, beside gorgeous." She began to groom, and the purr Twilight let out vibrated through her body. It felt like her soul was realigned as she sat there in the dusk and brushed the strange beast.

She had just finished the tail, when both animals jerked their heads up and looked to the depths of the mountains. Their shoulders slumped and they stood, walking to the edge of the gulley. One last glance back at Cam, then they disappeared into the gathering shadows.

"I swear, I hope those two are okay." Cam signed and went to finish prepping the rabbits and figuring out how to avoid her brother and the Reverend until they'd forgotten the strange "bear."

Twilight and Rhino flowed back through the dusk. The offal had been excellent, fortified with the vines that carried nutrients almost gone in their world. They stopped and got a few more mouthfuls of it, hiding it in their cheeks before slipping back through the portal.

"Report," barked out the scoutmaster and the two animals cringed, making them look smaller than they were. "What happened to you? Why are your coats brushed?" The scoutmaster strode out from behind the feed bins. "What did you find there? Have you achieved your objectives?"

~Yes. Scared away. Ate livestock. Found vines.~ Rhino responded, straining to hide Twilight in his shadow.

"And your coats? Are you consorting with those we must kill?"

Twilight and Rhino froze, not sure how to answer this.

"You two, get these creatures in their pens. No food until I figure out what is going on. Account for all the beasts. I'll be crossing over to inspect their actions myself."

Cringing Twilight and Rhino let themselves be dragged while their packs howled and cried. Twenty were still out in the wonderful place. But their cubs, their cubs were still here in pens, crying for their parents.

Locked up once more, close enough to smell, but not touch, Twilight carefully spat the vine she'd packed in her cheeks over to pack members who had been punished longer than her. They ate slowly while she looked at the opening to freedom. If they could get free.

Her mind drifted to the strange one, the one with kind words and touch. She had feared the wounds would fester and she would die far from her cubs and mate. But instead, she received tenderness and caring. Twilight couldn't remember ever receiving that from anyone not pack.

More lashes, and whimpers of pain, but they had learned not to fight back. Any measure of resistance, and you were killed and fed to your pack, who ate because they knew, from bitter experience, they would get no other food.

She longed to talk to Rhino and wasn't that an odd name for her mate. But all Scoutmasters could hear the speech. So, they waited as others slunk back, many with information, and most with food packed in their cheeks.

Twilight counted their numbers again. So few. She looked at the bleak sky and thought of the lushness on the other side. Maybe.

Shifts changed and she purposefully rolled in the dirt to muss up her fur as she listened to the plans. The scout that had seen them had not passed on any information, so their indiscretion had not been noted.

Two changes of shifts as more scouts came in and were shoved into cages. A small chain was formed to move the snuck in vines to the pair nearest the cubs. They shared what they had managed to sneak in, as not even the cubs were being fed. Not that the keepers had much more food.

Twilight chafed, but there was nothing they could do. Not here, where every word could be overheard. But for the first time in a generation, she felt a spark of hope.

Cam had successfully avoided both her brother and his desire to get her to sell her house, but the Reverend had talked her into doing three hours of manning the booth with Suzy Mae selling raffle tickets. Oh well. Suzy Mae would sell ten times what she did and spend the entire time telling Cam she'd only be pretty *if*.

With a snort of annoyance, Cam hiked through the woods hunting for some edible mushrooms, more berries, or to see if any of her rabbit traps had snagged a meal or two.

There was a weird low-pitched buzzing off towards one of the dry creek beds, that had dried up after a landslide had shifted one of the river tributaries, but no one had really cared back then.

"I really hope they ain't trying to set up another rave site. Ain't no place near enough to draw power." That had happened before, and the idiots had lugged in a generator and darn near burned down the mountain.

Hefting her harvesting bag up she headed that way, just in case. Fire sucked for everyone.

There was a bunch of shouting in a language she didn't recognize, which didn't mean much. She could order a beer in Spanish, but that topped out her languages. The words and sounds got louder, and one of them made her frown. She'd spent enough time around her brother's friends being show-off assholes that she knew the sound of a whip cracking. She crouched and moved through the shrubs to where the noise was coming from. She knew how to be quiet when she wanted to.

On her hands and knees, she peered through the bushes, still expecting to see a bunch of teenagers or stupid college kids setting up to drink too much beer and play their music so loudly it became a wash of noise, not notes. She scanned the clearing, but there wasn't a bunch of kids. It took her a second to see the man standing there, and her breath caught in her throat. He was tall, at least six-three, with no shirt, so she could see the muscles rippling over his chest and stomach. His thick silvery hair was caught back at the base of his neck. His face looked like it was chiseled out of marble, as his skin all but glowed in the summer sun. She felt her body flash with sudden interest.

Then the whip flashed up and back down on what had to be a pack mate of Twilight, cutting into fur that looked like it hadn't ever seen a brush.

Every emotion in her body went from interest to rage so deep that her vision tinged red. Cam was up and charging like a linebacker, before he could get the whip back up to strike the cowering animal again. She hit him like he was Lester Johnson, who in eighth grade had pulled her top off in class displaying her Hello Kitty bra to everyone.

Cam rarely forgave anything.

The man went flying with a startled oof, and Cam sprang up as soon as they quit rolling from her attack.

"I donna know who you are mister, but 'round here we don't take to people beatin' animals," she snarled as she stood, ready to teach him exactly what being beaten felt like.

The man stood, and her eyes widened. His attractiveness had vanished when he saw him whipping that creature, which obviously had not been trying to attack. But she hadn't expected eyes with horizontal pupils, ears that were almost flat holes against his skull, and an extra thumb on each hand.

"Jumping Jehoshaphat, what are you?"

The man spat a stream of syllables at her and lunged with the whip.

Cam reached out and caught it, expecting him to overpower her. He had at least two inches on her and looked like he spent more time working out than working, but his arm stopped moving.

"I don't think so. Ain't no one going to beat any creature while I'm here," she warned.

He spat more syllables tugging at his arm, but she held it. Not with ease, but the big dogs in the kennel gave her more problems. A fist swung at her face, and she dropped his arm to block, then came back with a haymaker of her own. Cam had never done well with the girly stuff, and by God, if you were going to swing at her, she'd hit back. He missed her by a Coke bottle. She didn't. He crumpled to the ground and didn't move.

"What in the world?" Cam stared at the unconscious man, or monster, or maybe alien? She didn't really know, but a soft whuff pulled her to look at the beast behind her.

The fur was a lighter shade of purple than Twilight, and only one of the lashes had broken the skin. But she had no doubt it was the same type of creature as Twilight.

"Oh my," she whispered as she looked past the creature into a ripple that didn't display the North Georgia mountains, but instead something out of a big movie production. She moved a bit closer, peering in. The air coming out of this portal thingy smelled and tasted stale and dry. The land was red and dusty, looking like it was from some place in Africa, and maybe she would have believed that, if not for the reddish sun in the sky and the broken moon hanging next to it. Scattered on the surface of this ugly place were tents, metal buildings, pens, and people scurrying to and fro. But no kids, no smiles, and everyone looked like they were waiting for a whip to come down on their backs.

"What in the world?"

~It is my world. We are planning on invading.~

A soft voice spoke in her mind, with weird pauses and a flavor to words that made no sense. Cam found herself sitting on her rump, staring at the beast.

"Did, did ya just talk to me?" The more stressed she got the heavier her accent, and she didn't think she'd ever had as many shocks before in her life.

~You are the one that helped Thinks like Wind?~

Cam blinked at the being and swallowed past a suddenly dry mouth. "If ya mean Twilight, well yeah. Her and Rhino needed some care is all."

The beast tilted its head, looking at her. ~They have our cubs. They keep them, hurt them to make sure we obey.~

It was odd. There was no anguish in the words, no begging for sympathy; just a flat statement that threatened to tear Cam's heart out.

"Now that ain't right. Ain't right to be holding chillun's as leverage." Cam avoided most politics, but she knew all too well the evils of the Department of Family Services. How they'd step in and just take kids, just cause they had some dirt or a bruise or two. Kids played and got dirty and hurt. It was called being kids.

Cam glanced over at the alien man lying on the ground, but he didn't rouse, though his chest rose and fell regularly. She'd take that as a good thing. Cam crawled under a bush near the portal and stared at the other world. Her overall impression was red and dust, but now she paid attention to the layout of the town, but it wasn't, not really. It reminded her more of the little cities that sprang up around rodeos. Everyone had their horses in shared pens and there was always some guy bitching at another about parking in his spot. Not a town, but a few permanent buildings that the fairgrounds owned.

But the rushing around and patterns screamed military to her more than rodeo. Which was too bad, an alien rodeo might have been kinda neat. "You're invading us?"

~Yes. We are scheduled to attack tomorrow.~

"Huh," Cam muttered, still watching. "Don't you have females?"

~I am what you call a female, in that I carry live young in me for a period of time.~ The voice sounded so matter of fact, not anywhere near as confused, excited, or terrified as Cam felt.

"I meant them. No women?" Even at rodeos you'd have girls about. They were just as horse crazy as guys.

~They are regarded as too weak. Women are fragile, and they do not let them go to war. They take care of the children.~ The creature lay next to her, and it smelled of burnt applewood. An unusual smell. But Cam was much too busy processing what she had said.

"And you can't be free until you rescue your cubs?"

~We will not risk our children.~ This time there was a bit of a growl in the words and Cam smiled as she looked back at the guy laying on the ground, still not moving.

"Perfect. Can you tell your, well the rest of you, that we'll get your cubs free? But you'll have to help us."

~If you free our cubs, we'll be yours for life.~

"Meh, we don't hold with the idea of slavery none. We'll figure it out." There wasn't anything right about doing this to animals, much less people, and by her reckoning, iffen you could talk, you were people. "What time tomorrow?"

The creature lifted her head to the sky, then at the portal. ~I believe before your sun is above the tree line, but that might be wrong.~

"No worries. I got this, Sparkle. You going to be okay if I skedaddle? I got plans to make."

The beast looked at the downed man, then back at Cam. ~Sparkle?~ A weird chuff. ~I will play injured. He will believe it.~

"Good. And you're a beautiful girl, Sparkle. Believe that, okay?" With that parting, Cam moved back out of the way, grabbing her stuff, and disappeared into the undergrowth, leaving the strange being behind. But she had a plan, and she'd be damned if it wouldn't work.

Twenty minutes later she was back at the house and had everything she needed. She reached down and pulled out her secret weapon—the church phone book for the ladies' auxiliary. Everyone knew they ran the whole town, and she'd kept in their good graces by working the church festivals. Ma had been the secretary for three terms. She had paid her dues and was calling it in. And she'd be starting with her Aunt Maribelle, Suzie Mae's ma.

"Auntie Maribelle?" She kicked her breath up a bit. Maribelle couldn't resist running to the rescue for anyone, and she knew it drove her crazy that Cam had never needed rescuing.

"Camilla? What is wrong?" Anxiety laced her aunt's voice and for a second Cam felt a sliver of guilt, but she had to rescue those animals. Besides, no Georgian was going to stand being invaded a second time. Once was enough.

"I hate to admit it, but I need y'alls help. All the ladies and even the menfolk."

A sharp intake of breath on the other end of the phone. "Camilla, you tell me what's going on right this second."

Cam had to close her eyes for a minute. That voice sounded so much like her ma's that the tears she'd been trying to fake threatened to become real.

"Yes'm." She'd thought this through carefully. It wasn't a lie, but it wasn't the truth. "There's some people coming that are planning on causing some trouble here, and they're going to be hurting some pretty animals." Cam thought they were gorgeous, so it wasn't a lie. "They think we're a bunch of yokels that will be easily intimidated and give them anything they want. They think we're easy marks to being invaded"

Cam knew playing that card was risky. Lots of the older folk still had a knee jerk reaction to invaders or revenuers. Made no sense to her, but she wasn't lying. Just hoped she wasn't wrong.

Getting a bunch of her friends and townsfolk killed would be wrong. But calling up the army or the police or even the national guard and say what? *Hi I have talking animals that say some weird guys from another place are about to invade us.* If she was lucky, they'd hang up on her. Worse they might send someone to see if she was on drugs, then what would she do.

"Are these furriners?" Maribelle asked, her voice going hard.

"Yes'm. They are from someplace totally different than Georgia. Not even this continent."

"Stupid furriners, always thinking they can come here and do whatever they want. We'll show them. Southerners take pride in our hospitality, but don't think you can ruin things and not pay consequences. Just tell me when and where child, and I'll make sure everyone is there."

Cam had forgotten about the bunch of illegals, from Russia of all places, that had squatted in a house and totally destroyed it. Maribelle would never forgive any foreigner for destroying a house on the Historic Register.

"Thanks, Auntie Maribelle. Tell them to come loaded. They'll have weapons, but I'm not sure what," Cam said slowly, the gravity of what she was doing registering.

"Sweet child, you don't get to be my age without knowing how to fight. We'll be there and any foreigners that think about hurting animals and invading our lands is in for a rude awakening. Now get going, child. Call your brother; I've got women to call."

Before Cam could even reply, Maribelle had hung up the phone, and Cam knew if she called back the line would be busy. Maribelle didn't believe in these fancy new cellphones. Steeling herself, she called Bobby Jo.

"Why hello sister of mine. You ready to sell that old place?" Cam rolled her eyes. The first words out of his mouth were that.

How much was someone offering him? Whatever, it didn't matter right now.

"I need your help. Got some people planning on coming out behind my place tomorrow and causing problems. They've been scoping the place out and are planning on doing an invasion thing."

"A home invasion on my sister? I don't think so. What time are they going to be there?" His voice had snapped from wheedling good old boy to hard and decisive. "Do they know you're alone?"

"I don't think they expect anyone to stop them. And they've got a bunch of animals they've been mistreating too. I found out roughly what time they'll be here tomorrow."

"Dogfighting? Now that's just wrong. Me and the boy's will be there tomorrow. How many you think are coming?"

Cam chewed on her lip. "Well, they've got about 30 animals penned, but I don't think more than a hundred or so?" She wasn't positive, but that camp hadn't been that big.

"Those assholes won't know what hit them. I'll be there. You make sure your shotgun is loaded, and door locked. You sure you don't want to come stay in town?" He sounded concerned, and Cam's heart softened a bit.

"Naw, I'm good. Going to load my shotgun with slugs, and I'll be ready iffen anyone does." They talked a minute more, giving him the location details before he hung up. She stood there for a long time, planning. As she was the only one who had any idea what they'd be facing, it was up to her to be prepared for everyone.

Cam was up and moving before the sun crested the Blue Ridge mountains to the east. She lugged two huge duffle bags and her shotgun with her. She'd spent the day getting ready, and she'd done everything she could think of. But if the aliens had blaster rifles or something, they were screwed. Then, she'd be calling 911 and the FBI or ATF. ATF wasn't good for much, but if you reported you found an active still, they showed up faster than a goose pooped.

She put the bags down in the brush and opened one of them up pulling out two plastic grocery bags full of brown round objects. Cam had started to collect them for a craft project she never quite got around to starting, no matter how often she told Aunt Maribelle that she'd have it before Thanksgiving; for the last three Thanksgivings. But Sweet Gum tree seeds would work just as well as anything else and give her animals a reason to avoid that area. Stepping on them hurt.

With quick movements, time was running out, she covered the area where the last portal had appeared with the seed pods, then scrambled back into the covering.

"I really hope she was right about the timing," Cam muttered as she heard people coming up through the mountains. She scooted back out from under the bushes and moved to intercept.

There was an old logging road that came up below the clearing, and Cam figured that was where most people would drive up. Even being quiet, cars made a shit ton of noise, and she glanced back hoping the portal hadn't formed yet.

"Shush. Ya'll sound like a pack of hogs rampaging round here," she ordered in a low growl as she looked at the people showing up.

Bobby Jo looked around with the Reverend and Aunt Maribelle right behind him. "Well Camilla? We're here. Where are these invaders you've been talking about?"

"Well, iffen you don't keep your voice down, they're going to hear you. So maybe shush your mouth before you ruin everything." Cam had to fight not to shout. Shouting at her brother just came naturally.

"Now Camilla, is that any way to talk to your brother?" the reverend protested, looking affronted on her brother's behalf.

"Now, she can talk to her brother any way she wants. But Camilla couldn't you dress a bit cuter? Look at how Suzy Mae is dressed, cute and practical."

Cam glanced over at her cousin and sighed. Suzy Mae, with her curvy figure and great chest, was dressed in form fitting camo cargo pants, a top tied at the waist, and a hunting vest over it. She looked adorable especially with her compound bow and quiver of arrows. Cam still wore her overalls, had her 1911 on her hip and a shotgun slung across her back, with her hair in a ponytail.

"Right now, that ain't what's important. We've got invaders to deal with. " Cam saw more and more people coming and swallowed at how many of the townsfolk came. "Wow. Everyone came out?"

Maribelle crossed her arms and glared at her. "Girl, I think you dress horribly and that you need a man to treat you like a queen, but don't think we don't recognize how hard you've worked. Your momma and daddy would be right proud of you." She cast a look at Bobby Joe. "You need to work on being a better human."

Cam felt the heat rising in her face, and she didn't know what might have been said if she hadn't heard a strange pop and words in her head.

~We are coming.~

"Shit, they're coming," she said and pulled up the shotgun spinning around.

"Camilla Jones, if your mother heard you, she would wash your mouth out," snapped the reverend, but he pulled around the rifle crouching as did most of the town.

"Next clearing. Be careful and don't hurt none of the beasts. They're my friends. They won't attack us. But I need to get inside and rescue their cubs."

"Wait? What beasts? And inside where? Camilla?" Multiple voices hissed questions at her, but Cam ignored them and headed right for the shrubs. This time she didn't crouch but swung the duffle up on her shoulder. She'd need it on the other side.

"Be careful and don't get killed." Guilt ate at her again, but she figured she'd drown it in Clyde's home brew if they lived. Hopefully if this became an issue, they'd have proof.

She reminded herself that surprise was the best weapon. With that she burst out of the bushes screaming the best battle cry she could think of. "Here comes LEEROOOY J.....!" The rest of the word was lost as she charged the emerging aliens.

~She's coming~ whispered in her mind in multiple voices, multiple levels of belief. But Cam fought to keep her feet moving forward, because she was scared senseless. Out of the portal streamed two columns of men, all armed with long swords, and a long stick with prongs on it. The aliens, all inhumanely beautiful yet wrong, spied her. They shouted out in a language she didn't know and charged her.

~Be careful, they want to kill you.~

That she had already figured out as she saw the snarls on their faces. It made it easier to pull up the shotgun and fire. The slug slammed into his chest and blew out the back as she chambered another round. The explosion of sound stilled the battlefield as the invaders looked at her with shock. Then they started screaming in their language and slashing at her. They were too close to use the gun, and Cam could hear her friends and family behind her cussing, and sharp cracks of gunshots. Cam ducked a swing and the guy stopped, an arrow in his skull, then fell backwards.

"I got you, Cam. Go!" Suzy Mae had never said sweeter words as Cam charged towards the portal.

~Here, help us.~

There were more aliens, though on their home soil maybe they weren't aliens. Either way she headed towards the pens, the duffle clanging on her back.

A few aliens were whipping the cat and rhino beasts that were trying to get to the pups. She had no idea what they were saying and didn't care. She charged in yelling.

"Get away from them," her voice a fierce roar. Cam realized she was moving fast and felt oddly light. Part of her realized gravity must be less here, but most of her was focused on the crying, tiny cubs. The whip cracked in the air, and she swung the duffle at one alien, hitting him solidly in the middle. He flew backwards like a horse had kicked him, but more were coming.

She fumbled in the duffle, trying to find the big bolt cutters she'd grabbed. They'd work as well as a club right now. She grabbed one of the squirt bottles first and grinned. Taking a deep breath, she whirled and squeezed it right in the face of the oncoming attacker. A cloud of cayenne pepper blasted into his face as she stepped to the side, eyes tightly shut.

He started to scream, and she headed a few steps closer to the cages, pulling the duffle with her.

~What did you do to him?~ A horrified voice asked in her head.

Cam cracked open one eye and saw others looking at the man lying on the ground screaming.

"Huh, it worked. Spicy powder. Burns like crazy." The bolt cutters were now needed, and she used them, making quick work of the cages. Running around like a headless chicken, she tried to release all the beasts she could see.

A scream of outrage came behind her, and she turned as a whip cracked and searing pain slashed across the left side of her face. A scream ripped from her throat as her knees gave.

"Nobody hurts my sister," came a bellow from the portal and the alien's head exploded, then she heard the crack of Bobby's favorite .30-06.

Cam forced open her eyes, but she couldn't see anything out of the left eye. Not now. She had to finish. She wanted to curl up and cry, maybe beg Suzy Mae for some of her fun drugs, anything to make it quit hurting. Instead, she levered herself to her feet and finished. The beasts swirled around her in a wash of fur, fangs, and claws. Cubs dangled from every mouth as they ran back to the portal.

Bobby Joe was standing there watching out for them as she ran back into less mayhem than she expected. Bodies lay on the ground, Maribelle stood in the middle, a baseball bat in her hand, and aliens kneeling before her.

"Aunt Maribelle, you okay?"

Maribelle looked at her and nodded sharply. "Better than you are. Get that seen to. Doc is over there. But we need to talk to these folks. Any ideas?"

Dizzy with pain and adrenaline Cam tried to look around. "Twilight? Rhino? Sparkle? Can you help?" Doc Rheen, the local vet came over and grabbed me.

"You need to sit down, Cam. Let me look at that. Maribelle here has Sheriff Glen on the way. They'll take care of it."

"Don't hurt them. They had to be rescued," she muttered as she sat. Warm fur brushed against her, and her hands found the pelt of Twilight.

"We won't. Trust us. We got this."

Cam leaned back and closed her other eye as she heard more footsteps and discussions. She ignored all of it and focused on the feeling of Twilight's rumbles.

Two months later.

Cam sat on the front porch of her house, a patch over her eye as she flipped through the college catalog. Doc Rheen said he'd sponsor her to get into Vet med school now that she had the money to afford it. But first she needed her degree.

She'd never thought Cam Jones would ever have a bachelor's degree. A whuffing sound made her look up and smile at Rhino and Twilight laying on the front lawn, two adorable pup-cubs at their feet.

Maribelle, once she had Sparkle translating for her, had identified the leader, some guy named Shalus, and cracked him open like a kid stealing cookies at church. Half the congregation almost fell over laughing when they realized the invaders were looking for kudzu and poison ivy. It hadn't taken Maribelle but fifteen minutes to set up a trade agreement. Cam got five percent of everything as the portal was technically on her land and she'd stopped the invasion. The aliens paid in rhodium, platinum, and black opals, all of which they had in abundance. In return Maribelle had a fresh, mulched, and cooked kudzu trade going and had even figured out what fertilizers they needed to get their soil revived. Apparently, they had never advanced into agriculture.

Cam just let them run it. She had two friends that were delighted to be here. She'd passed the vet tech exam and could start working on her degree. And best of all, Bobby Joe wasn't pestering her to sell the land and Aunt Maribelle wasn't comparing her to Suzy Mae.

It totally made losing an eye worth it.

It Came from the Trailer Park

Famous

By Kevin Steverson

Chapter 1

S lider Jones looked around. He wrinkled his nose. "What in the hell is that smell, Marty?"

Marty had his hand over his mouth and nose, so his voice was muffled. "It wasn't me. I had collards fer lunch with them pork chops Granny cooked, but even that wouldn't make a fella smell like he done died."

Slider looked all around, the LED light clipped to the brim of his worn ballcap splayed across the bushes, tree trunks, and the leaves up high. He put the cheesecloth back on the blue barrel and made sure the rope holding it on was tight. The one beside it was already covered.

He pinched his nose and said, "That dang smell gets into the mash and the next batch of shine won't be worth a nickel a jar."

"Well, it aint ready to run yet, so we aint got a choice. We can't seal the barrel."

"I know. Reckon we should slip off into the woods and see if can we find out what it is?"

Marty sat down on an overturned bucket. "You can go look iffin you want to, Slider. I'll stay right here until you get back."

"Chicken."

"Bwahk," Marty said, in a pretty good imitation of a chicken. "Ain't no shame in my game. That's a damn Bigfoot, sure as I'm sittin' here. This is as far as I'm willing to go up in these hills with that smell lingering."

"You think so?" Slider asked. He scratched under his beard. "Hell, you might be right. Lotta folks been talkin' about it again."

"Mary-Lou Ginfield said one took off with a goat," Marty said, "ran through her backyard and tore the clothesline off the poles when it done it. Said her drawers were all over the yard. Well, she didn't say that part, Fred Perkins did."

"Them's the only woman's drawers ol' Fred is ever gonna see these days," Slider said.

"I don't know 'bout that," Marty argued. "I mean, what in tarnation was he doing over at a widow's house at three in the morning, anyway?"

Slider pointed at his cousin and said, "Good point. Ol' Fred is doing the doings. I bet ya money on it."

"More power to him, I say," Marty agreed. "Get what you can get, when you can get it. At least she can cook. Everybody digs into her chicken at the church gatherings."

Slider sniffed a few times. "Whatever it was, it's fading now. Either it moved on or the wind shifted. Hell, it might have been something from the government compound. It's only a mile or so from here."

"Now I'm thinkin' you might be right," Marty said. "There's some secret squirrel shit what goes on behind those fences. Ain't nobody local knows what it is. Not even Sheriff Tanner and his buncha deputies."

Slider took his hat off and ran his sleeve across his forehead. The light played crazily in the dark. "I hear ya. When the dang law don't know what's going on, it aint good. Well, I mean 'bout normal stuff. Not making a batch of shine and runnin' it all over the county. Or…even a patch of wacky-terbacky like the Lowens boys have, next valley over."

"I heard they make good money," Marty said. "Still, it seems to me, shine won't get you near the jail time dang drugs will get ya."

"Yeah. It don't make no sense to me, but some like it."

Slider grabbed his shotgun and turned to go back up the steep trail to his truck, parked out of sight off the dirt road above them. Marty followed right behind him.

Two nights later, Slider and Marty stared at the wreckage of the still site. The big copper pot was dented and lay on its side, the top dozens of feet away. The rocks forming the base and home for the gas burner were all over the place. Both barrels were tipped over and all but empty.

"Damn Revenuers done got us," Marty lamented.

Slider stepped over the bucket Marty sat on a few days prior and looked around. It was late in the afternoon but still daylight. What he was looking for wasn't there. Something else was.

He sniffed to verify what he thought and said, "Marty. Don't say another word. Just turn around and go back up the trail. Now."

Marty shut his mouth, turned, and started moving. It wasn't often he heard Slider sound this serious. Whatever it was, he could ask once they made it back to the truck. The box of empty jars in his hands clinked against each other as he hurried. Slider walked backwards, shotgun gripped tight, while looking all around.

Without talking, Marty put the box in the back, making sure it was wedged between the cab and the spare tire laying in the bed. He threw a heavy moving blanket over it and they both got in the truck. Slider fired it up, put it in gear, and fishtailed down the dirt road for a quarter mile. Marty held on to the *oh shit* handle while his rear end grabbed for the seat like a pair of vice grips.

They were nearly to town when Marty got up the nerve to ask, "What the hell had you spooked like that? Man, my heart is still beating a hundred miles an hour."

"I looked for axe marks, or sledgehammer blows, pickaxe, …anything," Slider explained.

"And…?" Marty asked when his cousin didn't continue.

"There weren't none. Things were dented but there weren't no cut marks, no holes…Nothing."

"Well, what *did* you see?"

"I saw footprints."

"Combat boot lookin' prints? Them damn revenuers wear camo and army boots."

"No. You aint heard me right. I saw *footprints*. Big 'uns. Twice the size of my own. Five toes on 'em and all."

They were both quiet for a moment, each reflecting on what was said.

"I knew it!" Marty shouted, breaking the silence. "I knew that sumbitch was real!" He slapped his palm on the dashboard. "We're gonna be famous. We got to call the dang county newspaper, they run one every couple months or so, or channel two thousand and four on the ROKU…or something. This is big. This is real big."

"Are you crazy?" Slider asked. He gave his cousin a sideways look. "You want to take someone to our still site? So, we can be all: Look at these prints. Here's proof. Put some cement in 'em and make a copy or whatever y'all do." He shook his head. "Ya dang fool. You wanna go to jail?"

"Well, what do we do?"

"I don't know," Slider admitted. "I know this, though. We need to figure out what we're gonna do about getting those hundred gallons complete. Norman McGarner is expecting us to deliver them by the end of the month. We got less than three weeks."

"Norman is gonna be pissed," Marty said, "'cause ain't no way we can run shine in our old spot. And we need forty more gallons. I mean, we got our old set up we can use if there's actual holes in the pot or the thumper. We can get the pieces out of the back of the barn loft and dust 'em off, but we need somewhere else to run it. I ain't tryin' to meet one of them damn things face to face."

"We gotta find somewhere on that same creek," Slider argued. "You know good and well it's the water what makes the difference in a good jar and a great jar of shine. Hell, plenty of folks know how to make mash. There's some with the same recipe we use, I don't doubt. It's the water coming out of that mountain spring makin' ours the best around."

Marty was quiet. Slider knew he was trying to figure a way around it. They couldn't risk losing Norman's business. It allowed them to run it and sell to one person by the gallons and not sell jars to folks all over the area, risking one of them running their jaws and getting busted.

Marty sighed and said, "We gotta hunt us a Bigfoot, don't we?"

* * * * *

CHAPTER 2

Marty leaned his head back and finished his can of Busch Light. It was not his usual beer, but it was on sale. Slider watched him and shook his head. Ol' Marty could go through some beer.

They were in Marty's barn, in the back corner. The stall had been claimed by Marty as his man-cave. Right now, it didn't look like one. The pink edged chalkboard hanging on the wall ruined any semblance of a man's…well, anything. Slider studied the drawing.

"I don't know," Slider said. He scratched the side of his face and then smoothed his beard. "The last time we went with one of your ideas, we dang neared lost all our fishing gear."

"This is different," Marty argued. "This ain't a boat made of two-by-fours and particle board. Besides, that dang wood stain was on there thick enough it should have kept the wood dry."

"I'm just glad we didn't get in the boat right then," Slider said. "We went back for the cooler, and by the time we were back to the dock, it was sinking. We caught pure hell dragging it up the bank."

"Yeah…It was heavy."

"How bout you let me do the planning?" Slider suggested. "I'm not sayin' none of your plans have ever worked…I'm just sayin'."

Marty walked over to the chalkboard and wiped it off with the sleeve of his shirt. "You're probably right. A big-ass Sasquatch would tear apart a live hog trap… And I don't reckon we could get my tractor in there to use the bucket to dig the pit."

"Not down by the creek," Slider agreed. "Maybe we can dig one on the edge of an open field, disguise it and lure one there."

"I hope you're planning on using a barrel of mash to lure it, 'cause I sure ain't gonna be the bait."

"Come on Marty. It worked before."

"That was for a black bear. The dang thing only weighed about four hundred pounds. Nothing to that." He popped another can, drained three quarters of it, and wiped his mouth. "I ain't gonna be the bait for a Bigfoot."

"Come on Marty," Slider said. He started laughing before he finished what he was going to say. He laughed harder, and it took him a few minutes before he could talk.

"What in the hell was you going to say?" Marty asked when he calmed down a little.

Slider managed to get it out. "I was going to say we could go to the zoo over in Greenville and see could we get some kinda scent from the gorillas there. Or chimpanzees or whatever."

"Scent? You mean like doe urine or..." Marty's voice trailed off. His eyes widened. He threw his near empty can at Slider.

"You lost your damn mind! Ain't no way I'm gonna wear something like that. You trying to put a Bigfoot in rut? Damn thing will pick me up and run off to his cave or whatever." He shook his head in disgust and muttered, "Do all kind of unmentionables to me. I won't ever walk right again."

Slider laughed even harder.

"Some kind of cousin you are. You ain't right, I don't care if we are some kin. Hell naw, I ain't fixin' to be a Sasquatch's plaything. How 'bout you go fu..."

A small voice interrupted him. "Daddy, can I have my chalkboard back yet?"

Slider sipped his beer and giggled while Marty got the chalkboard down for his daughter. The glances from Marty didn't help in stopping them.

A pile of cans later, they had a plan. "Ok," Slider said. "So, we put five gallon buckets of mash out about fifty yards apart leading up to the shipping container, and we put the last in the way back of it. When the Bigfoot ducks in...crawls in, whatever, we jump down and close the doors. Then we call the law."

"What about the fact we used mash to lure him? Won't Sheriff Tanner try and get us for having it?"

"Naw," Slider said. "He won't say nuthin'. There aint gonna be no still lying around and getting pictures taken of it. He'll know it's good mash, but he won't mention it. The Bigfoot in the box is all anyone will be concerned with."

"If you say so," Marty said. "We best to gettin' some mash started. It'll need a few days to get right. Besides, we need to empty that container of all the truck parts, old lawnmowers, the washer, the 'fridge, six broken chainsaws, weed eater motors, both those..."

"Yeah," Slider interrupted. "We gotta empty it. Then we can use your tractor to help push it up on the trailer so we can move it as close as we can to that area. Not exactly by the trail to our still site, but close enough that a Squatch can smell it."

They drank another six pack apiece, while they unloaded the shipping container. They managed to get it loaded up on the flatbed trailer Marty used to haul his old truck to mud bog competitions years ago.

It sat behind his barn these days. The modern builds by folks with "Daddy's Money" started winning everywhere about five years ago. It wasn't worth competing, the same as dirt track racing, nowadays. Money won.

"I'm gonna crash on the couch in your barn," Slider said. "I've had one or two more than I needed to drive to my place."

"Alright," Marty said. "There's some water in the fridge. Be careful when you shut it. You need to poke the seal in all the way around the door. It won't stay shut, so scoot that cinder block back in front of it."

"Thanks. I'll do it. We'll move the container in the morning. Early. Say, about ten or eleven?"

"Sounds good. We'll get us some lunch at the Shaky Table and Wobbling Chairs. Tomorrow's lunch deal is frog legs 'cause it's Wednesday."

"Sounds good to me."

* * * * *

CHAPTER 3

The next morning, Slider woke up, blinking in the light coming in from the open doors. Chickens scratched in front of the barn. The dust kicked up, danced, and sparkled in the beam of sunlight shining in.

Slider sat up and ran his fingers through his hair. He smacked his lips and frowned. "Tastes like a mouse ran through my mouth and left a pile of pellets behind," he said out loud.

No one was around to hear him. Marty hadn't come out of his doublewide yet. It was only 10:30 in the morning. No self-respecting shiner would be up this early. A part timer…maybe. Those guys had jobs or farms to keep up. Not Slider and Marty.

He and his cousin ran shine for a living. They sold at least a hundred gallons a month at a hundred dollars per gallon. The man they sold it to put in pint jars and sold those for twenty-five dollars each. Slider and Marty had talked about selling by the pint, but it would mean taking a bigger risk when dealing with so many people. Besides, they split plenty of money after expenses. They didn't flash money around, but each owned a big piece of mountain land, mostly woods. Of course, they never set up a still on their own land.

Slider decided he wouldn't wait on Marty to come out. He grabbed his spare toothbrush out of his truck's glove box. He stepped on the porch and headed for the door. He saw Marty through the screen door. Marty had his bow in his hands and was checking it over.

Slider went in and asked, "What are you planning on doing with that? You better get your deer rifle. We might need it."

Marty shook his head. "I'm thinking this with a few of those arrowheads we made for the Fourth of July."

Slider tilted his head and pursed his lips. "You might be right. You still got the stuff to make some?"

"Yep. I got enough for a half dozen explosive heads. Ain't gonna be too accurate after twenty-five yards or so, but I'll still be able to hit a pie plate at thirty yards."

"Good enough, I reckon." Slider agreed. "We might as well get to making 'em after we get the mash workin'." He turned to go down the hallway. "After I brush my teeth."

When he came back to the living room, he said, "We gotta get that container put into place. We better grab a couple of biscuits to go."

"Yeah, good idea. Sarah left a while ago to spend the day with Granny and them. They're picking peas and spending the afternoon shelling 'em, so there ain't gonna be a lunch later. Supper neither."

"I figured. Aileen is going over there, too. Your wife probably told her where I was last night since I didn't come in at daybreak."

Four days later, Slider put the last bucket of mash in the back of the shipping container. "Well, the trap is set. I kinda wanted another few days with the mash, but we're not actually running a batch, so I reckon it'll do."

"I hope it don't work, to be honest," Marty admitted. "I don't think I'm ready to know there really is a Bigfoot."

"Well, whatever it is, it's done messed up our dang operation. We gotta run shine…" Slider paused for effect. "Or get jobs."

Marty looked around desperately for the ladder. "Oh, hell no we ain't. Let's get on top and wait for the Squatch."

Slider handed his shotgun and Marty's bow up before he used the ladder. Once he was up top, he pulled the ladder up after him. He adjusted his hunting vest with its pockets full of buckshot and rifled slugs. He lay down beside his cousin, and they waited for the sun to set.

It was near midnight and Marty's turn to keep watch. Slider was half asleep when he felt his cousin's elbow in his ribs. He blinked his eyes, and the smell hit him. He rolled over in the dark. They both heard the closest bucket to the trap hit the ground. Something had picked it up.

A few minutes later they felt the vibration and heard the shuffling footsteps as something entered the container. After a few seconds, they felt the movement below them as it shuffled to the back of the container. They both rolled off the top and hit the ground.

Slider landed on his feet and bent his knees with the drop to reduce the impact. It was no different than jumping from the hayloft to the dirt in front of the barn when he was a kid. He hit and rolled. He was up in a flash and closing the door on his side of the container. Marty did the same with his door, except he was scrambling on all fours.

The doors made the same loud screech they always did, but Slider was able to get them all the way shut and latched into place before the entire container reverberated with an impact against the doors.

"You reckon it will hold?" Marty asked, now on his feet. He jumped up and snagged his bow off the container. His next jump rewarded him with the shotgun.

"Maybe," Slider said. They both ducked when something slammed against the doors again. "I hope." The noise continued once or twice. Sometimes it was light and repeated.

Slider held up his hand to stop Marty from saying anything else. "Shhh,"

He put his ear up against the door. After a minute he turned towards his cousin with a strange look on his face. He grabbed Marty's arm and pulled him away from the container.

"There's more than one of them," Slider whispered.

"What? How do you know?"

"I heard lighter taps on the door," Slider answered.

"Yeah?"

"Then I heard…well, I heard crying, and something shushing it."

"Shushing?" Marty asked.

"Yeah, you know like you do when a young'un is scared of the dark or hits his head on the corner of the kitchen counter."

"You reckon it's a mama with a…a cub or young'un or whatever you call a little Bigfoot?"

"Gotta be."

"What'll we do?" Marty asked. "I'm all for hunting a Sasquatch, but a mama with a young'un? That don't set right with me."

"Me neither. Shit-fire, we got us a sitchy-ation here, Marty."

"Yep."

* * * * *

CHAPTER 4

They both inched closer to the door and listened. To their surprise they heard someone calling out. It was a deep voice, yet feminine. The accent was strange, like it was forced from the back of a throat.

"Out. Let out." After a few moments, they heard. "Out." The last was stretched and conveyed emotion even with the accent. It was not a demand; it was a plea. A crying plea.

"Shit," Slider said. "We gotta open the door. We might get killed, but it ain't right. Whatever is in there, talks."

"It might be a human," Marty said. "Maybe just someone who been in these mountains for years and don't never show themselves."

"You see these prints just like I do," Slider said. His headlamp shined on one. "Ain't no human makes a print that big or smells like what's in that container. Run back to the truck and get a lamp. It probably aint a good idea to shine a light right in its eyes. We can put the lamp on top above the doors."

A few minutes later, they were ready. A lamp was up top, and another was off to the side on one of the overturned buckets.

"We ain't gonna be famous, are we? Marty asked. He covered his cousin with the shotgun, never quite pointing it at him.

"Nope." Slider stepped close to the door. "Hey! I'm gonna open the door. Don't come out here and tear my dang arms off or whatever."

He waited with his hands on the latch. After a moment, he heard the voice again.

"Out? Open?"

"Yeah, now stand back. I need time to get away from them before you come running out and flatten a fella."

He gritted his teeth expecting the worst, lifted the handle and turned it out, unlocking the doors. When nothing happened, he pulled the doors slightly, opening a gap between them, then moved back quickly.

The doors swung outward and screeched to a halt nearly to the sides of the container. Crouched in the opening with a smaller version on its hip, a broad shouldered...ape-like creature waited. It was obviously a female. Her eyes darted around wildly looking back and forth at Slider and Marty with the gun in his hands. After almost a minute, she shuffled out and slowly stood.

Slider looked up at her, standing almost ten foot tall and covered with dark reddish-brown hair. The little one clinging to her had almost black hair and kept its face buried in her shoulder. Some of the mash was on her face and all over the little one's hands, smearing it on her fur where it gripped.

With what looked like concentrated difficulty, she said, "Out. Let out."

"Yeah," Slider said. "We heard your baby crying. We just couldn't do it, I reckon."

"Um, you can go," Marty suggested. He waved the barrel of the shotgun towards the trees. "Before you decide to tear us apart and all. I ain't tryin' to get killed."

"Kill?" she said. "Kill not good. Only kill food."

Slider was amazed. "Where in the hell did you learn how to talk?"

"Learn talk, study human." she said.

She shifted the young creature from one hip to the other. The movement was performed without thought, much like any woman would do while in conversation with a child on her hip. Slider stared, realizing this.

"What are you?" he asked.

"Yeah," Marty said. He lowered the shotgun. "What in tarnation are you? Bigfoot? Sasquatch?" He waved his hand in front of his face. "No offense, but I think Skunk Ape fits you best. 'Cause damn…"

"Am Rahtek," she answered. She stood taller. "Come long way. Study human."

"Wait. What?" Slider asked. Suddenly it dawned on him. "You mean you came from far away to study us. Like a scientist or whatever?"

"Yes. Study like your sy-on-tist."

"They's been sightings as far as Canada," Marty said. "I reckon that is a long way. Hell, they got the Abominable Snowman over in Russia or thereabouts. Sure 'nuff a long way."

"No," Slider said. "I think she means from a lot farther than that."

"That's clean on the other side of the planet," Marty argued. "You can't get no farther away unless…Unless." His voice trailed off.

"Yep," Slider confirmed. "They ain't from this planet."

"Shit." Marty said. "I reckon that explains the UFO sightings too."

"Not this shaynek." She paused, her face was close enough to a human's, it showed she was thinking of the word. After a moment she brightened and said, "Not this star system."

"Aliens," Slider said.

"Bigfoot Aliens," Marty agreed. "Man, this would be prime time on the ROKU. Dang."

"We can't tell anyone," Slider said. "They'd look at us sideways and lock us up for our own good."

"Say," Marty asked, "why ain't you wearing anything? Britches, a shirt, a flannel nightgown?"

"Rahtek do not wear...cloth," She answered. "That Human custom."

"Well, shit I reckon," Marty said. "Our women cover up, at least. Yours are out there for the whole world to see. Well, I reckon they are covered in hair...fur, whatever."

She grinned showing a mouthful of teeth. Four of them were longer and sharper, almost canine in appearance. She reached up and rubbed the back of the little one.

"Do you have a name?" Slider asked.

"Yes. Am called Nantharlithku," She turned the little one's face towards them. "This is Githarkunu."

"A male?" Slider asked. "Your son?"

"My...child. Yes. Human word. Child."

The little one kept his face away from his mother and studied them intently. Slider could see the childlike curiosity in his eyes.

"How old is he?"

"Twenty of your years," she answered after a moment's thought.

"Twenty? Dang how old are you?" Marty asked. "I mean, sorry. It aint right to just ask a woman that, I reckon."

"Over... one hundred... of your years," she answered. "On this planet... for thirty. Others here longer."

"Others?" Slider asked. He looked around, realizing she may have a mate of some kind. Wherever he was he wouldn't be happy about his mate and child being locked in a cargo container.

She grinned again. "Yes. Others. Here on this land and on other lands. You call Russia and Nepal. Where frozen rain."

"I knew it!" Marty exclaimed. "The dang Abominable Snowman. Yeti...whatever."

Slider sighed. "Don't encourage him. He believes in ghosts too."

"Hey, that shit's real," Marty said. "You know dang good and well they's Haints. Wanda Willoford seen a Haint over to the graveyard behind the church one night. She said it floated right over the dang fence."

"Wanda was out there smokin' that wacky-terbacky, too," Slider advised.

He turned back and asked, "Do you have a mate? Where is your youngun's daddy?"

Her whole demeanor changed. She slumped, losing a half foot of her height. "Vernohkolath is caught. In building behind fence."

"Behind a fence? Behind a fence?" Slider asked himself over and over out loud. He snapped his fingers. "The federal building. That whole area is off limits. Not even the local law goes near it."

"You really think he's in that secret squirrel building?" Marty asked. "I always wondered what was in there. He must be a prisoner or something. They might be experimenting on him." He looked over towards the little one. "Shit. I'm sorry."

He stepped closer to his cousin. "So, what are we gonna do about it?"

* * * * *

CHAPTER 5

Slider studied the guard shack and the fenced-in compound through the scope on his deer rifle. "I don't like it."

"What?" Marty asked. "The guards on the gate or the two walking inside the fence? They done come around twice since we been here."

"It looks too easy. Why aren't there more guards? It doesn't seem right."

"What mean?" Nan asked. Marty had decided her name was too long and too hard to say. Nan was the compromise.

"I'm worried there is not enough security, so your mate ain't there," Slider answered." Why only four guards?"

"Ah hell, that's easy," Marty said. "They can't have a bunch of security. If they did, folks around here would really get nosy. You know how it is."

"Yeah, you're probably right," Slider agreed. "The last thing they want folks to know is the UFOs are real, Aliens are real, and they are on the planet. It would be chaos. Children would starve."

"Wait…what?" Marty asked. "Why would children starve?"

"Because of religion," Slider answered. "Think about it. The largest charitable organization in the world is the Catholic Church. They run orphanages all over the planet. They feed the hungry, house families, run orphanages, and schools. I know there's some bad stuff in the past at some of those, but they've cleaned it up and are still working on it."

"Anyway," he continued. "They depend on tithing to pay for it all. If Aliens were proven real, that would screw everything up. Man is made in God's image. Aliens," he waved at Nan, "these guys, are not made like man, so that would cause many to question the Bible and think none of it is true. No one believing means no one tithing, and the money would dry up, leaving poor children in little pockets all over the world with no means to survive. It would be world-wide chaos."

"What about Area 51 and all that?" Marty asked. "Hell, they done said they have confirmation of UFOs."

"I think it's been a little sleight of hand. 'Hey look over here' kinda thing."

"So, nobody would look here in the Blue Ridge Mountains," Marty said. "Those slick sumbitches. What about them admitting some of the latest UFOs?"

"After all these years, they don't have a choice," Slider answered, still using the scope. "With cell phones, dang near everybody has a high definition camera with zoom capabilities on 'em at all times. Someone is bound to get good pictures or video, and then that shit would go viral on that inter-webs stuff."

"Yeah, you're right."

"They're easing the idea into society, so it won't be a shock when it happens," Slider said.

"Well, folks would sure be shocked to know Bigfoot is real and is an alien who can talk just like we do."

"Chaos," Slider advised. "Pure chaos."

Marty sat down on a rock. His feet were still in the creek as they dangled. Slider followed Nan across to the other side. They walked up the rocky bank towards a high cliff in the mountainside. As they got closer, Slider looked up, to the left, and to the right. It looked like many others in the area. No cave, only a bend in the creek with a few large boulders and plenty of rocks between it and the stone wall, left in place from when the waters ran high in the past.

"I don't see anything," Marty called out as he came up behind them. "And my dang feet hurt. I didn't know we was walkin' this far."

"I don't see anything either," Slider agreed.

Nan looked around one last time. "Not do this in light. This first time."

She reached up as high as she could, grabbed a small outcropping of rock far above where any human could reach, and pulled. A section of the cliff face pulled back and slid to the side. Nana waved them in.

As soon as they were in, she slapped a small square panel on the inside of the wall and the door slid back in place. Several lights came on, but the lighting emitted a strange red coloring. It wasn't so different they couldn't see, but it was noticeable.

Slider stood and stared. Before them, in the huge cavern was a round ship sitting on four thick struts. A long ramp extended to the cave floor. It was at least thirty foot tall and four times in diameter. The sight was so mesmerizing, he no longer noticed the sharp smell, even stronger in the cavern.

Marty eased up beside him and said, "Well looky there. That's a dang flying saucer. Well, it ain't flyin' right now, but I bet it could."

"It can if repaired," Nan said. She put her son down. The little one scampered across the floor and up the ramp, using all four limbs occasionally.

"Repaired?" Slider asked. "What's wrong with it?"

"Power cell," Nan said. "Must fly, charge cell. Not fly since mate captured."

"How did the hidden door work?" Marty asked. "And these lights?"

"Panel on cliff," Nan answered. "It charge different cell. There." She pointed to a waist high box. It looked to be made of the same metal the ship was. A cable ran to the door panel and above it to disappear in the rock wall.

"Well hell," Marty said. "Slider can fix it. He can fix just about anything."

Nan looked at Slider, hope on her alien face. "Can repair?"

"I mean…maybe," Slider said. "Marty's right. I can fix near 'bout anything. But I don't rightly know 'bout alien stuff."

He walked over to the box and studied it. He noticed a panel on small hinges. He opened it and looked inside. He turned on the light on his hat bill, scratched his chin through his beard and tried to figure out what he was looking at.

"Seems to me, it's about the fanciest battery set up for a solar panel I ever saw," Slider said. "But I can tell the battery from the adapter and the regulator's got a strange shape, but it's where one would be, anyway." He looked back towards the ship. "I'd have to poke around in there and see what's what. They's bound to be somethin' like the batteries out here or power cell, whatever. Then again, if that's some kind of fusion plant, it may be kinda hard to figure out."

"Don't let him fool you none," Marty said. "He spent eight whole years in one o' them tin cans in the Navy."

"Tin can?" Nan asked. "I know word, Navy. Human military. What tin can?"

"Submarines," Slider said. "I worked in nuclear powered ships."

"That's where he got his nickname," Marty advised. "I hear tell it was something 'bout how fast he slid down the ladders in a sub. He never touched a step."

"There was an ol' boy from West Virginia on the boat. They already called him Hillbilly, so they called me Slider." He shrugged. "Show me the power plant on your ship."

"Say," Marty asked. "You got any laser guns or glowing swords or anything in there? We may need it to break your ol' man out of the pokey.

* * * * *

CHAPTER 6

"So, what you're telling me is…nothing on the ship works right now," Slider said. "The power cell is depleted 'cause the plant is in shut-down mode. Without power, it can't be restarted."

"Yes," Nan said. She held a hand up to shield her eyes from the light on Slider's hat.

"Sorry," he said. He took his hat off, so it wouldn't shine in her face.

"My mate is pilot," she explained. "I not fly. Not make repair. I sy-on-tist."

"Makes sense," Marty said. "Ya gotta crank shit up every now and then iffin you want to keep the battery charged."

Slider laughed. "Something like that." He tilted his head and said, "Though a nuclear plant is not quite like a tractor, Marty." He put his hat back on and looked around the ship's power plant room. It was a fusion reactor. "But this ain't what I worked on. Hell, fusion power is not like fission either."

"What?" Marty asked. "Ain't nuclear…nuclear?"

"Not hardly," Slider answered. "Nuclear fission and nuclear fusion are completely different."

"Well shit. Can you fix it?"

"I wouldn't know where to start. Even if I could power it up, I can't read what comes up on the screen. I mean, look at that on the wall. I know it's a warning of some kind, but I can't read it. No human can."

"It looks like a chicken scratched it out," Marty observed. He tilted his head sideways to see if it helped.

Slider turned towards Nan. She was holding her child again. The little one had a six-legged stuffed toy. At least Slider hoped it was a toy. "Sorry. This is way beyond me."

"Understand," she said. She said something to her child. The little one's lips poked out as he pouted. She said, "He want favorite…food. No power, no make."

"Is that why you was eating our mash?" Marty asked.

"Yes, smelled good. Smell strong. Tastes good. Like food ship make."

"They must have some kind of food replicator," Slider said. "It ain't got no power either."

"If soured mash is the kind of stuff they eat, it ain't no wonder they smell ruint," Marty said. "No offense, Nan."

"It's probably why she didn't smell us on top of the trap." Slider said. "The smell of the fermented mash."

"Human stink," Nan agreed. She wrinkled her nose.

"Well, I can't fix it. I can rig it so the power cell is charged, but I'm not about to try and initiate the reactor. So, we ain't got a choice," Slider said. "The ship needs its pilot. Show us your weapons or whatever you got."

"Yep," Marty said. He rubbed his hands together. "We aim to break your ol' man out of the pokey. Leme hold one o' them lasers or light-knives or whatever've you got."

"What do you mean this is all you got?" Marty asked. He leaned closer so the light was brighter on the items on the chest high table.

"Not have kill weapons. Stun only," Nan explained. "Kill human not allowed. Big trouble."

"Well damn."

"We can use the stunners," Slider said. "All we gotta do is get close enough to use them. It looks like a shotgun. Kinda."

"A damn ten gauge," Marty observed. "Look at the size of the barrel...or whatever. Gonna need to use two fingers to pull the trigger. Reckon how big her mate is, anyway?"

"This big," Nan said. She held her hand about a foot over her head.

"He's a big 'un!" Marty said. "If we get in that building and get to him, how are we 'sposed to keep that big rascal from breaking us in half? He ain't gonna give a flip that we're the posse come to rescue him. We're just some more humans."

"He'll see the stun rifles," Slider said. "He'll know."

"Yes. See stunners," Nan agreed.

"The question I have," Slider asked, "is what happens after we get him out? The whole dang secret squirrel department is gonna come looking for the two hillbillies who did it."

Nan reached down and picked up a multicolored block. It looked small in her hand but when she handed it to Slider it covered his palm. "This make kethcola." She paused thinking of the word. "Make static."

"Static." Slider mused. "Static? Oh, I get it. It scrambles any cameras or recording devices. That'll work." He turned it over and saw a thumb sized indent to turn it on.

"Hell yeah. That's some o' that movie spy shit. How far does that thing work?" Marty asked.

"Long way. Can see, is static."

"Well, we got that figured out," Slider said. "What about the security guys, themselves?"

"Use stun, not remember anything whole day before," Nan said. She grinned showing those sharp canines again. "Help make settings."

"What?" Slider asked. "I forget, you study humans. You're saying you helped with the design of the stun gun. No wonder no one has proof of Bigfoot. Real proof anyway. Scramblers messing with video. Folks forgetting whole days."

"Say," Marty said. "When you study humans, do you like...abduct 'em and bring back here or to a lab or whatever?"

"Yes. Have before."

Marty reached back and covered his ass with a hand. "You don't...you don't uh..."

Slider laughed at his cousin. "I don't reckon it matters. You wouldn't remember."

"The hell I wouldn't," Marty argued. "Iffin that shit happened to me, I'd know."

"What do?" Nan asked.

"Never mind," Slider said. "He listens to talk shows in the middle of the night."

* * * * *

CHAPTER 7

Marty held the cube steady on the dash of the truck as Slider drove them right up to the gate of the compound. One guard stayed in the small shack while the other stood in the middle road behind the ten-foot-tall gate. Like the fence around the perimeter, it was topped with razor wire.

Slider opened his door part way. It blocked the view from the gate and of the guard with his weapon held across his chest in both hands. On the other side of the cab, Marty's window was down. The other two guards were out of sight. Slider had timed it right as he slowly drove towards the place. The two rovers rounded the big building on the far side right before he stopped.

"This is a secure facility," the guard said. He was a big man with a shaved face and a square jaw. His tone indicated he was all business. "Get back in the vehicle, back up, and turn around. If we see it near here again, it will be impounded, and you will be taken to a federal prison for processing."

Slider stepped around the door and fired from the hip. The weapon shook slightly as a pulse of blue energy exited the barrel, seemed to separate slightly as it went through the openings of the fence, and hit the guard in his chest. The man dropped his rifle and spasmed. Like a string puppet who has been dropped, he folded and hit the ground.

Marty fired through the open window as soon as the second guard stepped out of the shack and was raising his rifle. The man fell back against the building and slumped to a sitting position, his head on his chest, unconscious.

"Grab the scrambler, while I turn my truck around," Slider said. Marty obliged.

Slider backed up to the gate, got out and hooked a chain to his trailer hitch. He hooked the other end to the gate. When he stomped the gas it lurched forward, barking the tires. The gate followed it as the truck ripped it from its hinges. He unhooked the chain and threw it in the back of the truck.

"Come on!" Slider shouted as he ran towards the corner of the building. Marty followed, still holding the scrambler.

Three minutes later the guards stepped around the corner, still in conversation. One was complaining about the boring duty on weekends. The scientist got to go home but the guards didn't. They never knew what hit them.

Slider looked at the keypad on the door. He didn't touch it. He knew his fingerprints were in the system from his time in the Navy. He looked to his right. The bay door didn't have a lock showing. Slider figured it opened from the inside.

"Marty, take that bow off your back and get one of them arrows ready. Wait, let me see it."

He wiped it off with his shirt, scrubbing hard. "You got your glove? Good. Don't touch the arrow and leave a print. Let's get back. Hand me that cube. Now, blow that door open."

Slider and Marty entered the building, slipping past the door that hung on by only the bottom hinge. It was bright inside, the walls a clean white. They checked each room as they made their way towards the back of the building. They knew they were in the right place when they came to a door with warning signs.

Slider opened the door and looked around. He saw what he was looking for on the far side of the room. He looked through the glass and saw a cage in the middle of the closed bay. "No wonder they ain't no lock on the outside of that bay door. Take a look Marty."

Marty looked through the window. "Damn, he is a big 'un, huh? How we gonna get him out of that cage. Them bars are as big around as my leg."

"We'll figure it out."

They walked into the room. On the far side of the cage, Nan's mate crouched. He stared intently. His eyes widened when he saw the stun guns and the cube. He slowly stood to his full eleven feet and walked over to the door.

Marty studied the lock. "Shit, It's a keypad."

"Hey, don't get so close," Marty advised. "He looks mean as a wild hog."

Marty looked up between the bars and thought for a moment. He was almost sure he had Nan's name right. He said, "Nantharlith…"

The alien stepped closer. In a deep voice he said, "Nantharlithku."

"Yep," Marty agreed. "That's her name."

The alien slapped his hand against his chest. "Vernohkolath "

"Well, Vern," Marty said, shortening his name like he had Nan's. "We're the fellas what are fixin' ta break you out of this place. Maybe. If Slider can figure out the lock."

Vern reached through the bars causing Slider and Marty to step back. He gestured for the scrambler in Marty's hand. He did it again, urgently.

"Give it to him," Slider said.

"If you say so," Marty said. He put it in the big hand.

Vern held it close to his face with both hands. He twisted the top and pushed at the same time. His thumb moved a corner and a small panel opened on it. Inside several red lights glowed. He pushed two with the tip of his finger. The electronic lock disengaged, and the door was unlocked.

Vern stepped through the door, closed the cube, looked at it for a moment, and handed it to Marty. He gestured to the bay door.

Slider hit the opener with his elbow and the bay door rose slowly. A short time later he turned the key and started his truck.

"I hope it don't blow a tire," Marty said.

Slider looked through the back window at the Bigfoot crouched in his truck bed, looking over the cab. "Me too."

Slider watched Vern as he went through the startup procedure for the ship. He was right. He would never have been able to figure it out, even with his training from the Navy. Vern nodded at him as they both watched the readout on the screen. Slider couldn't read anything, and Vern didn't speak the human language. He relied on his mate to talk to them.

An hour later, Marty walked into the room. "Hey, try this." He held out a large metal bowl.

Slider looked at it, sniffed it, and dipped his pinky in. He tasted it and froze. He dipped his finger to try it again.

"That, hell...that's," he started to say.

"I know," Marty interrupted. "That's the best damn mash I ever tasted. We run a batch off o' that bitter shit, and we gotta raise our prices."

"We need to get a barrel of it and run it," Slider agreed.

"We can't tell no one about them," Marty said. "But we can still be famous for our shine. I wonder how hard it is to go legal?"

# # # # #

It Came from the Trailer Park

The Harrowing

By John Drake

Isle of Wight
United Kingdom
Present Day

"I've driven here every year for the last twenty-five years, Margaret. I don't need a GPF to help me,' said Alex.

'GPS, Dear,' said his wife, a lady for whom patience was measured in anniversaries.

'We'll be there by two o'clock, right on schedule. In all these years have you ever known me to be late?'

'There was that time we ended up in Exeter instead of Portsmouth,' said Margaret, rather bravely.

'That wasn't my fault now, was it dear? They were building the new motorway and whoever was in charge of the diversion signage sent everyone the wrong way. Can't really put the blame for that one at my door.'

'No Dear.'

Alex turned the volume up on the radio to signal an end to the inquisition. A droning voice broke through the static.

'*...and it was, until now, believed to be the largest collection of Toby jugs on the Isle of Wight. But today I'm here in Newport with Norman Price who claims to have gathered more than two hundred of the famous creations in his parents' garage over the last thirty years. Norman, welcome to Collector's Corner.*'

'Do we have to listen to this?' asked Margaret. 'It's the same every year.'

'I only get to listen to it twice a year, Margaret. It's one of the reasons we always arrive on the Isle of Wight on a Tuesday.'

'I thought you said it was because the ferry was cheaper during the week?'

'That's a happy coincidence.'

'And there were less children destroying the relaxing atmosphere.'

'Fewer,' corrected Alex instinctively.

'*...since I was about, oh, I'd say ten or eleven years old*' declared Norman Price.

'Quiet now, Dear. You know how much I love Toby jugs.'

They travelled along the quiet country road for fifteen minutes of Toby juggery until the radio station's hourly jingle indicated it was time for the news.

'*Good afternoon, Paul O'Connor here at the Gentle FM news desk, bringing you all the top stories from Yarmouth to Bembridge.*'

Alex pushed the power button on the radio and stared straight ahead with scrunched eyes.

'We should listen to the news, dear. We don't want to miss something important,' said Margaret.

'Quiet, I'm concentrating.'

He steered the old-but-reliable brown Volvo off the road and onto a narrow track of earth with grass growing up between the tyre tracks.

'Here we are,' he announced proudly. 'Lazy Heights caravan park, four minutes early too.'

'Well done Dear,' said Margaret flatly.

'Oh my! Would you look at that?' declared Alex, slowing the car to a stop below the arched entrance to the caravan park. 'Some ruffian has scrawled their graffiti tag on the sign.'

'What's a graffiti tag?'

'They're like a signature for unruly yobos. Marks their territory, so to speak.'

'And how do you know about them?' asked Margaret. In her almost-fifty years of experience with her husband she could count on one hand the number of times he had shown any knowledge of youth culture, and that included the early years when they themselves could be considered young and *with it*. In age, at least.

'Bill Jones told me about them in the Red Cat a few weeks ago. I never thought I would see such a thing at Lazy Heights though, I must say.'

'I'm not sure it's a tag, Dear.'

'And how would you know? You didn't know what a tag was until twenty seconds ago.'

'Well, I think it's just the letter *S* added to the middle.'

'That's just the sort of thing they would do though, isn't it? I'm sure they just slosh their tag on any flat surface without so much as a morsel of respect.'

'Yes, but placing the *S* where they have sends a rather different message, wouldn't you say? Look, it's just before the *H* in *Heights.*'

Alex studied the sign for a moment, then froze. 'Good Lord above, have they no shame?' He gathered himself, put the Volvo into first gear, and passed under the offending sign. 'I'm sure it has only just happened, and the staff will be along at any moment to clean it off. Savages. That's what they are, dear. Savages.'

'Yes Dear.'

Alex pulled up outside the first static caravan. There were two flags fluttering in the breeze, so weathered it was hard to tell their original colour. An overweight man sat beside an old, white plastic table. He was the sort of man you would expect spent his days playing computer games in a bedroom of his parents' house twenty years after he should have left. He took a large bite from a sandwich, placed it directly onto the table, and wiped his hands on his Legend of Zelda t-shirt.

'You booked in?' he said through a mouthful of cheese and pickle.

'Good afternoon' said Alex, pointedly. 'Mr. and Mrs. A. Raisbeck of Newbury. We have a reservation for ten nights in a Deluxe Two Bed Fotheringham A-Class.'

The sandwich eater hoisted himself upright and lumbered sideways through his caravan door. There was a sound of keys jangling before he returned with his arm outstretched.

'Forty-one' he said, with an absolute absence of emotion, before slumping back down onto his chair and picking up his sandwich again.

Mr. Raisbeck cleared his throat.

Mrs. Raisbeck rolled her eyes. Metaphorically, of course. *Actually* rolling her eyes simply wasn't worth the hassle.

'I was assured by your colleague Diane in the reservations department that I would be allocated number thirty-seven. We stay in number thirty-seven every year.'

'Forty-one' repeated the sandwich man, nodding slightly. 'That way.'

'Does forty-one come with the fold-up ironing board? Or the removable shaving mirror? I ask because they form an integral part of my itinerary for the duration of our stay. You can't just pop along to Chez Paris in town with creased trousers and a five o'clock shadow now, can you? No, they'd send you packing before you could hear the soup of the day.'

'Forty-one.'

'Well, I must say, between this and the graffiti at the entrance we will certainly be thinking twice before coming here next year. Not a good start, young man. Not a good start at all.'

'How long have you been coming here?' asked the man.

Alex stiffened his shoulders proudly. 'Thirty-four years. Haven't missed one since before Oliver was born.'

'Right, well we'll see you next year then.'

Alex scowled. 'What's your name?'

The man tapped a plastic badge that covered Zelda's left eye.

'Well…' said Alex, squinting. '…*Steve*. I'll be sure to include you in my usual feedback letter. I hope for your sake that our experience takes a turn for the better.'

'I wouldn't count on it.'

'Is it Stephen with a *ph* or Steven with a *v*? It wouldn't do to write such a letter with informal monikers.'

Steve made a 'V' with two fingers and waved them up and down.

Alex looked at the key, then at Steve. 'Right, well,' he said defiantly.

'Let's just find number forty-one, Dear,' said Margaret. 'I'm sure it will be just as nice.'

'Ha! Just as nice,' mimicked Alex. 'It's west-facing for one thing.'

'How do you know?'

'My dear Margaret. How long have we been married now?'

'You memorised the map of the park, didn't you?'

'Of course, I did! A man has to prepare for every eventuality.'

'What else have you prepared for? An encroaching plague? A marauding Mongol Horde? Aliens?'

'Don't be absurd, Margaret, we're on an island. The Mongols were horsemen.'

He opened the door of the Volvo, turned the ignition, and gave his wife a look that said she should get into the passenger seat without any more talk or walk to number forty-one herself. He drove carefully – very carefully – along the rutted path for a short while before taking a left turn and driving to the very end of the lane. Number forty-one was the last caravan on the right and was, to Alex's great relief, a Deluxe Two Bed Fotheringham A-Class model.

'I hope they have the same cutlery,' he muttered, half to himself. 'Remember nineteen ninety-seven, Dear?'

'How could I forget? The great bread knife scandal.'

'There's no need for that tone, Margaret. We're supposed to be on holiday.'

'Is that so, Dear?'

'Now, here's the key. You go in and put the kettle on while I unload the car.'

'Yes Dear.'

Margaret drew a patient breath, took the key from her husband, and got out of the car. She unlocked the door of the caravan, stepped inside, and froze.

'Bugger' she thought, most uncharacteristically. 'Alex, Dear? You know how you like everything to be *just so*? Well, just remember we're on our holidays. It's a good time to do something new, something different. Isn't it? Things don't always have to be the way they always are, do they? No, good to mix things up a little. Just don't be too hasty in your judgment, that's what I say.'

'What was that, Dear?' said Alex as he man-handled a suitcase through the narrow door. He looked up at his wife, then at the inside of the caravan. 'Oh no. No, no.' he announced. 'This won't do at all. What do they think we are, savages?'

'It's just a microwave, Dear. I'm sure it will be fine.'

'Fine!?' exclaimed Alex, in what constituted a roar for the Raisbeck family. 'Fine? It isn't fine, Margaret. It's an insult is what it is. How are we supposed to cook our coq-au-vin on

Thursday? Or our minted lamb roast on Sunday? Answer me that!'

'Perhaps we can use Chez Paris? It'd be nice not to have to cook every night for a change.'

'We go to Chez Paris on the first Tuesday and the second Wednesday, as you well know Margaret. I won't be conscripted to a change of schedule just because Lazy Heights have lowered their usual standards. No, this won't do at all. I'm going to see Steven.'

'Please don't, Dear. You know how wound up you can get after a long drive. Why don't we put the kettle on and have a nice cup of tea? I think there's a packet of custard creams in the bag.'

'And how will that solve our cooker problem? No, this needs swift action. If we don't say anything now, they'll have us over a barrel for using the facilities of number forty-one, and thereby declaring our satisfaction with its below-par amenities. Don't unpack a stitch, Margaret. Not a stitch!'

With that he left number forty-one and marched up the rutted path to Steven, his face set hard and his mind ready to deliver a stern lecture on the importance of basic cooking facilities on a modern caravan site.

When he arrived at reception Steven's plastic chair was empty. A half-eaten bag of cheesy puffs lay with its open end pointing to the chair.

'Steven?' called Alex, in his best Mr. Raisbeck voice. 'Steven? I need to speak to you about the amenities in number forty-one.'

He leaned towards the door slightly in the polite manner of a shop customer who would like the assistant to know they are looking for service.

'Steven?'

He stepped tentatively forward, past the chair that marked the unspoken boundary between guests and staff and peered into the caravan.

'Steven? We need to discuss the cooking facilities in number forty-one.'

A flushing noise from inside the caravan signaled an end to Alex's search. He stepped back quickly and stiffened his back.

'Ah, there you are. Good. Now, about number forty-one…'

'Forty-one' stated Steven.

'Yes, that's the one. Well, there are some features one would expect to see in a Deluxe Two Bed Fotheringham A-Class model that are not apparent in the one we have been assigned.'

'Forty-one,' repeated Steven, picking up a tatty piece of paper and thrusting it to Alex. 'Look'.

Alex peered at the rudimentary map of the site, and at the word *Raisbeck* scrawled beneath number forty-one. 'Yes, I have grasped the fundamentals of our predicament. Must I remind you that I reserved number thirty-seven at the time of my booking? No doubt a colleague of yours in the reservations department was unaware of the research that goes into these sorts of things. I have been coming here for over thirty years, young man, so I know which caravans have superior characteristics.' He tilted his head slightly. 'Which is why I chose number thirty-seven. Now, please reallocate our booking to another south-facing Deluxe Two Bed Fotheringham A-Class model at once. As I understand it, numbers seventeen and twenty-one are suitable.'

'Reservations' said Steven, as if that was all the information required.

'What do you mean, *reservations*?'

Steven let out what, for most people, would be an exaggerated sigh.

'I mean' he began slowly, 'that you will need to call reservations if you want to change your booking.'

'I haven't changed my damn booking!' cried Alex. 'I booked number thirty-seven! It's you who changed it. Bloody hell, man, what's wrong with you?'

'Reservations.'

'Fine! I'll damn well call reservations, but woe betide you when your manager receives my feedback correspondence this year. You'll be out on your ear before you can say *gas cooker with combination grill.*'

He snorted loudly through his nose to be sure Steven understood the severity of his grievance, pulled out his phone theatrically, and dialed reservations. Three haughty minutes later he presented an email from *Laura in Bookings* to Steven, who rolled his eyes before levering himself out of his chair and into the caravan.

'Thirty-seven' he announced, handing Alex a key.

'A pleasure' said Alex, nodding.

He arrived back at number forty-one and called out to his wife. 'You can stop folding the tea towels Margaret, I've secured number thirty-seven. Come on, pack up our things.'

Mr. and Mrs. Raisbeck filled the Volvo again and drove the hundred metres to number thirty-seven.

'This is more like it' announced Alex as they parked up. 'Looks like a newer model too. I've heard these have a television built into the walls, if you can believe it.'

'Marvellous, Dear.'

'Right, you start with the kitchen things, and I'll bring in the big suitcase.'

On the third attempt, Alex succeeded in hauling the overweight case from the boot of the car and let it fall to the ground with a thud. As he leaned on the luggage, the soft noise of the opening of a plastic window came from the neighbouring caravan.

'Afternoon, neighbours!' said a cheery London accent. 'Bloody lovely day for it, eh?'

Alex looked up from his suitcase battle and nodded non-committally at the discoloured window.

'Buggering Mondays! Is that really you?' said the voice.

Alex ignored him, took a deep breath, and manhandled the case into the caravan.

'It bloody well is you!' said the voice, now at Mr. Raisbeck's door. 'What are the chances of that, eh?'

'I'm sorry, I don't believe we've met,' said Alex from the far end of the caravan. 'Now if you wouldn't mind, we've just arrived, and we have rather a lot of unpacking to do.'

'*We've* just arrived? So, am I to finally meet the famous Mrs. Raisbeck? Margaret, if I remember correctly?'

'Are you from customer service? Because if you are there are a few choice words I'd like to have with you. We could start with the data protection breach. You should be asking me to confirm my identity before disclosing personal information willy-nilly. I've a good mind to write to the Data Protection Commissioner.'

'It *is* you, my old mucker!'

'Says who?'

'Who else would dive straight into privacy legislation?'

'Anyone who cares about how their personal information is used,' said Alex pointedly.

'Cauliflower won't believe this.'

'What does a cauliflower have to do with anything? And why would you be talking to it in the first place? You're quite mad.'

'There she is!' said the man, tugging politely at his tweed cap as he stepped over an assortment of saucepans to reach Mrs. Raisbeck. He gave her a light hug as if they were friends who only saw each other once a year or so, then stepped back carefully over the pots.

'Excuse me, young man!' snapped Alex. 'Do you mind explaining what you're doing here? This is not the sort of service we have become accustomed to at Lazy Heights. In fact, the whole experience so far has been very disappointing. Never, in all my years, have I known the staff to be as... *friendly*... as you are.'

'Oh, there's so much I need to tell you,' said the man. 'It's probably best you unpack your beers first.'

'Beer? It's wine, naturally. Not to mention the time of day.'

'Oh, I wouldn't worry about time, Mr. Raisbeck. Follow me, I'll explain everything at my place. Got a few cans in the fridge myself.'

They stepped over a one-foot-tall attempt at a hedgerow as they crossed over to the neighbouring caravan. The man disappeared inside, returning a moment later with three cans.

'Here, get some of this down you before I start.'

'What is this?' said Alex, turning the can in his hand as if it had been lifted from an Edwardian gutter.

'Cobbler's Knob,' said the man.

'I hope it tastes better than it sounds.'

'They've all got funny names like that these days. Gives you something to talk about at a party when the conversation dries up, I suppose. I'm happy with anything these days, to be honest with you, but they were on special offer. You know how it is.'

'What's your name?' asked Alex.

'You really don't remember, do you?'

'Well of course I don't. Why else would I be asking?'

'It's just that, well, when two people have gone through what we have it's hard to see past the confusion of having that person sitting right in front of you without the slightest clue who you are, know what I mean?'

'No, I'm not sure I do.'

'I guess time travel is harder on some people's brains than others. Alright, I'll do my best. My name's Scratch, and you and I have had some rather unusual adventures.'

'Right, that's it. You're clearly a lunatic with more time on his hands than he knows what to do with. I'm going to unpack the crockery.'

'Wait! I'll be quick. We were zoomed to a planet called Arcadia to help the local aliens save all life in the universe. We met all kinds of life forms, but once we were done you were sent back to Newbury to carry on your life where you left off. I chose to stay behind, but now I get to take the odd trip back to Earth to help me with the adjustment to living on another planet. Something about balancing your psycho-wotsits they say. Anyway, here I am. Holidaying on Earth like something from one of Basement Rodney's comic books.'

'Well that all sounds perfectly reasonable,' said Alex, standing up. 'Now, if you'll excuse me, I have some reality to deal with next door.'

'You bought a three-seater Belgian roll arm sofa in oatmeal beige,' said Scratch desperately.

'Oh, you can find anything out about a person online these days.'

'You drive a Volvo.'

'You can see it from all the way over there can you?' said Alex, pointing at the car parked within sloth-throwing distance of them. 'Please don't bother us again young man, we're trying to have a nice relaxing break from the rigours of Berkshire life.'

'You always wanted to be an Olympic Javelin thrower.'

Alex froze. 'What did you say?'

'And you had to move your mahogany Toby jug cabinet to make room for your new sofa. The picture of Oliver had to go on the opposite wall.'

Alex sat back down, picked up his can, and drained it in one go.

'So now you know,' said Scratch. 'I hope it doesn't cause any problems on Arcadia. Professor Doubt can be such a stickler when it comes to *The Rules*. Plays havoc with the space-time wotsits, so he says. I've never seen the harm in a bit of cross-contamination myself, but there you have it. Takes all sorts I suppose.'

'Say that again,' managed Alex.

'I said it plays havoc with the...'

'No, before that. The bit about the Olympics.'

'I said you wanted to be an Olympic javelin thrower. Not sure if *thrower* is the right word, but you get the idea.'

'How could you possibly know that? I've never told anyone, not even Margaret.'

'Well there you go then, proves I'm right don't it.'

'Doesn't' said Alex instinctively.

'Yes, it does.'

'I mean, the word is doesn't, not don't.'

'Doesn't what?'

'Never mind.'

Alex stared at an arbitrary point in the middle distance and raised the empty can of Cobbler's Knob to his mouth.

'I think I'd better have another.'

The next day

'Morning neighbour!' called Scratch from the deck of his caravan as Alex stepped out of his, stretching the previous night's sleep away. 'Looks like a good one for a spot of fishing. Fancy joining me? There's a river that runs across the edge of the campsite over there.'

Alex looked across to caravan number thirty-six and rolled his eyes. 'Not today, thank you. I have a number of very important matters I need to attend to.'

'Come on, you're supposed to be on holiday. I insist. It'll be good for you to get to know me as well as I know you, ain't that right?'

'Do you realise how creepy that sounds, Mr. Scratch?'

'I told you, it's just Scratch. Mr. Scratch makes me all nervous like I've done something wrong.'

'Have you?'

'Not in this world, no. Well, a little bit perhaps but not for ages. Now, how about a bit of fishing?'

'Oh, fishing,' said Margaret, joining her husband outside. 'You love fishing, Dear. It'll do you good.'

'Please, Dear,' said Alex with a ferrous glare.

Margaret ignored the look. No matter how clear the message was, it didn't stand a chance against the prospect of her spending the day with a Barbara Cartland novel and some ginger biscuits.

'I'll make you both a nice, packed lunch. Cheese sandwiches OK for you, Mr. Scratch?'

'Lovely.'

'I think we might have a couple of Scotch eggs and a pork pie in here somewhere too. You boys get yourselves sorted out, and I'll have this rustled up in no time. Best to get going soon, I hear the fish bite better in the morning.'

'Oh, you did, did you?' said Alex. 'And where, might I ask, did you hear that?'

'Sorry dear, no time for chit-chat. Got to make sure you boys have enough to keep you going for the day.'

'The day!? I'm not going for the day. I'll be back before lunch, Dear. No need to do anything on our account.'

'Oh good, so you are going then. I'll pack a nice flask of tea too, save you coming back. Come along now Dear, chop-chop.'

Half an hour later the odd couple were camped on the river bank. They sat in their dark green deck chairs, complete with drinks holders, studying the ripples of the water.

'Can't get better than this, can you?' said Scratch.

'Oh, I could think of something,' said Alex.

'So how come you ended up here then? Bit far from Newbury, ain't it?'

'Yes, that's the point. It was supposed to be a nice relaxing break.'

'What do you mean, *supposed to be*? This is bliss, this is.'

'It's been nothing but trouble since we arrived. The place has gone downhill, I can tell you. Wasn't like this when Oliver was a boy. No, there was a bit of class about the place then. The cutlery was made of metal for one thing, and the politeness of the signage was maintained to a high standard. Not that anyone would have dreamt of defacing it back in the day, of course. I mean, what kind of character would do something so... so crass?'

'Yes, well it takes all sorts, don't it?'

'Doesn't.'

'I thought it was quite funny myself.'

'Yes, I imagine you did.'

'Well, you're here now and that's all that matters' said Scratch placatingly. 'Caravans are lovely too. I reckon they're the nicest I've ever stayed in. They've even got wooden coat hangers.'

'And that's your benchmark, is it? Do you know they tried to put me into number forty-one? *Forty-one!* As if it's comparable to number thirty-seven. Bloody reservations messed up the booking, pardon my French. I've had nothing but disappointment since I got here.'

'Well, ain't it lucky they fixed it all up in the end, eh? We might not have met up again if you hadn't been in number thirty-seven.'

'The thought had crossed my mind,' said Alex. 'And there's no point in trying to get any action out of that receptionist, Steven, either. He doesn't even look at you while he's failing emphatically to solve your problem.'

'I thought he was a nice bloke.'

'More your type, I suppose.'

The two Day-Glo orange floats continued their endless bobbing in the water.

'Not much luck so far, eh?' said Scratch, nodding at the river. 'Perhaps we should have a cheese sandwich?'

'Don't you want to save that bit of excitement for later? How long have we been here without a single nibble from so much as a stickleback? Two hours? Three?'

'Twenty minutes,' said Scratch. 'And anyway, I wouldn't worry about having nothing to do. Look, here comes your friend Steven.'

Alex looked over his shoulder at the approaching figure. 'Are you sure that's him? He doesn't seem so... slouched.'

The receptionist lumbered slowly but deliberately across the grass towards Alex and Scratch.

'Good afternoon, chaps,' he declared when within earshot.

'Chaps?' muttered Alex.

'Bloody fine day, what? I dare say you've found *absolutely* the right spot for a bit of rainbow trout there. There are some damn fine examples about, too. Not as good a sport as picking off the deer in the woods there, of course, but still a jolly good barrel of laughs in the right company.'

Alex stared at Steven, then looked around him for signs of a hidden camera. 'I'm sorry, are you the receptionist here?'

'Oh yes!' said Steven enthusiastically. 'And a bloody marvellous place it is, too. Do you know, this land was used by Elizabeth I as a rallying point for her navy? There are some fascinating essays about it in the British Library too, you should read them.'

'The receptionist I spoke to when I got here? Steven? Steven with a V?'

'Ah yes. I have a thin memory of being less than courteous to you on your arrival. Please accept my apologies. I'm afraid I was feeling rather a little peaky at the time, but I'm over that now, I think. Feeling tickety-boo today. Back to one's normal self, you might say.'

'With the Zelda t-shirt?'

'Yes, I'm afraid that was me, my good man.'

'But you're in a full dinner suit? Look, you've even got an embroidered handkerchief poking out and a pocket watch slung across your waist?'

'My deepest apologies. I ran out of time, you see? Lots to do and not enough time to do it in, what? I'll straighten it out as soon as I am out of sight.'

'I wasn't referring to the *fitting* of the damn watch. And you've lost half your body weight. What happened to the sweaty, unhealthy looking sandwich stuffer?'

'Funny what you do in your youth, isn't it?'

'In your youth!? It was yesterday!'

Steven looked wistfully at the lapping water. 'How times change, eh? How times change.'

'Have you seen this?' said Alex, turning to Scratch at last.

'Seems a bit odd alright,' said Scratch. 'Probably just *one of those things*.'

'A bit odd!? Am I the only one with any sense left here? This man was a lazy, ignorant, computer geek in a sweat-stained t-shirt twenty-four hours ago and now look at him!'

'He scrubs up well,' said Scratch. 'Must be into those moisturising wotsits that men like these days.'

'And how many moisturisers do you know that would halve your weight and double your class?'

'It's probably a new one.'

'Right! That's it! I'm getting out of here. There's something fishy going on here and I'm not referring to the trout. Good luck with your sanity, Mr. Scratch.'

With that, Mr. Alex Raisbeck, retired human resources manager of Newbury stomped away towards caravan number thirty-seven.

'Wait! Alex!' cried Scratch. 'You forgot your fishing tackle.'

'You can have it. I'm getting the next ferry to Portsmouth. Good day, Mr. Scratch.'

'Margaret, pack our things. We're leaving' declared Alex as he stepped into the caravan.

'What do you mean, *leaving?* Are you taking me to Chez Paris?'

'No, Dear. We're going home. It's not safe here.'

'We can't go home today. I'm only on chapter four.'

'I believe it will be possible to read your book in the comfort of our own Belgian roll arm sofa. There's something going on here, and I'm not inclined to wait around to learn what it is.'

'Are you having one of your turns again, Dear?'

'It's not a turn, Margaret. Steven is in a dinner suit.'

'Who's Steven?'

'The receptionist. With the Zelda t-shirt.'

'Oh, I see. Going out, is he? Perhaps he has a date.'

'He's half the weight he was when we arrived, and he talks like an Old Etonian. If that isn't enough to send the willies up you, I don't know what is. Now come along, we'll have to fold the duvet cover together.'

'Maybe he's practising being all lah-dee-dah for the girl.'

'By losing a hundred pounds in twenty-four hours?'

'He must really like her.'

'You've been reading Barbara Cartland again, haven't you?'

'She's a very good writer.'

'She's prolific, I'll give her that. Now, can you please dry those dishes and I'll get the cases.'

'Yes Dear.'

Mr. and Mrs. Raisbeck condensed their holiday possessions into the boot of the Volvo with practised efficiency. All that was left to do was to make the flask of tea for the journey and to select the right biscuits.

'Bourbon?' suggested Margaret.

Alex concentrated on an arbitrary spot in the middle distance. 'Perhaps I will,' he muttered. 'Actually, no. It's too early, even for a day like today.'

'You could have one while you're driving.'

'Good God, woman, are you mad? I've never drunk driven, and I don't intend to start now. And certainly not at this time of the morning.'

'It's too early for a bourbon biscuit?' asked Margaret, missing the obvious.

'Oh, a bourbon *biscuit*? Yes, yes, whichever,' said Alex, waving an arm dismissively and pressing the car key to check it was unlocked. 'Right, let's get going.'

'There you are!' called a Cockney accent that made Alex's shoulders sag. 'Are you coming back?'

'I told you I'm getting the next ferry out of here,' said Alex. 'This place is giving me the creeps.'

'And miss out on all the fun? It was one man in a dinner jacket.'

'Suit, Mr. Scratch. It was a dinner *suit*.'

'So, if he was only in a jacket you'd stay, would you?'

'That's not what I meant.'

'Well come on then, I reckon those trout he was on about are just about ready for breakfast.'

'I'm not damn well fishing!' cried Alex.

'I'm going to return the key, Dear,' said Margaret, half to herself.

'I'm going home before anything else unplanned decides to rear its ugly head,' continued Alex. 'Now if you'll excuse me, I have a ferry to catch.'

'You can't tell me you've booked a ticket already,' said Scratch, a man for whom planning a means of escape was a professional necessity. 'Even if you called them as soon as you left, you'd still be listening to the hold music.'

'I have a flexi ticket, Mr. Scratch. I'm not a complete buffoon.'

'Of course, you do. Reminds me of that time we saved the universe.'

'And that's supposed to persuade me to stay, is it? A story from a stranger about how we travelled through space and time to an alien planet to save all life in the universe?'

'*Zoomed,*' corrected Scratch.

'Sounds more like a video conference call than an alien technology to me,' said Alex. 'You could at least have made up a new word for it.'

'Well, that wouldn't have been the truth then, would it? I could show you the portal when it opens up on Monday? They said I had until about half past one in the afternoon.'

'Who're *they*, then? The little green Martians?'

'Some of them are green I grant you, but they're Arcadians, like I said, not Martians. Plus, you could come with me if you fancied it. It'd be a nice little change.'

'*A nice little change?* You're a loony, Mr. Scratch. Even if I was to believe you, which I don't by the way, it certainly would not be nice, nor little. It would be a bloody great big one with a high probability of permanent death.'

'There is that, I suppose,' conceded Scratch. 'Haven't really thought about it like that.'

'Now, if we're quite done here, I think I'll be off. Margaret, come along dear, we're going. Margaret! Margaret?'

'I think she went to return the key,' offered Scratch helpfully.

'I'll pick her up on the way then. Goodbye Mr. Scratch, it was a pleasure to see what a lunatic looks like in real life.'

With that, Alex got into his Volvo and drove towards reception. He passed number forty-one and scowled. *Number forty-one indeed*, he mumbled to himself. A minute later he pulled up to an empty reception area and took out his phone.

'Hello, Mr. Alex Raisbeck here. Reservation number one seven two eight zero two. I need to…'

'Good morning' came a chirpy but vacuous voice. 'Welcome to Jameson Ferries, Deirdre speaking. Can I begin by taking your reference number?'

'Are you all like this?'

'I'm sorry, sir?'

'Never mind. One seven two eight zero two. Mr. Alex Raisbeck. My plans have…'

'One…'

'…changed.'

'…seven…'

'Can you just tell me if there is…'

'…two…'

'…space on the two o'clock sailing?'

'…eight…'

'Look, can you forget about the reference number please? I just…'

'…zero…'

'…need to find out if…'

'…two…'

'…there is space for me on the…'

'Ah, here we are. Can you confirm your name please?'

'…two o'clock sailing. What? Oh, Alex Raisbeck.'

'Perfect, I have your booking here Mr. Raisbeck. I can see that you have a flexi booking with us, travelling out on the…'

'Right, that's it! Stop talking and listen to me. I was a human resources manager for longer than you've been alive so you can show some respect and listen. I need to know if there is space on the two o'clock sailing.'

'No problem, Mr. Raisbeck. I can check that for you. What date were you looking to travel?'

'Today, Deirdre, today!' screamed Alex.

'Let me just check for you. I know there's a folk festival on tomorrow and that usually fills the boats a bit.'

'I don't care about the folk festival, Deirdre' said Alex, gritting his teeth. 'I care about whether you have a space for a Volvo and two people.'

'It's a lovely few days there. I took an old boyfriend once. The weather was unbeliev…'

'Do you have space,' interrupted Alex. 'Yes or no, Deirdre, that's all you need to say.'

'Right. No. I'm afraid we're fully…'

Alex hung up, threw his phone onto the passenger seat and got out of the car.

'Margaret? We've got a bit of a problem.' He peered sheepishly into Steven's caravan. 'Margaret? Come on, dear. I called Jameson's, and they can't take us today.'

When no reply came, he began to search the caravan with greater urgency. He checked the toilet, the shower and, rather pointlessly, under the thin, cloth-covered mattress and inside some cupboards that would struggle to fit a small dog, let alone a late middle-aged woman of a certain composure. Finding no sign of Mrs. Raisbeck, he stepped back out into the reception area.

A figure appeared from behind the caravan and began a bee-line towards him.

'Ah, there you…' he began, before falling involuntarily to the ground.

Scratch arrived beside him, panting. He gripped Mr. Raisbeck under the armpits and hauled him unceremoniously into the Volvo. Two minutes later they were parked up at the riverbank. Scratch lifted Alex out of the car, dragged him to the water's edge, and began scooping handfuls of water over his face. After a few attempts Alex twitched, then spluttered upright.

'Morning!' said Scratch cheerily. 'Looks like you had a bit of a turn there. Not half as much as good old Mrs. Raisbeck though, I shouldn't wonder.'

'Wha' happened?' said Alex groggily.

'Looks like your missus has got the same thing your mate Steven has.'

'She had a frilly collar,' managed Alex.

'She did at that, my old mucker. Nice bonnet too. I'd say she's straight from Victorian times. Public school girl now I reckon. Harrow, if I'm not mistaken. Don't quote me on that though, it can be hard to tell with the women. No school tie, see?'

'And you'd be an expert on that sort of thing, would you?'

'Yes, as it happens. You've got a bit of experience in that regard too. Not that you believe me o' course.'

Alex rubbed the bridge of his nose patiently. 'So, on the assumption that I'm not actually asleep at this very moment, my wife has turned into an upper-class Victorian student who attends Harrow, the rotund receptionist is now an Old Etonian, and I know all this because a man of dubious provenance has travelled through space and time to inform me of such. A man, I might add, who purports to be an old adventure buddy of mine from our days saving the universe on the planet Arcadia? Have I got that about right?'

'Not quite, no,' said Scratch.

'Well thanks be for that. I was beginning to question my sanity.'

'What I mean is, it's *mostly* right. We weren't actually *on* Arcadia when we were trying to save the universe. In fact, technically we weren't *saving the universe*, we were saving all *life* in the universe. Big difference, see?'

'I'm sure there is, Mr. Scratch. I, on the other hand, prefer to deal with things that are actually happening, so if you'll excuse me.'

'Oh yes, it's far more likely that everyone in Lazy Sheights…'

'Heights!'

'Fine, that everyone in Lazy Heights is turning into some kind of posh Victorian public-school character. Way more believable, that is.'

Alex sagged, not for the first time today.

'And what do you propose we do about it? Does your unexpected knowledge base extend to how to deal with upper class zombies?'

'Well,' said Scratch, rubbing his stubble in thought. 'I suppose you could shoot 'em with a crossbow.'

'A crossbow!' exclaimed Alex, throwing his hands in the air with faux relief. 'That's brilliant! We'll just pick up our bows, load them with our sycamore arrows and Bob's your uncle. Best not to mention how that'd kill my wife though, eh?'

'They're bolts, not arrows. Plus, sycamore wood's not practical. You want a good, cheap metal when it comes to crossbow bolts.'

'Oh, well then that's us buggered then,' said Alex. 'There was me thinking I'd planned everything, but silly me only brought my sycamore crossbow equipment.'

'Well, it's better than your idea,' said Scratch defensively.

'I haven't told you mine yet.'

'Oh good, so you've got one then?'

'Not exactly, no. But then, I've only just found out my wife has turned into a… into one of *them*.'

'Did you book your ferry yet? We could just bugger off and pretend it never happened?' said Scratch.

'That wouldn't work,' said Alex.

'Right, no way to get back to the portal. Good point.'

'I meant that the sailing is fully booked. There's no way there'll be a cancellation at such short notice.'

'Portal it is, then,' declared Scratch.

'As much as I would like to take a trip through your imagination, I believe I've filled my quota of it for today. Perhaps we could come up with some other solution? One that doesn't involve time travel and does involve reality.'

'It's not really time travel,' said Scratch. 'It can be, o' course, but most of the time it's just a change in your physi-wotsits.'

'I can see you're quite the expert.'

'Nah, Professor Doubt's the real expert. I'm just the binman.'

'Mr. Scratch, I have no idea what you're talking about. Can we focus on getting ourselves out of our current predicament, please? I'm rather partial to a quiet life as you would no doubt be aware if we really had, in fact, tried to save the universe.'

'Alright, but don't say I didn't try.'

'Try? Try to what? Win the Isle of Wight Crazy Madcap Award?'

'I mean try to get us out of this mess. Still, could be worse.'

'Don't start,' said Alex, glaring again.

'Look, maybe this bloke can help us.'

A tall, thin figure was approaching from the main caravan site. They looked an awful lot like Steven, but with a little less of an aura of latent slobbery about them.

'Good morning, chaps!' it announced. 'Bloody fine one, what? I say, one could quite fancy an old game of willow and bales in this weather, don't you think?'

'Who are you?' asked Scratch in the practised tones of one for whom strangers are a dangerously unplanned variable.

'I'm Gavin, the site manager. Not quite what the old man had in mind for me as a young one, but things are different these days, what? A man's got to experience life in all its forms.'

'The manager!' exclaimed Alex. 'Now, I have a few items I need to bring to your attention. Firstly, I booked caravan number...'

'Buggering Mondays, not now, Alex!' said Scratch. 'He's one of them, ain't he?'

'Are you sure?' asked Alex. 'Seems like a bona fide manager to me. He must be doing his rounds, checking on his guests and so on.'

'He's in a bloody top hat! How many caravan site managers do you know go around in a top hat and tails? He's a bloody Etonian.'

'Harrow, actually,' corrected the zombie.

'Well, that is a bit unusual I suppose,' conceded Alex. 'Oh dear.'

'I'm glad you've joined me on the side of the bleeding obvious,' said Scratch.

'No, I mean *oh dear,*' said Alex, pointing.

'Ah.'

Dozens of public schoolboy zombies were emerging from between the caravans in the distance. All were dressed in varying degrees of toffness; from simple, but high-end, double-breasted suits, to full dinner wear with white gloves and oversized cummerbunds. All were thin and all looked annoyingly real.

Scratch whistled a sound that could be broadly translated as *phew, that's a lot of them buggers heading this way and no mistake.*

'Better get a plan soon my old mucker or there's going to be a right palaver here, wouldn't you say? Did you get much experience in this sort of thing in your time as a human resources manager?'

'*Did I get...?* No, I bloody well didn't get any Etonian zombies knocking on my office door to complain about their pension contributions. They tended to be a bit more human and a bit less undead.'

'Shame,' said Scratch. 'Would have been useful if they had been zombies from Eton though, wouldn't it?'

'Yes, Mr. Scratch, it would have been very useful indeed if my colleagues had come to me with existential conundrums about their place in society as an under-represented undead Etonian, and not about their very human tea-breaks being five minutes shorter than they were back in the day. As it is, we're stuck with it. What about you? Any zombies in your line of work?'

'On Earth, you mean?'

'Yes on Earth! Of course on Earth! Where else... oh don't. Don't even think about it. I'm not basing any of my immediate escape plans on anything you come up with that has the slightest link to your time travel nonsense.'

The zombie site manager, who had been largely ignored during this conversation, cleared his throat.

'I say, do you lot want to fill in a feedback form?'

'Not right now, if you don't mind,' said Alex. 'We're trying to save my wife from... well, from you if that's not too rude a thing to say?'

'Too rude?' cried Scratch. 'Buggering Mondays, and you think I'm the crazy one. I'm the sanest person here as likely as not. Excepting these Etonians, o' course.'

The zombies continued to pour out from between the caravans. As with all zombie hordes, their numbers were far greater than could possibly have been nearby when the whole commotion began. Not that anyone ever really notices. There are often more pressing matters than population consistency when there's a zombie bite closing in.

'Wait a minute!' said Alex, turning back to the zombie. 'What did you say?'

'I said here's a feedback form.'

'No, you didn't.'

'Yes, I did.'

You said, and I quote, *I say, do you lot want to fill in a feedback form.*'

'Well that's the same thing, isn't it?'

'Alex?' said Scratch, nudging Mr. Raisbeck's arm. 'Look at that.'

Gavin's top hat was visibly shrinking. It reached a level similar to Scratch's tweed flat cap and stopped. Scratch peered around the zombie.

'His tails have shortened too, look.'

'Where's his pocket watch?' asked Alex.

'I didn't nick it!' said Scratch almost instantly, before quickly adding 'I would've liked to alright, but it wasn't me this time I swear.'

'Who the bloody hell are they?' said Gavin as his cummerbund popped out of existence. 'If it's those teenagers again I swear I'll bloody well call the police on 'em myself.'

'Why is he doing that?' asked Alex to the world in general.

'Well, it's obvious, ain't it,' said Scratch.

'Go on,' said Alex

'Bugger. I was sort of hoping you'd know. I ain't got a Danny La Rue mate.'

'A what?'

'Oh, sorry. I ain't got a clue. One minute he's an Etonian with a plum in his mouth and the next he's like one of us.'

'One of you, maybe,' corrected Alex.

In an instant, Gavin the site manager plopped back to his old self. He was wearing a shirt that was a fraction too disheveled for a manager and polyester trousers that were obviously standard issue. The zombie horde remained undead, however.

'Buggering Mondays!' said Scratch. 'Right, think Alex. Why has he gone and changed back to normal? What happened? What did he do?'

'He didn't do anything. He just, sort of, changed back of his own accord.'

'So your plan, if I'm not mistaken, is to wait until they decide to stop being zombies? Is that about right?'

'Well, it's the start of a plan, don't you think?'

'I'll give you that, but where, precisely, are we going to wait? They're heading right for us, and the river is behind us. Not much choice really, is there?'

'We could climb one of those trees,' suggested Alex, gesturing to a clump of silver birches.

'Silver birches are notoriously difficult to climb. The branches tend to point up, see?'

'You know all about tree climbing too, then?'

'Well, it pays... *paid* to know that sort of thing in my business.'

'I'm going to assume you mean you were a tree surgeon before you were Zoomed to a different planet.'

'Yeah, let's go with that. So, once we're up there, then what?'

'Like I said, we wait.'

'That's bloody marvellous, that is. You should write the next James Bond film. Imagine the tension in the audience as they watch Sean wotsisface scratching his initials into the bark to pass the time.'

'He hasn't been James Bond since nineteen eighty-three. It's more likely to be...'

'I don't bloody care who it is. My point is that the little horde over there is getting closer, and we ain't got time to chit-chat. Come on, it's the best plan we've got. I'll give you a bunk, and you can pull me up after you.'

As the two men squabbled, Gavin snapped out of his reverie. He had been transfixed by the oncoming zombies and was now moving rather quickly towards panic.

'Don't suppose either of you have a drink on you? Just a little nip of something fiery to keep me going, you know how it is? Erm, guys? I think we'd better get a move on.'

Alex and Scratch turned to Gavin. Or at least, Gavin was *one* of the people they turned to. They were now also looking squarely at the vanguard of the zombie mob.

'I say!' called one. 'Jolly fine day, what? The boys at the club were bally well right, we could have played all day in this.'

A second piped up. 'Let's gather up and pick sides. I dare say we could rustle up a few aperitifs and a nice Bordeaux to wash them down, what?'

Then a third. 'Bordeaux? Are you quite well? A Languedoc would be more the sort of thing old boy. Less of a weight to it, wouldn't you say?'

In a matter of moments, the three non-zombies were surrounded with offers of various wines and finger foods from the pallid figures whose arms were raised just a little too much to give them plausible deniability when the day of reckoning came.

'I reckon it's time we scarpered,' said Scratch, grabbing Alex by the arm and barging through the crowd towards the nearest tree.

'What about me?' cried Gavin. 'You can't leave me here with them!'

'He's right,' said Scratch. 'Can't leave a brother behind.'

'He's not a brother, he's a posh zombie,' said Alex. 'Now are you going to bunk me up or will we ask one of these nice undead folk to give us a hand?'

'Only if he goes up too,' said Scratch with moral defiance.

'Fine, but I'm still going first.'

A minute later, the three men were clinging to branches halfway up a birch tree and the horde was now surrounding their trunk.

'I suppose we'd better come up with the next part of our plan, *Mr. Raisbeck,*' said Scratch.

'Can you see Margaret? She must be in there somewhere.'

'No, I'm afraid I can't make out your zombie wife in the middle of an onrushing mob of them,' said Scratch. 'Perhaps you could sing her favourite song to her? That might get her attention, and she can give you a little wave?'

Several arms were now scratching futilely at the trunk. Alex let out an enormous sigh, then took a deep breath.

Here we go thought Scratch. *He's about to do something uncharacteristic I reckon.*

Mr. Raisbeck let out a roar, shouting as loud as his middle-class instincts would allow. 'Would you all please just bugger off back to your Victorian Eton lives before I lose my mind completely!?'

'That should sort them out,' said Scratch, rather unhelpfully.

As it happens, it helped quite a lot. The horde responded as one, in the tone reserved for those who have been deeply offended by a class-based slur.

'WE ARE NOT FROM ETON. WE ARE HARROW!'

'Now you've gone and upset them,' said Scratch. 'Fat lot of good that'll do.'

Before Scratch had made it to the end of his sentence, however, a series of plopping noises reached them. It sounded much like a hundred fingers flicking out from a hundred cheeks, only with less saliva flying around.

'Look at their hats!' said Gavin from the highest perch. 'They're shrinking!'

'That's it!' declared Scratch.

'That's what?' said Alex and Gavin as one.

'Call them Etonians as loud as you can.'

'Are we going to offend them into submission?' said Alex with a scoff.

'Yes,' answered Scratch honestly. 'That's exactly what we're going to do. After three, we're going to call them lazy Etonian bastards.'

'Do we have to swear?' asked Alex. 'Couldn't we just call them silly Etonians and leave it at that?'

'Sure, if you want Margaret to keep her frilly collar.'

The three men shouted their profanity as loudly as they could. A few seconds later the sound of pocket watches flinching out of existence and waistcoats fizzing away could be heard all around them. The bewildered faces of former zombies swayed to and fro as they grappled with events. Any thoughts of the rehabilitated undead rationalising their predicament were soon pushed aside by the remaining zombies, who by now had forgotten the tree-folk for the moment and were closing in on their former kindred spirits. People ran in all directions, some falling to the ground gracelessly as they tried to remember how to move faster than an elderly monkey with a sore leg.

'Why aren't the others changing back?' asked Gavin.

'Let me just check the rulebook, son,' said Scratch.

'That's handy,' said Gavin. 'I didn't know you had one. We'll be out of here in no time.'

Scratch looked up at Gavin's face for signs of sarcasm. 'You ain't all there are you?'

'Maybe we didn't shout loud enough,' suggested Alex. 'I mean, I'm not one for promoting anti-social behaviour, but the ones at the back might not have heard us.'

'And the well-dressed ones at the front here?' said Scratch. 'Are they just a little hard of hearing? Perhaps turning into a zombie damages your eardrums.'

'Maybe it does,' said Alex petulantly.

'What if they're not from Harrow?' said Scratch.

'None of them are from bloody Harrow!' shouted Alex. 'They're zombies, not time travelling public bloody schoolboys!'

'How do you know? Maybe they came in through the same portal I did. Stands to reason, don't it? Professor Doubt might have got things a bit mixed up and, hey presto, zombie mob.'

'And zombies were big in Victorian times, were they? Funny, I don't remember reading about them in Mr. Edwards' history class.'

'Alright, I'll give you that one. The zombie part is a bit hard to explain, but how about we...'

'I say fellows!' interrupted a voice below them. 'What say you chaps dally down the old bark there and join us for a bit of rugger? Cuthbertson has the pitch all set up. He's a bit of a Winchester College cad, but he'll do in a pinch. He's the only one with a ball, you see? Can't for the life of me see why we don't...'

'Buggering Mondays, that's it!' declared Scratch. He stood up on his branch, puffed out his chest and roared. 'Winchester! Bloody Winchester!' Several zombies flickered back to their original form. 'Here, Alex, how many posh public schools do you know?'

'Well, there's Eton,' offered Alex.

'Of course, there's buggering Eton. What others. And don't say Harrow or I'll throw you off that branch myself.'

'Winchester?' said Alex timidly.

'Any others,' said Scratch with more patience than may have been expected. 'They're not all from Eton or Harrow. Or at least, they don't all *think* that's where they're from. I presume your dear Margaret didn't go to one, did she?'

'She went to Our Lady of Pity Independent College, and a damn fine example it was too,' said Alex defensively.

'I couldn't give a fiddler's elbow where she went so long as it wasn't one of the fancy ones. If we can remember the names of the good ones, we can turn them all back.'

'Our Lady of Pity *was* a good one, Mr. Scratch. One of their alumni became a world champion swi…'

'Shut up about your bloody pride, would you?' snapped Scratch. 'Think!'

'We could just Google it,' said Gavin, half-forgotten above them. 'People never just Google things in the movies. Always seem to lose their phone just before they need it, have you ever noticed that? Here, have either of you got a little something to calm my nerves? A nice Irish, maybe? I'd even take a little Scotch if you promise not to tell anyone.'

'I ain't got a phone no more,' said Scratch. 'Signal isn't great on Arcadia. Alex, where's yours?'

'It's in the car.'

'Gavin?'

'Yeah, I've got mine here. Always have it with me in case of an emergency.'

'And the battery?' said Scratch through narrowed eyes.

'Seventy eight percent. I always make sure it's fully…'

'Signal?' pressed Scratch. 'Tell me you've got a bloody signal.'

'Let's see,' said Gavin, peering at the corner of the screen. 'Yes, four bars.'

'Right, so we're not in a movie then,' said Scratch. 'Get a list of posh English Public Schools, quick.'

'How do you do that, then?' said Gavin.

'What do you mean, how do you do that? You bloody well Google it!'

'Right you are. How, erm, I mean, how do you Google something? Is it one of these little squares?'

'You can't be serious? How long have you lived in the twenty-first century? Give it here, I'll do it.'

Scratch took the phone, tapped the screen, and puffed out his chest again. 'Copy me, lads. Ready? Gordonstoun! King's! Westminster! Wycombe Abbey! St Paul's!'

The air filled with fizzing and plopping. The last of the horde of public-school zombies morphed back into checkout operators and civil servants.

'Buggering Mondays, we did it, lads!' said Scratch. 'Who'd have thought it, eh?'

'Where's Margaret? Can anyone see Margaret?' said Alex, shading his eyes with a hand.

'Can we get down now?' said Gavin. 'Only, I'm not a fan of heights.'

'Don't,' said Alex, glaring at Scratch.

'Don't what?'

'Make a joke about Lazy Heights.'

'Wouldn't dream of it,' said Scratch. 'Now, are we going to get down or are we waiting to see if they change back?'

They scaled back down the tree and meandered through the crowd of stunned ex-zombies. Alex called his wife's name every now and again. This time the cliché *was* just like in the movies. Margaret appeared from behind a post office clerk.

'Hello Dear,' she called. 'Are we leaving?'

'Yes, I think we better had. Not sure we'll make it home today, Margaret. The whole itinerary has been shot to pieces, but I'm sure we'll find an acceptable bed and breakfast for the night.'

'You could come with me,' said Scratch. 'I reckon the prof could Zoom you back to Newbury in no time. And I mean *no time*. He could even send you to before you booked the holiday, and you could choose somewhere else instead. How about that then, mate?'

'Don't be ridiculous, Mr. Scratch. I booked the trip in February.'

'Don't make no difference, that,' said Scratch. 'He can send you anywhen.'

'I'm sure he can,' lied Alex. 'That isn't my concern. Margaret's sister came by in March, and we had to sit through three hours of photographs from her trip to Eastbourne. I'm not going through that again, I can assure you.'

'Right, well that's that then, I suppose,' said Scratch ponderously. 'Still can't believe it's you. After all this time, eh? Maybe next time we'll have that fishing trip, but without the undead popping up to stunt the conversation?'

'Yes,' said Alex, wondering how to get away from this madman. 'If I'm ever in Arcadia and all that.'

'You don't believe me, do you?'

'What? That you arrived here through a portal from another planet? One that I myself have visited? Why wouldn't I believe that?'

'I could prove it to you if you like?'

'With what? An anecdote?'

'How about a portal?'

'That would do it, I suppose. Now if you'll excuse me, Margaret and I must be going.'

Scratch cleared his throat. 'Zen horseface.'

'You are quite mad, do you know that?' said Alex. 'Goodbye Mr....'

The sight of a swirling purple and black vortex stopped Mr. Raisbeck from finishing his sentence. On this timeline at least. A man stepped out and nodded at Scratch. He was certainly a scientist of some sort; he had the pens in his breast pocket to prove it and his glasses appeared to be slightly too weak for his requirements.

'Mr. Raisbeck!' he said, grinning wildly and grasping the retired human resources manager's hand. 'How good to see you again. Everything going well in Newbury? Right, well I can see you're a little thrown by all this. Forgot you wouldn't remember it all, what with everything that's been going on.'

'What's happened?' said Scratch. 'Has Corporal Cauliflower finally tried the top shelf drink in Moon Shots?'

'Oh nothing as bad as all that. Just a little declaration of war from those buggers in the Convoluted Nebula.'

'What's on the top shelf?' asked Gavin. 'A nice little nerve-calmer?'

'You wouldn't believe me if I told you,' said Scratch.

'Excellent! And it's this way, is it?' said Gavin, gesturing to the vortex.

'Sort of,' said Professor Doubt. 'Much like a spot on a teenager's face is *sort of* a volcano.'

'Great,' said Gavin, and threw himself into the purple and black spiral.

'That won't end well,' said Scratch. 'Come on, prof, we'd better help him out.'

Scratch and the professor stepped towards the vortex. Scratch turned to Alex. 'Bye then, my old mucker. Just remember to come and visit, eh?'

'I'll be sure to jump into the next vortex I see,' said Alex.

'Great, can't wait mate! Just say the codewords and you'll be sipping melancholy in Moon Shots before the echo has died.'

'What codewords?'

'The ones I just used. Can't say them again, can I, or there'll be all kinds of existential-wotsits? Cheerio!'

Scratch and Professor Doubt stepped into the vortex and disappeared with a satisfying *whoosh*.

'Did that just happen?' said Alex to his wife.

'Which bit, Dear?'

'All of it.'

'Yes, I think it may have. Come on, let me get you a bourbon before we get going. You know how bad the roads can get here at this time of day.'

'Good idea, Margaret. Maybe not the biscuit type this time, though.'

Black Teeth

By William Alan Webb

It was a crazy story, and I didn't know nothin' about it 'til Hiram told me. Hiram not bein' the most reliable of sources, I called on Spaghetti Jones to verify. It's not that Hiram lies, exactly, he just sometimes gets confused by what he calls a hangover. Doc Whitfield looked it up in one o' his books and called it Meth Psychosis, which are big words meanin' that Hiram's brain's all turned to bobcat scat from that stuff he cooks up. Most folk around here like 'shine, but Hiram calls himself a chemist and mixes things that probably ought not to be mixed.

Anyway, Spaghetti Jones backed up Hiram's wild-ass story about these mole-things the size of a yearling white-tail, comin' up outa the ground, hundreds of 'em, with chipmunk teeth the size of a Ka-bar. Black teeth, too, all shiny black, not black like maggoty-roadkill black, but black like the feathers of a fat, old crow who's been eatin' good. According to Hiram, the moles could turn into people so's they could snatch victims. He didn't say *why* they wanted people, 'cause I guess he probably didn't know. I didn't figure it took too much imagination to figure it out.

Now, some people call me a Doubtin' Thomas, but where I lived you heard stories like that all the time. With television gone, and mostly no electric power, there ain't a whole lot more to do at night than swap whoppers. I don't usually pay 'em no mind, but sometimes that policy came back to bite me on the butt. Like later that day when a herd of them things came chasin' Mattie McCoy over the soybean field, down by Deep Cut Creek. Once I saw the first few come runnin' out of the tree line, I believed.

It Came from the Trailer Park

Lucky for me, nobody in Mississippi stepped out their front door without a firearm, not since…well, no reason to go into all that again. With most of the people gone now, there ain't nobody left to thin out the wildlife. Deer won't bother you none, except for eatin' up your crops, but thousands of hungry boars lookin' to eat anything they can sink their tusks into, and that includes your leg, well that's a different story. Bears, cougars, bobcats, hell, we even got rattlesnakes back down here again. There's all kinds of critters now that you gotta take count of, and that don't begin to mention people. Don't nobody I know trust a stranger, and ain't no stranger I've met who expects to be trusted. It's a shoot-first world now.

I took, and still take multiple guns everywhere, under my daddy's theory that you could have too little firepower, but you can't never have too much. That way if the boars showed up, then we'd all be havin' barbequed ribs for supper.

I saw right off that Mattie wasn't gonna make it before them things caught up to her. Young as she was, an' fast the way only people feared of dyin' can be fast, them things was still faster. I liked Mattie, liked her a lot, maybe *more* than a lot, so instead of pickin' up my single-shot long rifle, I grabbed the AR-15 with sixty-round magazine and went to work.

Whatever them things was, I called 'em Black Tooths for obvious reasons, they had a weird, lopin' sort of gait. Made it hard to keep the scope on 'em, but I was what you call motivated. I don't usually miss what I shoot at, and I didn't that day, neither. The first round hit one of them things square between the eyes, the closest one to her, and damned if that bullet didn't bounce off. I thought Daddy had a hard head, but compared to them things, his skull was mush. It stunned the ugly sucker, though.

Mattie got away, took about five steps, and then stumbled. The same one jumped toward her leg, but this time I aimed for its right eye. It stopped in mid-jump and flopped around like a bluegill on a hot river rock. That gave Mattie time enough to get back on her feet.

"Dig into it, girl. They's right on your heels!" I yelled at her. The rifle cracked and punched backward into my shoulder. Through the scope I watched another one o' them weird things roll over. There must've been two dozen at the least, but the ones further back quit chasin' Mattie and went for their wounded brothers. Through the rifle's scope I watched 'em dig into the one I'd just shot, with their long black teeth comin' up bright red as they tore out chunks o' flesh. It weren't pretty.

Mattie didn't need to be told twice to hightail it my way. I covered her o' course but switched out the AR for my black powder rifle. Ever since The Shit, as Daddy called it, you cain't hardly find store bought ammo, but I could mix powder and cast shot afore I was knee-high to a grasshopper. Every boy an' girl could. Without thinkin' about it, I also made note o' where I was in the field so later on I could 'police my brass', which meant pick up the empty shell casings.

We hadn't had rain for a while, so Mattie kicked up quite a dust cloud as she jumped and dodged the half-grown soybeans. I waited to shoot 'til one got too close and put it down with a shot to the neck. Mattie didn't stop but jumped up onto the tractor's runnin' board. Once she'd climbed up there weren't nowhere for her to sit 'cept my lap, which I didn't mind, but *was* a little distractin' as I cranked the tractor hard left and hit the gas. What with her arm around my neck so she didn't fall off an' all, I couldn't see the way I usually could. Not that I minded much. My heart started thumpin' from havin' Mattie in my arms, and I kind o' lost track of the situation for a couple o' seconds.

"Perry Joe," Mattie purred in my right ear, "maybe we should go. Them things is after us again," and damned if they wasn't. I shifted into third gear and stepped on the gas, although if we'd been usin' actual gas for fuel then I would've felt better 'bout our chances of gettin' away. But if machine made ammo was scarcer than a cigarette-smokin' armadillo, gasoline weren't to be found nowhere. Some folks used 'shine for fuel, like I'd asked Daddy to do. He said no, that was a waste, and that wood worked just fine.

Truth to tell, if them Black Teeth wasn't lopin' after us, I wouldn't have been in such a hurry to get away. I didn't want Mattie to ever get off my lap. I could see the sweat runnin' down her cheeks an' makin' her hair stick to her skin. Her shirt was soaked too, an' I didn't exactly see that as a bad thing. Unlike my brothers, an' even my sister Billie, Mattie didn't stink like a pissed-off copperhead when she got sweaty. Not to me anyway. I thought she smelt kinda nice. And if she was bothered by my obvious reaction to her sittin' so close, she didn't mention it.

Then one of them moles bit the plow hitch so hard we skewed sideways a might, an' I quit moonin' after Mattie so I could save both our lives. It didn't do much good to be in love if you was dead.

"You good with an AR?" I asked, which was a stupid question, as I already knew, and Mattie reminded me.

"Perry Joe Deloach, you've known me your whole life. You know I'm a better shot than you'll ever be."

I started to say somethin' about not wastin' ammo, but that was even stupider than askin' if she could shoot. Plus, the moles was gainin' on us, and savin' ammo didn't seem to be our most pressin' concern.

But shootin' from a tractor that was bouncin' down rows of half-grown soybeans weren't the easiest thing, even without all the smoke from the wood-burnin' engine. I had my replica 1851

Colt Navy Revolver on my left side, but if it came down to me usin' it, we was in big trouble.

We was in big trouble.

A Black Teeth jumped on the runnin' board next to my left foot, its big old curved claws grabbin' onto anything to keep from fallin' off. We hit a rut about then and it bounced up, which is when it lost grip and raked them sharp claws against my shin. The heavy denim of my jeans kept it from tearin' me up too bad, but when it started clackin' them six inch teeth together and starin' at my thigh like it was a hambone, I confess I might've panicked for a second or two. And maybe it got worse when those teeth chomped on my boot. They didn't penetrate the snake-hide, but I sure as hell felt them points diggin' into the top o' my toes.

Hangin' onto the steerin' wheel with one hand, and with Mattie squeezing off shots from my lap, I somehow managed to pull out the Colt and put three rounds down the mole's right ear canal. I couldn't hear much over the tractor, but I think it grunted before it fell off. My leg was bleedin' and hurt worse than a cottonmouth bite, which I can attest to from personal experience. I had to ignore all that and keep drivin', hopin' they get tired o' tryin' to kill us.

By this point we was in sight o' the homestead, and I prayed to baby Jesus that my Daddy or brothers heard all the shootin' and came to investigate. Turns out I was in better with the Lord than I thought, or maybe it was His shock at hearin' from me, but for whatever reason I saw my whole family runnin' toward me carryin' guns.

"Hang on Mattie, we's almost there!" I yelled out, but when she didn't say nothin', I turned and saw her face all covered with blood. I got mad like hadn't happened since Roy Kramer tried to steal some o' our goats. What I wanted to do was stop the tractor, get down and kill one o' them moles with my bare hands, which would've resulted my death, but I didn't much care. I thought Mattie was dead, and that set off a red rage inside me.

Good thing I didn't stop the tractor, 'cause it turns out she weren't expired after all. A moan lemme know she needed doctorin' more than buryin', so I kept drivin' until my family opened fire like the Sword o' God, which after all maybe they was. He does work in mysterious ways.

Wasn't nothin' mysterious about the lead they pumped into them moles. When you gotta load your own ammo, you work up to bein' a pretty good shot. Even my littlest brother Toddy could hit a runnin' rabbit with a single-shot shotgun…leastwise, he says he did. Anyways, Daddy'd spread everybody out in a kind o' skirmish line, and when they let fly, wasn't no part o' me that worried about gettin' hit. Hot lead ripped into them Black Teeths.

I aimed the tractor at a gap between my sister Clemmy and our cousin, Betty June. They was yellin' at me but I couldn't hear what they said over all the noise. The tractor engine didn't much like a wood-fired steam engine and backfired a lot, not to forget how loud the cylinders was even when I weren't pushing the gas pedal to the floor. The moles' squealin', the shootin', the yellin', Mattie's moanin', it all combined to make such a ruckus it was all I could do to keep the tractor from doin' a header after hittin' a rut.

Somehow, I held onto Mattie. I gripped her pretty hard, and unlessin you get the wrong idea, it weren't nothin' untoward. My leg hurt pretty bad by then, and she was turnin' pale under all that blood, so doin' somethin' I ought not do wasn't nowhere in my mind. Asides, I planned to spend the rest o' my life doin' that with her, so I didn't see no need to hurry.

Once I got to the house, I put the tractor in park and lifted Mattie down as gentle as I could. The collar of her shirt was all soaked with blood. Stiffness in my left leg gave me a limp as I carried her up the porch steps. That's when I saw Rotten Roger Rodgers comin' out our front door.

I'd swore to deck him if I ever laid eyes on him again, but I didn't expect even Rotten Roger would be so low as to rob my family in a moment o' crisis. It just goes to show that you shouldn't never underestimate the wickedness in the heart of a wicked man.

Roger was big and hairy and always had a grin like he'd slipped a fifth ace into a hand of five-card stud. When he saw me, I figured him to bolt toward a horse I hadn't recognized that was tethered over in the shade, 'cept he didn't. At first, I figured it was 'cause my hands was full o' Mattie McCoy, and he figured I couldn't hurt him without puttin' her down, but that weren't it. He had a rifle and brushed by me on the way to where Daddy and the others was shootin' at the moles, stoppin' just long enough to see that Mattie was hurt, but alive. Then he patted my shoulder.

"We'll get 'er back," he said, "don't you worry none, Perry Joe. Your Momma's as good as back home."

"What do you mean by that?" I called after him, but hefty as he was, once Rotten Roger got up a head o' steam there weren't no stoppin' him.

When The Disturbances happened, Daddy rebuilt the house usin' field stone and hardwood. He said it needed to be stout, in case somebody tried to take what we had, like a fort. That only happened a couple o' times, but Daddy was right. When you're getting' shot at, it's mighty nice to have a big ol' rock between you and the other fella.

'Cause it gets pretty damned hot in Mississippi, he cut a bunch o' new windows, put some vents in the roof, and covered 'em with stout shutters. All them hard surfaces meant things echoed, so when I called for Momma to help with Mattie, my voice rang like I was down a well. Momma didn't answer. I hadn't much listened to Rotten Roger, only now I had a sinkin' feelin' in my guts.

I couldn't think about that right then, though. Mattie was still moanin' and twistin' in my arms, and while I carried her inside, I had a momentary thought about it bein' a threshold. I couldn't think about that, neither. So, I laid her down on my bed and fetched a bowl o' water and a clean rag. That's when she woke up.

"What happened?" she said.

"Them Black Teeth got hold o' ya," I said, "you're over to my house. Now you hold still while I clean you up."

Sticky blood run down her cheeks and nose from the gash on her forehead, right about the hair line, but it looked a lot worse than it was. She reached up and touched my cheek, and I kinda got lost lookin' in her eyes. They was the color of cornflowers. Ever since her boyfriend, Eskell Parveneu, went missin' a few months back, I'd set my sights on marryin' Mattie McCoy, and there weren't nothin' I would do to mess that up.

"You're sweet to take care o' me like this Perry Joe," she said, showin' off her white teeth. "But you make sure your hands stay off my naughty bits, you hear?"

"Don't you worry none Mattie," my Daddy's voice called out from behind me, "I raised him better than that. And if I didn't, I'll box his ears. Move aside son, let me look at her."

I stepped back to give Daddy time to inspect Mattie and clean her up a bit more. Clemmy, Toddy and Betty June was standin' right outside the door to the room I shared with my other brother, Dustin.

"Where's Momma?" I said.

"They got her," Toddy said. Clemmy hit him on the arm. "Oow, stop it!"

"Daddy said to let him do the talkin'," she said.

"Momma's gone?" I said, not havin' time for no sibling rivalry nonsense. "Who is 'they'? Who got her?"

"The Black Teeth, that's who," said Rotten Roger, who'd meanwhile come back inside. He was so dusty, and sweatin' so much, that it dripped off his beard like drops of mud. "I saw it happen. She was outside feeding the chickens when a whole bunch of those things came out of the ground, snatched her up, and dragged her back down into their hole. They grabbed a couple of hens, too."

Given how I didn't much like Rotten Roger, my first reaction was to not believe him, and said so.

"Go look for yourself," he said, "the hole's out there by the coop."

"What were you doin' around our house?" I asked, puttin' as much suspicion as I could into the way I said it. That's when Daddy came out to join us.

"I asked him over here," he said, the way he does when he don't want no arguments. "Gabi Crockett told me that Roger knows more about the moles than anybody else around, and I wanted to talk to him about it. He was nice enough to come over, and he's a guest in this house, so I expect my children to show him courtesy. If we're gonna get your Momma back, and we *are* gonna get her back, I want to know what I'm up against."

He's here to see what he can steal or mooch, I thought. I daren't not say it out loud, though. I might be a lot bigger than my Daddy, but when it comes to meanness ain't nobody holds a candle, and he don't never get meaner than when you talk back. Daddy invited Roger to sit at the dinin' table, and set Clemmy, Betty June, Toddy and Dustin to bring out whatever food we had that didn't need to be cooked, with somethin' to drink. No 'shine, though; we was goin' huntin', and alcohol don't mix with shootin'. Then we talked.

First, Daddy explained they'd dropped four moles dead, but hit more'n twice that many more. "Harder to kill than a boar, that's for damned sure," as he put it. "Curved black teeth longer than my hand, with other teeth further back. Jaw is wider than a plain old mole, but the claws are the same, only a helluva lot bigger. If we hadn't been in such a hurry to get chasing after your Momma, we'd have dragged one back to see if they're good eating."

"They ain't," Roger said, shakin' his head. A curled-up lip showed the roots o' his teeth was damned near as black as them moles. "They taste like a day-old carp, but stringy, and oily. Not sure I could choke it down if I was starving. Hogs seem to like 'em, so I figure your best bet is to fatten up the local boar by letting them dispose of the carcasses, and then have a big ol' Hi-wah-yun barbeque."

"You've eaten one?"

"I have. One came at me right after I got done using the outhouse. I killed him out of sheer reflex, it being the dead of night and all. Figured I might as well eat him, that's when I figured out I'd rather eat an old tire than one of them moles."

"Huh," Daddy said.

I started tappin' my toe, tryin' to keep my yap shut. Time was wastin' and none of that was gettin' us closer to findin' Momma.

The others brought in some cheese, dried meat, bread, butter and some peaches, along with a pitcher o' water, which we passed around.

"Touch o' 'shine wouldn't really hurt nothing," Roger said, putting his fingers close together and checkin' Daddy's expression. It was his best frown, so Roger shut up. That's when we all turned as Mattie came in to join us. She looked sickly and walked kinda slow. I went over to give an arm to lean on until she sat down at the table.

"Child, you're better off in bed," Daddy said. I thought the same thing.

Mattie waved a hand. "No sir. They got my folks too."

"Ah damn."

"I'm a-gettin' 'em back, Mister Deloach. Wherever you're goin', I'm goin' too."

"I can't allow that."

"No offense meant, but I wasn't askin'. I'll go by myself if I have to."

Betty June giggled until Daddy shut her up with a side glance, the way only he could do. Toddy and Dustin looked my way. It wasn't much of a secret that I intended to marry Mattie one day, even if she didn't know it yet, so they must've figured I'd speak up to keep her safe. I weren't that stupid. I'd seen Mattie shoot, and she didn't need me fightin' any battles for her. Apparently, Daddy thought so too, 'cause he did somethin' he'd never do with his own progeny, he gave in.

Ain't anything in the world I'd rather stare at than Mattie McCoy up close…unless my Momma had gone missin'. As it was, I leaned forward to hear better everything Rotten Roger said. I already told you I trusted him less than I did a cottonmouth and hoped Daddy wouldn't neither. He's a damned smart man, my Daddy, but sometimes he tries too hard to see good in people where there ain't none to be seen, no matter how hard you look.

Indian lore of the Choctaw Nation told about things crawlin' out o' the ground somewhere in Central Mississippi, things in the shapes of animals that could also take on the form of men. The Black Teeth first showed up maybe four months earlier, about the time Rotten Roger came back from somewhere in Alabama. That's how he first noticed 'em, they'd dug holes in his yard and was draggin' a big ol' boar down into the Earth. Apparently, the pig took a chunk out o' one of the Black Teeth, and then hightailed it back to the woods."

"Why didn't you tell somebody afore now?" Daddy asked.

"I did!" Roger said, with a might too much vigor for my taste, "I told Hiram right away!"

"Hiram's lucky his brain hadn't leaked out his ears yet," Daddy said, and I heard some o' the suspicion I'd begun havin' touch his voice. "Why in the hell did you tell him?"

Roger spread his arms. "Why wouldn't I? No offense Virgil, but we ain't exactly what you'd call close friends. I did what I did, and today I came over here in good faith, 'cause Gabi said you wanted to see me. I didn't make you come to my place, now did I? No, I did the neighborly thing. But if you don't want me here, just say the word and I'll head back home."

Say it, Daddy, I thought. *Say it, say it*…I never trusted Rotten Roger before, and in that moment, somethin' made me trust him less than ever. I wanted Daddy to send him on his way, so's we could go after Momma. By then I didn't believe anything Roger'd said and was fixin' to ask if I could beat the truth out o' him when Daddy answered.

"My apologies Roger, what with Beth missing I guess I'm a little jumpy. What would you suggest we do?"

"I'd get my firearms and go down that hole after your wife and Momma, Virgil. That's what I'd do."

"All of us?"

"Well, maybe not the girls, or the boy." He nodded at Toddy when he said that last part.

"I ain't no boy!" Toddy said.

"And you ain't leavin' me here neither!" threw in Clemmy. Betty June bein' Momma's sister's daughter, and nearly as old as me, she didn't say nothin'. I guess she figured Daddy's words didn't apply to her.

"Hush!" Daddy said, and silence fell real quick. The look he gave us made sure nobody would speak up again. "Go on Roger, please forgive my over-enthusiastic offspring."

"It's alright, they're worried about their Ma," Roger said, in that greasy way of his, "they wanna go down and get her back."

"You think that's what we should do?"

"Sometimes a man's just gotta take action."

"Uh-huh...sure, that makes sense." Now I could see Daddy's hackles gettin' up. I don't think Roger did though, 'cause Daddy was mighty good at lettin' you talk yourself into trouble. "Of course, there is one part of this I don't understand. See, we could've gone down that hole right off, except you told us to make a plan first, and then we heard Perry Joe fighting off them Black Teeth. That's some coincidence, huh? If it hadn't been for you talking me out of it, we'd have been down that hole when Perry Joe needed us, almost like you knew they were coming. And now here we are, all circled back to where we were two hours ago."

Roger sat back a little as everybody looked his way. I guess it finally dawned on him that Daddy wasn't buyin' the manure he was shovelin'.

"Why would I do that?"

Daddy glanced my way and gave a little nod, then turned back toward Rotten Roger. Roger was facin' Daddy, so he didn't see when I used my left hand to slide the Colt out o' my holster. I hadn't reloaded but still had three shots left.

"I can't say why you'd do that Roger. It's not something that would enter my mind."

"What in blazin' Hell are you implying?" Roger said. He stood up so fast his chair fell over. His fists balled up and he towered over Daddy. He was tremblin', like he was so mad he couldn't hold himself back. I didn't believe none of it, men like Rotten Roger are cowards, not fighters. Leastways it didn't last long, not after I laid the barrel of the Colt to the back o' his head. It made a loud *click* when I cocked it.

"Whatever you're thinkin' about doin'," I said, "you might wanna rethink it."

"I ain't moppin' up no brains," Clemmy said, "you shoot him Perry Joe, you clean up after."

"Might be worth it," I said.

"Whoa now!" Roger said, holding up his hands. He tried to turn and look at me, but I nudged him with the gun so's he couldn't. I felt his tremblin' shakin' the pistol's barrel. "What the hell're y'all mad at me for? I'm just trying to help."

"Maybe so," Daddy said, "maybe this is all just a big misunderstanding, and if that's true, then you will get my most sincere apology, Roger. But see, here's the part I don't quite understand. You said...what was it? You grilled up them moles?"

"He didn't say how he cooked it Daddy, just how it tasted," I said.

Daddy pointed at me and nodded. "That's right. So how did you cook it, Roger? You grill it, boil it, sauté it in a cast iron skillet? How'd you do it?"

"I, uh–"

"What?" Daddy grinned some, and sat back, waitin' for Roger to answer. When after a while he didn't, Daddy went back to talkin'. "See, the reason that's important is because of the ones we dropped out there in the field. Once they'd been dead for a might, they sort of changed, you see, from what looked like a mole, into what sure as hell looked like a human being, a person, just like me, and my wife and kids…and you, Roger, what about you?" Any friendly edge remainin' in Daddy's voice turned into nothin' less than a threat. My daddy was a great man, but he could be dangerous at need. "Are you a human being, Roger?"

"You son a bitch," Roger said, "what the hell kinda question is that? You invited me here, remember?"

"It's hard not to remember when you keep saying it, but that didn't answer my question."

"Why would you ask such a thing?"

"You been gone from this community for a long time Roger, going all the way back to right after the Disturbances, and then you come back, and right about then these moles show up. And you supposedly see them, but only tell the most unreliable soul in this whole area. Why's that?"

"I told Gabi Crockett!"

"No, you didn't. I asked her before I invited you over here. Hiram told her, and said you told him, but you didn't tell her direct. You said you did, but you didn't. That makes a man wonder what else you're lying about."

"I ain't gotta put up with this!"

Roger meant to turn, as if darin' me to shoot, so I did. Nobody told me to do it, and I figured Daddy'd get on me about it later, but in the moment, I was too mad to care. I moved the barrel to the back of his left ear and pulled the trigger.

The ball blasted off half his ear. Hot gunpowder sprayed his neck, and the sound blew out his ear drum. In case you don't know, ears bleed real bad and his was no exception. Blood gushed down his jaw. Roger bent over and danced around, howling like a dog scared o' thunder. I re-cocked the Colt and kept it aimed at him. I still had two shots left.

Daddy watched him a few seconds, and then took his favorite shotgun down off the wall. He used the barrel to smack Roger on the head, drivin' the fat man to his knees. Then Daddy stuck the shotgun under his chin and lifted Roger's head until their eyes met.

"One more chance at the truth, Roger," Daddy said, "just one more. Lie to me again, and I'll paint your brains on the ceiling. I won't think twice about doing it. Now what the goddamned hell is this all about?"

I'd never heard Daddy take the Lord's name in vain afore, which told me exactly the depth o' his anger. Apparently, Roger got it, too, 'cause he started blubberin' somethin' awful. I holstered the Colt, since Daddy seemed to have it under control. By this time Roger was rockin' back and forth on his knees.

"Alright, alright, I'll tell ya!" Roger yelled. "Just keep that fool boy of yours from shooting again. Damn that hurts!"

"Maybe he should take off the other, too, just so you don't forget," Daddy said.

"No! They made me do it! There, you happy? The moles made me do it."

"That's gonna require a bit of explaining."

So, Roger opened up, and there weren't no doubt that this time he told it straight.

By this time, you might be wonderin' why we hadn't gone straight away down that hole to get Momma back. We was worried, sure. I kept picturin' them Black Teeth doin' terrible things to Momma, but Daddy always taught us to center on the target afore you shoot. The best I can tell you is that she weren't no wilted daisy, our Momma. We loved her, don't get me wrong, and that's not to say that usin' the word 'adore' would be puttin' too fine a point on it, but we also knew what happened when you got Momma's hackles up.

Oh, and remember when I told you that nobody never went nowhere without bein' armed? From the time I was old enough to use the outhouse alone, Momma made sure I had firearm and she never failed to take her own advice. If she'd gone to feed the chickens, she'd been armed with at least two pistols and knew how to use 'em. Daddy told me he'd once seen her pluck a chicken at fifty paces, usin' nothin' but some help from Mister Smith and Mister Wesson. Not sure I believe that, but not sure I don't, neither.

Rotten Roger told us that he'd once been like everybody else, a regular person, that is. Not a nice one, as he readily admitted, and that's what got him turned. A long time afore, back when some people still put a value on cash money, somebody invited him to a cock fight. I'm sorry to say that has become a major form of entertainment among the belly-crawling folk who like seein' animals die for their own pleasure, and Rotten Roger went, lookin' to make some easy money by wagerin'. He'd been to many such in his young life, only that one was a trap. What occurred weren't a case of a good man gone bad, but more a case of a bad man gone worse.

Roger described the fightin' ring setup like most such, some rusty metal sheets lined up a circle so's the roosters couldn't get out. Just afore the first bird was about to be tossed in to fight for its life, the organizers pulled out shotguns and lined up all the ones come to bet on the fights. They was led into a sorta tunnel dug into the side of a hill and taken underground, where they got turned.

Momma made sure we could read and write, and Daddy brought home every book he came across. My favorites were monster stories with werewolfs and vampires, so's the idea of a man turnin' into a giant mole wasn't so odd to me as it was the rest o' my family. 'Cept accordin' to Roger, that ain't how it happened. He went into great description about some kinda ceremony, much o' which he said he didn't remember, but couldn't place any of them moles bitin' him nowhere. To his recollection, the whole process took some long while to happen.

So, Daddy, Mattie and me armed ourselves each with a repeating rifle, a sidearm and lots of ammo. Mattie had another cloth tied around her head as a bandage. When she saw me carryin' my AR, she seemed relieved.

"I thought I lost it."

"The others picked it up, cleaned it while we was talkin' and refilled the magazine. Once't we get back, I'll have to go search around for the shell casings, I can't be losin' too many o' those."

"I'll help you if you want," she said, "seems the least I can do."

I damned near fainted, but tried to keep from showing how much I'd started tremblin' in the last two seconds. Unfortunately, my voice shook.

"I–I'd l-like that."

She laughed, really pretty like, and patted my forearm. Then Daddy said it was time to go. I have to admit that when I stared at Mattie, I kind of lost track o' everything else, even Momma.

It was early afternoon and bright sunshine cooked on our skin, as we was fixin' to head down to rescue Momma. We took the two flashlights that we charged-up with the bicycle generator Daddy built, since it didn't seem there'd ever be a better use for 'em. The batteries was rechargeable, but everybody knows you can only do it so many times afore it don't work no more. The others wanted to go too, but Daddy refused. Told 'em it was their job to defend the homestead, from inside the house. Under no circumstances was they to go outside. Rotten Roger didn't wanna go, he offered to stay back and help Clemmy and the others in case they found trouble, only Daddy didn't give *him* no choice. He weren't only goin', he was goin' *first* down that hole. Unless Daddy was mistakenated, we was headin' for a skunk fight. Best that Roger get squirted first.

When I talk about the hole we went down, it was somethin' like a crawdad volcano, only a lot, lot bigger. We had to climb over all that dirt just to get into the hole. It didn't go straight down, neither, but kinda sideways like, and it was big enough we could crawl without rollin' down into the blackness ahead. I followed Rotten Roger with the AR slung over my back and holdin' the Colt in my right hand. Weren't no danger of it going off by accident, since I only half-cocked it.

The crawl was about as nasty as nasty gets. Once't you got maybe three feet underground, the soil was mighty wet. For a while they was roots in our way, which I guess them Black Teeth slid past. Me bein' the biggest of our bunch I nearly got snagged on one, which is when my Ka-bar came in handy. It cut through that tap root clean and fast.

Moles are a lot like mice and rats, they don't much care where they do their business, and while I didn't go lookin' for Black Teeth scat, even assumin' I'd know it when I saw it, from the smell I assumed we crawled through some. It was cold, the way it is when you're too deep for sunlight to warm the ground, but we was sweatin' so hard it soaked our clothes. I might not have minded had Mattie been ahead o' me, I could think o' worse things than watchin' her sweaty backside swing back and forth, but seein' the same sight when them buttocks belonged to Roger, that weren't so pleasant.

Eventually the tunnel leveled out, and from up ahead I saw a glow o' light, which ain't somethin' you 'spect to see down below. I'd been assumin' that Black Teeth was mostly like the moles what eat up crops from underground, and I always assumed they could see in the dark. Or maybe they was like snakes, what smelled with their tongues. Whatever it was, I didn't 'spect they'd have what looked to be a fire goin'. I poked Rotten Roger's buttocks with the barrel o' the Colt.

"What is that?" I said, quiet like.

"It's a fire you damned fool," he said, kind o' snappish, which I didn't much like considerin' the situation.

"You might wanna think about where this pistol is aimed at," I said.

He must've done that, 'cause next he said "I'm very sorry, Perry Joe, forgive me, it's the stress I'm under right now."

"You'll be a lot more stressed if you speak to me that way again." I think he nodded. "Now what cause do them Black Teeth have for makin' a fire underground…and where's all the smoke goin'?" Truth was, I couldn't smell nothin' 'cept a general rotten smell, there weren't no wood smoke in it.

"I don't know, honest," Rotten Roger said, "but that fire means…we gotta hurry, Perry Joe."

Daddy wanted to know what we'd been sayin', so I told him. He then crawled up close to me and talked to Rotten Roger direct. "If you're leading us into a trap, be aware I'm using my first two shots on you. You understand?"

"I sure enough do, Virgil," Rotten Roger said, "and I'm so sorry for all of this."

"Put that manure back in the bull."

I'd kind o' forgot about my leg. Back at the house I'd wiped off the wound and smeared honey on it, then wrapped a clean piece o' cloth around it as a bandage. It got tight as we conversated about how to find Momma, but all the crawlin' loosened it back up. Only in doin' so it started hurtin' again, throbbin' like when you're too close to the wood stove. Since a fight was likely any time now, I figured that havin' loose and sore was the better part o' limpin' on a stiff leg.

Once't we'd gotten close enough, I could see where the tunnel let out into a sort o' chamber, with room to stand up, that was maybe forty feet across. I don't know what got into Rotten Roger in that moment, and as things turned, I couldn't never ask him. But about five feet from where the tunnel ended, he started crawlin' real fast like.

"Stop it!" I said, not all that low. "I'll shoot you dead if you don't stop."

I don't like killin' people. Never have, even when they needed killin', and I didn't want to shoot Rotten Roger, neither. You could argue that if anybody deserved lead for lunch, it was him, but still, I didn't want to be the one to feed him a bullet. Only he didn't give me no choice.

Once through into the room beyond the tunnel, Roger stood up and started wavin' his arms, shoutin' somethin' I couldn't make out. It didn't sound like any words I knew, mostly bein' grunts and somethin' akin to the way a squirrel chitters. O' course, the Black Teeth in the area, they was maybe fifteen of 'em, they all turned to see what all the commotion was about. Pretty soon they knew.

I fired twicest, puttin' two shots into Roger's back, and then finished crawlin' out o' the tunnel so's I could distract the moles while Daddy and Mattie joined me. Roger didn't fall right away, he kind o' lurched at me, so I put a third ball atwixt his eyes and that did the trick.

What I saw reminded me o' somethin' in a book Daddy read once't to us kids, fairy tales or somethin' like that. Four other tunnels emptied into that room, kind o' like streams into a lake. There was another room too, right off that first one, with a door made out o' bamboo poles the way they used to make jail cells and grippin' them bars was the fingers of my Momma. They was other people in there, too. I recognized Mattie's parents, but it was Momma's sweet face what distracted me for half a second, I was so relieved at seein' her alive.

"Don't look at me, Perry Joe, you damned fool!" she yelled out, in that kindly way she had, "get me out of here!"

Oh yeah, them Black Teeth.

In the middle was giant cast-iron pot, with some kind o' soup boilin' inside. A fire underneath gave off a flickerin' light, and the smoke went up through a hole overhead, which I assumed went all the way up to the surface. Three Black Teeth stood around the kettle, stirrin' it with wooden paddles. I'm not one to know how a giant mole would look when surprised, but I'm guessin' it was like them, squintin' at me down a long nose.

One nearest me must o' been a guard or some such, 'cause he hefted a rusty sickle and charged at me. I emptied the Colt into his chest, but his momentum carried him forward so's he crashed into me, and we rolled over in a heap. He was dyin' but not dead. His black teeth, the long, sharp ones that some folks call incisors, was champin' no more than six inches from my neck. The only thing keepin' him from rippin' out my jugular vein was my hands around *his* neck, but I knew right off he was a lot stronger than me. Unless he died quick, he'd take me with him.

Gunshots, squeals, screams and all kinds o' mayhem went around me as I fought for my life. Hot blood poured over my body from the holes in his torso. A mixture o' blood and saliva dripped onto my face, getting' my eyes and mouth and makin' it harder to see. Them got closer as my arms trembled. I strained against his might, but it weren't enough. I could feel my veins pulsin' against his teeth...

Then a loud *crack* sounded in my right ear. It jerked and I let go, and should o' died, 'cept most its head got splattered all over me and the wall. I blinked through all the gore to see Mattie standin' beside me, the twenty-gauge braced on her hip as she pumped out rounds o' double-ought buck.

I scrambled to my feet and unslung the AR. Some o' the Black Teeth was runnin' for the other tunnels, some was rollin' on the floor and some was on the floor but not rollin'. Blood was all over the walls and soakin' into the dirt. Next I knew there wasn't nothin' left to shoot at, 'cept for one wounded Black Teeth that Daddy put out o' its misery. That was the one what made me vomit in the corner. Maybe half a minute after it took its last breath, the oversize mole kinda blurred, and turned into somebody I recognized; Jeremy Howell, a friend o' mine who drowned the previous winter. But his body weren't never found, and now I knew why.

Kneelin' off to one side, tryin' not to let anybody see me in my moment o' sorrow, I didn't see Daddy and Mattie release Momma and the other prisoners. I was still there, not heavin' no more but gulpin' deep breaths, when I heard Momma across the room. I wiped my mouth, I don't know why I did that, since I were all covered with guts and brains, and then I stood. I wanted to hug Momma, but I wanted to hug Mattie more, and figured this was as good a time as any. 'Cept she was already huggin' somebody; Eskell Parveneu, her former betrothed, who'd gone missin' a few months back.

Once't I got over my shock enough to inspect my surroundin's, I saw what was in that black kettle. At first, I thought it was noodles o' some sort, then upon a closer look I realized it was mixture o' worms and snakes, all boiled up so's their guts exploded into the stew. They were other stuff in there too, only nobody knew what. It seems them Black Teeth was brewin' up a mixture that turned ordinary people into one o' them. Couldn't nobody say exactly why they was doin' it, or where they might o' got off to, but once't everybody were out o' there, I used a wooden paddle to dump it over. I would've asked Eskell to help me, but he and Mattie seemed to be otherwise occupied. Asides, he's pretty scrawny.

After getting' back above ground, Momma sent me straightaway over to the pump house near the creek to wash up. I stripped down to bare skin and wrung out my clothes, then unwrapped my leg and cleaned it good. The honey kept it from getting' infected so far, and I knew I had to keep applyin' it for at least a week. That meant flies and mosquitoes would be followin' me around like a new puppy, but there weren't nothin' for it.

After I got back to the house, I found Mattie and her folks waitin' for me on the porch. Her Ma and Pa thanked me for savin' her life and made me swear I'd accept a blackberry pie as token o' their appreciation. Mattie's eyes was filled with tears when she lifted up on her toes and pecked me on the cheek. I reckon my eyes was too, 'cept for a different reason. I'd lost the only girl I ever loved.

Eskell Parveneu shook my hand and thanked me for all I'd done. Said he'd name his first-born boy after me, like that somehow made up for my heartbreak. I smiled real nice and took his hand like a man ought to, but what I really wanted were to punch him in the nose.

Momma invited them to stay for supper, but Mattie figured she and her folks needed to get back home afore it got too dark. I offered to escort them. Even if I'd lost Mattie, I could still admire her womanly shape from afar, but Eskell said that weren't necessary if'n he could just borrow a firearm. Daddy made sure they was all armed, since they was plenty of predators out there besides just Black Teeth. As I stood on the porch watching the love o' life walk away into the sunset with another man, Daddy laid his hand on my shoulder and spoke to me gentle like, which I didn't hear too often.

"I'm sorry son, I know you felt strongly about Mattie, but she wasn't the one for you. You think she was, I know that, except the Lord has a different idea about that. One day you'll meet the right one."

"I don't want the right one, Daddy," I said, feelin' kind o' bitter in that moment, "I want Mattie."

I hadn't heard Momma come up behind.

"Stop mooning over that girl, Perry Joe," she said, "stop it right now. It ain't right, and I won't have it from any son o' mine. And don't you think you can mope around here, I won't allow that, either. I didn't birth you to have you pining after somebody who don't love you back."

"But Momma–"

"I said stop. Let's get your mind off this Mattie McCoy nonsense. You take Dustin and you boys go get something for the pot," Momma said, as if the day's doin's weren't nothin' out o' the ordinary. "Take your mind off that foolish girl. Whatever comes across your sights, shoot it up close if you get the chance. Black powder residue makes everything taste special."

On that point, I had to agree.

The End

The Enchanter of the Highland Estates

By Benjamin Tyler Smith

"It's looking good already, Mr. Wishman!" old Mrs. Yoder called from down below.

"I haven't even started yet," I called back, my voice pitched to carry over the wind. I stood on an old wooden ladder that leaned against an equally ancient barn, my feet spread wide on the third rung down from the top. A round hex sign had been painted into the red wall directly in front of me. Once full of flowers and feathers and the colors of spring, this bit of Pennsylvania Dutch artwork had faded over the last several years.

"Well, it's good to see someone hard at work on it, then!" Mrs. Yoder crossed her thin arms and looked up at me, a smile on her wrinkled face. "Past time this barn got the care she deserves."

I'd have been here months ago if you'd let me, I thought. I'd done everything short of begging on my hands and knees to get out here and take care of this before pandemonium erupted. Mrs. Yoder didn't know this, but the hex sign on her barn wasn't there to keep evil spirits away, like most thought. It was there to keep a particularly nasty demon sealed in. By the looks of the hex sign's condition, I was barely in time. "Give me a little while, and I'll have this sign looking like new."

A sudden gust buffeted the rickety ladder. I gritted my teeth and shifted my stance. *Provided the wind doesn't kill me first.*

I opened my backpack and removed a picture of what the hex sign looked like the last time my grandpa touched it up. Thankfully, it had been during a time when color film was readily available, so I could really make out the colors. White chamomile flowers mixed with vibrant peacock feathers in a display atypical of most hex sign paintings. I studied the design for a long moment, my gaze shifting from what the picture showed and what was still on the barn wall.

The outlines of most of the flowers and feathers could be seen, even if the color was almost gone. The hex sign's circular border had once been painted a solid gold. That gold—and it *was* real gold, another thing Mrs. Yoder didn't know— had largely flaked away as the magic that powered the sign faded. Once that circle disappeared, the demon contained within would be free. Part of my job was to make sure that never happened. It was a duty passed down the Wishman line ever since my family came to reside in Berks County back in the 1700's.

Something tickled my nose, and I turned my head to sneeze once, twice, and again. "Damn pollen," I muttered.

"God bless you!" Mrs. Yoder said. "Would you like some lemonade? The vitamin C would help fight off that cold."

"It's just my allergies, but some lemonade would be great. Thank you!" It would go nicely with the lunch I'd packed in the John Wayne lunch tin Grandpa had given me back when I was kid. It was still my favorite way to carry a meal.

As she turned toward the farmhouse about twenty yards away, I placed the picture back in the rucksack, then removed my palette, a set of horsehair brushes, and three bottles of paint to start with. Time to get to work.

Something tickled my nose again. When I rubbed at it, my finger came back with flecks of gold on it. I turned my attention back to the hex sign. The golden ring had gotten worse. Paint continued to flake away, deteriorating much faster than could be accounted for with the wind.

A piercing crack rent the air. I winced and resisted the urge to cover my ears. That didn't sound good.

"Mr. Wishman, are you alright?" Mrs. Yoder called.

A split had formed in the wood next to the hex sign. An eye peered out at me, malevolent energy radiating from it. *Yeah, definitely not good.*

"Everything's fine, Mrs. Yoder!" Everything wasn't fine, but she didn't need to know that. "Just the barn settling. You know how these old buildings can be."

"Oh, don't I know it. There was this one time back in—"

Four more eyes appeared in the ever-widening crack in the barn's wall. "Mrs. Yoder, don't forget about the lemonade!"

"You're right! Where is my head?"

Mrs. Yoder's self-deprecating laughter covered up the sibilant hissing that rose up from the crack-o-eyeballs in front of me. *"Tremble, Hexenmeister,"* a multitude of voices whispered. *"You will die a thousand deaths as Mal'Heru watches on."*

I ignored the demon's taunts and unstoppered the bottle of Verdant Grass and dipped one of the brushes into the green liquid. Normally I'd pour it out onto the palette and do a bit of mixing to get the shade just right, but the time for proper form was past. I daubed big globs of paint onto the background portions of the hex sign. I concentrated on the brush and urged the bristles to "stay in the green." Even with my hands shaking, I filled in the background without a drop of paint winding up inside the lines of faded flowers and peacock feathers.

The crack-o-eyeballs stopped its expanse, and the infernal orbs glared at me in impotent rage. A rumble emitted from the other side of that split, deep enough to shake the ladder and the ground beneath. I tried to press myself against the barn wall, but a clawed hand reached out of the crack toward me. I drew back my head, then dipped the brush into the paint and splashed some into the crack. Mal'Heru the Watchful One let out a gasp of pain, and the hand disappeared. *"You wretched little—"*

"Yeah, sorry, that stuff burns if it gets in your eyes. Be careful." With the green portions of the hex sign finished, I dropped the bottle of Verdant Grass back into my backpack and withdrew two more bottles, one white and the other yellow. I dropped the green-stained brush into an open bottle of paint-thinner that hung at my waist, then drew two more brushes from the opposite end of my utility belt. Again, normally I would carefully clean one brush and use it the entire time, but I always brought spares in case of emergencies like today. I opened the bottle of white and got to work. Chamomile blossoms soon stood out against the green background, their delicate petals shining with vitality once more. Little splashes of yellow soon completed the floral portion of the hex sign.

A shudder ran through the barn, and Mal'Heru let out a groan that was carried away on the wind.

I dropped these brushes into the paint thinner, pulled another from my kit, then grabbed a bottle labeled "Hera's Essence." Made from the feathers of wild Staten Island peacocks, the paint appeared iridescent in the late afternoon sun. I uncorked the bottle, dipped the brush into it, and started slathering it on the wood. I murmured words of control under my breath, urging the paint to flow into the feather outlines, to alter its color to suit the pattern of a real feather, and to soak into the wood.

I had just started to color in the last peacock feather's "iris" when something buzzed in my pocket, and a generic ringtone played. The noise startled me, and my concentration slipped. Still-wet green and blue paint began to run. I put the paintbrush's handle between my teeth and jammed the now-free hand into my pocket to mute the phone. Whoever the hell it was, it could damn well wait!

Mal'Heru must have sensed my broken concentration, because he threw himself against the crack in the barn. Clawed hands grasped either end of the tear and began pushing it wider in a shower of splintering wood. My hand wanted to reach for the S&W 640 in its Galco KingTuk holster, but I urged it to take the brush from my mouth and get back to painting. I was almost finished and stopping to put a few enchanted rounds into Mal'Heru's body would just be an annoyance to the demon and would mean he'd spend three eternities devouring me rather than two.

I put the finishing touch on the last peacock feather, dropped the brush into the reservoir of paint thinner, then made the sign of the Cross over the painting, touching the top and bottom edges of the golden ring, followed by the left and right. "Return to the Abyssal Sleep, Mal'Heru. Until He comes again to judge the living, and the dead, *and the demonic.*"

Mal'Heru recoiled from the words. He howled wordlessly in an explosion of wind, but his many eyes soon closed. The clawed hands lost their purchase, and he sank back into the wood. The interdimensional rift closed, and the barn went back to looking as it had when I first ascended the ladder.

Crisis averted.

Mrs. Yoder returned a few minutes later, as I was cleaning my brushes and wiping off my painters' palette. She set a tray laden with sandwiches, glasses full of ice, and a pitcher of lemonade onto a wrapped hay bale next to the barn doors. She shielded her eyes with a hand as she looked up, a grin stretching her lips from ear to ear. "I can't remember the last time that hex sign looked so good! Well done, Mr. Wishman!"

"Thank you, Mrs. Yoder."

"No, thank *you!*" She filled the glasses with lemonade, then handed one to me. "Sorry I took so long. My granddaughter called while I was preparing lunch, and you know how chatty she can be."

If she's anything like you.... I left the thought unspoken, and instead reached for my own phone. I brought up the missed call notifications, and grimaced. Tim Quintrell, an enchanter and sorcerer who lived in the area, had called, and he's a real pain in the ass to deal with. It figured he would be the one to call and nearly get my soul ripped from its body.

Mrs. Yoder held out a plate of sandwiches and chips. "Dig in. You must be hungry."

As if on cue, my stomach grumbled, long and loud. "That must be the case. Thank you."

I dropped the phone back into my pants pocket and dug in as Mrs. Yoder instructed. Whatever Tim needed help with could wait until a little later.

"A little later" turned out to be three days. In my defense, I never specified *when* later was, and a lot came up. First it was a hex painting job down in Oley that I needed to give an estimate on, and after that a crime scene the regional police were investigating needed to be photographed. The latter wasn't my preferred method of making money, but that was the life of an artist, especially one with as niche a profession as me. If I wasn't painting hex signs—whether magically charged or plain folk art ones—I was working my photographer's skills for civilians and police alike. If I wasn't doing either of those, I was teaching art and photography. That meant my schedule went with the wind, and it wasn't always possible to get back to someone right away.

That, and I was still pissed off at Tim. He only ever called when he needed something, it was almost always something stupid, and he rarely paid on time if at all. This last call of his nearly killed me and unleashed the real world equivalent of a Lovecraftian Great Old One on us all. So, seeing what kind of inane crap he needed assistance with wasn't exactly high on my list of priorities, not with paid work to be done.

By day three my work ethic got the better of me, though, and I decided to make the drive out to his home in the Highland Estates. Well, the eleven missed calls and subsequent voicemails might have helped in that decision, too.

The Highland Estates was a trailer park off of Old Route 22, at a point between Krumsville and new Smithville. The park occupied land on both sides of the roadway. The north side was comprised of streets and cul-de-sacs lined with single-wide homes. The southern side occupied a hill, and was filled with newer mobile homes, many of them of the double-wide variety. I was impressed the first time I ventured into it several months back. It does not fit the stereotype of most trailer parks, with broken down cars on cinder blocks in front of trailers that had seen better days. This was a managed neighborhood where management actually did a decent job. Yards were kept up, homes were in good repair, and the people were generally nice. There was even a neighborhood swimming pool at the bottom of the hill, right along the road.

Now, as nice as this neighborhood is, a trailer park is still a trailer park. That begs the question: why would someone with the level of self-worth that Tim exhibited want anything to do with a trailer park? Like most magic-wielders, much of Tim's power came from what he could draw out from the environment rather than his internal reserves. As it turned out, the Highland Estates had been built upon a convergence of ley lines, making it an excellent source of magic power. That isn't too uncommon in Berks, Lancaster, and Lehigh Counties, as this area had an unusually high concentration of ley lines running through it. It was why at various points in its history it was known as a haven for witches and even for priests and pastors who wielded what has now become known as Christian folk magic.

It had also attracted demons and other dark forces to the area, to feed off the ley lines and use that power to influence and possess priest, witch, and any in-between. This had led to the development of hex sign magic and was a large reason why so many demons had been sealed away in this area, in barns and homes that had been built on or near ley lines.

The entrances to the Highland Estates lay at the bottom of a valley. I crested the hill to the west and coasted toward the bottom, my foot hovering over the brake pedal. From here I could see many of the homes on the gently sloping southern hill. My eyes swept upward until they fell on an odd site at the top of that hill, at the center of the recently-paved Raven Drive: a pyramid, and not the kind one was used to seeing out of Egypt. This was a pyramid fashioned of trailers. Two double-wide modular homes served as the base, with another double-wide on top of that. This was followed by a single-wide as the third floor, and on top of it was a shed.

As ridiculous as it looked, there was a reason for this. Structures in the shape of pyramids and towers are able to enhance the magic drawn from the ley lines they're built over. Tim wanted the most bang for his buck with this property, but he hadn't gone through with his original plan to build an actual tower. No builder in the area could do it to his satisfaction, and he also thought it would stand out too much. The trailers, he decided, would help him to better blend in.

I parked the Roadmaster in front of Tim's "Tower O' Power" and stepped out. Marble steps led up to a set of ornate double-doors. A sign hung next to the door, and its etched surface read, "Tim the Enchanter: Magic, Marvels, and Notary Public."

Oh, yeah. He was blending *really* well.

I climbed the steps, but before I could knock the doors opened, and out stepped a man in bright purple robes, a silver rod in his hands. "Welcome, Madame Groff! What enchanted baubles do…you…seek…?"

Tim the Enchanter trailed off entirely as his eyes focused on me. The smile that had split his bearded face was soon replaced with a scowl. "Oh, it's just you." He crossed his arms. "Tell me, Wishman: did you actually listen to my voicemails, or did you finally get sick of all my missed calls?"

"The latter." There was no use in lying to the man. Enchanters and sorcerers were great at discerning the truth, even as they attempted to alter it. "Sorry, I was busy."

Tim snorted a laugh. "Busy, right. Busy with people you'd rather be dealing with, you mean."

Before I could object, he spun around and walked back inside, throwing off his robes onto the sofa to the left of the door as he did so. Beneath the robe he wore a set of slacks, a button-down shirt, and a tie. I assumed this was his notary public attire. "None of that matters, Wishman. What does matter is that you're here, and I need your help."

That piqued my interest. While Tim and I were colleagues of sorts — even if we got along more like bitter rivals rather than friends — it was rare for him to ever call on me for magical help, and that was common with most sorcerers. Many times, our different magical styles conflicted with one another. "What do you need help with?"

He turned toward the desk to his right and glanced at the cell phone there. He grunted. "Ah, Madame Groff had to cancel. Well, all the better with the way things are. That gives us time before my next appointment."

He turned back to me and stepped outside. "Follow me. It's just down the hill."

I opened my wagon's driver's door. "Wouldn't it be quicker to drive?"

"I wouldn't be caught dead in your jalopy, Wishman."

"It is *not* a jalopy!" I reached into the car long enough to snatch my backpack. "It's got a leather interior! This was top of the line for its time!"

"Right, right. Just hurry it up."

Grumbling, I followed as Tim led us down Raven Drive. When we crossed onto Pheasant Drive, locals who were outside enjoying the weather and grilling dinner waved and called greetings to us. I waved back, but Tim continued to face forward. I didn't know what his neighbors thought of his enchanted notary service, but they didn't appear to mind his presence.

Tim stopped a few minutes later, right after we turned onto Grouse Drive. He pointed. "We're here."

We stood in front of a double wide covered in beige vinyl siding that didn't appear any different from the rest of the trailers in the park. However, Tim didn't point at the home. He pointed at the shed next to it. This shed was made of wood, and very old at that. It had originally been painted green, but that paint had long since faded away. Years of merciless sun had changed much of its flaking surface from a vibrant green to a pale, sickly color. I shrugged. "You want me to paint a shed for this guy?"

"Look closer."

The shed had a single door on it, its brass handle tarnished to a dull brown. What looked like a black shape had been painted in the center of the door, and that shape was surrounded by a faded brown ring. It was a hex sign, a real one! And in such a state of disrepair it made Mrs. Yoder's original sign look brand new. I studied it for a long moment, frowning. How had this gone unnoticed for so long? Neither I nor my grandpa had....

"Wait," I said after a moment. "This wasn't originally here, was it?"

"Very astute." Tim crossed his arms and glared at the structure. "It arrived a few weeks ago, and it's been interfering with my work ever since. Particularly over the last few days."

My eyes widened. A shed with a demon of some sort housed in it had been moved from its original location? "Do you have any idea where it came from?"

"None. One day it wasn't here, and the next it was." He glared at me. "I called as soon as I noticed how leaky the seal had become. It's gotten a lot worse since then."

I grimaced, unable to hide my discomfort. As a mage sanctioned by the Parliament of Owls, Tim knew all about the hex signs and what was sealed within them. While a regular person could do nothing to damage a hex sign short of burning the entire structure down, a magician of Tim's power could easily damage or disrupt the seal, whether he wanted to or not. "It's that bad?" I asked after a moment.

"Indeed. I've been unable to properly tell fortunes for close to a week now, and my object enchantment has gone from a sure thing to a hit-and-miss affair. This needs to be resolved, preferably back when I first called you, but we're past that point."

He didn't sound like he was past it. I swallowed my pride and bowed my head. "I'm sorry, Tim. It's just—"

"You were busy, or didn't want to deal with me, or your wagon was in the shop." He waved a hand. "I don't care. All I care is that you're here now, and now is when you can get started fixing this mess. I've already lost a week's worth of revenue and research with your dawdling. I'll not lose a second more."

I don't know how much revenue Tim actually made on his magic versus his abilities to navigate government and regulatory bureaucracy, but any lost income was a bad thing these days, especially for freelancers. I knew that better than most.

I also had a vested interest in this. If the hex sign broke, a demon of unknown origin, power, and motive would be unleashed. It could be anything from a mischievous demon to one of the Four Horsemen of the Apocalypse. With what little I currently had, there was no way to know.

Hmm, a horse. I stepped closer and studied the faded hex sign. The black smudge in the center of the circle *did* have a horse-like shape to it. It could also have been a cow or an ox, but something told me those weren't correct. I removed my camera from my backpack, turned it on, and started snapping pictures.

"What are you doing?" Tim demanded after a moment.

"Taking pictures so I can check it against Grandpa's old records. I'm hoping he'll have a picture of it after he finished repainting it."

"And if he doesn't?"

"I'll have to improvise."

Tim grunted. "Why do I get the feeling you won't be finishing this today?"

"Because I won't." I inspected the images I'd snapped, then returned the camera to the bag. "Once I know what I'm dealing with, I'll have to gather the necessary paints. We're looking at a couple of days, maybe three."

Tim's eyes looked like they were about ready to bug out of his head, and his face grew red as a beet. "A few days? Do you have any idea how much work I'm going to lose? Do you have any idea what this Saturday night is?"

"Hot date?"

"Very funny. A rare astral conjunction will take place Saturday evening, and I need my magic at its peak so I can enchant several artifacts for high-paying clients."

"Can't you just wait for the next conjunction?"

"Well, sure, provided I live another four hundred and fifty-seven years."

Ah, one of those situations. I studied the hex sign for another moment, then shook my head. "Either way, Tim, this is something I'm going to have to investigate."

"Investigate quickly, then."

I held up my hands. "I will, I will. First order of business is my grandpa's records. I also need to find out where this thing came from."

"I can help with that." Tim strode to the front of the trailer and banged on the door. "Open up! I have questions!"

I sighed.

In the end, we found out from a neighbor that the owner of the shed—a Mr. Meckes—was away on a cruise and would be for the next few weeks. The neighbor had no idea where the shed had come from, other than it was from a farm that a late relative had owned. That narrowed things down a little, and I promised Tim I'd get to work immediately when we parted ways at the door to his pyramid.

"Be quick, Wishman," he urged, his usual haughtiness tinged with unease. "I fear we don't have much time."

After seeing the state of the hex sign, I could only agree.

I picked up dinner from Spectators Bar & Grille just down the road from the Highland Estates, then headed home to the farm.

I drove past wheat fields I rented out to a neighboring farmer, a barn full of hay I sold to whoever needed it, and finally pulled up to the one-story guest house I'd made my own since moving back from Florida several years back.

After a deliciously greasy burger and fries, I washed my hands and retrieved Grandpa's old records from the basement safe. The old man had maintained meticulous records of every hex sign in the region. This included when they were painted, what type of structure they were painted on, what sort of paints were used, who or *what* was sealed within, and the date the last time it was touched up. Included with most was also a photo, similar to the one I'd had of Mal'Heru's peacock seal. I set the stack of manila folders on the bedroom's desk, pulled up a chair, and got to work. This should have been an easy, if time-consuming, thing.

...Except for the fact that half of Grandpa's records had gone up in smoke in the fire that claimed his life a few years ago, right as he was ready to hand the reins off to me. The farmhouse had been gutted, with very little surviving fire and smoke damage save for some of his precious hex sign files. I'd taken what could be salvaged—and even some that couldn't be—and moved them to the guest house. From the bedroom window, I could see the remains of Grandpa's old home. It was made of stone, so the structure had survived the fire, even if much of the interior was too damaged to save. It was my hope to one day have the money to properly restore it, but that was a long way off.

I spent the better part of the evening checking and rechecking what records had survived but came up dry. Failing that, I shifted to the pictures I'd snapped. I loaded the high-resolution image files onto my PC and studied the badly faded hex sign for any clues. "It's a miracle it's still containing anything," I murmured as I played with the contrast settings. The border was all but gone, along with whatever background color had filled the circle. Only the black, horse-like smudge in the middle remained. The more I studied that part of the image, the more I was convinced it was a horse and not some other four-footed farm animal.

That said, it seemed a little...off-center, for lack of a better term. The horse wasn't in the middle of the circle, but was instead closer to the bottom, as if something had once been above it. A bird? Another horse? A date or a name? Most hex signs did not contain writing, but there were exceptions to every rule. If there was, I hoped it wasn't in fraktur script. That was a completely different kind of magic, and not one I had much affinity for.

I switched to an image that showed the whole shed. There was something familiar about it, and I wasn't sure why that was. Most sheds I'd encountered had a set of double-doors on them, like what one would see on a full-sized barn. This one had a single door, as if it had only ever been meant for storing hand-tools and other supplies that didn't need a wide entrance. Where had I seen it before?

After a few minutes of racking my brain, I gave up and went to get ready for bed. Going by the assumption that it was a horse of some sort in the image, I at least knew where I could go to get the paint supplies I'd need.

Witchcraft Road is a short road not too far off Old 22, deep in Berks County farm country. Whatever its history, there isn't much on the road now except fields of wheat, corn, soy, or sorghum depending on the year and what was in the crop rotation schedule. Scattered amid this rolling farmland were a few houses, as well as a small horse farm run by a family that had been on the road for generations. The newest addition to that farm was a bakery shop close to the front of the property. A wooden sign bearing the name "Callie's Cupcake Cauldron" hung from what looked like a witch's broom over the front door.

Most would think this was just a clever bit of marketing by an entrepreneur who lived on a road with a strange name, but in this case, it was an exercise in "hiding in plain sight." Callie Reichard was indeed a witch of some renown, but only in certain circles. Her family had long dabbled in witchcraft of some form or fashion over the decades since settling in the area, but they had wisely kept it to themselves, especially at the height of the witch hunts.

I pondered this as I turned up the drive and rumbled past the unoccupied store. During the workweek she wouldn't open her store until the late afternoon, so she could usually be found either tending to her father's horses or tinkering in her "lab" near the back of the property. I parked about a hundred feet back from the workshop, just to play it safe.

No sooner had I stepped out of the car than I heard a muffled explosion from inside the workshop. Green and purple smoke poured out of the windows. The door flew open, unleashing more smoke. A young woman stumbled out of the colorful haze, coughing and laughing. "That didn't quite work out the way I intended it!" she shouted.

As she tossed her head back, the morning sun made her red hair look like it was on fire. Wait, it actually *was* on fire, and Callie had only just noticed! I ran over to her and helped beat the flames out of her scalp, which only elicited more laughter from the woman. Once she was well and truly put out, she threw her arms around me and pulled me into a bear hug. "Jim! It's good to see you!"

"And you, too," I said, "especially now that you're not on fire."

Callie pulled back so she could study me with her bright green eyes. A broad grin split her ageless face. Witches were among some of the longest-lived magicians second only to necromancers. She could've been in her late twenties like me or about to celebrate her hundredth birthday. I had no way of knowing, and I wasn't about to ask her that. Instead, I said, "What were you working on?"

"A new potion that got a little away from me. You know how some of those reagents can be. Mixing with things they don't like, and you have a fight on your hands!" She shrugged. "It's the risk one takes when dealing with live ingredients."

This was why I always dealt with ingredients that had already been processed. I never tried making my own paint out of anything still breathing, although in Callie's case she wasn't necessarily dealing with living animals or insects. She was talking about elemental and spiritual essence from the various reagents she used. When those essences were unleashed, they had a tendency to clash with essences of a different affinity. Light and dark, water and fire, things like that.

"So, what can I do for you today?" she asked. She grinned. "Are you here for horseback riding lessons?"

"Maybe later." I reached into my backpack and pulled the camera out. "I do have need of your equestrian talents, though. In the painter's realm, anyway."

I turned the camera on, loaded up the zoomed-in image of the hex sign, and handed it to her. "It's faded pretty badly, but I know I've at least got a black horse to paint, and maybe something else."

Callie squinted at the image a moment, then shook her head. "I can't see much with this glare. Can we—" She hit a button, and it switched to another image of the shed. She cocked her head to the side. "Where is this from?"

"The Highland Estates trailer park off Old 22, but the shed was moved from somewhere else."

Callie pursed her lips. "Maybe…." She glanced back at the workshop's overhang, and at the smoke still coming out of the windows and doorway. "I need to get out of the sun. Do you mind if I take this back to the house? Or maybe—" She turned back to me, eyes bright. "Let's take it to the bakery! I've got a new cupcake for you to try!"

My stomach rumbled at the thought of food, even as my brain hesitated. Callie was a phenomenal baker, but she also had a tendency to make strange concoctions from time to time. The potion-maker in her loved to experiment. "Well, I don't know—"

"Splendid! I'll get some tea going, too." She hiked a thumb at the workshop door. "Can you do me a favor and put that out? There's a fire extinguisher just by the door.

"I—"

"Thanks!" She pressed the camera against her chest and ran down the dirt driveway, giggling like a schoolgirl.

I turned back to the workshop and heaved a sigh. How'd I get roped into these things?

After fifteen minutes and multiple lungfuls of smoky air, I traced Callie's steps back to the bakery and entered through the front door. The strange smoke from whatever she'd been brewing in the workshop clung to my hair, skin, and clothes, making me look like some sort of Mardi Gras experiment gone awry. Lord only knew what color my lungs were, but it wasn't a natural pink anymore, that was for sure. My throat and lungs burned from a coughing fit that hadn't really stopped.

The bakery had a few small tables for customers to sit, and part of the long countertop had been converted into a bar. Two mugs, a teapot, and a tray of cupcakes sat on this bar. Callie pulled one of the stools around to the employee-side of the bar, then motioned for me to sit across from her.

After I sat, she poured a steaming red liquid into both mugs. "This is called 'Lungsoothe Tea,'" she said. "We make it for the volunteer firefighters around here."

Whatever was in the bittersweet tea, it worked. After just a few sips, my throat no longer burned, and my lungs felt clear. "I'm not one for hot tea," I murmured, "but I'll make an exception for this."

"High praise from someone who prefers his beverages iced!" Callie pushed the tray of cupcakes toward me. "I went to Pop's for the first time in a while last week, and they inspired me to create something new."

Pop's Malt Shoppe was a landmark in nearby Kutztown, known mostly for its variety of ice cream flavors. I picked up a cupcake and studied the yellow icing. I tried to sniff, but my nose was still filled with the smell of smoke. "Lemon?"

"Not even close." She shook her head. "What other fruit is yellow and not part of the citrus family?"

"Banana?" Intrigued, I took a bite. There was definitely banana, along with peanut butter and chocolate chips. "It's Monkey Bones!"

"Bingo!" Callie laughed. "You've always said it was your favorite flavor, and I finally tried it the other day. You don't think they'd mind if I used this flavor with my cupcakes, do you?"

"As long as you let people know it's where you got the idea, I'm sure they'd love it." Free advertising was free advertising, after all.

We spent a few moments eating and drinking in companionable silence. I ate two cupcakes, while Callie managed to pack away three in the same amount of time. Based on her slender figure, you'd think she hardly ate anything, but this was the norm for her. She used a lot of magic each day and that burned calories.

As she peeled the wrapping off the bottom of her fourth cupcake, she said, "I took a good look at the hex sign. Good guess on it being a horse, when it could've been any kind of farm animal."

"There was something about it that—Wait, you say that like you know I'm right."

"That's because I do know you're right." She pointed to the far side of the room, a sly smile on her face.

A number of photographs and paintings adorned the walls of the bakery, most of them related to horses and farms. The one she pointed to took up a large section of the far wall. It was a color photo of a stable, its doors thrown wide, and horses being led out by handlers. The camera had been set back enough to catch some of the surrounding landscape, including a small shed off to the side of the stable. A shed that looked eerily similar to the one at the trailer park, although it was a vibrant green without a hint of fading or flaking.

"I thought I recognized it," Callie said. "That's from the Wollenweber farm down in Oley."

I walked over to get a better look, with Callie a few steps behind me. Even though the shed wasn't the photo's centerpiece, the detail of the hex sign was plain to see. A brown ring surrounded a yellow field. In that field stood the black horse, with what looked like a Renaissance nobleman riding it. The man's style of dress was a bit strange, but a painting of a rider did match the farm's purpose.

Another nonstandard hex sign, I thought as I pulled out my notebook and pen. "We'll need something for the horse, for sure. And that looks like sunflowers in the background. I should have that back at the house."

"I've got some here, too," Callie offered. "No need to go back home if you don't have to."

A peal of thunder rolled in from the distance. I frowned. It wasn't supposed to rain today, or for the next week. "I'll take you up on that." The last thing I wanted to do was waste more time and end up having to paint in the middle of a storm.

Callie returned to her workshop, leaving me to continue my study of the photograph. I wish it was a close-up shot, but it would have to do. Fortunately, the design didn't appear to be too complicated, and so long as the proper paint was used, my magic could take care of the rest. Still, I didn't want to mess anything up.

While I worked, the thunder continued to rumble in the distance. While it didn't draw any closer, it was growing in frequency until it sounded like horses galloping along pavement. It was affecting my concentration, and after a few minutes I gave up and stepped outside to see what was going on.

The sky was completely clear in and around the farm, but that wasn't the case to the east. A single black cloud hung low, with bolts of lightning arcing out of it toward the ground.

"Wow, that doesn't look good!" Callie called. She walked toward me from her workshop, a satchel similar to mine slung around a shoulder. She handed me two vials of paint, one black and the other yellow. "Sable Courser and Sunflower Morning," she said. "We can settle up once the job is done." She turned back to the east. "And it's looking like the job needs to be done sooner rather than later."

"So it would seem." I had a bad feeling in the pit of my stomach about that cloud. I packed the vials away, then jogged toward the wagon. "I'll be back when I've dealt with this!"

To my surprise, Callie jogged behind me. "You might need a witch's help for this one, so I thought I'd come along!"

"Are you sure?" Callie was afraid of lightning. I couldn't imagine how she'd be riding into a storm like that.

As if reading my thoughts, Callie laughed. "Oh, come on, Jim. How bad could it be?"

Callie screamed as lightning struck the Roadmaster for the third time. This bolt struck the hood, leaving stars in my vision and a ringing in my ears. "It's all right, Callie!" I shouted over the constant rumbling of thunder.

She just continued to scream. I ignored her and focused on the road before us. "How bad could it be, indeed?" I muttered.

We'd left her parents' farm only about fifteen minutes ago, and the difference between there and here was stark. As we sped along Old 22 through the village of Lenhartsville, the dark cloud in the distance had grown larger. By the time we reached Krumsville and blew through the four-way stop near Dietrich's meat market—running a college-age kid in a beater Civic off the road in the process—the sky ahead was completely black.

I'd offered to let Callie off at the Krumsville Inn, but to her credit she insisted on continuing on. The constant thunder and flashes of lightning had her wide-eyed, but she refused to back down. "It'll be fine," she said in a high-pitched voice. "I have this feeling you'll need me."

So, we'd pressed on. The screaming hadn't started until lightning was raining down around and on top of us.

Gale-force winds buffeted the Roadmaster, and I was thankful for the heavy car's low center-of-gravity as we crested the final hill and began the descent toward the Highland Estates' entrance. The black cloud hung dead center over the trailer park, blocking the sun so much that it looked like a moonless night rather than close to 11:00 AM. That darkness was pierced over and over by bolts of lightning that struck trailers and vehicles all along the hill.

We entered the trailer park and maneuvered around several upended garbage cans and even an SUV that had rolled over from the wind. I turned us onto Grouse Street and pulled up next to Mr. Meckes's trailer, or what was left of it. The trailer had partially collapsed. Worse yet, the shed that had originally been on the Wollenweber horse farm was gone. Not knocked over. *Gone*, leaving only a bare patch of earth. "Well, that's not good."

Callie had her hands pressed against both ears, but she looked where I indicated. "The shed's gone? What's that mean?"

"It means our demon's on the loose, but I have a good idea where it went." I pointed up the hill. Most of the bolts of lightning coming down around us were striking Tim's pyramid. To be more precise, they were striking a barrier surrounding his pyramid. "Looks like he could use our help."

Another bolt of lightning struck next to us. Callie let out a squeak, but she nodded. "I'll do what I can."

I pulled the wagon as close to Tim's front steps as I could. The double-doors shimmered with prismatic light, visible even with the near-constant flashes of lightning threatening to blind us. It seemed that Tim's barrier extended even to the doors, and his was a magic I couldn't easily crack. "All right, Callie, you're up. We need to get inside."

Callie rummaged around in her satchel and held out a bottle to me, her eyes shut and her teeth chattering. "S-s-suspension of S-s-sesame Oil. Pour this o-o-over the locks and r-r-repeatedly s-s-say 'Open Sesame.'"

Really? That's the best magic release phrase she could come up with? I shook my head. "You know your potions only work when you activate them. You're not getting out of it this easily."

"Can't you t-t-treat it like one of y-y-your paints?" she demanded.

"It doesn't work that way." I grabbed the door handle with my left hand and lifted the center console with my right. Once the console was out of the way, I grabbed her wrist. "Come on, let's go!"

"Wait, no—"

I opened the door and jumped out into the gale, dragging her with me. She fought me until the first lightning bolt crashed down near us. Then she leapt into my arms, wailing wordlessly. This threw me off balance. We stumbled up the steps and crashed against the door. "Do your thing!" I shouted, struggling to be heard over the roaring wind and booming thunder.

Callie muttered words I couldn't hear, but she unstoppered the potion bottle she'd attempted to give me and poured it over the door handles. She then took some in her hands and smeared it against the corners of the door frames, chanting her spell all the while. As she completed the spell, the shimmering around the doors vanished. I twisted the doorknob and began to push it open—

A gust of wind slammed into our backs and threw us inside. We flew into the entry and slid to a stop in front of Tim's notary desk. The rushing wind sent books and papers flying. I staggered to my feet and pushed the doors closed. Even with the lock engaged, the wind crashed against them again and again, causing them to rattle against the deadbolt.

The noise of the wind abated, but it was replaced by crashing and shouting from higher up in the pyramid. What sounded like hoofbeats rather than thunderclaps vibrated the floors and walls, accompanied by muffled chanting and a high-pitched shrieking that echoed down from the spiral staircase in the center of the first floor. I looked down at Callie, who still lay where she'd fallen on the floor. "Got anything to use against demons?"

"You know that's not my specialty." Callie sat up and pressed a hand to her chest. She took in several shuddering gasps for air and shook her head. "I'll stay here and try not to die of this heart attack I'm having."

I knelt down long enough to squeeze her shoulder. "You did good. Dinner at Ozgood's is on me."

"Dinner at Ozgood's for the next month is on you, you mean."

I smiled. "See? If you can joke like that, you're not having a heart attack."

"Who says I'm joking?"

That hit me where it hurt most: my wallet. Still, she'd earned it. "All right, it's a deal. We'll make Tim pay."

I ascended the spiral staircase. For the first and second floors of this redneck pyramid, the stairs were open like you see in most modern homes. So, as I reached the second floor, I saw a living room with hallways branching off in either direction. Past this, the staircase became enclosed, almost like one would expect in a fantasy tower. I had never left the first floor in the few times I'd visited Tim's place and was surprised to see a stone façade on the steps and walls as I climbed higher. Whatever his quirks, Tim took his wizard's tower seriously.

A locked doorway on what I assumed was the third floor bore the word "Library" on its oak surface, likely where Tim kept his prized collection of magical tomes. I had yet to see the collection, but he had shown me a few manuscripts. Provided the tower survived, he'd have to show me his library.

There was a loud crack, followed by a thunderous crash that shook the whole tower. It knocked me off balance, and I slammed into the stairwell's stone wall. "Foolish mage!" a voice bellowed from the open hatch just above me. "Enough of this farce! Release me at once, and power unimaginable will be yours!"

"You're not the first of your kind to make such a promise, Balforst!" Tim called, his voice haughty but strained. "I doubt you'll be the last, either!"

"Not if I strip your flesh from your bones, mortal!"

I crept up the remaining few steps and peeked over the rim of the hatch. The top floor of Tim's pyramid looked as if it were a real wizard's tower from some epic fantasy, with more space in it than its eighteen by thirty foot physical dimensions should allow for. Torches giving off unnaturally yellow light illuminated a room in disarray. Tables and desks had been overturned, scattering books and baubles. The walls, floor, and ceiling all shimmered with the same prismatic glow that covered the outside of the tower.

Tim stood on one end of the chamber, a shimmering barrier surrounding him. On the other end, a man sat astride a black destrier. No, not a man. No man had eyes that burned red as this one did. He and his horse shouldn't have fit in the room, but the chamber's already strange physical dimensions seemed to warp even further around the demon.

What had Tim called him? Balforst? The name suddenly clicked in my memory. Balforst, Duke of Hell, Master of Horse to the Lord of the Eighteenth Circle. That a duke would be relegated to such a duty meant that the demon he served was incredibly powerful, yet it hadn't stopped him from being sealed away by one of my ancestors. I swallowed hard. I only hoped I could do my family proud.

As if sensing my fear, Balforst turned his gaze my way. He and his horse grinned, revealing white fangs in both mouths. "Ah, the Hexenmeister has arrived."

"About time you got here," Tim muttered. He hadn't once taken his eyes off the demon. "What kept you?"

I climbed the last few steps. "I was trying to do things correctly. I didn't think the seal would fail this quickly."

"Well, about that—" Tim began.

"Oh, it wouldn't have failed," Balforst said. "I still had a few more days of chipping away at the seal to go, but this mortal decided to release me by...how would you say, taking matters into his own hands?"

I hiked a thumb at Balforst. "Tim, what does he mean by that?"

"I thought I could repaint the sealing ring." Tim shrugged. "Turns out I was wrong."

I gaped at him. "No shit you were wrong! Why would you do that?"

"Because my enchantment magic is still too weak!" Tim snapped. "About all I can manage is barriers like this right now, and it's killing my business! I thought if I could strengthen the hex, I'd...No, don't look at me like that, Wishman!"

"Yes, *Wishman*!" Balforst snapped his fingers. "That's the name of your cursed line. *Wishman*." He turned his red-eyed gaze back on me, and I felt my blood grow cold. "And which generation are you? Which of your ancestors did I swear to destroy, and if not him then his son, and if not the son, then the grandson, and all the way down until all his offspring were gone from this earth?"

I shivered but tried to cover it up with a chuckle. "Well, I'm the sixth of my line, so if you were sealed by the first, you're way behind on your payback plan for my family." I pulled the palette from my backpack, along with a set of brushes. "Speaking of which, it's time I do right by my ancestors and seal you up again."

"Oh? And how will you do that? I destroyed that paltry little shed I was sealed into."

I kicked the hatch shut, and the shimmering that surrounded the rest of the room covered the hatch, too. "I don't need the shed, Balforst. I can seal you just about anywhere I want."

"What do you mean?" Tim snapped. "What are you planning?"

I stepped over to a clear space on the wall and removed a bottle of brown liquid. It was a mix of three different browns: Rich Soil, Aged Timber, and Rusty Earth. I had no idea which was correct, so it was my hope that an equal-parts mixture of the most common colors I used would suffice. "What does it look like I'm doing?" I asked Tim.

"It looks like you're about to seal Balforst into the top of my pyramid."

"Very astute!" I unstoppered the brown and poured a little onto my palette.

"If you do that, how badly will it interfere with my magic?"

"That's a journey of discovery you and I will have to go on together, my friend." In truth, I had no idea, nor did I really care. All that mattered was sealing Balforst away before things got any worse, for the trailer park and for my neck. The members of the Parliament of Owls already would be displeased with me letting things get to this point. If Balforst escaped, it'd be a race to see who killed me first: the demon, or the council of magicians.

"Outrageous!" Tim stalked over toward me. "I will not allow this! You cannot use my home as a prison for a demon!"

Balforst growled. "You mortals dare—"

"Shut up!" we both yelled. "We're trying to have a discussion here," I added.

"There is no discussion!" Tim stomped his foot. "You will *not* seal Balforst into my home, and that's final!"

"If you have a better idea, I'm all ears!"

Tim stood there for a long moment, then finally said, "I don't have a better idea, I'm afraid."

"Okay, then." I turned back to the wall.

"But I know how we can get one." Tim snatched a torch out from one of the wall sconces nearby. As it left the sconce, the sorcerous light went out. Wielding the now extinguished torch like a club, he swung it with all his might at the closest window. The glass shattered, and with it the shimmering barrier that had surrounded the entire chamber.

With a roar of triumph, Balforst put spurs to his destrier's flanks. The black horse reared, then galloped through the now-open window. As they approached, the window warped and expanded until it was wide enough to allow him. They dashed out and immediately nose-dived toward the ground. The window snapped back into its original shape, and I leaned out to see Balforst's horse galloping along the roof of the pyramid's third floor before he reached the edge and his angle abruptly shifted downward again. His horse was running along whatever surface its hooves touched as if it were level ground.

I leaned back inside and glared at Tim. "Why'd you do that?"

Tim crossed his arms and looked at me with a satisfied air. "Necessity is the mother of all invention, my friend. Now, you and I will have to think quickly about how we're going to seal this demon up in a *proper* structure."

"You're insane. You know that, right?"

"So I've been told." Tim smiled as he watched the retreating demon. "I wouldn't worry too much. He will not get far, but we should hurry."

Tim pointed, and I watched as Balforst continued to drive his horse downhill toward the trailer park's entrance. The demon lord turned toward Old 22, crossed the grass that separated the neighborhood from the highway, and was repulsed by a crackling force field. The impact blew Balforst off his horse and sent the powerful steed onto its backside.

"I erected that before I attempted to repair the hex sign." Tim shrugged. "In case it didn't work."

I couldn't argue with the results. Tim may have been an arrogant blowhard, but he was good at what he did. I turned back to the stairs. "Let's go!"

We pounded down the steps, reaching the bottom in a matter of seconds. Callie had pressed herself against the bay window near Tim's desk. Her mouth was agape as she looked back. "Did I see what I think I did?"

"You did! We've got to chase after him." I unlocked and threw open the door. With Balforst on the loose, much of the wind and lightning directed at the pyramid was gone, and daylight peeked out from behind the dissipating black cloud. "Into the wagon!"

Callie climbed into the backseat. I motioned for Tim to go around to the front passenger seat. He looked at the Roadmaster with utter disdain. "You expect me to—"

"Ride in this monstrosity? Yes, I do." Without waiting, I grabbed him by the scruff of his neck and flung him through the open driver's side door. I continued to shove him over into the passenger seat as I climbed in. I quickly clicked my seatbelt on, fired up the engine. "Hold on!" I ordered, then stomped the gas.

The rear wheels spun for a moment until they could gain traction. I know I left a good size rut in the grass right before Tim's front steps. "Sorry about the turf."

Tim clutched at the handle above the passenger door. "No, you're not!"

"You're right, I'm not."

We tore down the hill at top speed, my steering wheel held far to the right as we rounded the circular Raven Drive and hit the Pheasant Drive straightaway. Tim held on for dear life with one hand while he tried to fasten his seatbelt with the other. "You're insane! You know that, right?"

"So I've been told! Just ready another barrier spell!"

Tim muttered some very unenchanting things under his breath, but eventually that subsided into a proper spell. His hands glowed with magic.

We rounded the last bend that brought Pheasant Drive parallel with Old 22. Balforst had mounted his destrier once more, and he stood facing the trailer park's entrance with a sword in his hand. He raised the weapon, and it glowed with black light as he brought it down. A slash appeared in the shimmering barrier, and then another as he made a crosscut. He took one look at us, then spurred his horse through the gap.

"That's not good," I said for what seemed like the tenth time since this week began. I hit the brakes and slid to the left to get into the entrance driveway. I then stomped the gas and made a sharp right to get us onto Old 22. The engine roared through the firewall as we chased after the galloping horse.

The fastest horse in the world couldn't do much past fifty-five miles per hour, and only for short bursts. So, in theory we should have caught up to Balforst in no time. Unfortunately, the demon lord rode a demon horse, and that infernal animal was keeping pace with us even as we shot uphill doing ninety. Still, I could see *something* was wrong with it, as its gait was slightly off. Maybe crashing into Tim's barrier at top speed had hurt it somehow. Because of this, we were slowly gaining on them.

Balforst must have sensed this as well, because he suddenly turned left, onto a farm's asphalt driveway that cut through a partly harvested field of cucumbers. The day laborers had vanished for the day, likely when the demonic storm had erupted over the nearby Highland Estates.

As we turned up the drive to give chase, I saw the laborers had left behind stacks of crates for crops, a tractor, and one of those blue portable toilets you see at public events and construction sites.

Balforst's horse stood nearby, head lowered in exhaustion. As for the demon lord, he sat on the tractor, working the wheel and the pedals in a fruitless attempt to get it started. I could only assume the farmer had taken the key inside his house, because it wasn't going anywhere. Balforst looked up at our approach, gave the tractor's wheel one last spin, then jumped off it in disgust. "I'll just take your steed, Hexenmeister!" he bellowed, his voice ringing loudly in my head.

He drew his black sword and charged toward us. I had no doubt his sword could have pierced the windshield and killed all three of us with minimal effort, except he never reached the windshield. His sword bounced off the barrier Tim finished encasing the Roadmaster in, and then I slammed into him. Once again, Tim's barrier held and sent the demon lord flying without a scratch or dent on my car's hood or bumper. Balforst flew over the tractor and crashed into the stack of cucumber crates.

I parked the wagon and stepped out, my backpack of painter's supplies slung over one shoulder and my Smith & Wesson 640 in my right hand. I reached into a pants pocket and removed a blue speed-loader. It held enchanted .357 magnum rounds, each bullet and casing painted in miniature hex signs. I dumped the regular ammo out of the gun, then shoved the magical rounds into the now-empty cylinder. I shut the cylinder and twisted it until I heard a click.

As I finished this, the upended stack of cucumber crates stirred, and Balforst burst forth. With a rage-filled scream, he charged at me once again. I took quick aim at the demon lord's center mass and squeezed the trigger. The lightweight pistol kicked hard in my hands, but the recoil was nothing compared with what struck Balforst. The magically enhanced bullet shattered against his armored chest, but the demon still staggered from the blow. Two more rounds, and he dropped his sword. My fourth round missed, but my fifth caught him in the shoulder as he spun. His knee struck the ground, but then he leaped into the air and disappeared into the pile of crates once more.

Before I could reload, one of the crates rose into the air and flew at me. I rolled to the side, barely avoiding the thrown crate as it hurtled through the air.

The crate slowed and spun around to face me again. I gaped at it a moment, then dove to the side as it sailed past. This was an ability I'd never seen before. I'd fought demons in my time, but never one that could possess objects like this. Was this part of his power as a "master rider?"

With a keening cry, Balforst's destrier charged at me just as I finished reloading my gun. I took aim, but Callie threw herself between us. She held a charm necklace in one hand and an open potion bottle in the other. The horse slid to a halt and reared up on its hind legs. Its hooves lashed out for Callie's face but missed by scant inches. The woman didn't flinch. "I'll handle the horse, Jim. You deal with the demon!"

The crate flew toward Callie this time, but it bounced off a barrier that had surrounded her. Tim had stepped out of the

Roadmaster, too, his hands glowing with power. "He won't get away from us this time," he declared.

The crate crashed into the ground, and Balforst leapt out of it, once more his full-size. He ran to the pile of crates, but three of my bullets found his back. He howled in pain and jumped into the only thing close at hand: the portable toilet. It trembled and started to rise.

"Don't let it get away!" I shouted to Tim. I holstered my pistol and ran toward the toilet.

A shimmering barrier encased the toilet, and it sank back to the ground. I passed through the barrier and hurriedly pulled out my paints, brushes, and palette. I really didn't have time to mess around, so I poured the brown paint onto the palette, then mixed it with the colors Callie had given me. Drawing deeply on my magic and the image of the hex sign I'd etched into my memory, I dipped a brush into the mess of colors and slathered it onto the toilet's blue door. Instantly, the brown separated from the rest of the colors and formed a perfect circle that contained the rest of the paint.

As the magic started to take hold, the toilet stopped shaking. "What are you doing?" Balforst demanded in a muffled voice. "And what *is* this structure? What is that awful odor?"

I slathered more paint into the circle and willed the colors to separate out into their respective shapes. Sunflower background, black horse, dandy-man rider. "You'll get used to the smell," I said through gritted teeth.

Balforst must have been significantly weakened by repeatedly being struck by Tim's barriers and my bullets, because he fell silent as I finished my hasty work. That, or he was just so embarrassed at being trapped in a toilet that he didn't know what to do. By the time he realized what was happening, it was too late. All he could do was shout impotently from inside, but no regular human would be able to hear him. In fact, only the person who performed the sealing would be able to hear him, so he could rant and rave all he wanted.

I staggered out of Tim's barrier a few minutes later, carrying a palette that desperately needed cleaning and a pounding headache that needed some kind of pain relief. Tim leaned against my Roadmaster, his hair plastered with sweat. "I could use some brandy," he muttered.

"That makes two of us," I said.

Only Callie seemed to be in good shape. She'd forgotten all about her earlier terror as she led the red-eyed, fanged horse over to us. "Looks like I've found a new friend," she said with a wide grin. "Can I keep him?"

"Uh, we'll have to see," I said. *What can one do with a demonic horse, anyway?*

"What do you intend to do with him?" Tim nodded toward the toilet. "You can't mean to keep him there."

I shook my head. "No, I'll have to transfer him to a proper structure. I'll get him into something portable, then move him to a barn or another shed."

"When were you planning to do that?"

"A little later."

"A little later" turned out to be three weeks. In my defense, I never specified *when* later was. And I didn't realize how quickly they would be done harvesting cucumbers.

I was on my way to DeMarco's for a pizza to take back to the house, when I saw a truck pull out of the farm. Carried on the back was a blue portable toilet sporting a lovely hex sign that hadn't been there all that long ago. As the truck passed by, a deep muffled voice called out to me:

"Wishman, heeeeeeelp!"

I had to follow the truck for twenty miles before it delivered the toilet to the next farm in need of harvesting. Once the truck departed, I reproduced the hex sign inside the only container I had on hand: my John Wayne lunch tin.

"I still cannot believe you have me sealed in this metal box, Wishman!"

"Well, believe it." I sat at my kitchen table, a bottle of bourbon next to me as I scoured a map of ley lines for a place I could seal Balforst. So far, no luck. "Until I can find somewhere to properly house you, you're stuck in that tin. And it's a collector's piece! They don't make stuff for the Duke like that anymore."

"I care not for this Duke fellow." There was a loud sniff from inside the box. "How can a little man share my title?"

"He wasn't little, and he rode horses as well as you. Possibly better, since I don't remember him ever getting blasted off a horse like *somebody* I know."

"Those were extenuating circumstances!"

"You know, you've gotten a lot more petty since getting re-sealed." I leaned close. "Hey, if you don't like the Duke, I can always get a My Little Pony lunchbox. I don't care what I eat out of, but how much would you enjoy being a Brony, Master of Horse?"

There was a long pause. "I *suppose* the present accommodations are satisfactory."

"That's a good demon." I held up a bottle. "Bourbon?"

"Is it top-shelf?"
"Only the best."
"All right, then."

END

It Came from the Trailer Park

Frack and Blue

By Philip K. Booker

"*Henry Bryant Cantrell*, have you been paying attention to a single word I've said to you?"

"Not really," I answered absentmindedly, kicking my work-boots over to the entryway of our shared double-wide. I was still shaking off the drenching I'd taken in my sprint from my truck to the house. I had to look like some kind of giant shaggy dog. It took another couple of seconds before I realized my brain had let that bit of fatal stupidity fly out of my mouth, instead of rumbling around my thick skull.

Aw hell.

Fire burnt its way up the tips of Darlene's ears, sharply contrasted against the raven-black locks she had tucked behind them. Between that and the hard set of her mouth, I knew that not only had she heard me clearly, but that I'd stepped in one heck of a hornet's nest.

It's not like I was trying to be an ass. I'd just come through the door; I desperately needed aspirin, a cold beer, and a towel.

Raising my permanently grease-stained hands in the air, I turned and gave her my best apologetic grimace. "Hell's bells, darling. I don't suppose you'd allow me a cold one before you kill me dead?"

The murder in her eyes softened a bit, but she still swatted my arm with the back of her hand. Damned if the edge of her engagement ring didn't bite at my shoulder like an angry half-carat yellow-jacket. "You're lucky I've already put too much damn effort into training your stubborn ass to waste it on putting you down, ya' big ole lug." She reached into the fridge, pulling a pair of longnecks out. With a practiced ease, she smacked the caps off on the edge of the countertop and handed one to me. "Don't you get too comfortable. You're going right back out after you finish that."

"What the heck for?" I asked as I poured out an infantryman's ration of painkillers, washing the handful of pills down with my beer. "I just pulled a Twelver at the shop! Can't I dry off and rest my bones for a spell?"

"If you'd been listening, you'd have heard me telling you why. Carol Jenkins rang me up from down the way. There's been a big fuss up at Free State Farms. A bunch of their herd has gone missing, and they're looking for help in finding them."

"Please tell me you did not volunteer me to go poking around the hills of Bankhead, aimlessly looking for a lousy bunch of hairy spitting-goats."

"They're alpacas. And you're damn right I volunteered you. I've got money wrapped up in those critters. If we can't find them, I'll lose a chunk of my investment on their wool."

"That'd be a damn shame. But really, it's alpaca wool. How much money could we possibly be talking about? The shaggy critters can just grow more." I shrugged, taking a cool pull from my beer. "It can't be worth going back out there tonight."

"I've got upwards of fifteen-grand put into that co-op. I'll be damned if I'm gonna take a hit on my profit-line on account of you being too lazy to at least go and look! As I see it, you've got two options: Be uncomfortable for a few hours tonight, and find those critters, or figure out how to squeeze your big-ass onto that couch for the next month—cause that's where you'll be sleeping."

I glanced down at said couch. The well-worn Naugahyde three-seater might be just fine for relaxing on. But there was no way I could fit my six-foot-seven frame onto it to sleep, at least not without destroying my back.

"You're bluffing," I laughed, and tugged at her arm playfully. "Besides, you couldn't go a month without Hank the Tank."

She yanked her arm back. "Uh-uh, don't go thinking you'll be sweet-talking your way into our bed. And I never said I wouldn't still be getting *mine*–that little jackhammer in my bedside can tide me over *just* right."

Beer shot out of my nose as I sputtered and gasped.

About forty minutes later, I begrudgingly pulled up the gravel drive of Free State Farms hauling my off-roader behind me in my old Ford F-350. The summer sun was setting, but I could see Carol's husband, Darren, in khaki shorts and an orange and blue striped golf shirt. He was loading gear into the back of his new Polaris Ranger. I'd teased him mercilessly when he'd bought the four-wheeler, saying it looked like the bastard child of a pickup and a golf cart, but I had to acknowledge that it could get around. It helped that Darren usually had a foam cooler filled with cold ones, too. Which also went a long way in overlooking the fact he's a diehard Auburn fan. There are just some things that you don't do this close to Tuscaloosa.

I hopped out of my truck and walked over to help.

"Damn boy! Your wife let you walk out of the house like that? You look like you're auditioning to be the junior caddy at Auburn! You know we're gonna end up trudging through the woods, right?"

He grinned at me. "So, I should have schlubbed out here in a pair of coveralls, like you?"

It Came from the Trailer Park

I gave him a friendly slap-hello on the back, "You're gonna wish you came out in waders and a pair of Carhartt's when you're picking ticks out of your nethers. You doing all right?"

"Can't complain. Darlene kicked you out this way too, huh?" he asked, wiping the sweat off his thinning hairline with his sleeve. "Didn't you just pull a double at the garage?"

"That's the price of being with fiery women." I shrugged. "At least the rain stopped."

"I'll take the rain over the humidity."

"*Please* don't let him start bitching about the weather again," Faith said as she came out of the barn. She had a pair of climbing rope bundles slung over each of her shoulders. "I can't listen to it anymore. He'll blow right through the rest of your daylight."

Faith Harrigan had moved to Winston County from somewhere out west a few years ago. She'd bought ten-acres of cleared grassland abutting the southern edge of Bankhead National Forest, and christened it Free State Farms, in honor of the region's antagonism against the Confederacy during the war. Alpacas had been an eyebrow-raising decision to the area, but it seemed the scrappy young bohemian woman with her tie-dye tees and bell-bottom denim overalls was onto an untapped market. She bred the animals, but also harvested their wool for crafters, and rented space for weddings and photography spreads.

"Well then, what's the deal?"

"I rushed out this afternoon to bring the herd in, before the storm rolled in—heard what I thought was thunder beforehand, but it must have been miles off. I rode the length of the ranch, but I'm missing four head. One of them is a proven breeder too."

"Any sign of damage to the fence line?"

Darren pointed to the far-end of the property. "I found a break on the northern border. Not terribly big, but there was a snag of wool nearby. There's a trail running up along that ridge, so that's where I'm thinking we ought to start."

I thought about that a bit. "Karla Moore lives up that way. We should pay her a visit."

"Crazy Karla?" They asked in unison.

I frowned. Karla was eccentric, sure, but she didn't deserve that moniker. Most days, at least.

Faith's eyes narrowed. "Why on earth would you want to get her involved in this?"

"Well, Karla grew up in these woods. There are twenty-year veterans in the Forest Service that don't know them half as well as she does. She might be the best hope you have in tracking down these damn runaways."

"That's assuming *she* didn't poach them herself," Faith muttered, arms crossed. "Hell, she's probably the reason they're missing. Lured them up there because she got tired of living on squirrels and moonshine. She'd already have them butchered and on a spit."

I'd forgotten Faith and Karla had a history of bad blood. They'd had a squabble over water rights after Faith had moved in, culminating in Karla taking a shot at her.

"Hey, Faith," I hedged. "Maybe you should hold the fort down here. Things might go over better and end with fewer bouts of gunfire that way."

The first of the orange *No Trespassing* signs started just after we pulled onto the trailhead in our four-wheelers. More of them were pinned to the massive beech trees that flanked the barely visible path in regular intervals. The load in the trailer hitched to

Darren's four-wheeler rattled noisily along the gravel-dusted road.

"Shouldn't we call her? Let her know we're coming?"

"She doesn't believe in phones. Signal's garbage up here, anyway." Jerking my handle about, I maneuvered around a pothole, which Darren *ker-thunked* right on through. I glared at him. "Besides, she's gonna hear us coming long before we see her place. Especially with all that racket you're making."

"Sorry," he said defensively. "Be prepared, that's the Scout's motto. I've got extra fuel and enough rope to wrangle the alpaca, if we find them. More to haul them out of a crevasse, if we need it, and then some."

BOOM! CRACK!

A papery birch beside Darren's head exploded, bursting into a cloud of pulp and splinters. He froze in place—I couldn't blame him, getting shot at is a mind-killer. It also ranks stupid-high on my list of things I hate to experience. I dove off of my four-wheeler. It rolled a few feet further uphill as I tumbled painfully down an embankment.

"I done told you miserable corporate sons of bitches I ain't selling ya my land, and I'd put air-holes in ya the next time ya trespassed!"

I recognized Karla's voice in the shrill ranting. She was unhinged about something. And there was no mistaking that the shots had come from her compound up the hill.

"*Stop shooting, you damn fool!*" I inched over the embankment, palms up in surrender. "It's me—Hank Cantrell, and that's Darren Jenkins. We ain't here trying to take your land. We came up here to ask you some questions. Now, can we talk?"

A hundred yards up the hill, Karla Moore's grease-painted face and wiry nest of faded brown hair popped out from behind a cluster of old oak trees. "That depends. What kind of beer have you got in that cooler?"

We were sitting in Karla's front living room fifteen minutes later, drinking watery IPAs that Darren claimed were good—they weren't. Now, *living room* would be a generous description. Karla's home was a hodgepodge of cinder block lined bunkers and pieces of broken-down vehicles, all dug into the hill. Her living room was the carcass of an old school bus, minus the wheels, with the seats ripped out and turned about to line the walls. You entered through the front door of the bus, and the back door led into her maze of tunnels. As a diesel mechanic, I couldn't help but be a little impressed by her ingenuity. I've spent many an hour tinkering under the hood of some of the County's fleet of buses. Not even once have I ever thought, *gee, this would make an excellent addition to my house.*

"So, you see our predicament, don't you, Karla?"

"Happy wife, happy life," she said with a nod. "That's what my Pappy used to say."

"Precisely," I said.

Then Karla burst into a sputtering cackle, which brought tears to the corners of her eyes, as she howled, "Of course, ain't no man ever been *stupid* enough to pop the question. So, I ain't had to worry about it!"

Darren frowned, and bit back with, "But you have *so much* to offer here."

"*Damn right I do*. This is *my* land. Ain't nobody getting their hands on it!"

The tension ratcheted up immediately. I set my crappy beer down on the floor beside me, in case I needed to do something quickly, like keep Karla from gutting Darren. I could easily thump both of them in open-ground or in a bar fight, being at least a head taller than each of them. However, a bunker chamber made of an old bus body isn't exactly roomy. My size was more a hindrance than a blessing.

"Darren, shut your trap." I shot him as hard a warning glare as I could manage. "We're guests in Karla's home." Turning my attention back to Karla, "When you shot at us earlier—"

"I said I was sorry about that!"

I sighed. "Yes, you did." Like that made it better. "Anyway, you said something about a bunch of corporate types coming up here. What did these folks want?"

"They want my land," she said, as if that should have been obvious.

"Yes, but why do they want your land, Karla?"

"They want to buy it up so that they can drill test samples. They've already snatched up most of the private lands up to the southern border of the Bankhead and have gotten permission to test on several of the Bureau of Land Management lots. Gonna check to see if they can confirm a good source of natural gas in the shale. That way they can try to buy leasing rights to drill in the forest."

Darren blinked. "They think the Bureau of Land Management is going to allow them to frack in the Bankhead?"

"Sure enough. They think there's a whole butt-load of untapped shale down there. They've already been pounding away in wells they've made. You folks downhill might not have noticed it, but my bunker's been trembling like a prom-night virgin, and it's been getting worse the closer the bastards get to my land."

As if on-cue, the room groaned and shook. I saw dust fall from the tunnels beyond the bus-room. I sprang to my feet and braced myself against the wall and ceiling. Damned if I was going to die in some hillbilly spider-hole after making it through a tour in the Dirt intact.

"*See! I told'ya!*" Karla jumped up from her seat excitedly.

"Earthquake?"

I shook my head, relaxing as the shaking stopped. "Not like I've ever felt."

"This is those drilling bastards," Karla insisted.

"*Now?* It was pouring for hours, and the last bit of sun was fading when we were pulling in. I'm only up here under threat of forced celibacy. You're telling me a bunch of out-of-town speculators are out there pounding sand in the dark?"

"You don't believe me? Their latest test site's up the way, just south of the lumber mill. I'll show you."

"It's not that, Karla," I hedged. "It's just we've got to find these alpacas."

"Oh, come on, Hank—if it ain't that far from here," Darren slurred, "what's the worst that could happen?"

"Just off the top of my head, your IPA-drinking dumbass rolls your golf cart-on-steroids off a ridgeline, into Collier Creek."

He dismissed my observation with a wave of his hand. "If this group is causing quakes in the area, we've got to let folks know."

"No, what I've got to do is look for these woolly bastards. I can't be spending the next month on that couch."

"*In the dark?* This entire trip was a farce from the get-go. Those critters are dead or bedded down in a cave for the night— *most likely the former*. The odds of us fumbling into them tonight are ludicrous. We'll hop up the road, see if Karla is right about these jerks, and then go back home. Hell, shine your flashlight around a bit on the way. That way you can honestly say you looked and come home the dutiful fiancé. Let Harrigan come out her damn self in the light of day."

"That's some half-assed thinking there," I grumbled.

Karla piped up, "Ain't nobody gonna take my word on this alone, Hank."

"Well damn, Karla, maybe if you stopped *shooting* at folks, they'd listen to you!"

"Boy, you're like a dog with a bone; you just can't let that go, can you?"

"*No!*" Darren and I shouted in unison.

As much as I didn't want to venture out to the drill site, I also didn't want to be out alone looking for those alpacas either. We'd settled on riding up the trailhead to the bluff that overlooked the drill-well. Karla would drive for Darren—since I wasn't sure just how much of his bravado was beer-induced—and, in a sad state of affairs, I trusted her more at the moment.

The site wasn't but a couple of miles up the trail. It wasn't as large a setup as I'd been expecting. A foreman's trailer sat in a dirt clearing, with a portable generator humming loudly enough to almost drown out the night's serenade of crickets and katydids. Several active floodlights sat around two large tanker trunks and a crawler-crane; a massive white tube being supported by its hook.

And not a person in sight.

"That just doesn't track," Karla said, scratching her chin as she squinted at the site.

Darren shifted in his seat to get a look. "Shouldn't there be somebody there?"

I nodded. "A whole crew of folks, if it were in use. And there ought to be at least some kind of security presence there now."

Karla pointed, "The trailer door is open."

"Are you sure?" I got off of my four-wheeler.

"You questioning my eyes, boy?"

"You shot at us tonight from half that distance, because you *thought* we were these people. *Yeah*—I'm gonna question you seeing a cracked door from here. Darren, have you got a set of binoculars?"

He turned to fish through a bag in his Ranger and pulled out a hefty black Nikon model. "Be prepared."

I took them and adjusted the focus. "Son-of-a-gun. You were right."

Karla smirked. "*Told ya.* Don't be questioning my eyes."

I gave her a sidelong glance over the binoculars. "Fine. You have the eyes of a hawk."

Eyes of a hawk, and mind like a sack full of rabid weasels.

"Well, that means somebody's got to be down there, right?" Darren shrugged. "Maybe they're just using the bathroom or something."

"All of them? *Woo-hoo*—Pee-party in the port-a-potty." I shook my head, then kept panning around the site, searching. Nothing. "I don't know. This feels... wrong. You don't just up and leave a site like this. I'm going to call the Sheriff's department. Let them check it out." I pulled out my phone and swore.

"What?"

"No bars. How about you?"

Darren laughed, "That's why I don't use that cheap-o service that you—*son-of-a-bitch*... Nah, I've got nothing either."

Karla cackled with laughter. "Of course not! That's why I like living up here. You young folk are too damn dependent on those cellphones. Bunch of new-fangled junk, if you ask me."

"Fine," I sighed. "With the signal being so bad out here, there will have to be a radio down the hill. Something feels off about all of this. Keep the guns ready, but out of sight. No shooting unless *I* say so. Clear?"

Navigating down the ridge in the dark with the four-wheelers took another hour. Darren monitored the site with his binoculars. Not once did he notice anyone come out of the trailer.

"Steady," I said as we edged up to the clearing. "I'll go check and see if anyone is on-site. Y'all watch my back. If there's nobody in, I'll see if I can scrounge up their radio and patch a call in to the Sheriff or the Rangers. If not, I'll just leave a note and lock up shop as best I can."

Darren and Karla nodded, and I pulled out into the lot.

The foreman's trailer, a thirty-foot double-wide with white aluminum siding and a gray dust-skirt, had a pair of chrome-covered steps leading to the two doors. I pulled up beside the trailer, doing my best not to seem imposing as I got out and approached the ajar door. The last thing I wanted to do was wheel-up on some security guard who'd fallen asleep on the job. That's practically asking to get shot.

The lights were on in the trailer, but there was an obnoxious flicker coming from one of them inside. Yeah, that did nothing to ease my disquiet.

I knocked on the door. "Hello? Anybody 'round?"

No answer.

Well, hell.

I opened the door and took a pair of slow steps through, "Listen, I'm just checking to see if y'all are—"

The words caught in my throat.

Stunned.

I stood there for a solid minute. Just a slack-jawed fool, trying to take in just what it was that I was seeing.

All of the cabinets, drawers and desks were upturned. Doors were broken or hanging from their hinges. Papers and office equipment were strewn all over the floor.

And the floor.

There was a giant hole in the center of the trailer floor. It was like something had violently ripped it apart, from underneath the trailer.

I eased slowly back out the door, not daring to turn to face my allies until I heard the latch on the door click.

"Guys…" I said, waving them over with increasing urgency.

"Holy hell!"

"I wouldn't stick my head too close to that hole, Darren," I said as I pushed around the debris. "No sign of a radio."

Darren kept his shotgun trained on the hole but kept craning his neck to get a better look. "Do you think this is blowback from their drill or something?"

"Nah," said Karla, shaking her head. "This was some kind of critter. A big'un too."

"Yeah. If this had been an explosion, it would have blown out the windows and damaged the roof as well," I said, pointing to the gypsum ceiling. "There's some puncture marks here and there, but nothing like I'd expect to find."

Clink, clank, clack!

Karla and I whirled our attention back toward the hole. Darren's face had a sheepish grimace.

"Sorry! I bumped a stapler with my foot, and it fell in." He let out a low whistle. "That's one deep hole. Sounds like it might lead to an old cavern."

"Tons of caves and the like 'round here.," said Karla. "Hank, there ain't no radio anywhere in here. How you wanna handle this?"

"With about five beers, after a call to the Sheriff's department…" I sighed. "The Ranger Station is a bit closer, but both are further than I'd want to go by four-wheeler on. I say we double-back up to Free State. We can use Harrigan's phone to file a report with the authorities, and then call it a night on this weirdness."

Karla's jaw stiffened at the mention of Harrigan's name.

"That's assuming *you* can play nice, Karla."

"Fine. I can deal with that water-thieving hippy for one night."

"We can cut our drive time in half by using the access road, you know," Darren said, pointing to the cleared dirt road that left the clearing. "It'd be easier on the four-wheelers too."

"Fine. If you're set, take the wheel on your cart. Karla can ride shotgun with you, and keep an eye peeled for this critter. Let's take no chances. As soon as we hit asphalt, gun it to Free State."

Take the access road, he said. It'll be quicker, he said…

"Darren, if this goes tits-up, I'm officially leveling the blame on you."

We'd made it over the hill and around the corner before plans went sideways. The bright lights from the drill site had given way to the darkness. I'd spotted a faint glow illuminating the roadside. The 'road' out was still barely more than packed dirt and the 'glow' had turned out to be an overturned pickup. It used to be a Chevy Silverado. *Used to be* being the operative phrase.

Something had flipped the truck, or otherwise smashed into it and caused it to roll upturned down a small crevasse. The windows were in various states of breakage, but I couldn't get a clear look inside the cab.

"Just add it to the police report. There ain't no sense in wasting time going down there," Karla had said when I'd pulled over.

"Bad juju," I said, unspooling the cable from the winch on my four-wheeler. "Besides, imagine how shitty you'd feel if they find a body down there and then determine they were still alive when we came by. How would you feel about that?"

"Wouldn't lose a lick of sleep over it," she said, spitting.

"Damn, that's cold, Karla," Darren said.

"Fools would've brought it on themselves. They probably drilled into some bear's den or something."

"I've seen some angry bears before," I said. "But never one that'd climb out of a tunnel and rip a trailer apart like that." I draped the cable down the embankment and wrapped a few loops around my hand. "Karla, cover me with that rifle of yours. Darren, watch our backs with your shotgun—and maybe make sure Karla doesn't shoot me for my own good."

Damned if that didn't make Karla laugh a little.

I'd turned the wheels to the side on the four-wheeler, but I still felt the vehicle shift a little when I let all of my three-hundred pounds hang on the rope. No lie, that was a pucker-moment. I could have turned coal into diamond. It held though. I finished going down the slick rocky embankment.

Reaching the upturned Chevy, I gingerly tested my foot against the frame, along the passenger-side wheel-well. The truck groaned, shifting slightly.

"Hello?" I leaned over. The window below me had spiderwebbed, obscuring the interior. "Is anyone in there?"

No answer.

I added more of my weight onto the truck, dropping to a kneeling position. The metal protested but held. Inching up to the window, I pulled my phone out. Still no signal, of course, but I activated the little flashlight on it.

Something moved inside the cab.

"Hey!" I shouted back up the hill. "I've got movement!"

More movement.

"Take it easy, buddy," I said, turning back to the window, a bounce of excitement in my chest. "We're here to hel—"

A long, chitinous limb burst from the glass, rocketing barely past my face. The window crumbled inward around it. Another limb, five-feet in length, also shot out of the window. The two arms were a translucent-yellow easily and as thick as Louisville Sluggers. They bent inward at odd angles and hooked themselves into the truck, hoisting up a chittering body. Multiple glossy black orbs of what could only be called the biggest damn spider that I've ever seen stared back at me.

A pair of fangs lashed out at me.

"Oh shit!" I fumbled backwards. My phone fell from my hand, skittering into the rocky crevasse behind me.

"Move, stupid!"

I'd barely pushed myself along the bedside panel of the truck when a hail of gunfire erupted from above me. The impossibly large spider shrieked in pain as the mixture of Karla's bullets and Darren's shells tore and peppered it into a splattered mess.

The gunfire stopped, and Darren's voice called out to me, as a blinding flashlight beam hit me in the face. *"You all right, Hank?"*

"What…the…hell…was…*that?*" I huffed.

On the insistence of both Darren and Karla, it was decided that we should bring the remains of the spider back with us. Otherwise, who would believe our story. Of course, *neither* of them was volunteering to come down and help. They sent down a pair of the thick, corded ropes that Darren had packed for alpaca-wrangling.

Even though the thing hadn't done much more than twitch after the barrage of gunfire, I was still not taking any chances, and shoved my hunting knife into its head. The blade crunched through its carapace and squished nauseatingly into its innards. The blood had a weird blueish-gray tint to it, and I did my best to shake it off my knife before I sheathed it. And the smell… It was a sour mixture of rot, rancid vinegar, and something I couldn't put my finger on. It would make the busted gut on a deer smell like daisies, by comparison though. I had to back up and take a few good breaths to continue lacing the rope around its body.

"All right," I hollered back up the hill. "Keep it slow, until it's completely clear!"

Foot by foot, they hoisted the damn thing out of the truck cab. Fully exposed, it was massive. The segmented trunks alone were each a good two-feet in length, and more than half as wide. Its legs had a hard, armored chitin material around them. Four legs faced forward, with the other four to the back. The inner-legs on the front and back were easily five-feet long when straightened out, with the outer legs being only slightly shorter.

I made a final scan of the interior of the truck, while Darren and Karla fussed with loading the spider onto the back of my four-wheeler. The windshield was completely knocked out of its frame. I didn't see any sign of the owner until—

"Hey guys?"

Darren's head popped over the edge, "Find something?"

I lifted the severed arm into the air. "You could say that."

The arm was a waxy pallid white, wrapped in the sleeve of an oxford-blue dress shirt. Both the shirt and arm were covered in blood and caked-on mud and ripped away roughly about the shoulder.

"*Jesus!*"

"Safe to say we're not looking for a survivor now," I said. "There's a *lot* of blood down here."

"Where's the rest of the body?"

I shrugged. "Must have dropped through the hole in the windshield."

"Bring the arm up too," Karla said, coming back over.

Darren looked even more horrified. "Are you kidding?"

"What? He's already dead, and maybe it'll help identify the man. That's assuming they can't find the rest of him."

Ugh.

"*Fine,*" I said, disgusted. "But if I'm hauling an arm up with me, I need y'all to use the winch to help pull me up."

Something was bothering me.

And I mean that something *more* than scaling up a slippery ravine with a severed human arm in my hand. The spider that had attacked me was huge, for sure. Assuming it had been the thing that had attacked the trailer—which tracked—it had been in the cab of the truck with this guy. However, it had also struggled to break out of the damaged window of the truck, to get at me. Granted, we hadn't given it a lot of time to do so, but I had to wonder if it could have caused all of the damage at the trailer. That had been a gigantic hole in the floor, not to forget the tunnel leading to it.

I felt the ground shake under my boot.

I really hate being right sometimes.

"Hurry up, guys!"

The cliffside *exploded.*

I was sent flying against the rockface as arms tore through the ground, multitudes larger than the spider we'd killed. The cable pulling me from above sped up, dragging me clear. I scrambled up the last couple of feet of the hillside on all fours, throwing the cable along with the severed arm clear as soon as I was on even ground again.

"Go! Go! Go!" I screamed, as I jumped into my four-wheeler and gunned it.

It's not like I had to sell that sentiment too hard. Darren was peeling down the road, his tow-trailer barely managing to stay level as he did so. Karla had strapped herself *into* the back of his trailer and was reloading her rifle.

The dirt road doubled back on itself ahead of us, to handle the downhill turn. Which immediately brought the problem of trying to outrun this monster into perspective. We might be able to burn rubber at nearly sixty-mph in a straight-a-way, but we were racing against a creature that was intelligent and did not have to abide by roads.

It screamed through the trees, toppling whole timbers as it went, and cut us off down the road. It filled the breadth of the road. Its legs were at least twenty—if not thirty feet long—and its massive body was at least as large as my four-wheeler. Playing chicken with an earth-bursting monster-sized spider felt like suicide. Then I had an idea.

I yelled to Darren as we skidded to a stop. "Turn around!"

"Are you crazy?"

"At this point? Probably! We need to get back to the drill site!" I lined my four-wheeler up to the angry spider, tied some of the rope hanging from the dead one in the back, and shoved a piece of timber into the accelerator. My four-wheeler careened downhill toward the beast, and I jumped into Darren's cart. Darren wasted little time and we tore back up the hill, hoping that maybe that bought us some time.

"I can't believe that *actually* worked!"

We'd briefly caught a glimpse of the massive spider charging after my old four-wheeler as we fled. We'd heard the commotion of the aftermath for a while longer. There was no way that beast hadn't ripped my old four-wheeler to pieces, by the sound of it. I was going to catch all kinds of hell from Darlene, and Allstate about that.

Darren whipped his four-wheeler behind the foreman's trailer and stopped. "Okay, now what?"

"We've gotta make our stand here," I said.

Darren restarted his engine, "Now I know you've lost your mind!"

I reached over and shut the engine off again. "Think about it. There is no way in hell that we're going to outrun that thing out of these woods. The roads are too loose and windy for us to make speed, not when it can just charge through the woods like that."

"There ain't exactly a lot working in our favor up here either, boy," Karla said. "There's all kinds of things up here that beast could throw at us. And there's no telling how many of those critters are up here."

Darren blanched, "You think there's more of them?"

"Just think on it," she shrugged. "We already killed one, then that one comes tearing out of the ground. Spider-Kong screams angry woman to me. Figures that was either its offspring or its mate. Female spiders are usually the bigger of the species. There could be a whole egg sac full of those things waiting to hatch beneath us."

I'd watched an egg sac of spiders burst in the back of my shed once. My blood ran cold at the thought of the damage even a handful of these creatures could do.

"We can't let these things live. We're going to have to hit this beast with everything we can to stop her, and then we need to make sure there aren't more down below. Got any more guns back there, Karla?"

She checked the chamber of an old M1 Garand and pushed it over to me with a fresh en bloc clip loaded in the top.

"This isn't a weapon," I said, taking it wearily. "This is an *antique*."

"Watch yer mouth, boy. That weapon was good enough for my Pappy in the War. It's good enough for the likes of you."

"Yes Ma'am," I said.

Darren shook his head. "Man, I brought my shotgun in case of coyotes or something. I wasn't prepared to go to war. I've only got three shells left."

I looked around.

When I'd first met Darren, he'd been doing roadwork with the DOT. As I understand it, the pay was decent, but the work in the area had dried up, and he'd moved on.

"Well, think you can still operate one of those?"

Darren followed my gesture. "Yeah, probably."

"Then here's what we do."

There hadn't been a lot of time to prepare before the shrieks of the massive beast filled the night air. We'd turned on every bit of equipment we could find, so as to overwhelm its senses with the excessive vibrations and sound.

It tore right up the roadway, until it had reached the primary cluster of the equipment. For a moment it just stood there, bobbing up and down. Fangs—taller than me—flexed back and forth, dripping with a silvery venomous ooze. I was willing to bet that whatever nastiness was in that hellish substance, it would be a damn painful way to die. And that was assuming the bite alone didn't rip you apart.

Just a little bit closer.

Kneeling by one of the site's floodlights, I lined up my shot. It'd been *forever* since I'd used something with iron-sights and the hefty Garand weighed much more than the Weatherby Mark V that I like to use for hunting. Taking a deep breath, I did my best to control my rising nerves. The long day was wearing on me. I hadn't wanted to be here in the first place. I'd just wanted to be curled up with Darlene on the couch with a hot meal. Instead, I was cold, wet, and risking being chow for a spider big enough to spin a web for Mothra.

I eased out my breath and pulled back on the trigger.

CRACK!

The 30-06 round slammed into one of the beast's massive black eyes and it jerked, spinning about to focus on me. I definitely had all its attention.

Gulp.

BOOM!

Karla's rifle smashed another shot into the flank of its abdomen. The monster pivoted again to target the new threat, as it favored its damaged side.

"Leeeroy...!" Darren roared before the roar of the crane engine drowned him out as he whipped the crane around, extending the jib as he did so. The massive white hydraulic tube hanging from the end of the crane's hook slammed hard into the backside of the spider, sending it flipping end over end. The creature flailed about wildly, as it landed on its back.

"Now!" I screamed as I charged out from my position, unloading each of my seven remaining shots into its underbelly at closer range.

Karla and Darren charged it after me, each giving the massive beast every bit of firepower they could.

The creature twitched and spasmed with each blast, and eventually stopped. Just like with the smaller male, I didn't hesitate. Too many schlocky horror films in my youth had taught me there was no such thing as overkill. I pulled out my hunting knife and jammed it into repeatedly into where I guessed its brain to be.

I was covered in the sticky blue-gray blood of the spider when I turned back to face Darren. "Leeroy Jenkins?"

He shrugged, "Leeroy's my middle name, and some kind of an internet joke. My boy thinks it's hilarious."

I couldn't help but burst out with laughter. Strands of the oozy spider blood dripped off of the bill of my hat with each shake. I slung another stream of the stuff off my hand and then wiped my face clear. "All right, empty out your cooler. We've got more work to do."

It was a little surprising how quickly the Styrofoam foam cooler broke down in the gasoline. We salvaged a little more foam from the remains of the foreman's trailer. It wasn't the most elegant recipe, but it was effectively napalm when we'd finished. We'd fixed it in a hefty chem-bucket, which wasn't ideal, but would still hold for our purposes. That was, assuming there were more of these things, they hadn't hatched yet.

I'd toweled off as much of the spider ooze as I could, from the remains of the trailer's bathroom supplies. There was still a layer of sticky residue all over me, but I looked less like someone who'd wrestled the Blob.

We dropped several lines down the tunnel hole in the trailer, the first being attached to an electric Coleman lantern. After waiting several minutes and not seeing anything stirring below, Darren went down, then Karla, followed by me and the bucket of napalm.

"Look at this," Darren said excitedly, as we finished coming down.

It was a smooth-sided cavern, mostly limestone if I had to guess, and easily a couple stories high at this point. On the wall where Darren was pointing were some faint etchings in the stone.

"They look like the petroglyphs at Kinlock Shelter," he said. "These could be thousands of years old!"

"Or they could have been done by a bunch of drunk college kids, twenty years ago. Looks like just a bunch of scribbles to me," Karla said, squinting in the low light.

I swirled one of the chunks of wood we'd brought down with us in the napalm mixture. It was thick and sticky and should be perfect for what we'd intended. Pulling the wood back out, I lit the glob at the end and the torch flared to life. An orange/yellow light filled the area.

There were definite markings on the wall. They were crude, for sure, but seemed to offer a coherent tale. Massive spiders swarmed on villages and feasted on groups of ancient people and their livestock. It was exactly the thing I'd feared. The people had risen up and fought back. It looked like they'd made some kind of a trap and buried them underground.

"Look!" Darren scurried over to a spot on the cave floor. There was what looked like a small axe made of sharpened rock. He picked it up and ran his finger over the edge. A small cut formed on his finger. "Ooh, still sharp."

"All right then, so these things are ancient," I said. "They must have cocooned themselves or laid dormant for years after this. The drilling surveyors likely exposed them while they were testing the area."

"Well then," Karla said, taking a chunk of wood and making her own torch, "let's go bug-hunting."

Darren made a torch too and kept the axe head he'd found with him. We'd used up all the ammo killing the mother. So, I *really* hoped we were dealing with eggs now. Still, I kept my knife at the ready as we moved deeper into the cave. The system narrowed dramatically around the bend and a vinegary smell caught my nose.

"There. Do you two smell that?"

They nodded.

Karla pointed into the distance ahead. "I can see something reflecting over there."

I squinted but couldn't make out what she was talking about. "Dammit woman. I swear you must be part-falcon or something."

"Don't start knocking my sight now. I might not be able to appreciate cave-drawings, but I can see there's something over there."

"No, she's right. I see something too."

Who was I to argue with them? We pushed on and—*she was right again!* I was going to need to up my carrot intake or something. Glossy strands of spider silk hung along the walls in a massive web. It would have been beautiful, but the pattern wasn't quite symmetrical. There were big globs of webbing that were—

My stomach sank.

Those weren't flaws. They were bodies. Dozens of *human* bodies.

"How many people did you say should have been working at a site like this?" Darren asked, gulping.

"That's about right..." I said.

Karla pointed closer to the floor. "Ain't that some of them pesky spitting-goats you boys were after?"

"Alpacas," I said numbly. Turning to follow her motion, I could plainly see the bodies of a pair of alpaca, bloodied and wrapped in more spider silk.

These things had come as far out as Free State. Mere minutes from my home. From Darlene.

My blood boiled. "Let's finish this."

"I found them!" Darren pointed to a pulsing mass along the cave floor. Tucked into a ridge about eight-feet high and twelve-feet long, was a concentrated weaving of spider silk, along with dozens of yellow gelatinous spheres. Each sphere shook and wobbled with the silhouette of a spider as large as my head.

I slung the rest of the contents of the bucket at the mass and shoved my torch into it.

The nest erupted in flames as the torch contacted it and the napalm. The fire spread the entire length of the egg sac in seconds. Shrieks came from some of the eggs as they shook violently and exploded. One egg rolled loose to Darren's feet, and he drove the stone axe head into it, splitting the baby spider in two.

We thoroughly eradicated every single spider we could find.

As the fires burned out, we cut down the bodies of the people on the web. We'd hoped that we'd find someone still alive, but it wasn't to be. Most of them had been impaled by the fangs of the female spider, and either bled out or succumbed to the toxins in its bite. A few looked as if they'd simply asphyxiated in their webbed cocoons. At least we could notify the authorities later, and their families could give them a proper burial. A small consolation, but one that would hopefully be better than not knowing.

I. Hurt. Everywhere.

I was going to have nightmares about this for weeks to come—worse than the ones from my time overseas. Fortunately, I had a good woman to come home to.

And I would not have to try and sleep on that damn couch.

Trailer Park COUS

By J. F. Posthumus

Chapter One

"*R*ed's dead! The bastards killed Ol' Red!*"*

That's really how it started. No one knows how it's all going to end, but I can tell you for certain that's the exact moment that the war began.

Sure, you can argue that tensions were high. Wasn't it that way everywhere? Yes. Some will say those with weapons and too much down time were looking for any excuse to use them. Hell, for that? I can't think of a time when there wasn't an adversarial, even violent, altercation ready to start -over anything- between Captains Everly and Duddlemyer. Maybe we all could have been more prepared. Or just left. I can say I was personally impressed and even gosh-darned proud in a patriotic kind of way at how the Somner family rose to the occasion. I mean, especially when you consider their circumstances.

Still... war means the ugliest parts of humanity are on full display. Maybe that's why the tiniest gems sparkle so bright in those circumstances.

People died that didn't deserve it. Same with animals. And there are those that most certainly *did* deserve it.

Ah, well. That's life at a trailer park, I suppose.

Argh, bad writer! Getting ahead of the real story. Good thing I can go back and edit this later. Just trying to get all that happened while my mind has a grip on it. So much happened, even since the beginning! Gotta pace it out, not lose anything.

Okay.

I say "that's life at a trailer park, I suppose" because I've only spent the past couple of years living in one. Not like some of the residents here at Stoney Knob.

That's Stoney Knob Trailer and Campground Park, to be clear. Emphasis on stony. I swear, the landowners could have made a fortune as a gravel business. You only have to scrape off maybe two inches of topsoil before you start finding rocks of each size possible along with clay, sand and worms.

But, nope. Due to the proximity to one of the many small lakes in this state, and a pretty good underground river, along with the view of mountains, some genius looked around and said "yup, we gonna make big money here lettin' people park their RVs for long or short term!"

Yeah, I live *there*, and have been long enough to meet, and observe, everyone long before… well, *before*.

Just to be, y'know, transparent and all that- I am not tearing down life at a trailer park or people, in general, that live in or ever have lived in one. Or make an RV, or trailer of any kind, their residence. Nope, nope, I've spent my time in a big city, a small city, also towns of various sizes. People are people wherever you go, as the song declared. But there are reasons for cliches, stereotypes, profiling, and all that. It's because enough people fit roughly into a generalization for it to ring true. Doesn't matter if that's a tiny truth overshadowing much bigger ones. Anybody says "trailer park," and there are mental images that spring up. Quite a few of them are less than complimentary.

That's just the way it is. That's society at work right there. We tell ourselves it's getting better, when what has happened is the focus for such lazy thinking has shifted to a group different than the ones which have dealt with it for a while.

Anyway, we do have the full gambit here at Stoney Knob. Only one person trying to deal drugs, but they'll get run out soon enough by the long timers and lifers. Yeah, addicts abound, from chocolate to booze to harder stuff, but we've kept out of the "meth market," and there isn't enough in the illegal opiate fan club to keep a pusher in business. If someone got it in their heads to run a little liquor, tobacco and vape shop out of their residence, they'd be swimming in money before the third round of welfare checks cleared.

I suppose we could say that's what the so-called convenience and grocery shop at the front of the park is actually doing, but they only have a license for beer and wine. If they're making hard liquor available, I haven't been inducted into the secret club. Aside from really good internet, that's my one vice, decent tequila and rum are required for my personal libations. Fortunately, UPS still delivers out here, and my favorite brands started shipping last year.

Before the naughty ideas start getting a voice, let me backtrack. I need reliable internet for my job. I'm a writer and writing means research. Since the advent of the interwebs, no one has to drive everywhere or spend ridiculous amounts of money to learn about anything. But you gotta have that sweet refresh rate if you want to keep your sanity. If I had lived here back when the best to be bought was five minutes or more to reload a web page, I'd have bought a gun just to eat a bullet. I don't have any hobbies to eat up that kind of downtime.

Most of my neighbors do, though. Listening to music, watching shows or social media. Trying to play music on whatever instruments they can get. Drinking. Watching everyone, although I guess I do have that as part of my profession, too. Weapons, that's another big one. Collecting stuff. All kinds of stuff. From Coca-Cola bottles and cans, to tin signs, little figurines, trading cards, anything a person can think of and more. Some of the fellow "parkers," that's what I call myself and my fellow park occupiers, seem to make a hobby of collecting or breeding kids, or kittens, or both, because there seems to be more and more of them around the same lots every few months!

While we have plenty of "crazy cat people" and mega-moms, we do have a few dog aficionados as well. Only a couple of the parkers here have more than a pup or pair of them. Those two, the Smiths and Whetsalls, are constantly talking trash on each other's little packs. What all of the dog owners have in common is a deep love and appreciation for canines of any kind and age. Really, though, just about everyone at the Knob appreciates a good dog.

Which brings us full circle to what started it all.

Red. Ol' Red. Good Ol' Red.

All those titles were used to acknowledge Mr. Addison's bright red retriever. When I first moved in, I wanted to nickname him Clifford, after the character in children's stories. That got frowns so deep from everyone else around here I wondered if I was going to be lynched for suggesting it. Good Ol' Red was the epitome of his moniker, though, so it was easy to fall in line. That canine fellow must have weighed close to a hundred pounds, and was the quintessential "Man's Best Friend," especially for Mister Addison. Tyler Addison, a retired music teacher in his eighties, was older than his companion, even in dog years, but only just. Something else to know is that Addison is nearly six feet tall and barely over one hundred fifty pounds.

Hearing that the arguable favorite of the park dogs was dead was unexpected enough. Seeing Addison cradling that big pooch's dead weight like a spouse who'd lost their life partner? That would've put the shock, sorrow and anger in anyone with a thriving pulse. It sure did to the inhabitants of the Knob. The ones who cared about anything besides themselves, at least.

I had been in conversation with George Duddlemyer, the pair of us standing in the small patch of bluegrass between my 1970 Dodge Glastron Motorhome and the gravel road that connected us to the rest of the park, and points beyond. The motorhome was an heirloom from my grandma on Dad's side. Fortunately, she had it parked in an unused barn, so it was still in pretty good shape. The fifty-gallon gas tank was a bitch to fill in any year. But between that and the solar panels I put up everywhere? Easy living by comparison. Sure beats a gas and electric bill every month, especially in the winter. Add in the cheap monthly fee for the lot I stayed on and my cell bill with internet connection, and you have the bulk of my expenses. That's why I moved here, after I took possession of the Glastron. Cheap, easy living, baby.

George had been regaling me with details of how the military ranks broke down in the good old USA Army. He'd spent his four years in service between 'Nam and any of the skirmishes in the Middle East, so he wasn't a current or war vet. He was free with his advice and information, though, and a fellow human being to talk to. He was tall like me, graveled but friendly voiced, still kept the buzz cut hairdo from his time in the military. He was also the best person in the Knob to talk to about anything technical in regards to guns. For the story I was thinking of writing, I needed all the accurate info I could get about who ordered who around in the Army, and the weapons they'd use. For the sake of ease, I decided to make the story set in the time frame when George would have been in. Why scour the interwebs when there's a darn reliable source living nearby, and didn't hate me for my sense of humor?

"Great flying shit balls, Ed, what the hell is this?" Duddlemyer stage whispered to me.

"Don't know, George," I replied, "Poor Red looks dead to me, though. What's your take?"

My informed conversationalist exhaled loudly through his nostrils while he peered at his next door neighbor. Addison was struggling as he walked with the limp form of Red in his arms.

"Don't you worry, Ty! We gonna get them sombitches!" George roared. "I'll be right behind ya!"

Addison appeared to barely notice that he was being spoken to. He kept shuffling on, towards his own abode down the road.

"Did you see the huge wounds on Red's neck and shoulders?" George asked me via stage whisper. I doubt Addison would have paid any attention if we spoke at normal levels, but I respected Duddlemyer's intention. I whispered an affirmative.

"Puncture wounds. After the sombitches jammed 'em in, they ripped 'em out, hard. Vicious, like. He probably went down fighting, but he wouldn't last long with injuries like that," Duddlemyer observed. "Ain't no way for Good Ol' Red to go."

"Not many who deserve going out that way, George," I said somberly.

"No, not many. But some." he answered. I could hear his anger growing just in those few words. No doubt about it as he concluded by saying, "I gotta go get things ready."

He didn't wait for me to reply. He just began his brisk walk after his next door neighbor.

Maybe I should have realized how bad things would get at that moment. Aside from arguments with Everly, Duddlemyer hardly ever got angry. Should have expected less reserved personalities, and by that, I mean most of the adults around, to be just as enraged. And none of them were the type to stifle their impulses.

Chapter Two

There was a cynical part of me that toyed with the notion of grabbing either the "red" rum or mezquila, a few mixers, a tall glass, and just watching while everything unfolded. Nor would I be doing it alone. More than a few of my fellow parkers did just that, although it was cheap light beer they drank.

There again, considering what happened to most of them, it's a good thing I didn't.

After George had left, I watched the surrounding lots from my kitchen area. It so happens I did this while blending a large mojito. No matter what was going to happen, I was going to need a good drink. Everyone was yelling, literally running back and forth, getting worked up. Yeah, I'd seen similar behavior from these people. A docile existence makes for over-reacting, and a docile existence is what you're often in for at a trailer park. But this wasn't like someone's party getting out of hand, or the occasional tragedy that happens in everyone's life, or even the weather forecast calling for snow. No, this time it looked like people getting ready for a conflict with real consequences.

Okay, for the people who had no interest in being a part of the conflict, they acted like we were going to get snowed in. Mass quantities of groceries, alcohol, and toilet paper were purchased or brought out of secreted stashes. The Johnsons, Eggletons, and Martha and Bruce Ford were just the parkers in my field of view who did that. An argument between Edna Johnson and Martha Ford broke out when they got back from the store. Edna had grabbed every case of PBR at the local Food Lion. Martha, as a result, had to settle for paying the convenience stores' exorbitant prices on single cans in order to stock her supply. When Mrs. Ford witnessed Mrs. Johnson pull up with her small truck burdened with what looked like at least half a dozen 24 packs of the preferred brew, she stormed over and started yelling.

I still wonder why the hell it's Dr Pepper, milk, eggs, and canned corned beef hash that many people around here consider to be "vital emergency supplies", and that they buy enough to last weeks. It's true. I've seen people pass up getting their favorite brewskies to make sure they got those four all-important items. Everyone else grabs bread, and what's left of the eggs and milk. They should have taken the advice from my favorite tv chef. Always have a stocked pantry, and you're never without options.

While Edna unloaded her truck and argued with Martha, the little Johnsons scurried out of the large double-wide they called home and started helping their mom bring in the supplies. The two boys, Herman and Johnny, grabbed the bags with chips and pork rinds, leaving Nichole to struggle with the cans of hash, Spam, and tiny six packs of soda. No sign of Mr. Johnson.

The Eggletons, consisting of Jenny, Scott, siblings Hunter and Matthew, had been preparing for an outdoor feast. Lawn chairs lined up, coolers set nearby, while daddy Scott had gotten the gas grill going. Now, the parents were yelling at each other about supplies they needed to get at the store. The boys were clamoring to get into the back of the family minivan. The way Mom and Dad Eggleton were carrying on, you'd think they had a visual on Godzilla and had to make sure they grabbed the right kind of hot dogs, milk, and bread that the boys would eat before the critter's big feet hit the edge of the park.

Don't forget the corned beef hash and soda.

The minivan peeled out less than a minute later. Inside my place, I took the first sip of the mojito. Ahhhh, just right. I pondered if I should make a full pitcher of the elixir and put it in the fridge for later.

That's when Stacey Miller blew down the road between the lots. Walking faster than I had ever seen her move, in three-inch heels, no less. Probably leaving a vapor trail of the latest pop star fragrance in her wake.

Years ago, she'd been in a country club family, complete with weekends playing golf. She'd also been the girl that looked like she should be on a California beach. Don't believe me? If you spent five minutes talking to her when her photo albums were nearby, you'd know her youthful years. Might take your memory a few episodes to retain the details, but not to worry. She'd remind you.

Every. Single. Time. If you went by her place and didn't escape before she started going.

Not saying she was exaggerating. Much. The photographic evidence she loved to present over and over backed up most of her tales.

Stacey also wanted to remind everyone that she was a very pretty teen and young adult. She hasn't aged badly, still fitting in size 4 to 6 clothing that looked good on her. But the excesses of her youth could be seen in the lines on her face. And even if she was living out of what could only be a retired touring bus from the 90's, she was still living here instead of near any country club. Also, she never talked about the forty or so years between those pictures and today.

Ms. Miller did try to live her life like she was at a country club, though. Wearing elegant brand clothing right down to her bathrobes. Boxes were delivered weekly to her lot. All of them with logos and brand names stamped on them, each one a company connected to celebrities of one caliber or another. She walked around with a chihuahua named Tinkerbell. I think it was because some celebrity, of some kind, had one as well. That dog had a pink jeweled collar with a large oval plate hanging from it. The name "Tink" was engraved on it in a fancy script. And to be honest, I think that collar and tag cost more than my laptop.

I should say the dog *had* a collar, and Ms. Miller walked around with her tucked into her arm all the time. Tinkerbell was, in theory anyway, the first victim. That's how I saw it, and how Stacey saw it. No one else cared or wanted to give the dog any more acknowledgement than she already had. Stacey Miller was the kind to take the dog everywhere, especially where pets weren't allowed, in her arms, in her purse, even tucked in Stacey's expensive long coats. Made me wonder if the little ankle biter was crippled. Until, of course, Stacey decided she wanted to walk around the park and pond in a little two-piece outfit that would have suited her in her glory days. Having nowhere to tuck Tinkerbell without taking away attention from how much skin she was showing, she had the dog on a leash that matched the collar. The dog's short legs worked hard to keep up, but she never had to be dragged along. Tinkerbell even had her nose pointed slightly upwards, just like her owner, when they walked.

All of that wasn't the problem. It was how the owner wanted the dog to be treated like a human princess everywhere and by everyone, without exception. And an infant one, at that. So, when Tinkerbell went missing, those who cared about every animal or just being neighborly assisted Stacey in her search. That does not mean they brought their best efforts. Enough effort was done so that Stacey had no foundation for holding any of the parkers here accountable for not finding Tinkerbell, but only just. When other pets began disappearing, and then some being found mangled to death, Stacey immediately announced to anyone and everyone that her beloved dog had "obviously" been the first victim.

Actually, it wasn't just her impressive dexterity that grabbed my attention. She was hurrying down towards the end of the road where George was talking to a slumped and grieving Tyler. They were standing in front of Tyler's place.

And Stacey was nearly there.

Suddenly my mojito and I were out the door and making a quick pace to intercept. Stacey did not get along with either fellow. Things could go very badly, and I wanted to try and intercede. I honestly wasn't going for story material. Mostly.

"No, ma'am, it's not a matter of I don't have what you're asking me for," George was slowly explaining to Stacey when I got within listening distance, "it's that I have no intention of handing out ammunition to anyone until I am sure of their intent. Shotgun shells, 12 gauge, in birdshot, I have in quantity and don't mind parting with some. Same with roofing nails. But you are going to tell me what you have in mind."

"If poor Mister Addison's boy has been done in, probably like my beloved Tink? I expect we are going to have those devils at our doorsteps soon, and I intend to protect what's still mine," Stacey replied in her usual, get-me-your-manager tone.

George used his most neighborly voice as he explained, "I didn't think you'd be making burgers with shells and nails, ma'am. I need to know how you plan to use them, or, sorry to be un-neighborly, you'll need to ask someone else."

The well-tended teeth in Stacey's mouth ground together. She spoke between them as she detailed the plan.

"I intend to dig shallow holes around my yard, leading up to my door. In each hole, I will bury a nail, point-up. Each nail to be secured with dirt and rock. Then a shotgun shell will be placed atop the nail point, and then filled around with more dirt and rock. The last half inch of the shell, that is to say the top part, will remain above-ground. Do I need to explain further?"

"Ah," George replied, and his manner left no chance that he'd misunderstood her. "Improvised landmines, then. Alright. Be right back." He hurried off towards his place.

Stacey folded her arms, watched him go, with a smug look on her face.

"You can't... there are children who live around you..." Tyler's voice interrupted the scene. He still looked numb, even sounded that way, but he looked right at Stacey.

"If anyone keeps their children out when we are about to be raided, then whatever grief comes, they've earned it." Stacey countered without ever looking at Tyler. "Besides, no children come around *my* yard. They've all learned better."

Tyler's eyes showed a brief flash of anger. A moment later, though, they took on that numb, dazed look. He looked back to the corpse of his beloved canine.

"I suppose the same goes for any of us adults? Especially those who aren't around to hear what you have intended? Know what to look out for, in case they come to check or aid you?" I interjected.

"No doubt everyone will be informed. You have never kept anything you learned to yourself. Or found a pair of ears you didn't want to talk off, I'll warrant," was her cool rebuttal. She didn't bother with eye contact towards me, either.

Fred Everly prevented any further words between the two of us. His big "Texas" voice preceded his lanky, tanned strutting form by only a heartbeat. The still full blond hair blew back in the wind, along with the tails of his old button up blue cotton shirt. His tan skin shone out below the turned-up cuffs, and above the unused button holes above his navel. Faded blue jeans ended in even rougher looking cowboy boots. The oversized belt buckle was the only bit of wardrobe in pristine condition.

"What do we figure, Stacey? Eddie? Time to finally take it to those bastards?"

I opened my mouth to say something, even if it was just to remind him that I didn't like to be called "Eddie" by anyone still alive, but of course he was already smiling and talking over anything anyone else might have to declare.

"You should have come to me, Ms. Miller! I'd get you some a' my fine hand-loaded 8-gauge shells! That'd do twice the job any store bought 12 gauge rounds that ol' George has. Teach them bastards up right! And why bother with nails? Probably have some extra detonators and a remote you could make use of?"

He leaned back on his heels and gave a beaming smile. Probably waiting for her to be impressed or wooed. Nah, he always wanted both.

"I have no intention of making this more complicated than it needs to be, Mister Everly," Stacey replied. She did, I had to note, make eye contact with Fred.

"Suit yourself!" He continued in his cheerful drawl. "I see Eddie already has a drink in hand. Guess he's as prepared as he needs to be! Oh, wait!" He pivoted on one heel to fully face me. "Where's your typewriter?"

"I use my smartphone for something other than a detonator, or trigger, Freddie." I tried to growl.

He didn't blink at my use of a nickname. "So do I!" he assured himself. "Security cameras, dim the lights in my homestead, turn on the television! Fantastic thing, technology is!"

Stacey made a dismissive snorting noise beside me. George reappeared on the lawn, holding two boxes. He held them out to the woman in our midst. She took them without a word and began her way home at the same breakneck pace.

"Still a fine lady," Fred observed aloud, but not too loud.

"You're no gentleman," George countered. "What the hell are you doing on my side of the park, Fred?"

"I came to give my condolences to the one gentleman among us," Fred said before pivoting his whole body again to face Tyler. But his voice and demeanor were somber as he said, "Tyler, I am sorry as hell about Good Ol' Red. He was a good one. Gonna make things right for both of you."

This seemed to get through to the former music instructor. He seemed to sink inwards a bit more, sobbed for a second, and then nodded.

"Thanks, Fred."

"While you make with the nice words, I'm going to actually get this place ready to do something about those sombitches." George rejoined.

"You do what you think will help, my fine friend, and I will do the heavy lifting as usual." countered Fred.

"That's only going to happen when you start using shot *placement* and *accuracy* over fancy hardware and bigger ordinance."

"I'm sorry you're jealous of my gear, George, but when it all comes down…"

I'd heard this argument too many times. Walking over to Tyler, I knelt next to the mangled remains of a good dog.

"Hey, Tyler? Can I help you bury an old friend?" I gently asked.

Tyler nodded. By the time he and I got Red into a bag, taken to the vet's to be incinerated, and drove back, the sun was starting to wane in the sky.

Chapter Three

Tyler parked his old Toyota behind his trailer, gave me a hug after we'd departed the vehicle, and then he went into his home. I stayed in his yard, watching the door, waiting for I don't know what.

When nothing happened and no noise came from his place for several minutes, I began my walk home. My half-drank mojito was where I'd left it on a stump. Flies had tried to finish it off for me, so I tossed them and the watered remains of my beverage into the nearby grass.

Guess I'd be making that full pitcher after all.

Tyler had shared stories of Red the whole trip. Most of them I had already heard, but it was the listening that mattered. I'd gotten swept up in the history of a human being and the companion that had made widowed life bearable. It wasn't until the first shot rang out that I was brought back to the circumstances around me.

My eyes swept all around, looking for the possible source of the shot. Fred and George were nowhere to be seen, so there went the most likely candidates. Down the road a bit, I caught sight of a group of people on top of a trailer. And then I realized it was a bunch of kids. With a small .22 caliber rifle. Regardless, I moved closer to get a better fix on what the hell was happening.

George came jogging up beside me. He panted a bit while talking.

"Those kids of Judy's are really impressing me," he confessed, pointing at the small group of four kids. "They've got their shit together on this. Grabbed some high ground. Got Markus on the binoculars, sweeping the area. Little Pauly has a running chart of what everyone has, as well as a map of the area that he's marking as there are sightings."

That explained why it looked like the blonde kid was playing corporate exec, complete with an easel and clipboard. The younger boy, dark haired and always looking ready to get into anything, lay on the roof of their home, binoculars against his eyes, slowly looking around.

"Got one, two… four!" Markus barked out, sounding much older than any of them were. "Moving west by northwest at 10 o'clock!"

Little P pivoted like a military officer, toward the easel. He tossed a blue colored refrigerator magnet shaped like the number 4, the kind moms buy for their preschool kids, at a spot on the map. It was a little disturbing to see it was not the only number attached. The rifle cracked again, and after I recovered from the involuntary jump, I took a closer look at the rest of the kids.

Jackie, the only girl in the bunch, was manning the old .22 rifle with a scope. Behind her, the Roth clan's cousin, Johnny, stood with his lanky arms crossed and a big smile on his face. To either side of him was another easel and a large cooler. Bags of chips and jerked meat sat beside the cooler. The easel at Johnny's side had a small chalkboard, where Pauly was occupied by a magnetic dry erase board with the hand-drawn map of the Knob. Johnny used a large chunk of blue chalk to make a mark under Jackie's name. She now had two slashes under her listing. I looked over the chalkboard and saw many of the Knob parkers listed, with a final one called "everyone else". Only Jackie had any marks under it at that point.

"So, Jackie is the sniper and Johnny is, what, the bookie?" I asked.

"Supply master!" Johnny said with glee. "Not accepting any wagers, just keeping score!"

"Uh huh!" I replied to the youngster. Stage whispering to George, I asked, "Are we putting the safety and survival of the Knob on a cluster of kids and a pre-teen?"

"Just amazing." George continued, as if I hadn't spoken to him. He was looking up at the kids and smiling. "Their dad would be proud of them, God rest his soul. They jumped right into action. Nobody gave them instruction or demanded anything."

"And Judy is working another double shift, I bet."

To that, George acknowledged that I'd spoken. "Yep, won't be home until after eleven this evening, if there's anything left to come home to."

"Wait a minute, we haven't been invaded." I insisted. "It's lousy that Red is dead, and precautions should be taken, sure. Maybe if no one goes and tries to stir up the woods, we-"

George grabbed my chin and pivoted my face towards the kids. His voice was more than a little testy when he spoke.

"See that map of the Knob? All the numbers that Pauly has stuck on it, all around?" he demanded. "That's *them*. Single scouts and groups, surrounding the area. If we haven't been invaded, then it's only a matter of when."

I nodded, and he let go of my face.

"Whoooo! That was a fine shot!" the loud, drawling voice had returned. Fred strode up from the other end of the road. He carried a modern American military rifle, slung over one shoulder. I could see a backpack strap over the other. Four handguns were visible on his person. Part of my mind wondered why Fred wasn't wearing a black trench coat and sunglasses. Though, I had to admit, the real question was why he wasn't riding on a horse.

Hey, I've watched too many movies. I admit it.

"There's no way you could have seen the hit." I deadpanned.

Fred aimed his big smile at the kids, particularly at Jackie.

"Especially since you managed it with that pithy thing!" Fred continued. "I can grab my spare one of these, if you like?" He swung the rifle around and pointed it to the sky. "It won't have the laser sight, bayonet, or grenade launcher like this one does, but it'll fire faster and give you a bigger bullet!"

"The only two requirements that Fred lives by." George grumbled in a low voice.

"No thank you, Mister Everly." Jackie responded. She had lowered the small bolt action firearm to chest level and continued to look around the area. Eye contact with Fred apparently was more manners than she felt the situation warranted. "I'm really comfortable with this one, and our ten-twenty-two rifle. Got plenty of ammo for both, too."

Johnny triumphantly held up a small plastic bucket and shook it. From the sound, not much had been taken out. The printed writing on the container (that was visible to us) read "500 round bucket" just below the ammunition manufacturer's name.

"Alright, alright, just know it's available!" Fred called back.

Little Pauly tapped his clipboard, a droll expression on his tiny face. "It's noted, sir."

With an energetic wave, Fred walked past me and muttered, "That kid gives me the creeps, sometimes."

"Where's the biggest concentration, kids?" George asked, not paying attention to Fred.

Pauly stood a little more erect. His time to shine, I guessed.

He pointed to a pink number 8 magnet that was east and slightly south of the woods by the main gate.

"This location, sir." Pauly announced. His tone was brisk and formal. "We have packs of four and five moving at the outer perimeter to the north and west. Looks to be patrols. The largest group has been, so far, stationary."

"Are they all the same kind?" I asked, with no idea I even had the question in my head before it blurted out of my mouth.

"Yeah. Nothing different. Have you seen any different ones?" replied Markus. He was still peering through the binoculars.

"I've only glimpsed two. The one that we all saw at the cornhole competition, and the other which ran down our road two nights ago." I admitted.

"We don't need anything different," Fred called from over his shoulder. "We just need to know where they are."

"Has anyone thought about calling the police about this," I asked. "Or better yet, that specialized group the government put together?"

"You mean you didn't call them?" George teased. "C'mon, you know nobody is going to come here unless human bodies start stacking up."

I groaned internally.

"That's very comforting."

George shrugged before asking me, "Can I interest you in taking advantage of your Second Amendment rights, Ed? I still got that nine mil Glock you felt pretty comfortable with."

Ah, yes, that firearm. I hadn't had much practice when I moved to Stoney Knob, but still managed to not embarrass myself the one time I'd accepted Fred and George's offer to target shoot with them. I put most of that on how comfortable and easy to operate that Glock had been.

Fine, I hadn't embarrassed myself much.

"Maybe you should get that. I don't think I can beat these guys with a strong drink."

After barking a laugh, George smiled at me and said, "Good man. I'll go grab it."

"Uh oh."

That was the voice of Markus. George and I glanced back to the roof of the Roth trailer. Markus had the binoculars aimed at somewhere to our right. He had leaned out so much that his chest was peering out over the roof.

"Report!" snapped Little P.

"That group by the burnt tree is gone. I don't see them anywhere around that area." Markus sounded a bit strained, and worried.

The burnt tree meant the huge, centuries old oak tree that had been struck by lightning last summer. The tree was the centerpiece of the gazeboed oasis that the landowners had placed at the far end of the "hiking trail" through the North West end of the surrounding woods. Charred debris had fallen onto the roof of the gazebo as well as the paved walkway and park benches. That had been cleared away, but the burnt skeleton of the once mighty oak hadn't been cut, trimmed, or otherwise touched.

Jackie swung the business end of the rifle towards where the tree stood about a half mile from where we were. She looked hard through the scope. Began moving the rifle on a downward trajectory.

"Not seeing any," she declared. Her voice was constrained, as if she were holding her breath. I think we all were, to be honest.

Everyone started looking around. Okay, everyone except Pauly. He just turned back to his map and plucked the yellow number 6 magnet away from the map's rendition of the burnt tree oasis.

Regardless, I was pretty sure I wasn't the only one starting to panic. Fred had moved the rifle on his shoulder into both his hands. The barrel was pointing upwards enough to be clear of everyone.

George tapped my shoulder with something heavy. I looked over.

He was holding a handgun out to me, his big fingers wrapped around the barrel. It looked like a smaller version of the gun he had offered to go get for me. My eyes looked past this weapon and noticed his trusty military .45 ACP in his other hand. I took the offered one.

"That one only has seven shots." George warned me, nodding to the gun I was holding.

"Is it loaded?" I asked. Which isn't as dumb a question as one might think. The proper question was "is it chambered", since there's no way that George would have offered me an empty weapon. Fortunately, he knew what I meant.

"Rack it," he instructed.

I was looking at the gun, trying to discern the best way to grip it with both hands so I could rack the slide back and put a bullet in the chamber, when the sound of multiple feet moving rapidly through woods and grass came from nearby.

Make that multiple feet with claws.

"We got incoming!" George roared.

"Get to cover!" Fred yelled just as George was finishing his last word.

From above, I heard Johnny's voice sarcastically call back, "Aye, aye, captain!"

And that's when it all cut loose.

Chapter Four

There were only six at the beginning. Six against four parkers with firearms. I don't know when the others started pouring in, but for a while my brain couldn't keep up and it seemed like they would never stop coming.

Five feet tall.

The furry bastards were five feet tall when they stood up. Most of the time they were running on all fours, sure, but when that one stood up right in front of me? I swear to you, it was as tall as a few of my exes. No lie.

What? I have a weakness for petite ladies. So, sue me.

None of my exes had eyes like huge black marbles, though. Or stank like rancid swamp water. Even the craziest one didn't try to kill me with her nails or chew my face off with mighty incisors.

At least not ones as big as what that mega hog had.

I watched and counted when the pack first burst through the woods on all sides. I had counted the fifth when the sixth one stood up right in front of me. There was a moment that stretched out, when I was looking into those big black eyes I mentioned, and it was doing the same to me. Then it came at me, teeth first.

Sure, I had a gun in my hand. It was a gun that didn't have a bullet in the chamber. Something I didn't remember at that pants-dampening moment. So, when I swung the gun barrel up into its face and pulled the trigger, there was nothing to stop the incoming incisors that were as long as my fingers. Except that barrel.

Let's hear it for Austrian craftsmanship and ingenuity! Whatever that gun was made of, the material was hard enough to make those giant teeth shatter as it bit down. We were both unsettled by that unexpected turn of events. The furry bugger got angry and started swiping at me with the claws on its front… paws? Hands? No, it was still a groundhog, even if it was now several hundred pounds worth of groundhog. So, paws. Yeah.

Sadly, my favorite Hawaiian shirt got shredded on the right side. I loved that shirt. The skin underneath got scratched, but it was the shirt that really took the hit.

My ears were ringing at that point, since the other guns in the immediate vicinity were definitely loaded and being used. I know I yelled something at the mega hog in front of me, might have even been "That's my favorite shirt, you furry bastard!" But I didn't hear a word of it. I do know that I kicked straight out, and because of the height between us, that means I landed the blow somewhere in the waist to crotch area. The hog stumbled back and landed on its side. Didn't act like it was used to standing. While it scrambled to get back up, I had time to properly rack the slide and put two bullets in its head.

Only when the hog slumped flat and did nothing else did I look around and nearly got bit again by another as it ran into me.

I shrieked.

Not too proud of that, but I admit to doing it.

The beast knocked me over. I bounced on its back once before hitting the ground. I heard its paws hitting the ground. Gunfire and explosions wrecked my hearing. After the third big bang, I couldn't tell what was what. Everything was muffled, a high-pitched whine rang constantly. I got up, expecting the second hog to run me over, but it didn't come. I got to my knees and looked around. Someone in Bermuda shorts and white loafers was on the ground, being chewed on by two "mega hogs". I pointed the gun and fired at both of the critters until they collapsed. Unfortunately, one fell onto my unlucky neighbor.

Fred was shooting some weapon that was even larger than the rifle he'd arrived with. More of the giant groundhogs were circling him. Over a dozen dead ones littered the ground.

George was herding the Eggletons, or at least most of them, back towards his place. There were hogs approaching and getting dropped with single shots from George's pair of .45 pistols.

From my position, I couldn't see the Roth kids, or their cousin. Couldn't see much of anything else, honestly. It was time to get up and get grooving.

Something struck me from behind.

I was pushed along for I don't know how long. I fired until the gun was empty, which was one or two rounds at most. Tried hitting my attacker with the empty firearm. Felt an enormous THUMP! nearby just before I was covered in blood and chunks of fur. Pushed against the back of the hog that was dragging me along. Then there was another heavy thump, everything in my field of vision was obscured by blood, dirt, fur and then blackness.

Sometime later, I came to, laying askew on the steps of Stacey Miller's fancy touring bus home. The mega hog had apparently tripped one of her homemade mines with, lucky me, its back hooves. They had been torn up by the exploding gunpowder and steel pellets of a shotgun shell. Maybe two, considering the mess. I had to push the remains off of me before I could stagger back to where George, Fred, and the others had been before I'd been carried off.

What a mess.

The other mega hogs, lay all around. Some more or less intact, others not so much. One was missing most of its back half. Another was gone from the front shoulders up. There were some human bodies lying around, none in a condition for me to identify anyone with a quick glance.

Discarded firearms and empty ammunition magazines were scattered everywhere.

Fred and George looked to be arguing, as usual. Fred had the tricked out military rifle from when he first arrived again. George was loading a magazine for one of the .45 pistols without looking at either the magazine or ammo.

Jackie and Johnny were jumping and dancing. Markus held the bolt action rifle in his lap, still looking through the binoculars. Little Pauly stood by his easel. The semi-automatic .22 rifle was leaning on it. Little P looked very disappointed, or maybe that expression was skeptical.

Several of the surrounding trailers had been damaged. Claw marks, gashes, torn siding. Large holes in almost every home, and broken windows. There was blood in a few places. The widow Hardkin's Winnebago was on fire. Tyler and one of the neighbors from further down were trying to contain the blaze with fire extinguishers.

Somewhere in the back of my mind, I knew I needed fresh trousers.

The ringing in my ears began to abate. Of course, the first thing I heard was the usual suspects arguing.

"The kid was not officially giving you the title, Fred! He was being sarcastic!"

"Seems the boy recognizes leadership at his young age, George." Fred was calmer in tone but no less loud than George. "Be jealous if you have to, but as the leader, I say we take the fight to the East, where they've obviously set their base."

"What in sweet Jesus's name do you think you're going to do?" George demanded. "Waltz in there and take them by surprise? This is just so you have a chance to fire that grenade launcher, isn't it?"

Fred frowned for a second. George threw his hands to the sky and laughed. It wasn't a happy laugh.

"Anyone want to follow Captain Big Shot into gloriously stupid doom?" George shouted, his arms straight out while he turned to look around at the survivors in eyesight. "On the bright side, he won't be close enough to put any more bullet holes in our homes!"

I suddenly realized how much of the surrounding damage couldn't have been caused by oversized animals. At least the kind that walked on four legs more often than not. Guess I was lucky to have not been hit by "friendly fire", over-penetrations or ricochets. Was anyone else hurt?

"Y'all can certainly stay here with Captain Cautious. And hope you survive the next wave of super-sized varmints without my help. Just remember, only be attacked in a clear line of fire! That way George doesn't have to worry about what he might hit behind you!"

"That's only a concern if they're around someone that takes three to ten rounds to hit the target, no matter *how* big it, or the bullet, is!" countered George. "I happen to hit what I shoot at!"

"Excuse me, *oh captains*, but we have wounded, fires, and a need for an actual plan!"

That declaration came from Scott Eggleton. He approached while supporting his wife, Jenny. She was limping, having sustained what looked like a huge bite on her left foot. I didn't see either of their kids.

"I'm with 'Captain' Everly." announced Stacey Miller. She was storming towards us, although her outward appearance had gone through a rough time. The expensive heels had been replaced with fluffy bunny slippers, which were filthy. In fact, there wasn't much of her that wasn't covered in something, or torn, or ragged. "Let's go stomp their heads in!"

Fred, of course, beamed that unblemished smile of his.

"Mister Eggleton," Little Pauly interjected, "You'll find first aid supplies in our place. Retired Nurse GiGi is in there as well. Misters Addison and Dillard are tending to the fires while we await county fire and rescue.

"That's Ms. GiGi to you!" The elderly woman who'd recently retired called out from within the Roth's trailer.

"So, the police are on their way?" I asked.

"There's been a lot of monsters hurting people today." Jackie replied from her place on the roof. "The fire and rescue will get here first."

"How does that work out?" Mister Eggleton wondered aloud as he helped his wife toward the trailer.

Markus passed the rifle back to Jackie while explaining "They have to write down what everyone saw, right? That's worse than taking notes in class. After the firefighters and rescue people are done, they're still writing stuff down."

"I'm guessing Pauley called 911? He sounds more like an adult than most people." I surmised.

The trailer door opened, and Ms. GiGi stepped out to hold it for the Egglestons. She was wearing faded scrubs, like most days- said she wore scrubs more than any other clothing in her life, so that was what she felt most comfortable in- with her gray and bleached blonde hair tied back in a severe ponytail. "I called the first responders, thank you. Since most of them know me, I got the scoop on what's been happening."

George chuckled. He finally finished loading the last magazine and tucked that onto the pouch attached to his belt.

"Knowing you, the instant they said there might be a wait? You demanded all the reasons why. Probably in alphabetical order." he teased.

"Time's a wastin', people." said Fred. "We need to move on them now, before they have a chance to regroup and attack again."

"Give me a gun. I know how to shoot one, even if I've never owned one." Stacey demanded.

"That makes you more qualified than 'Dirty' Freddie to go," George observed.

Fred ignored his rival and turned to Stacey. "I have just the thing for you," he said then hurried off to his car.

"Hey, Scott? I know Jenny is out of the fight for the moment," George said gently, "but since you've both served in the Army, we could use you. You know how Fred can get."

"You mean you want someone who'll make shots count, next to Ms. Miller here." Scott said from the trailer doorway. Stacey smiled at his vote of confidence. "Sorry, I've got the boys holed up at our place. Getting ready to head back there and protect the homestead now that Jenny's being tended to."

"Fair enough." George said with a sigh. He looked back at me. "Seems I will have to go along. Care to be part of the 'last charge of the Knob parkers', Ed?"

"I, uh, dropped the gun somewhere when I was getting dragged around like a rodeo clown."

George smiled and pulled the gun from the small of his back.

"Found it after we cleared this wave of hogs. This time it's ready to go."

"Oh," I said, carefully taking the gun. "Okay, sure. Let's see how the story ends."

Chapter Five

The walk to the entrance side of the property didn't take long. We didn't try to be stealthy, or strategic. We just strode like we were big damn heroes, right down the center of the road. When the front gate was in sight, we took the side path to the east that followed the hiking trail. Not a single bit of opposition met us from when we'd left the Roth's patch of lawn until we came into the trail's first clearing.

Seemed all the remaining opposition was, actually, right there. The Roth kids had counted thirty-nine of the mega hogs in total before the fighting started. We had thirty-one dead furry jumbos in a pile on Tyler's property. There were eight here. They were all standing on hind feet, in two rows of four. When we came into the clearing, they all turned at the same time. They looked at us as if we were late for dinner. Then they parted, and at the end of the rows was the ugliest monstrosity I'd ever seen or even heard of.

Remember, I had been practically nose-to-nose with one of the mega hogs. Also, I'd seen pictures of some of the other reported critters of unusual size seen in the area. Humongous rats, bigger than hounds, a pair of grey foxes that were as big as bear cubs, and a few others.

But the creature sitting on the stump of a hundred year old tree was something I struggled to comprehend. The fur was a sickly pale yellow. Patches of it were missing. Grey, mottled skin was visible in those places. I could only guess at how much it weighed. Swollen, taut muscles covered its whole body, even around the ankles. Its paws were the size of a basketball player's hands. The nails were ragged, broken, and filthy in ways I didn't want to think about. That head, though... that was the craziest part. Long-nosed like a rat. Fiercely intelligent brown eyes burned at us from above that nose. The ears were large and tapered to points. Kinda reminded me of a bat's ears. One stood erect, the other at half-mast. Below the nose, black lips were pressed down in a deep scowl. A studded metal ring hung from the nostrils.

Wait a minute.

That wasn't a ring or a band. That was the collar of a small animal. The studs weren't metal. They were garnet stones, crusted with old dirt. The remaining tatters of cloth looked like they might have once been pink. The dented and scratched oval plate hung beneath the collar.

"Tinkerbell?!?" Stacey shrieked.

The creature snarled and narrowed its eyes at the sole female member of our little party.

Stacey's response was swift.

"Bad dog!"

"Oh, we're dead," George sighed, "so very dead."

Tink spoke. The voice sounded like someone who was trying to speak a second language that they were still in the process of learning. While gargling gravel.

"*You not own me, stinky bitch.*"

Stacey's mouth snapped shut. She looked as if Tink had taken one of those massive paws and slapped her with it. Her eyes went wide in surprise.

I'd read more than a few comic books in my youth. This seemed to be the super villain moment, so I did what any hero would do.

I gave Tink a chance to monologue.

"Uh, good to see you, girl! What happened? Where have you been? Everybody looked for you when you disappeared!" I said as enthusiastically and evenly as I could manage. The fact that we were all holding firearms was suddenly a worrying point, to my mind.

The groundhogs stood to either side of us, waiting.

"Stinky bitch took too long talking to another horny male. I wandered, followed nose. Someone grab me." Tink grumbled. "Could not escape cloth cage. Pulled into light and stung many times. Pain all I know for long time. Woke here in the dark. They found me."

She pointed at the groundhogs with one huge paw.

"They want land back from stupid homans. I lead them. Will sit in stinky bitch's precious chair when she dead. Eat all the food. Do all she told me I was bad dog for-"

A single shot rang out right before the bloody hole appeared between the brown eyes.

Tink fell off the trunk.

Fred, George and I looked dumbfounded at each other. The groundhogs looked stunned but didn't move. Stacey held the spare rifle Fred had given her at the hip. Wisps of smoke rose from the end of the barrel.

"Nobody calls me a stinky bitch." Stacey growled.

There was silence.

"That's what I'm talking about!" George suddenly shouted, startling all of us. "Shot placement! Boom!" He pumped his gun hand at the trunk. "Yeah! Good work, Stacey!"

"Oh, come on!" Fred groaned.

"One shot, one kill! Yeah! That's how it's done!" George carried on, with the biggest shit-eating grin I've ever seen on his face.

Fred made a disgusted sound, right before he opened up on the row of groundhogs behind George. As if they'd been doing this for years, George followed suit against the other row, behind Fred.

To be fair, George fired four shots, and a groundhog fell each time. Fred went through the whole thirty round magazine The remaining four critters were just as dead as the ones on the opposite side, if a bit messier.

I stood there the whole time. Looked at the gun in my hand at one point and decided there was no point.

Stacey, meanwhile, sauntered over to the dead pile of Tinkerbell, nodded, and looked satisfied with herself.

While my ears were ringing yet again, Fred and George looked around to see if there were any other surprises. Fred reloaded his rifle without a pause. Stacey walked past the three of us. She paused long enough to lean Fred's other rifle against a tree and then continued to walk away, towards her lot.

If I'm going to be honest, I don't know exactly how long I stood there, staring down the path that led back to the main road. I didn't really snap out of that stupor until the first aid and fire trucks flew by, sirens and lights going full-tilt-boogie. At that point, I looked around and discovered Fred and George sharing a drink from a flask. I had no idea who brought it.

Their weapons had been leaned up against the same tree that Stacey had made use of.

"Uhhhhh…" I managed.

Fred and George looked over at me.

"Oh, sorry, Ed. Forgot you were still there," Fred said in an oddly sincere voice. "Best put that gun over with the others." He glanced over at George. "Guess we better go wait at the front gate for the police to show up. Can give our statements first, let them gather up whatever they need to."

"As long as we aren't the ones who have to clean up the mess, I have no objection." George replied amiably.

Still a bit confused, I watched them move past me, towards the front gate. Finally, I laid the handgun on the ground next to the tree and followed after.

I hoped the police were on their way. I'm sure they would have a lot of questions.

And I had a story to write.

-- End --

Better to Receive

By Rob Howell

Medieval Cajun Santa Claus walked into the site's industrial kitchen staring at his phone. Nothing terribly unusual about that. He was in charge of that event's feast since it was in our home group.

I'd come to Louisiana as a fresh-faced biochemist determined to change the world. I hadn't wanted to work for a petrochemical corporation, especially not with things like natural gas and oil, but the opportunity had been too good. And, I'd thought, maybe if I was in the system, I could mitigate the harm petroleum products did to the environment.

My friends at medieval events back home assured me I'd find new friends doing the same thing down south, but even so, I'd been terribly nervous going to my first event in flyover country.

At first, when I ran into JT, I knew my fears were warranted. He was paunchy, bearded, and jovial. When he wasn't wearing a stained t-tunic and faded jeans over muddy, slop-covered work boots, he wore overalls, often without a shirt, over those same dirty boots. He leered at me, all the other women, and many of the men throughout the day.

In short, he was everything I hated.

Then he went into the kitchen and ensured everyone feasted on accurate re-creations of Hundred Years War-era dishes.

I'd been amazed. I'd soon realized JT just liked making everyone happier, which explained why his leering just made me feel sexy instead of skeeved out.

After that, I spent nearly every event helping him cook. He even taught me to love gator, shrimp, and crawdads, at least when I'd learned how to prepare them.

So, when he came into the kitchen that day, I didn't pay any attention to him. My sweetie had traveled to the event from DC, and she got all of my attention. Bri and I were cutting pastry shells and giggling like two schoolgirls instead of a top flight biochemist and a mathematician gaining worldwide recognition.

It didn't help that we were exhausted because, of course, it'd been a year since we'd been able to do *anything* together and we'd done some catching up.

Then JT said in a tone I'd never heard from him, "Kelsey. Look at this."

"What is it?" I asked.

He seemed at a loss for words. He was *never* at a loss for words. I leaned over to look at his phone. There was a report of a riot in DC. No real surprise that, ever since the turmoil began in the early 20s but I could see what bothered him. The rioters weren't rioters, they were attackers. They had no signs, no symbols. They weren't chanting slogans. They were fighting through the riot cops.

Bri and I looked at each other and then back at the video.

That's when whoever it was recording the scene dropped their phone. Everything after that was a blur of figures rushing past the phone's camera. It got stepped on, which cracked the screen, after which, it went black.

But it didn't stop picking up the sounds. Crunching, yelling, wailing, and a weird gurgling receding off into the distance. I almost retched.

Then JT swiped to another story.

Bri's eyes widened, and she grabbed the phone. "That's Georgetown! *My* neighborhood."

She'd hated JT at first sight, even before she saw him leer down my bliaut. He'd helped us pitch our tent, ignoring every subtle and not-so-subtle hint she'd made to let us do it ourselves.

But when he yanked the phone out of her hands to swipe to a third video, she didn't say anything. She just stared at me, eyes wide.

I gasped when I looked back at the phone, though, because I'd spent many an hour walking near Faneuil Hall during my time at MIT. Now, bleeding corpses stained its steps crimson.

After it ended, JT growled, "Alright, girls, time to get this lot movin'."

"What do you mean?" I asked.

"If we're saving anyone, it's getting them to my farm."

"But those riots are in DC and Boston," I protested.

"Girl, that's every zombie trope I ever read, and I read everything."

The word 'trope,' which I would have never expected this Cajun hillbilly to even know, seemed not at all odd at that moment. He was right. It was just like every stupid zombie apocalypse movie. *Exactly* like it. As dumb and crazy and completely impossible as those ever were. And yet, we could see it happening.

Still, I couldn't believe it. "But—"

"Lass, trust me on this. We gots to get what we can save to someplace we can hold." His eyes held no humor, only a cold intensity that hinted at something he'd seen before.

I'd never seen those eyes without a Santa-like twinkle, so I made no more protest as he chivvied us out to the event hall.

Halls at medieval events are never quiet. Too many people geeking out on calligraphy, brewing, armoring, the political situation leading up to William's conquest of England, the Secret History of the Mongols, and, of course, the musicians blithely playing hurdy-gurdies and lutes in the corner.

Our footsteps echoed in *that* hall. They'd all pulled out their phone and were staring at them with wide eyes.

"Alright, everyone," said JT in the silence. "Them as wantin' are welcome to come to my place. Bring what we got here and what's in your car. If you're within a half-hour of home, go get what you can. Guns, ammo, all your tools, canned food, clothes, raw materials. In that order."

For a moment, people protested.

Bri was one of them. "You can't be serious! I've got to get home!"

He snarled in a voice that shocked everyone, including Bri, into silence. "Y'all don't hafta come. You can stay here. Go back to Baton Rouge or N'awlins. I don't care. But them as wantin' are doing as I say now."

He turned to me. "You're comin'."

"You can't—" protested Bri.

"You're comin' too," he snapped. "Back east is death and I'm not letting Kelsey's sweetie die." He strode off.

"You can't—" she started again, but I stopped her from following him.

I said, "I don't want you going home either. I love you too much."

We hugged, and I ruffled her hair.

She always hated that. Her hair was short and straight, and she kept it combed neatly. She hated disorder. But this time, she just hugged me tighter.

"Do the math, love," I said. "Worst case, this means more time for you and me together. Your bosses aren't going to be mad you stayed here from these reports, will they? Besides, you can work from here."

"I guess. It's just, he's such a jerk."

"True, but he's an honest jerk. How many jerks have we met back home who always just lied?"

She sighed and leaned in to me.

I whispered. "Go pack our stuff. I'll get the group's things organized. Can't leave it here, no matter what."

She nodded and went away.

JT came back into the kitchen followed by a couple of sweaty fighter-types as I started putting the group's utensils into their tubs. "You got things at your lab you can get quickly?" he asked.

I blinked. "I suppose. What things?"

"We're going to need all the help we can get, so bring enough beakers and stuff you can set up a small lab. Also, it's likely the internet's going to go down, so bring all the reference books."

"But—"

He turned to the two who'd followed him. They were clearly in the military. "You don't have time to get back to Polk and if it happens that this all blows over, I'll testify that you were helping save people here. Go with her. Tote what she wants. Make sure them as gettin' in the way know you're forged for war."

I didn't understand that last bit, but those two sure did.

"Yes, Sergeant!" snapped one.

Sergeant?

Before I could ask, the other turned to me. "May I suggest my truck, ma'am? It's got a camper top and can hold more stuff."

I blinked and before I knew it, I was on the road to my lab. Everything was crazy, like you'd expect, but the guards knew me well enough to let me in. They didn't argue, much, with the two kids while we carried stuff out. They didn't know what to do either, and soon they both left and went to their families.

The day passed in a blur. Bri and I actually slept in my tent that night, and for many nights to come. She and JT had taken it down at the event and brought it to his place. In fact, in the morning, when I stumbled out, it looked like any other event with a dozen pavilions and some dome tents crowded between buildings.

Except we were in the bayou.

The ground squished.

The bugs buzzed.

Fish jumped and splashed.

Birds called. Weird bird calls.

Every once in the while I heard a big squeaking sound, which I learned later was an alligator.

His farm was not terribly big, but it had a number of massive outbuildings, a good-sized garden, and a large chicken coop. The bayou formed the southern and eastern boundaries, with a small creek cutting across the north. The west was mostly empty and barren.

If I'd had any chance to really think about it, it would have made me nervous, but things had happened too fast.

I smelled coffee and followed the scent to find JT up and looking as fresh as ever. He seemed jovial as he handed me his particular style of coffee.

"Here you go, lass."

"Thanks." I looked into his eyes. The gleam absent from them suggested his joviality was a pose. "It got worse overnight, didn't it?"

He simply said, "I got a shed I'm thinkin' might work for you. It ain't big, but it's got electricity. I's usin' it as a workshop."

"What do you expect me to do?"

"I got several nat gas wells on the property, plus an oil well."

"You do?"

He said, "How do you think I play all the time?"

"Never thought about it. You want me to refine that into stuff we can use to heat?"

"Sorta." He grinned and his old self was back for a second. "Honestly, my shine still will be doin' most a' that. No, I like to make things go boom. We'll need more gunpowder, too. Plus, a little napalm might be comin' in handy here and there."

"Explosives? Gunpowder?" I blinked. "But—"

His eyes turned grim again. "Can't be too careful, if any of us are makin' it."

"But—" I repeated, then stopped. "You mean we use explosives on... *people*?"

"They're not people anymore, at least not that I see on the video. This ain't like them protestors blocking roads and throwing bricks and painting everything. This is something else."

I shook my head. I'd seen the videos. I knew he was right, but I didn't *believe* he could be right. It was all too much. "No, I can't do it."

He grinned. "That's my lass! Stick up for what you're believin' in!" He sighed. "I wish it were different, but I have to think it'll be as bad as it could be. At least do me this, set up the lab for all the things you want to do that might help. Soaps will be good, especially in this bayou. Pesticides will be handy. Fuel for heating, like you were sayin', when we get closer to cold temps."

I looked at my feet. "I can do that."

"It's going to get worse, lass. I hope I'm wrong, but I ain't."

"I just can't... I mean—"

"I'm understandin', lass, but at least be payin' attention, okay? And take care of your lass, too."

I nodded. What else could I do? And besides, there was that clearly rational part of me that said he might be right.

I still didn't know if I could kill a person even to save myself, but I hoped I wouldn't ever have to cross that bridge.

The next week we watched all the videos. People died in front of us and with terrible fascination we couldn't take our eyes off the screens. But then we adjusted, and those videos became meaningless.

I guess it's a human thing to lose that humanity at some point. Besides, it became easier and easier to ignore the outside world as fewer and fewer people could record anything. Except for JT and a few others, the rest of us ignored all the news as best we could.

Besides as places got overrun, news got more infrequent. Plus, the internet got slower and slower as hubs went offline.

So, we focused on our tasks, of which we had plenty. Everyone did something.

For myself, I got up, worked on projects in the lab, and slept. Bri helped in the lab, as I needed an assistant and her math skills helped. Frankly, Bri and I ignored as much as we could of everything. We barely acknowledged any of the others in the camp, which wasn't too tough as everyone worked dusk to dawn.

It was the first time in our relationship we'd ever really been together. We'd been a couple for six years or so, by then, but we'd been off doing our postdocs.

Strangely, these medieval events had brought us together. I say strangely because she never seemed to fit with these groups whether back east or here. She was all angles and sharp, pointy clarity, and medieval reenactment is often a place for rounded romanticism. But she loved making garb because it was all math to her, and she liked cooking with me.

She hadn't wanted me to move to Louisiana. She'd known it wouldn't change our relationship much. Fewer weekend events where we'd meet up, but the distance between us had always meant vidcalls.

No, there was always the small added tension because Louisiana was a variable she could never really account for. Flyover country that one avoided for a reason. Full of, well, full of people like JT.

Now she was stuck in this bayou around people she despised. Plus, we had to deal with all the little things that married couples have to work around. It wasn't always easy.

Most people would have gotten angry and hateful, but not Bri.

One morning, she woke me by brushing back my hair. She said, "These might be some of the best days of my life, despite the mud, mosquitos, and fear."

We were late getting to the lab that morning.

Day after day, Bri and I did what JT suggested. We made soaps and shampoos. Creams to hold off the rashes from the bugs and crappy conditions of the bayou. Lubricants to keep the few machines we had running, not to mention helping to convert them to using straight nat gas. We made a few medicines but couldn't do much without some of the raw materials. Penicillin wasn't a big problem, though, and we made lots of that.

I did everything I could to avoid making something that could be used as a weapon, but I hadn't counted on JT's cunning. He asked me to come up with a process for expanded polystyrene, saying we'd need insulation sheets for the huts they were building.

Even Bri hadn't thought of the ramifications because the point made sense at the time. Besides, it never dawned on me that JT had converted our vehicles to nat gas almost immediately and saved all that gasoline for the precise purpose of making napalm.

What we did see, each day, were all the others converting JT's farm into a fortress. They opened the bayou on the west side to serve as a moat. Figuring they didn't have much in the way of good wood to make walls, they built berms too steep for the alligators to climb. Then they encouraged the gators to sun themselves on the far side.

We figured the gators would be the best guardians we could have hoped for. I kept thinking they'd be enough, and I'd never have to really sacrifice what I'd always been.

But one morning, Bri said to me, "I think you should consider making what JT wanted you to make. Explosives, gunpowder, the rest."

I was stunned. We were cuddling and she said *that*?

She sighed. "I've been working on the disease spread vectors."

"Yes." I'd known she'd been doing something to avoid getting bored.

"Much as I hate to say it, but that asshole was right."

"JT?"

"Yes. It's coming."

"Even here?"

She ran a hand through her hair. "I didn't want to be here. Not in flyover Louisiana. But we'd be dead back east."

It was the first time either of us had said it. I'd known it, but I hadn't wanted to say it.

"Our friends?"

"Dead. Have to be. They wouldn't be avoiding what's left of social media if they weren't."

Sometimes her cold mind chilled me, but I couldn't argue.

"Just think about it, my love," she added. "I knew I loved you years ago, but now, after being here with you, I won't give this up without a fight."

"But you—"

"I never had an equation where fighting added up. Now, I do." She sighed. "I still think JT and a bunch of these rednecks are idiots, don't get me wrong, but I can't argue with the math."

I shook my head, tears flowing.

She rubbed them off my cheek. "Just think about it," she repeated.

JT came into the lab. "Y'all maybe are going to have to reconsider, lass."

"Why?" I asked.

"I just got a message from a cousin in Pierre Part."

Pierre Part? Why that's less than a hundred miles away.

"I hadn't been a-worryin' with Baton Rouge or N'awlins. They's too many up and down that corridor and I's surprised took a month after it all started for this thing to take them down."

I blew out a breath. Pierre Part was as flyover a place as it could be and in the six months since Baton Rouge, we'd all hoped it would stand.

"How many live there?"

"Thirty-five hundred or so," he said. "More'n a few are cousins and such-like. Not much, I'm supposin', given that all them places with a million or more have fallen, but still, they's family."

"How'd it happen?"

"I ain't knowin'. They's doin' what all us small places doin'. Settin' up barricades and the like." He sighed. "We's been workin' hard, lass, but I's still seein' holes."

One of the soldiers from Fort Polk ran up. "Sergeant, there are people across the berm."

JT sagged. A font of inexhaustible energy he'd always seemed to be but now I could see he wasn't a young man.

"Alright." He turned to leave.

"Wait, we're coming." I turned to Bri. "Come on."

We rushed to the berm separating what had once been the road from the north to JT's farm. He'd dug that out first, but it was still the easiest way in since the gators hadn't really taken to that section.

"JT!" called the older man standing next to the car. He pointed at the other soldier, who had a wicked looking rifle in his hands not quite aimed at the newcomers. "Let us be comin' in."

"I can't, Billy Joe Bob. I jess can't."

Billy Joe Bob gestured at his wife, son, and daughter. "But we's got no other place."

"I's knowin', but we can't. We got no way a-knowin' whether you's one o' them or not."

Tears streaked down JT's cheeks.

Mine too.

The other soldier from Polk lifted his rifle. JT didn't have a rifle, but he had his hand on what he called his Moses gun. I'd found out it was an old .45 caliber and apparently the guy who'd designed it was named Moses or something. At least, all those who knew about guns caught the reference.

"You cain't be jess leavin' us out here." The man made to start crossing the moat.

JT pulled out his gun and fired a shot over the man's head.

I'd heard gunfire before since this had all started. Most of these people knew the basics, at least, but they'd practiced shooting to make sure. However, I'd never been so close to one getting fired. I hadn't realized they were so loud, and I staggered back to be caught by Bri.

I looked up in her eyes and saw sorrow... and something else. *Calculation?* I wondered.

"Dammit, JT!" said Mark. He'd been at the event and was a calligrapher of some note. Now, he was just another laborer inside the berm. He'd not ever gotten fully reconciled, as he was from Memphis and had no place to go when it happened. He grabbed at JT's .45.

"Don't be doin' that agin, Mark," growled JT.

"Show some humanity, you damn redneck!"

"At the risk a' them as is in here? Ain't happening."

Another shot rang out. One of the soldiers had seen Billy Joe Bob thinking to take advantage of the quarrel and stepping forward.

Mark grabbed for the .45 again and this time got a bit of a hold.

I saw the moment when JT's eyes shifted to something I'd never seen before. Not sad. Not intent. Not all the things he'd had to be to keep us all alive. Cold, now. Empty.

He wrested the gun away. "Mark, don't be doin'—"

But Mark tried again.

JT shot him.

I jumped back.

Mark collapsed, blood gushing from his chest, his eyes wide.

"I's sorry, Mark," whispered JT. "We's just can't." He looked around the stunned group. "Be leavin' if you're wantin', but I's—"

I heard a snarl of rage. I thought, at first it was one of us, but then I realized it was Billy Joe Bob's son.

The boy pulled his sister's hair, yanking her head back and exposing her throat. He opened his mouth, but before he could rip through her jugular, his mother jumped on him with a rage all her own.

JT lifted his .45 and shot the son, taking off his head. That didn't stop the other three, so he took a breath and drilled Billy Joe Bob in the chest. The two soldiers killed the mom and daughter.

Then, as suddenly as it had started, the echoes of the gunfire disappeared and all we could hear was the bayou.

JT called to someone. "Be bringin' me a couple bottles a' shine and some o' them old rags."

I didn't see who. I was too busy throwing up. Bri held my hair back.

When I finished, JT had a bottle in his hand, rag stuffed in the top. "Y'all be gettin' back." He waited until we all had moved back so far we could barely see anything. Then he lit the rag and tossed it.

A moment later, I heard a small boom, and then a bigger one as the car exploded. I thought it was enough, but JT tossed the other bottle, and I heard another small boom.

JT then went to the top of the berm and watched.

I don't know why, but I went up next to him and held his hand. Bri never let go of my other hand. Together, the three of us stood in a line watching as the remnants of the family burned next to their car.

It smelled too much like pork, but I had nothing to throw up at that point. I retched a couple of times, but none of us could leave until the pyre had burned itself out.

Then JT and one of the soldiers picked up Mark's body. I never did find out what they did with it, but we had a small memorial at dinner. We finished by singing one of those songs where the hero dies but lives forever in our memory.

Bri and I didn't say anything that night. We just held each other close.

The next morning, Bri said, "I don't think you need me desperately in the lab today."

I thought about it. "No, I guess not. Why?"

"I have something to do." She kissed me and left.

I didn't ask her about it, because I was already thinking about my tasks for the day. Mostly I made up a new batch of pesticide.

I heard gunfire, but I didn't hear any shouting or commotion, so I figured they were just practicing.

But Bri smelled like gunpowder when she got back to our tent.

I peered at her. "Did you go *shooting*?"

She nodded. "Yes."

"But… You hate guns. Anything to do with them."

She nodded again.

"It's yesterday, isn't it?" I asked.

"Yes, love. I've been working out the probabilities and I think our chances are better if I can shoot."

"That much better?"

She turned away. "Yes."

I stood there stunned. Then I asked very quietly, "Is that because we really don't have any chance to survive?"

She didn't say anything for a moment. "I wish I'd never fallen in love with math." Then she gathered her shower clothes and went to clean up.

I fell onto the bed and wept. *What's to become of us?* I thought. I didn't leave the tent for dinner. Bri brought me some gator sausage and I ate it.

After I finished it, I sat there. Bri came and held my hand. Then, for a while, I forgot everything as we tried to bring some joy to each other.

It turned out more awkward than our first time. It was like we'd both forgotten what pleased each other. Afterward, I wept myself to sleep, Bri holding me throughout the night.

Bri spent a part of each day for the next week at the range. At the end, she came home with a pistol. I didn't say anything. *What was there to say?*

JT spent a lot of that week telling me jokes. They were dad jokes, as bad as you could expect. I laughed despite myself, but I also clung to him too.

We woke up two mornings later to yelling and crunching. When we rushed to the berm, we discovered that gators had eaten their fill of some things that had once been human. We couldn't recognize anything, which was something to be thankful for. JT tossed another Molotov cocktail, and we went about our business.

What else was there to do?

Two people didn't have an answer to that question. They climbed the berm and walked into the bayou, never to be seen again.

I hadn't known them well prior to all of this, but we'd all been forced to bond together during this time. They hurt more than Mark, because we could all remember he'd been wrong, and that JT had actually saved us.

Bri had to hold me again that night.

She always had her new gun with her, from that point on. Dinner. Bathroom. Next to us in bed. Everywhere.

"The math says I have to," she said.

I was too tired to argue.

I did try to argue the next day when JT came to us and said, "We've one of the huts open for you two now. Time to get you two inside solid walls."

After these months, the bayou had taken a toll on all of our things. Our tent, especially. Sunforger canvas is tough, but not designed to be out for months in a row.

We needed to move, but I yelled, "No!" when I saw which hut it was. One of those who'd walked over the berm had lived in it, along with a couple of other people without family. JT had moved the other two into other spots.

The argument lasted all night long. I finally gave up because I had no energy to keep going.

It took weeks for me to sleep in that hut without nightmares. Those nightmares turned into dreams of walking across the berm myself.

A month later, we got our first major rush by the zombies. We'd had a few more come in ones and twos like the family. The gators got them all.

The beasts made sure we'd never needed the bell that JT had rigged for an alarm until this point.

So, it took Bri and I a moment to realize what it meant when we heard it.

She rushed off.

I followed, wondering if I should help. Even now, I still thought of the zombies as people. *What could I do, anyway? I should just be hiding, not getting in the way.*

But I couldn't let Bri go alone.

JT, the soldiers, and those others with guns lay prone on the northern berm, firing steadily.

Bri ran up and added her fire, as did others. She fired deliberately, but with confidence.

I kneeled behind her and watched. Each of her shots struck her target. Most hit the target's head. I could see that she'd had an aptitude for shooting. *Probably something to do with angles and such*, I supposed.

There were at least a hundred of the zombies. No clue where they'd come from.

They didn't make it past the moat, and the gators ate well for days.

After it was over, JT turned back. His eyes held that coldness I'd seen when he'd shot Mark. "You shouldn't be here, lass."

I gestured at Bri. "I couldn't let her be here alone."

Bri nodded, and we clasped hands.

JT ran a hand through his thinning hair. "I's seen worse reasons."

One of the soldiers asked, "Hey, JT, should I get some more moonshine?"

JT stepped back up to the berm and looked out. Then back into his farm. "No, I's thinkin' we's lettin' the gators take care of it all. They's spread out too much and we ain't got too much that'll burn. Hopefully, the wind will be blowin' its normal ways and it'll keep most of the stench away."

"Yes, Sergeant."

"Now all of you, be gettin' yer guns a-cleaned. Make sure we's ready for another like this."

We all went back to our lives as if this had been a normal thing.

"You have to," snapped Bri. "The probabilities change to our favor."

We stood in my lab, Bri in my face and JT leaning against the wall not saying anything.

I looked at him. "But we're holding off all the rushes, right? The first charge was the worst, wasn't it?"

JT sighed. "It was, but we're running out of ammunition."

Bri added, "JT's had people reloading all we can and it's a good thing he had so much powder, but that's almost out. We *need* you to make more."

"But I—"

"You know how to do it, and we have the ingredients. Maybe not for the good powder we've had, but enough to make the guns fire."

"Yes, but, I just—"

"Can't?" She pressed her lips together. "You *have* to. And you *have* to make something more than those Molotov cocktails. We're making moonshine, no problem there, but we're running out of bottles. Besides, they aren't that powerful."

I didn't get much sleep that night.

Nor the next day because we had another rush.

I don't remember much about the rush itself. I do remember running from place to place to get ammunition and what few Molotov cocktails we had to those who fired from the berm.

And fired and fired and fired.

Afterward, I held an exhausted Bri. Gunpowder colored her face around her glasses. I tried but couldn't wipe away the smudges.

Her hand shook from the fatigue.

Even so when about ten minutes later another alert came, she rose as if nothing had happened and did it again.

This rush wasn't near as bad, thank goodness. Just a few dozen this time and the gators had already swum over to feast on the first rush.

Just as well, as two zombies got all the way to the berm and started climbing before JT jumped up with a double-barreled shotgun and blasted them.

Neither Bri nor I could sleep.

We tried, but in the end, we crept over to the lab.

I wept with each task I did that night. They were all I'd sworn I'd never do, but I couldn't let Bri go through another day like the previous one without doing *something*.

No zombies came the next day and we breathed a sigh of relief. Those in the shops reloaded as fast as they could.

I spent the day learning how to mix black powder quickly. JT insisted he could use it in a pinch for some things and I didn't question him.

The second day, we expected another attack, but one didn't come. I didn't really notice as I was in my lab gathering the ingredients to make black powder in significant quantities.

Two of the three were easy. JT had hundreds of pounds of potassium nitrate in fifty-pound bags. Plus, JT had used our waste to create beds to make more.

He also had some sulfur in bags, but I could extract all I wanted from the natural gas and oil in his wells using the Claus method. After my time with the petrochemical company, I knew that process backward and forward. It was routine enough I taught Bri the process so I could work on other things.

Oddly, perhaps, charcoal proved the most difficult since we didn't have that many trees within the perimeter. However, JT arranged a couple of lumbering excursions on the outside of the berm and set some people burning everything they could find inside. My tent poles, for example, went into the fire.

Fortunately, by this point they'd built all the berms as much as they really could so all they needed to do was maintain them. That left extra hands. Some dealt with the charcoal, but JT sent three over to help me produce powder.

So, by the time they ran out of real gunpowder, we'd started churning out black powder in big lots. Not only that, they learned how to do it all themselves so I could start researching explosives in those books JT had insisted I bring those months ago.

I didn't actually know how to make such things after all, but there the instructions were in plain, dry prose. I also researched fulminate of mercury.

I plowed through that research. JT asked for naphtha first, so that's what I focused on. I didn't know why he needed as much as he said, but it was easy enough to learn.

I made all the things I'd hoped I wouldn't ever do. I could feel myself changing.

I didn't like it.

I tried to keep to myself, and so I didn't notice the days passing. They were all much the same, anyway.

But Bri did.

I realized at one point she'd gone to the wall each day expecting a rush of zombies, but one never appeared. The other guards did much the same. As the days went by, they got edgier, thinking the next rush would come any time.

One morning Bri pushed me out the door and to the gun range. JT waited for me with a pistol in his hand.

"There are you are, lass," he said, holding it out. "It's a Sig Sauer 9mm. Should be fittin' you nice."

"What's going on?" I asked.

"I'm going to teach you the basics," said Bri.

"What? No? I'm not—"

"Yes, you are. You need to at least know some of this. I won't have you die simply because you haven't ever touched a gun."

We had our worst fight ever. But in the end, I learned enough about this gun to be able to load it, take it off safe, and fire it. And trigger discipline. It only took once for JT to snarl *at* me, something I'd never expected to hear, for me to realize how important that was.

Then he gave me a holster and instructed me to keep the gun with me at all times.

I went to sleep crying. Bri tried to hold me, but she wasn't the best at comforting, and I pushed her away. Fortunately, I relented by the morning, and we were both late to our tasks.

We'd needed the relief.

So did the others, but most didn't have anyone they were as close to as Bri and I. People just can't stay keyed up for that long without a break, but we couldn't see any hint of one coming.

Occasionally, something would come in through those internet nodes that survived showing the fall of another small town. Places I'd never heard of, had not cared about in another life, but each hammered into me. Coldwater, Kansas. Carbondale, Illinois. Sikeston, Missouri.

The last bothered JT the most. He actually made chicken fried gator steak with some of our last remaining flour in honor of a restaurant there.

I suppose it tasted good, but none of us had the energy to compliment him.

It's hard to tell, some days, when the seasons change in Louisiana. JT kept track though, and he wasn't going to let Christmas Day pass, zombie apocalypse or not. He shortened the watch and rotated them frequently so everyone could get a chance at dinner.

Somehow, he made gator look like a turkey. It didn't taste like one, of course, but at first glance it had the same rounded appearance. No clue how he did it.

I also had no clue how he'd hoarded enough to come up with all the trimmings as well. He made mashed potatoes, instant of course, but still amazing. Dressing, two kinds. Cranberry sauce. Thick gravy.

Then he brought out presents. He had something for all of us. He gave Bri an old book on mathematical philosophy that she immediately buried her nose inside. For me, it was a new pair of boots. My old ones had been falling apart.

"When did you have time to sew these up?" I asked, hands on my hips.

"Here and there, lass. Be seein' if they fit."

They were tight, initially, just like leather boots are supposed to be, and I could tell they were almost a perfect fit.

"And how the heck did you size it right?" I demanded.

"Santa can't be tellin' all his tricks." He wandered off to give out other gifts, all equally targeted to their recipient. We all shook our heads at his ability to figure out just what we needed.

We didn't worry about it much, though, because he started caroling.

Bri had always hated caroling before. Despised religion in general as it messed with her sense of order. But she knew all the songs, something I'd never even guessed at, and she belted them out with all the rest of us.

We were in the second verse of *Hark the Herald Angels Sing* when the watchmen on guard heralded another attack.

"Damn these assholes," yelled JT. "It ain't right for zombies to be attackin' on Christmas!"

I'd never heard him say any curse word like that before, so I knew he was angry, but we'd all been through the drill before. Fortunately, there was still enough light outside for us to get to our spots.

JT lit a Molotov cocktail and tossed it out on the approach. Thanks to my work, it didn't need to hit one of the zombies. It landed in a patch of naphtha I'd brewed up and the flames rose. He lit several other patches the same way, setting up lanes the zombies had to rush through.

I'd asked him why he hadn't just ringed the entire area with naphtha and he'd said, "We's wantin' them to attack, iffin' they're here. Fire might be stoppin' them for a moment, but it ain't lastin' forever. This way, we can be shootin' them in a line."

Months ago, I wouldn't have understood that.

"Now you be helpin' yer lass. Don't be shootin' less it's needin'. Got it?"

"Got it."

I found Bri in her spot. She started firing that .45 slow and steady. She only had four magazines, though, and it was now my job to reload them from the boxes of ammunition.

She fired a magazine empty, replaced it, and handed the old mag back. We'd practiced this, and I focused on filling them.

I kept up as best as I could, but I lost track of how many magazines I handed back.

Suddenly, she cursed, "Damn this thing!" She was fussing with the .45. "JT said they might jam with reloaded ammo." She pulled, then a shell fell out, and she was back at it.

However, I could see the zombies had gotten close. Too close.

Bri stepped onto the berm, blasting away.

I had to step up to hand her the next magazine. The smoke made my eyes tear up, but I could still see zombies filling the lanes and charging.

"Get off that berm, girl!" yelled JT.

She ignored him. I tried to keep her supplied but stepping up that far made it harder on me. I had to run back and forth to the box, as there was really nowhere else to put it at the moment.

I didn't realize what had happened immediately. I mean, I did, but my mind wouldn't let me *know*.

It was a hand. It reached up and grabbed Bri's ankle. She fired once more and her .45 clicked empty.

Then the grimy, scarred hand pulled Bri off the berm down to the moat.

JT jumped into the gap blasting with his shotgun. He emptied it, then pulled out a gun.

"Get up here, lass! It's needin'!"

Shocked, I stepped up, pulling my pistol out.

I missed my first shot. And the second.

I couldn't see well because of my tears, but that wasn't why I missed, of course. I just—

But then the practice kicked in, and I hit a zombie in the chest. I shot again and again. I wasn't quick exchanging magazines, but I'd been given four of them too.

I emptied another. Now the horror had gone, and they were just targets. They'd hammered in "center of mass" when they'd trained me, and I put every round in that magazine into a zombie's center of mass.

The third time the slide clicked open, I slid in the fourth magazine and readied to shoot when I realized I had nothing else to shoot at.

Then I saw Bri. She lay on the far side of the moat, having been dragged there by the zombies. She had wounds across her chest. A zombie had torn a bite out of where her shoulder met her neck. Blood covered her arms.

But she still moved.

JT jumped off the berm and swam across the moat before I could say anything.

At first, I thought he was trying to save Bri, but even I knew she *had* to be infected with whatever this was. She struggled to get to her feet, but I couldn't see our love in her eyes. I couldn't see her thinking through an equation. I couldn't see anything but rage.

That mind, that lovely mind, the mind I'd wanted to grow old with, was gone. I knew it.

But I couldn't believe it.

Nor apparently could JT, as why else would he go to her?

But when he got to Bri, I saw that claws had shredded his right leg. Blood flowed. Not arterial blood, but blood where a zombie hand had ripped him.

And undoubtedly infected him.

He knew!

JT grabbed Bri before she started back across the moat. His eyes held something.

I started down the berm.

He snarled, "Hold!"

I stopped. "What."

The snarl left his face, mostly. He took a deep breath. "It's fast. This thing. It's very fast. Remember that. I haven't been this angry since my last tour. Good thing I've spent my last few years pushing anger away."

"What?" I repeated.

He held my girlfriend tight and said to me. "Well, lass, we had some good times." He nodded at the gun in my hand. "I'm glad it'll be you."

"JT... Wha—"

That which had been Bri fought and clawed and strove to reach me, but JT, rage in his eyes, held her. Held back all the rage of the world.

"Do it, lass," he demanded.

I raised my pistol.

"Hurry, lass," he growled.

And then I saw it. The moment when he lost it. Lost all that made him jovial and wonderful and giving. The moment when he died, and the rage was released. The pair of them started into the moat.

I took aim.

But I didn't fire.

The two soldiers had gotten to the berm and saw what had happened.

I sighed, relieved. "I'm glad you're here. I would've shot them, but now, you can do what's needed so I don't have to."

One nodded and raised his rifle.

Then I stepped down into the moat.

The soldier protested, "Kelsey, what are you doing?"

I turned back before what had been Bri and JT reached me. "It's okay, guys. Without my one true love, and without Santa Claus, why would I want to stay in this world?"

He nodded again. Took aim.

Sometimes, it's better to receive.

Heeta's Place

By Jenny Wren

"**S**o then he comes stompin' in with leaves in his hair, grass stains all up and down his front and a huge tear right up the seat of his pants with his rear hangin' out and yells for me to get him a beer." The woman in the kitchen chair said, laughing. The front of her hair was parted down the middle and each part curled up, held in place by mismatched neon hair clips. The spring in the neon pink one on her right was starting to come loose so she had to keep pulling the bun on that side back up.

Heeta laughed as she combed out another section of the seated woman's hair and started working down the hair with her crimping iron. She still had the older crimping irons from the eighties, the ones that made the really tiny, close crimps. As the eighties had given way to the nineties and the crimped style phased out, she'd put them in a cabinet with the rest of her hairstyling tools, certain that they would come back as all good fashions eventually did. She'd been waiting almost thirty years – though that wasn't something that was spoken about – and the tiny crimping irons were still on their shelf. The women here in the Wispy Pines Trailer Park Community stuck with what Heeta thought of as the pinnacle of feminine hairstyles. Big hair made a statement. The woman wearing that confection was one who could whip you as quickly as she could kiss you and do it all while looking fabulous.

"Oh, Gale, no! What did you say to him when he came thunderin' in like that?" Heeta asked.

Just as Gale started to deliver the punchline, the kitchen door slammed open with a bang that let rain and enough wind in to temporarily blow away the permanent bleach smell.

Viola Mae White stood in the doorway, soaking wet and covered in mud. The broken neon pink clip went flying as Gale and Heeta dashed for the girl gripping onto the doorjamb like it was the only thing holding her up.

"Viola Mae, come in here and sit down!" Gale led Viola Mae over to the chair she had just jumped out of while Heeta arm wrestled the door closed. Reaching around without looking she grabbed some of her beach towels out of the closet and laid one down to soak up the water that had blown in.

Heeta turned around to see Gale helping to get Viola Mae's wet cardigan off as the younger woman sat and shivered. Her lips had turned blue, and she was as pale as the bleached platinum blond hair that some women had walked out of Heeta's kitchen with.

"Here girl, let's get you dried off." Heeta brought another huge beach towel over and got her wrapped up in it while Gale started drying her hair with the closest thing to hand; a dish towel that had hung from the handle of the fridge. Even folded in half the beach towel was big enough to bundle up most of Viola Mae. Heeta had a brand-new hair dryer chair with a big clear hood she'd just gotten two weeks earlier. She wouldn't say it in so many words, but she was really proud of it. She felt like it gave more of a professional feel to her business and made her feel like she ran a real salon, but there again, she'd never admitted that to anyone. The fact that the only place she had room to install it was in her living room was one she ignored.

"Come on, let's get you over here and under the heater." Gale led Viola to the hairdryer, sat her down, lowered the hood and turned the heater on high.

Heeta opened one of her accordion pantry doors just a crack and tossed Viola's cardigan up over the open "V" shape at the top to drip dry. Picking up a hairband from the counter she walked over to Gale and pulled her hair up into a messy bun.

"There goes all of the work. Well, at least we hadn't done more than half." Heeta mumbled as she leaned over to hear what Viola was saying.

"I was driving home from work, and it started raining. After the 'S' curve I saw it. It was a bright light, like as bright as when Leon's using his arc welder. Then there was someone there. I slammed on the brakes and skidded off the road. My car got stuck, and I was so scared that I wasn't thinking, I just got out and... I ran. All I could think of was to get as far away from whoever they were and to get home. All I wanted was to be back home."

It was hard to hear Viola over the hair dryer on full blast, and her shoulder-length brown hair was fine enough that it dried quickly. Heeta reached up and turned it down to low.

"Viola Mae, hun, what do you mean 'someone' was there? Was it someone dressed up in a big raincoat maybe? Could they have been camping and the light was from that?"

Viola looked at Gale and said "No, it weren't any kind of raincoat that I've ever seen or hunting gear or a Ghillie suit either. They were tall and wearing something almost like what astronauts at NASA wear when they're going up in a shuttle. They even had these big glass domes on their heads."

Gale and Heeta looked at each other.

"What happened to your car, sweetheart?" Gale crouched down so far, she might as well have been sitting on the floor so she could look up at Viola while the hairdryer hood was still down over her head.

"I don't think I actually hit anything. It's just off the road." Viola said, thinking back.

Her skin was returning to something closer to normal, not as blue and sheet-white anymore. Reaching up, Heeta turned off the hairdryer and lifted the hood. As soon as the dryer went silent, it sounded like every dog in Wispy Pines was barking.

"What in the world is that about?" Heeta asked, looking between the other two.

Suddenly the unmistakable sound of a gunshot could be heard over the storm. They ran outside, Heeta leading in a raincoat and Viola huddled up with Gale under her umbrella.

Dogs barked all over the park, and someone was yelling. All the lights were on at Donny's. He had the most dogs of any resident. He'd adopted a whole litter of eight hounds as pups. His reason at the time was that by having that many when some got tired from hunting, he could let them rest and use the others, doubling his hunting time. Everyone else knew that he just couldn't pick one or two; he was too soft-hearted, falling for their big bright eyes. Of course, no one pointed this out, or even said it within earshot.

"Donny's," Heeta said decisively, then set off with Gale and Viola following close behind in her wake.

They ran through the playground in the middle of the park, zig-zagging between the areas that were the least muddy, usually around the least-favorite pieces of playground equipment. Heeta even got on the merry-go-round; she kicked off of the squelchy grass and rode it around to the other side before jumping off, avoiding one of the bigger mud puddles.

"Donny? Everyone alright in there?" Heeta called.

"Come on in, Heeta. The door's open. Just be careful not to trip over the monsters."

As soon as Heeta started to crack the door, she was met by a half dozen wet black noses all trying to get a sniff of who was coming in at the same time. Trying to get in the door with nearly the full pack of wet, agitated hounds was a trick. She pushed them out of the way while trying to keep them from tumbling over each other too much.

Donny was sitting on the couch holding one of his soaking wet, muddy, sixty-pound pups in his lap. Most of poor Julep was stretched out on the couch next to him. She'd long since outgrown being able to curl up like a lap puppy, but tonight it didn't look like she cared. She shivered with her tail tucked up under her. Donny soothed her, completely ignoring the wet and mud. The others kept going up to sniff her and check on her, getting up on the couch to nuzzle her and jumping back down.

"Shhhh girl, you're ok, I've got you. You're ok, you're safe. Heeta, if y'all don't mind trying to calm the others down please? If we're calm, they'll calm," Donny asked in a quiet voice.

"Of course," Viola dropped down on the floor where she had been standing and started petting the hounds as they came within reach and took turns sticking their noses in her face to sniff her. "Oh, you're ok, she's ok, she's safe. Come here you brave pups."

Gale sat down on the couch and started petting the ones nearest her or who jumped up next to her while Heeta sat in the armchair next to Donny.

She reached out slowly to let Julep sniff her hand, then started petting her gently. "Ohhhh, you're ok, sweet girl. Your daddy has you, you're safe." Heeta said quietly and soothingly.

"Donny, what in the free world happened?"

"I let these guys out back to run and do what they needed to do; they're really good about telling me when they need to go out, you know." Heeta nodded, still petting the shivering pup. "Sure, you've got a good pack here."

"Well, they started barking, which by itself isn't all that weird. But then their bark changed to a 'warning bark' and all the other dogs in the park started chiming in. I had my hand on the door to go out and see what the fuss was about when this little girl yelped."

Donny's expression was furious, but he never stopped petting his scared pup and neither the tone nor volume of his voice changed.

"I grabbed my rifle and ran out the door. Poor little Julep here was huddled in the far corner of the fence, terrified, and there was something standing over her, just looming. The others were circled up around it like they'd treed a coon. When I yelled, the pups turned and ran back to me, and I shot at whatever it was. I shot it right in its damn head." Heeta's eyes got wide, but she never stopped petting Julep.

Donny continued. "I ran over, scooped her up and we all came running inside. Whatever it is, it's dead and it's still out there."

By now the other hounds had started to calm down and Julep's shivering was starting to slow, but she didn't look like she was going to be leaving Donny's lap any time soon. Just as Heeta was about to suggest that they call the Sheriff, the dogs started barking again but this time it was their greeting bark. "Donny?" a voice called from outside the trailer.

"Come on in, Nolan." Donny called over the barking. "Hush you lot, you know Nolan!"

Donny explained everything again for Nolan, who sat silent for a few moments, petting the agitated hounds. Nolan's pauses could be longer than other people's, but for those who knew him, it was just the way he worked through what he was going to say before he spoke.

"We need to call the Sheriff and get whatever that is out of your yard. We don't want its smell making the pups more nervous."

Donny nodded. "Yup. I definitely want whatever the hell that is out there gone as soon as possible. It's going to take me a while to get the pack to go out there again without freaking out."

Heeta called the Sheriff's office. In a town this small they didn't have to call 911, they could call the actual Sheriff's office; whoever was working at the front desk was both the desk staff and the 911 dispatcher so one was as effective as the other.

"Hmm, that's weird," Heeta said, hanging up. "No answer."

"Heeta," Donny said, "if you'll hand me my phone, I'll call Luthor and Jackson. We'll load whatever that thing is up in my truck and take it over to the Sheriff ourselves if you three ladies will stay here and keep an eye on the pups."

Twenty minutes later, the rain had slowed to a drizzle. Donny, Luther, and Jackson were pulling up in the sheriff's office parking lot. The body of whatever it was that had threatened Donny's dogs was laying in the bed of Donny's truck where it had been dumped. No one had seen anything like it or could have guessed what it was. All everyone could agree on was that it was not human.

"What the hell happened here?" Luthor asked, leaning out of the passenger window. The sheriff's office building had broken windows and only had half as many lights on as it should have.

"Come on boys, let's go see what the hell's going on. There's too much weird happening for me," Donny said as he turned the truck off and got out. Walking in, they realized the damage was a lot worse than it looked from outside. There were lights pulled from their mounts and wires hanging out of the ceiling. It looked like there had been a riot in the office. Computer monitors had been tossed on the floor; the phones had been ripped out by their plugs and thrown across the room, and paperwork carpeted every clear space. Even the ubiquitous coffee maker had been picked up and thrown across the room, leaving a dark fan of coffee splashed on the wall along with pieces of mugs scattered everywhere.

"Hello? Is someone out there? Come on, let me outta here!" Someone yelled from the back of the station.

Coming around the corner into the holding area they found a man locked in one of the cells. The man was wearing dirty jeans, worn work boots, and a flannel shirt that had one sleeve ripped. The smell of alcohol rolled off of him every time he moved or breathed.

"Otis Shetler, you lush. What in hell happened here? Where is everyone?" Luthor demanded.

"Come on guys," Otis pleaded. "I don't know nothing about what happened. But you're gonna let me outta here, right?"

Ignoring Otis' question Donny asked him "What did you hear? What in hell happened out there?"

"I don't know. I was dozing in here, and I woke up when I heard crashing and yelling. Then nothing until y'all showed up." Otis explained.

Luthor nudged Donny and nodded back at the door. "Sit tight Otis, and don't you go nowhere," Donny snickered as they turned around and headed out of the holding area. "Yeah, you're really funny guys, really," Otis said sourly as the men walked back out into the office.

"Do we let him out?" Jackson asked as soon as they were out of Otis' earshot.

Donny considered. "Well, we don't know how long it's going to be before there's anyone back to get him, though he's probably safer in here."

"I wish the Sheriff or the National Guard or someone was here to take care of these things. This is too weird for us to have to handle. Who knows how many more of these things are out there," Luthor muttered.

Donny nodded in agreement. "Ok, so let's get a move on. Luthor, you and Jack get that disgustin' thing out of the back of the truck and put it in the morgue. We don't know when someone is going to come along to let Otis out, so I'm going to open the cell. He may be a drunk, but I don't want him starving to death on my conscience. That done, we can figure out where everyone went," Donny waved them out the door, nodding at the truck as he turned to hurry back inside.

Donny grabbed the keys for the holding area off of the wall and headed to the back to let Otis out. As he unlocked the cell door, they heard someone yelling. "Aw shit, now what?" Donny asked. Both men rushed outside and found the thing from the bed of Donny's truck bed on top of Luthor. Jackson lay in a heap on the ground against the outside wall of the sheriff's office.

Luthor let out a low roar as he wrestled with the thing, barely holding it off of him. It growled and grunted, snapping its jaws in Luthor's face.

Donny ran to his truck and dove for the toolbox in the bed. "Go check on Jackson!" he yelled at Otis.

Grabbing a crowbar, he turned around and saw Otis frozen in place, staring at the monster "Otis!" Donny yelled as he ran toward the monster and Luthor.

"I'm... I can't. I'm outta here man! This shit is too crazy!" Otis yelled and was off at a sprint.

Donny ran up behind the monster and hit it hard in the head. It didn't react, so he kept hitting it. It looked over its shoulder at him after three or four more hits. It was gruesome – reddish-brown and goopy-looking, like pudding that's boiled and bubbled over. It was thin, with long gangly arms and legs dressed in some kind of suit with hookups and valves all over it. Around its neck were jagged pieces of broken glass from where Donny's shot had broken the dome and taken out a big chunk of its head.

It stood up and tilted its head looking at him the way someone looks at a kitten that's trying to attack and moved toward Donny. As Donny backed up, he saw Luther draw his handgun. Donny jumped, throwing himself off to the side. Luthor fired twice, both shots landed square on the side of the creature's ugly head, and it dropped where it stood.

Donny and Luthor scrambled over to Jackson's side. He was unconscious, and bleeding from a large gash across the back of his head.

"Careful, he probably broke something," Donny said.

Luthor replied, trying for humor but his voice was shaking. "Well, if he did, it weren't his thick skull. That gash is just skin-deep."

Jackson was still breathing – barely.

"Jack, come on buddy, you've got to wake up. Jackson!" Luthor gently smacked Jackson in the face. The shaking worry in his voice got worse as he kept talking.

"Luthor, man, don't. He'd probably rather stay unconscious than feel everything that just happened to him," Donny took slow breaths to calm himself.

"Think, think…," Donny mumbled. "We need to get Jackson out of here, and I need to get that thing in a cage just in case we didn't kill it." Donny snapped his fingers and jumped to his feet.

"I've got an idea, but I need you to stay here with Jackson." He shook Luthor's shoulder to be sure he had his attention. Luthor just nodded absently.

"Ok, look. I'm going to take that thing inside and lock it in Otis' cell, then I'm going to see what they have that we can use to help Jack until we can get him to the hospital. When I come back out here – don't shoot me, ok?"

Luthor nodded. "Right. Good idea. Donny, hurry though, ok?"

Dragging the stinking body into the cell was one of the grossest things Donny had ever dealt with. He grabbed it by the ankles, so he didn't have to be near the squelchy, pulpy remains of its head. The second he had all of it in the cell he dropped the ankles, jumped out, and slammed the door good and hard. He searched the station but didn't find much of anything that was useful. He'd hoped for a stretcher or one of those board things that looked like a surfboard that emergency responders used. Instead, all he managed to scrounge up was a box of bandages and a couple of slings.

He carried it all out to the parking lot where he and Luthor bandaged Jackson's head as best they could. Using the slings, they tied his arms snuggly to his chest. "I bet he's got some broken ribs to go with these broken arms. Keeping his arms tied down should help keep him from flopping around and getting hurt worse." Donny explained. He pulled out his phone as soon as he had Jackson and Luthor loaded in the back of the truck. "Dammit" he growled when his phone beeped at him. "No signal."

Donny opened the sliding rear window and yelled out as he pulled out slowly onto the street. "Luthor? You got any signal?"

He heard Luthor swear as he checked. "No, I've got nothing."

"Ok Luthor, hold onto Jack nice and tight," Donny snarled, then gunned it down the street.

Back at Wispy Pines, the residents had been busy. "Clyde! Get your ass in gear! We need to move those old cars of yours now! If there are any gaps in this barricade because of your lazy ass, I'm throwin' you to them monsters first!" Leroy yelled out the passenger window of Nolan's wrecker as Nolan pulled up next to Clyde who was working on excavating his junkers from the overgrown field where he'd parked them as they died.

"Yeah, yeah what'n hell does it look like I'm doing?" Clyde yelled back, while he continued to dig out around the front end of an old Chrysler that was all but grown over. Nolan had been driving his wrecker since he was ten when he helped his dad. He could put it anywhere he wanted to, with or without a car on it. He executed a skillful three-point turn and backed the bed up to one of the cars that was newer to the collection and easier to get out.

"I can get this one loaded on my own Leroy, you stay and help Clyde." Nolan told Leroy who nodded and jumped out to pick up one of the extra shovels Clyde had brought with him. Walking over to the Chrysler he started furiously stabbing at the ground around it.

At least it wasn't still storming.

I'll take a drizzle, thought Nolan as he hooked Clyde's junker. He didn't bother with taking a lot of care with how he hooked up beyond making sure that nothing would damage the wrecker. The car was a late model compact sedan, three of its wheels were gone and it was sitting cattywampus on one flat tire and three rusty rotors.

As soon as he finished hooking the car up, Nolan got back in and put the truck in gear. At first nothing happened, the car had been sitting there for a little bit and the rotors had gotten sunk in the clay after ages of rain and weather. He gave it more gas; he could feel the mud start to give way as he pulled on the car. This was not going to be good for the field where Clyde had been parking the cars or the gravel road for that matter. After the story of the monster in Donny's yard got around, it started coming out that others had seen or heard things that they couldn't explain. Someone heard strange snarls while taking their trash out, another resident saw something moving in the woods while taking their dog for a walk. One at a time the experiences started adding up. Clyde, the resident mechanic, even swore that he saw something skulking around just outside the fence that surrounded the park. Clyde's experience was the breaking point. Residents who had seen or heard things started to gather outside Heeta's place. "That fence isn't going to keep these things out!" Someone in the back yelled.

"It already isn't, one of those things got into Donny's yard and attacked his hounds!" Someone else shrieked. Panic was starting to rise, and everyone started talking at once.

"Now just hold on. Let's not start losing our heads!" Heeta snapped. The noise stopped.

"That's better," Heeta nodded. "Now what we need to do is figure out how to keep them away from the fence and out of the park. Does anyone have any suggestions?"

"Why don't we use Clyde's junkers and line them up outside the fence?" Nolan suggested. "If we can get them dug out, I can haul them out and line them up like the county does with the cement barricades on the highways."

"I don't see why we gotta use my cars, Nolan has lots of wrecks at the junkyard," Clyde grumbled sullenly.

"All in favor of using Clyde's junkers to build a barrier?" Heeta gave Clyde a warning look and raised her hand.

Nolan started dropping the cars at the end of the park that was closest to the woods where these things had been seen. They had to pull the cars out of the field outside the trailer park fence where Clyde had left them and up the gravel road that ran along the outside of the fence. Normally the road was used by the city to get to the power poles at the back of the park where the power lines connected. They were the last stop for the gas, and for the power from the back. So the city had to be able to get to both ends of the park easily.

Lucky for us the city preferred to pay for a couple dump truck loads of gravel. It makes this easier than dragging these junkers through more mud. Nolan thought as he hauled the car to the back of the park. He'd been able to get this one mostly on the flatbed, so he wasn't dragging anything to leave gouges in the gravel.

Every time Nolan went back for another car there were more people helping to dig out Clyde's cars. It didn't take long before there were so many people working on freeing them that Nolan couldn't keep up with hauling them on his own. On one trip back, after dropping off his sixth car, he passed a pickup dragging a car with a tow chain, leaving large gouges in the gravel behind them. Out of the window he saw Raymond Clay driving, so focused on where he was going that he barely looked up and nodded at Nolan as they passed by each other. With both of them taking it in turn to haul the junkers, they started keeping up with the ones that had been dug loose. Nolan noticed that there were more cars being added from other park residents and that the barricade got put in place faster than Nolan would have thought possible.

Just as he finished dropping the last car off and got turned around, there was a series of screams from the woods. These were screeching, growly screams echoing through the woods.

"Nope," Nolan said. Throwing the truck in gear, he tore down the road, flinging gravel up behind him.

Heeta knew that Clyde didn't have enough junkers to make a barricade all the way around the park, but he had a fair number of them, and they were already outside the fence. While they were getting the woods side of the trailer park barricaded, she sent some of the other men to the other residents with junkyard cars with the message that they needed to get the junkers dug out and added in with Clyde's. "If any of them have any issues with that, you tell them to come over here and see me." Gale had stepped into the kitchen where Heeta was giving out assignments from. Gale was an emergency room nurse, and when she chose to, she could employ a look that would have all but the most obstinate following directions. The men looked at her and nodded with a simple "Yes ma'am." before taking off to go collect more cars.

"You think that's going to be enough?" Gale asked.

Heeta sighed. "No, not really. But it's a start. I've sent Jasper and the Mitchell kids out to Nolan's junkyard. I asked them to start pulling hoods, trunk lids and any tin roofing panels they can find, anything that we can start layering over the chain link fence. People will feel safer when we have something up that feels like a wall, even with Clyde's junkers making that barricade."

Gale looked up at Heeta and smirked. "Smart move, the Mitchell kids have been destroying things since they could toddle. I can just see their expressions when you told them they were supposed to be tearing things apart. And at least the rain has stopped, that's something good."

"If we don't figure out what these things are and how to stop them, it's not going to amount to a hill o' beans," Heeta said.

Horrible, growling screams suddenly filled the air. Both women jumped.

"Sweet fancy Moses on buttered toast!" Gale swore. "What in this sweet life was that?" She looked at Heeta, eyes wide, face pale.

"That, my friend, is the signal for us to get a move on." Heeta said quietly then stepped out on the porch. Jasper and the Mitchell kids were rolling back from Nolan's. They managed to scavenge every hood, trunk lid, and piece of tin flashing they could get their destructive little hands on. They had even torched the beds of two wrecked pickups from their cabs and done some quick welding to add tow arms on them, effectively turning the beds of two junked pickups into trailers for their two working trucks.

"Well, aren't you a bunch of clever little hooligans." Heeta smiled at them as three of the Mitchell brood jumped out of Jasper's pickup. Christie, the oldest Mitchell, climbed out of their truck with Neil, the littlest Mitchell.

"We got what we could on the first trip, Heeta. I'm going to stay and help add this stuff to the barricade. I stopped by the garage already and picked up my welder. That's why poor Jasper had to carry the others. If we can get our trucks unloaded, we can disconnect the extra beds, and the others can go back for more. There are some other things out there that we have some ideas about. Holden can drive our truck," Christie tossed the truck keys to her younger brother. The younger Mitchells looked at each other and smiled.

"Suits me, but we need to get moving," Heeta said. "Gale, do you mind scaring up some more help for us please? Here kids, we'll put it all right up there in front of the office. It'll be easier for folks to come up and get pieces." Heeta hurried to help get things unloaded.

Heeta watched in amazement as the Mitchell clan worked with the efficiency of an ant nest, crawling over everything somehow getting the parts unloaded. With the extra help Gale had sent over, they had both trucks unloaded and back out in under twenty minutes.

As people finished tasks or ran out of materials, they headed up to the office to see what needed to be done next. The sound of an engine roaring got everyone's attention immediately.

Donny's pickup came skidding around the corner, his back-end fishtailing. He slid to a stop in the parking lot, jumping out of the truck almost before it was fully stopped. "Quick, help! It's Jackson!" Heeta ran around to the back where Luthor was holding Jackson with one arm and holding onto the side of the bed with the other. "Gale, we need Gale…." Donny was so worked up that he was breathing like he'd been running for miles. Heeta started to open her mouth to tell him to take a breath and calm down when Luthor yelled for someone to help him get Jackson out and everyone's attention was on Jackson and Luthor.

"Quick now boys. Get him into the office. Come on, move." Gale stepped in, taking over without missing a beat. "There's a bedroom in there that the owner has for show when he's trying to get new residents to move in. We'll use that." She directed everyone calmly.

Luthor helped carry Jackson into the office, leaving Donny at the center of everyone's attention, and the questions were coming at him from everywhere.

"What the hell happened out there Donny?"

"Where's the Sheriff?"

"What happened to Jackson?"

"Everyone just stop!" Heeta snapped, raising her voice high enough that the people closest to her flinched. She took control of the conversation by moving so she was directly facing Donny, flapping her hands at everyone to get them to back up. The crowd went silent. She took a breath and hid her shaking hands in her raincoat pockets. "Donny, take a breath." After Donny took a couple of deep breaths, Heeta asked "What happened to y'all out there?" She was trying to use the same tone that she did with Julep. Donny looked right at Heeta as he explained. He had a pale, blank expression like he was in shock. "We took that thing to the sheriff's office, but there was no one there and the whole place was torn up like there had been a big fight. Otis Shetler was there in the cells, drunk."

Someone in the crowd snorted and several people nodded "No surprises there," someone muttered.

Donny kept talking. "Otis hadn't seen anything, and we couldn't leave him in there by himself, so we decided to let him out. There probably wasn't anyone left to go by there and see to him, and we didn't want him to starve.

"Or dry up," someone else in the crowd snarked. Heeta gave the probable speaker a warning look and nodded for Donny to continue. "We were going to leave that thing locked up in the morgue, so Luthor and Jackson went out to the truck to get it, and I went to let Otis out. When Otis and me got back outside, Jack was laying on the ground by the wall and he was all messed up. That thing was on top of Luthor like it was trying to, I don't know, bite him or something. It was grumbling like it was tryin' to talk." Donny scrubbed his face with hands that were shaking as much as Heeta's.

Everyone stirred uncomfortably and started mumbling, the volume quickly getting louder. No one cracked any jokes.

"Hush your mouths, all of you! Let the man finish talking, or we're never going to know what happened." Heeta raised her voice again, hoping no one noticed that it shook a little.

Donny picked the explanation back up. "Otis ran off like a coward, and I grabbed my crowbar and hit the thing two or three times. I'm not sure how many, but all I did was get its attention. It barely even moved when I hit it. It stood up and started coming at me, but Luthor shot it right in the head with his pistol. After that, I dragged it into the sheriff's station and locked it in one of the cells. We loaded Jackson up as best we could and tried to get to the hospital over in Jefferson."

Heeta frowned. "But you didn't get there."

Donny shook his head. "No ma'am. The sheriff's deputies from Jefferson had the roads closed off; they weren't letting anyone in. It didn't matter that they could see that Jackson was hurt. They weren't making any exceptions." Donny's expression changed to anger.

The tone of the crowd changed from panic to disbelief.

"Ok, ok – so we know that whatever's happening Jefferson is ok. That means they'll be able to call for help." Heeta said. "That also means we need to get a move on and get ourselves looked out for in the meantime. If you don't have anything to do, come see me. If you do, then get back to it!"

Donny headed inside the office to check on Jackson as everyone who had walked away from a task scattered back to what they had been doing and the few with nothing to do waited to find out what needed to be done next. Heeta sent some of the folks out to the stores to start collecting supplies.

While Nolan and the others had been moving Clyde's cars to the tree line, the rest of the Wispy Pines residents had been just as busy. There was now a solid barrier of trunk lids and vehicle hoods welded to the fence that ran the entire length of the park on the side facing the woods, across the backside, and half of the way up the side facing the town. After they ran out of car parts, they started riveting together the old sheet metal, tin roofing, and the flashing from around the bottom of the trailers. They covered about a third of the way up the city-facing side. It was just going to have to be good enough to serve.

On the Mitchell kids' second trip, they surprised everyone by bringing Nolan's forklift from the junkyard on a flatbed trailer with a very long rectangular box that was almost as long as the trailer itself. Behind that, they were towing the big fifteen-seater van that the local church had used until its engine overheated enough to crack the engine block. They stopped outside the gate to the park and started disconnecting the van.

"What?" Holden said defensively in response to the looks they were getting. "There's a method to my madness."

"Sure, but it seems like more madness than method right now." Gale said softly enough that only Heeta, who was standing next to her, could hear.

Heeta nodded her agreement and walked up to Holden at the same time as Christie did. "Ok kids, what's the scheme?"

Christie looked up. "Well, we've come up with a way to keep the gate safe. Or at least half of it." While they were talking Jasper had jumped in the forklift and was lifting the huge box thing off of the trailer.

"Hey! Isn't that the brand-new car lift I just ordered?" Clyde protested, loudly. Jasper and the Mitchells carefully ignored the question.

"What do you mean that's your new car lift?" Heeta asked.

"I just ordered a brand new four-arm car lift for the garage. It's big enough that I can lift a truck with no problems and wheel it out of the way." Heeta just gave him a raised eyebrow.

"What? I'm getting too old to be wheeling around on the floor, scooting under vehicles, and the wheels on it lock, so I can put it wherever I have room for it in the shop," he said, just a little defensively.

It was a solid three hours later by the time the four-post lift had been set up, so it was perpendicular to the entrance to the park with the van loaded on it. As people left to go get supplies someone would hit the button and activate the lift, raising the van up and out of the way.

"Ok you hooligans, I'm impressed. That's a damn good idea you all came up with. Running the power lines through a hole in the fence and plugging it into the park's power was a good idea too." Heeta said, sounding genuinely impressed.

"Thanks Ms. Heeta, but we still have to figure out some way to block the other side of the gate." Christie said. Her face was a dirty mess from all the welding and cutting she'd been doing.

Nolan stepped up at that point. "I've got an idea, but it's going to take the flatbed you've borrowed and my wrecker. Care to help out?"

"Yessir." Holden said immediately.

Christie declined, "I'm going to stay here and see what I can do to help make the barricade more solid. I have an idea about welding the frames of the cars together to make them less likely to get knocked apart."

At Heeta's look, she rushed to explain. "Don't worry, I'll stay on the inside and bring Jasper with me.

Heeta nodded, "Good call Christie. You go get Jasper and get to it."

Three weeks later the National Guard arrived, rolling through town and heading straight for Wispy Pines. The captain stepped out of the lead vehicle as it rolled to a stop in front of the trailer park entrance and gave a low whistle. Soldiers deployed, checking the scorched and decomposing bodies of the creatures scattered all around in front of the makeshift gates. The captain inspected the solid barricade of car panels with a dumpster and passenger van blocking the entrance into the trailer park. The sound of generators could be heard from inside the barricade.

Off to the left side of the gate, a gas door on what used to be a retired police cruiser popped open.

"Who are you?" The stern question was called through the hole behind the gas door surprising the soldiers standing near the gate.

"Uh," the closest soldier said, mildly confused. "We're the National Guard. There have been reports of…. difficulties in this area, and we're here to help."

"So, you're here to help?" The man on the other side of the gas door asked with no change in his tone.

The soldier hesitated, turning to look at his captain and shrugged before turning back to the voice. "Yessir, that's what we do."

"Humph." The voice behind the gas door snorted as a wire attached to the gas door was yanked and slammed the gas door shut. Someone yelled from inside the park, then the van started to lift up.

As the lift raised the van up to a comfortable door height, three people walked out. A shorter woman with a pink camo baby-doll tee shirt, rhinestone-covered jeans, pink cowgirl boots and some of the largest blond hair that the captain was sure he'd ever seen. With her was another woman who was taller, also with large blond hair, a pink t-shirt with "Juicy" on it, jeans and regular boots. The third person who came out was the only male. He was skinny, but wiry with a sleeveless white Dale Earnhardt tee shirt, dirty jeans and boots, but his dark hair looked as though it had recently been trimmed into a very tidy mullet. They all looked tired but determined as though they had settled into what they had to do.

"Y'all made a barricade.... out of scavenged car parts?" asked one of the soldiers.

"Yep. We had to keep those things out and keep ourselves safe. One of our residents owns the junkyard, so we went over there and grabbed what we could. I'm Heeta, this is Gale and Donny," The woman gestured to the two people who had come out with her.

The captain nodded. "I'm impressed," he said, smiling. "I'm Captain Thomas Michaelson, and we're here to, well… help."

"Well, y'all better come in, but that tank isn't going to fit. We're going to need you to back it up a good ways off to leave a decent space between it and the gate." Heeta said in a no-nonsense way. "We don't want to give those things something to hide behind." She looked up to check the position of the sun. "We've got a little while before dusk when they start coming out, but there's no sense in taking unnecessary risks."

"Yes ma'am. We can do that. It seems like you're pretty good at this," Michaelson risked a joking tone, nodding at the goopy bodies scattered everywhere.

Heeta and Gale laughed, while Donny's expression didn't change.

"You could say that, Captain." Gale finally said as they led the way into the Wispy Pines Trailer Park Community.

As soon as everyone was inside and the van lowered, blocking the gate again, Michaelson looked around and realized that these people had been completely serious about surviving. They had turned the green areas into gardens that were just barely starting to put up green shoots. There were generators hooked up here and there and cables running up and down the trailer park. They had dug their heels in against these monsters and dug them in hard.

"I've got to say Ms. Heeta, we were sent to rescue whoever was left, but looking around and going off of the scorch marks outside, y'all are more likely to teach us a thing or two," Michaelson said, respectfully. Heeta looked up at Michaelson from her five foot-nothing and smiled. "I believe we can help each other out, Thomas. But I've got Gale coming for her hair appointment in fifteen minutes, so you can either wait or come with me, and we can talk it over while I work."

The captain nodded and smiled at Heeta in agreement. "Yes, ma'am."

Scorpions of the Scorned

By Amie Gibbons

"Please be careful?" Sarah Blakely said, the worry in her voice as obvious over the phone as it'd be if she were right in front of Beau.

Beau Caldwell shook his head, laying his Southern accent on thick as honey in winter. "Why Miss Sarah, ya know I've been shootin' since I was five, and huntin' since I was eight. I'm not fixin' to get into any trouble."

"Stop that," she said. "You know that's not what I meant. Though, you did say you're going with some of Nate's friends from New England, so good luck with that."

Beau snorted. "I knew what you meant. I got all my usual weapons in that respect, too. Father Martin already checked the signs. There aren't any showing up in Georgia, except Atlanta, and we'll be further away from that than you."

"Yeah, but... Chattanooga being this quiet is freaking me out. They were here, and they left... *traces*. We don't know if we can track all the demonic omens."

"I will be on watch for anything. And y'all can call me if anything shows up on tracking. Honestly, I'm more worried about shooting with a couple of Yankees."

Sarah snorted. "Oh, come on," she said in her sweetest tone, "it's not nice to stereotype. I'm sure they'll be *great* shots."

"One's from Boston; the other's from New York City."

Sarah burst out laughing. "Have fun babysitting the city boys out there."

Beau grinned. Sarah'd been on edge and stressed, so knowing he made her laugh for a few seconds made something in his stomach loosen up.

He was far more worried about watching over Sarah than corralling a couple of city boys for Nate's birthday hunting trip. She'd assured him she'd be fine. She had Father Martin, her mom, and her new puppy to keep her from going over the edge unexpectedly again, along with all the spiritual protections the Church could come up with for her. But still... she was vulnerable after what'd happened.

The bar's front door squeaked open, and two of Beau's oldest friends walked in, Nate Jameson slamming the door behind them.

"Watch it, jackass," Judd Branson said, grabbing his buddy around the neck and twisting him into a headlock. "I'm gonna tell your mama you're disrespecting my girl."

"No, that's what I did last night to your girl." Nate broke the headlock, and twisted around Judd, yanking his arm up.

"Please," Judd scoffed. "Scarlet would kick your ass if you tried."

With battle yells, the guys broke into a grappling match just like they had when they were kids.

"Sarah, I gotta go," Beau said.

"Fun starting already?"

"At least the drinking has. These numbskulls are acting like we're in high school and not almost thirty."

"Okay," Sarah said in a tone that reminded him of her mother. "Play nice with the other boys, unless one of them wants to fight. Then kick the other boy's ass. Have fun at school, sweetie."

Beau snorted and hung up. "Y'all done?"

"Dude!" Nate broke off and slapped Beau on the back. Nate the Stringbean had put on some muscle after joining the Army, but he didn't have nothing on Beau's broad shoulders. Sarah said Beau had a farmer boy build. Beau laughed and slammed Nate on the back, knocking him forward.

"Thought the Army taught you how to fight, Stringbean?" Beau said as he and Judd slapped palms and gave a bro hug. "Civilian life making you weak already?"

"Beau, man, where ya been?" Judd asked, going behind the bar. "We're starting this off right. Bourbon."

"I've been working," Beau said, taking a seat at the bar as Nate flipped on the lights. "Not playing behind a bar and kicking out drunks all day."

"I'm offended," Judd said. "I work at night. Not some nine to five chump like you. Come on, son."

Nate took the barstool next to Beau and tapped the bar. "It's my birthday; I want the good stuff."

"You sure you can take that at your age?" Judd asked.

"Don't even fuck with me, man."

"Don't dudes become complete prisses after moving to Northern cities? Especially when they hit thirty? You sure you don't want an appletini or something?"

"I will kick your ass." Nate smirked. "Give me a Manhattan."

"How the *hell* did you just ask for that with a straight face? I can't believe we're still friends."

"Too highbrow for your hole in the wall here?"

"Your Yank friends coming soon, Nate?" Beau drawled.

"Yeah," Nate chuckled as Judd turned around and grabbed a bottle. "That's why we gotta get this out of our systems now. I have to be an adult when they get here."

That didn't sound like the Nate Beau had known since he was seven and helped Nate beat the shit out of a group of other fourth graders pushing and slapping around some of the girls in their class.

"Since when do you act like an adult with friends?" Beau asked.

"Since I work with them," Nate said.

"And?" Beau and Judd asked as one.

"If they can't take their booze, I'm not letting 'em into my hunting cabin," Judd said, shaking up a covered metal cup, then pouring the liquid into an actual Manhattan glass.

"Dude, when did you get fancy?" Beau asked.

"While you were dicking around in Tennessee," Judd said, sliding the drink over the bar to Nate, "I even got a craft cocktails menu. No shit. I get bands in here on weekends, sports on the TVs, and started getting in fru fru craft beers and mixing cocktails. And I'm killing it. The ladies love me, because I make all this fancy shit they see on TV. We got voted one of the best hidden gems in Georgia."

"Now who's prissy?" Nate asked, taking a drink, and doing a double take. "Dude! That's awesome. What... when did you learn how to do this?"

"I don't just run a bar and ring knuckleheads' bells when they get violent up in here. I took a course online, ordered some good stuff, and like I said, killing it." Judd spread his arms out with his wide, shit-eating grin.

Judd had done really well for himself since growing up dirt poor on the edge of town. Went from bartending and sleeping around to owning a successful business. Beau was proud of him. Judd was the friend he'd prayed for the most when they were younger because of his wild, reckless ways, especially with women. Judd had had an actual girlfriend for two years now.

Judd slid Beau a glass of amber liquid across the bar.

"Scotch?" Beau took a sip. It slid down smooth, with a rich, clear flavor that said it was the good stuff.

"Twenty-five-year McCallan," Judd said. "Only the best for my boys."

"It's gonna be hard not to get drunk tonight," Beau said. "This is *good*." Judd gave him a look. "Dude, we're fixing to go hunting tomorrow. Can't do that hung over."

"And the pussy hat goes to Beau," Judd said in an announcer voice as the bar door swung open.

"Excuse you?" a nasally voice that sounded like something out of Gossip Girl said. Beau had never watched it, of course. He'd been studying while his girlfriend at the time was watching it on Netflix.

"Hey cowboy, we're closed for the weekend," Judd said.

"They're my work buddies," Nate said. Beau did a double take as Nate got up. Nate's voice had gone from normal to holding a generic American accent.

Beau checked out the newcomers. While him, Nate, and Judd were wearing typical weekend in the woods clothes of boots, jeans, and flannel over Ts, the two men who'd walked in looked *city*. They wore slacks and button-downs with sneakers that cost more than most people in this town made in a month, and the taller black haired one had a navy sweater tied around his neck like he was a preppy in the nineties.

"This is the bar you were telling us about?" the blonde, short guy said, tone holding that Yankee edge that always made Beau feel like he was gonna need to throw down any second.

"Yeah, it's cool," Nate said, shaking hands with them before locking the door behind them. "These are my friends from way back when. Judd, Beau, this is Trayson and Skylar."

Judd snorted. "Y'all having me on with those clothes and names?"

"The bartender's rude," the dark haired Trayson said with a sniff. "Nathan, I know it's your birthday, but-"

"He's joking around," Beau said smoothly, getting up and shaking hands with the men. "Nate tells me y'all are engineers with Northrup, too. What area?"

"Computers," they both said.

"Mechanical engineer," Beau said.

"And I'm the cocktail engineer. What can I get you, gentlemen?" Judd put a note on the question, making it clear to anyone who knew him he was mocking these guys.

"When in the South, I guess I'll try a mint julep," Trayson said, snapping his fingers. "If you have fresh mint. And put a step on it."

"Snap those fingers at me again, and we're gonna have a problem this weekend," Judd said, throwing his bar towel over his shoulder and leaning over the bar. "Ya got me on that, Yank?"

"Obviously they don't understand the meaning of service here," Trayson said, straightening his sweater.

"This is my friend Judd," Nate said. "He owns this place."

Why did it sound like Nate was justifying being friends with a bartender? Like he wasn't from redneck roots too? He used to be proud of where he came from, like any hardworking Southern man. Maybe he'd been up North too long.

"I'm busting your balls, gentlemen," Judd said, making Beau jerk. Maybe Judd caught the hint of desperation in Nate's voice too, and manners won out over kicking some ass. He really *had* grown up. "I'm the one hosting this weekend. We'll be doing some drinking tonight and hunting tomorrow at my cabin."

"You were serious about hunting?" Skylar said to Nate. "I thought that was a joke since you're from the South."

"No, guys," Nate said. "I said I'd teach you how to shoot. It'll be fun."

They looked like he'd just said playing in a pit of copperheads would be fun.

"Mint Julep," Judd said in a completely flat tone as he slid it across the bar. His brown eyes used to turn near black when they were kids, and he used that tone.

Now his face was blank. So, despite the tone, Beau figured he was okay, just getting pissed at the guys.

"We should head to the cabin soon," Beau said. "Get up there before dark. I got fish fixins."

This weekend was looking less like a hunting trip and more like babysitting by the minute. Maybe the Yanks would loosen up once they got comfortable with the strangers.

"Drinking and shooting?" Skylar asked. "Sounds... very Southern."

"No," Beau said. "You don't shoot after you've been drinking. Any man who knows the first thing about gun safety could tell you that. Anyone's hungover tomorrow, they ain't shooting. Anyone drinks tomorrow, they ain't shooting."

The door busted open, and Beau had his gun out and zeroed in on it before his mind caught up to the reaction. Out of the corner of his eye, Nate had done the same, and he'd bet a hundred rounds of ammo Judd had his gun up too.

Cold flooded the bar, freezing Beau's ears so he barely heard one of the Yanks curse and yell about them having guns out.

Nothing came through the door.

At least, nothing visible.

"Judd," Beau said slowly, "anything weird been happening around town lately?"

"Weird how?"

"People seeing things, animals disappearing, weird weather, anything?"

"It's pretty cold for November down here," Judd said. Beau risked a glance over. His friend had his rifle pointed at the open door. "We got snow two weeks ago. Chickens and pigs have been disappearing. We went on a coyote hunt a few nights ago but couldn't find nothing."

"Chickens and pigs?" Beau asked, the cold seeping into his stomach. "Any strangers in town?"

"Yeah, we've gone tourist, I done told ya," Judd said, voice tighter than a chastity belt. "Bunch of strangers in lately."

"Any... feel wrong to you?"

"How would I know? I don't know what you're talking about."

"Anyone feel evil?" Beau said flatly. "Like you wouldn't let any locals leave with them drunk? Like you had to watch them?"

"What the fuck is wrong with you Southerners!" one of the Yankees screamed. "You're so fucking xenophobic, you try to shoot strangers? Why do you have guns on you already? We're not at the hunting cabin."

Beau glanced over. The hysterics came from Trayson. He was pale and looked like he'd fall over if he wasn't already cowering in the corner.

"Beau?" Nate asked, not putting his gun down either.

"Ghosts, demons, they're as real as we were taught in Sunday school," Beau said. No time to sugarcoat it. "And last month... something real bad happened. A lot of them got out."

"Out of where?" Skylar asked from the sidelines, sounding oddly calm.

"Hell," Beau said. "Some folk opened a door and let them out of Hell. We've been tracking signs of them for the Church since."

"The wind blew the door open, and you think it's demonic activity?" Skylar said, still in that same calm voice. "Why don't we just put the guns down, gentlemen, and look at this like rational men?"

"I locked the door behind y'all," Nate said. "I'm sure of it. I don't know about this demon stuff, but something forced that door open, and it sure as Dixie wasn't the wind."

As though on cue, something flew through the open door, landing with a crash just a few feet from Beau's boots.

A simple brown bag tied with a string lay on the floor, and Beau's blood ran cold. "Nobody touch it," he commanded, tucking his gun away before pulling out his phone. He snapped a picture of it, though the inverted cross carved into the leather told him he already knew what this was.

He texted it to Sarah and called her.

"Sick of guy's weekend already?" she asked.

"Just sent you a picture," Beau said. "Should show up in a moment."

"Okay, just got it," she said, followed by, "What the fuck! Beau, where are you?"

"I'm back home in Townshead, at Judd's bar. That what I think it is?"

"If you mean one of those fucking spell bag things, then yeah!" she snapped. "What happened?"

"Locked door blew open; this thing was thrown in a moment later."

"Shit! Don't touch it. I'm coming."

"It's a six-hour drive," Beau said.

"Five with me driving," Sarah interrupted.

"Shit's going down *now*. Sarah, I need you on the books."

"For what?"

"How to block witchcraft." Beau ground his teeth together. It wasn't Sarah's fault.

"Yeah, that narrows it down," Sarah said, voice high. "Beau, if it's-"

"Pretty sure it is."

"We don't know how to block those kinds of beacons. You have to find the witch who planted it. Destroy her altar or her. Who knows you're there?"

"These friends, my dad, y'all," Beau said.

"And you don't do social media, so it's not like you posted about it there. Duh, who else is there?"

Beau quickly told her.

"Northern snobs, a guy with a birthday, and a bartender," Sarah said. "Only one who's been in town is this Judd guy? You said he was a man whore, right? My money's on him."

"Why now though?"

"To get back at him when he has friends in town? Listen, I'm going to start working on this, at least narrowing it down. Give me his full name, I'll search databases for anything obvious. But Beau, I don't know how you protect yourselves. I... I can't help. The beacon's already *there*."

"We'll head to the church," Beau said. "Call me if you get anything." He hung up. "Judd, buddy, any women pissed off at you lately? More than usual?"

Judd raised his hands. "What the fuck, dude? I'm not twenty-five anymore. I stopped fucking around, and I've been with my girl almost two years. I'm proposing on our anniversary next week. I'm *settled*."

"Fuck," Nate breathed.

"Seconded," Beau said. "Anyone know you're proposing? Any old girlfriends?"

Judd's mouth hung open. He closed it, licking his lips with a slow nod.

The door to the bar slammed shut, and the lights went out, dousing the bar in dim daylight streaming through the windows.

Beau pulled out his gun and marched to the door, pushing on it. His scapular warmed against his skin as electricity shot through him in a warning. "Locked," he said. "Cover your ears." He shot at an angle at the window. The bullet ricocheted off the glass and hit the roof. His bells rang from the blast. "Something's sealing it."

"You're insane," Trayson breathed, visibly shaking when Beau looked back at him. "This whole thing... just insane."

"No arguments here," Beau said. "Judd, any religious iconography here?"

"My Bible," Judd said.

"Get it. Nate?"

"Scapular," Nate said, pulling it out from under his shirt.

Beau nodded. "I got a lot more in my truck but didn't think I'd need them waiting for y'all in the bar."

"I have a cross my mother gave me," Skylar said, pulling out his keys and holding up the tiny silver cross to the light.

"Good," Beau said. "Trayson?"

The man shook his head, eyes wide and searching.

"Beau?" Judd asked.

"Short version," Beau said, "Demons, ghosts, and witches are real. Some witch threw this bag in here to act as a homing beacon. It makes it easier to direct spells at us, might even have some shit in there to attract ghosts to us. I've heard of them being planted to set someone up for possession, but that's a lot more difficult. Whatever kind it is, we need to get out, and now. Judd, what ya got in here?"

"Booze, bar towels, cleaning supplies, toilet paper, mixers." Judd shook his head and snapped his fingers. "The garage. Downstairs. We got all sorts of shit in there."

"Like what?" Nate asked, holding his scapular out and looking around with quick jerks of his head.

"Stuff for the grounds, tools, oil for the lamps when power goes out, and..." Judd pumped his fist in the air. "And fucking fertilizer. The good stuff."

Beau's mouth fell open. "Where is it?"

Judd ran out from behind the bar and shoved a door to a backroom open without a problem. The guys followed him through the storeroom and down the stairs at the back to another door into a garage.

Beau held his phone's flashlight up for light, noting there was no signal. He already knew that it'd be the first thing the witches would cut off when they sealed the place, but he had to check. He hit the garage door opener. Nothing.

"Must've sealed the building in general," Beau said.

Judd ran to the edge of the garage and hauled over a huge bag of fertilizer. "This, some of the oil, and pack it into something. We got the makings of an HME."

"Homemade explosive," Nate said before the Yanks could ask.

"We're going to blast a hole through the wall?" Skylar asked, still with that same oh so reasonable voice. But he had his cross clenched in one hand.

"Yeah, let's go through the wall, backed up by dirt," Judd drawled.

"Garage door," Beau said, looking around. Judd had a pile of two by fours and plywood up against a wall, probably for the back deck he'd been saying needed mending. "Anything to pack it in?"

"Bottles?"

Beau shook his head. "Anything bigger?"

"I got the coffee cans for target practice."

"We still got to set it off," Nate said. "We can prop it up against the garage door with some of the wood over there. And if we pack it tight enough, in the right mixture, yeah, it'll blow a hole through it. But what do we have to set it off?"

"How do we know it will blast a hole through?" Skylar asked. "Your bullet bounced off the window. I've never shot a gun, but I'm betting it should have gone through."

"He's got a point," Beau said.

"Would a bigger blast be more likely to go through that shield or whatever?" Nate asked. "Is it like breaching a wall? You just have to get the blast big enough to get through."

"I don't know," Beau said. "Never had to face witches before. But, it's all we got, so we do it."

"We're gonna need all the oil we can get packed in there for the bomb," Nate said, holding up the obviously near empty jug. "Judd?"

"All I got," Judd said.

Beau looked around, brain whirling. He was the mechanical engineer. He may not know how to make homemade explosives off the top of his head, but he sure as shit could figure out how to set one off.

"I'd kill for some det cord right now," Nate said. "We got so much of that shit in the Army. We blew rocks out of the way to set up that base in Afghanistan with it."

"I believe you," Beau said. "But I don't think you can pray for det cord to appear."

"Booze burns," Judd said. "I got some high proof moonshine. It burns, trust me."

"So, we just make a bomb and hold a lighter under it?" Skylar asked.

Nate glared at him. "If you want to get your ass blown across the room, sure. We need a fuse."

"Bar rags?" Judd asked.

"I don't think that'd do it," Beau said. "Maybe if we had a line of them tied together and soaked through, but there'd be too much smoke, and that'd only be if they were something like cotton. We need something thinner. Judd, any towels here real cotton?"

"How the fuck would I know?" Judd said. "Are cheap bulk towels usually?"

The air weighed down on Beau, heaviness in his heart making him gasp for air.

"Y'all feel that?" Judd asked, looking around.

"Yeah," Beau and Skylar said as one.

Beau crossed himself, praying under his breath to the Lord to protect them. Whatever this presence was, it was the opposite of the Holy Trinity, which meant it could be fought with such.

Bang, bang, bang, echoed off the garage door, loud as a gunshot.

"Fuck!" Trayson yelled.

The three bangs came again, so loud they all pressed their fingers in their ears.

"I'd say that's a yes," Beau growled as it banged again. "Something's close, and it's pissed. We need that alcohol, Judd, and something that can act as a fuse. Nate, get on packing the coffee can."

Nate grabbed one of the empty coffee cans in what was obviously Judd's target practice pile, got the fertilizer and oil, and got to work, flinching with every set of three bangs. Judd ran up the stairs before Beau could tell him not to go alone, vanishing into the dark.

Bang, bang, bang. Bang, bang, bang. Bangbangbang.

If Sarah was right, and this was some scorned woman looking for revenge since the playboy of Townshead was settling down with someone, then Judd was the one person that shouldn't be left alone.

Beau prayed under his breath, running to the stairs. Judd thundered back down, a jar of clear liquid without a label in his hands.

"My homemade moonshine," Judd yelled over the banging. "About a hundred-eighty proof."

Beau nodded, pulling his shirts' necks around to check the tags. Both blends. He went around checking the other guys' tags to see if there was something that'd burn. All mixes of stuff, but nothing that was just cotton. Their jeans and slacks obviously weren't.

Beau looked down at his boots. His usual footwear, with the nylon laces, meant to be more durable than... than cotton ones!

The banging kept up, bombarding them. They wouldn't hear it if a whole coven of witches was upstairs and coming for them, but something told Beau whoever was doing this wasn't looking to get into it face to face. That she'd rather fight her battles from a safe distance. If it was a girl...

Beau shook his head. *Fuck that. You're fighting for your life; you don't worry about pounding on a girl. You don't fight fair, and you take the bitch down.* Nate and Judd were wearing boots similar to his, sturdy hiking boots with tough, durable nylon laces, he was sure of it.

But sneakers?

"Shoes!" Beau yelled over the pounding.

Skylar mouthed, "Why?"

Beau marched over to him, shoving him on his ass as gently as he could while still getting the man down. He said, "Sorry," as he yanked the sneakers off, and felt the laces as he undid them.

"Cotton!" he yelled, pulling the laces out quick as he could. "Thanks!" he said to Skylar and ran them to Judd, who already had the lid off.

Beau tied the edges in a cherry knot and pushed the laces into the jar. They were fat, white cotton ones. If anything was going to burn, it'd be them.

The banging cut off as suddenly as it'd started. Beau crossed himself, ears ringing in the silence.

"What..." Trayson whispered.

"Don't know," Beau said. "Nate?"

"Working on it!" Nate said. "Can't guarantee a shoelace will set this thing off."

"Pack it in tight as you can," Beau said. "You get that fertilizer pressurized enough, it won't take too much heat to set it off."

"Fuck you! I know that!" Nate growled under his breath. "I didn't survive six years and two tours in Afghanistan to get killed by some magic bitch. I got Maddie and the kids at home."

"Yeah, and we're going to get you back to them. Guys, anything you can think of for this?"

The stench of rotting meat blew through the garage, and Beau gagged, the others right behind him. Skylar turned and threw up, the puke adding to the noxious stench.

"Is that some spell?" Judd coughed and breathed through his hand over his mouth, pulling off his overshirt and wrapping it around his face in a makeshift mask.

The same icy cold Beau'd felt when the hex bag flew into the bar invaded him, freezing him down to his soul.

Trayson opened his mouth and bent over like he was about to puke.

Beau handed the jar of booze back to Judd, rushing to the man's side. Trayson reared up, and Beau saw it a second too late.

Trayson's empty, fully dilated eyes bore into Beau's as he shoved a handheld shovel into Beau's middle.

Beau doubled over and fell to his side, curling up, the dull pain telling him the trowel hadn't been sharp enough to slice into him, but it'd been bad. There'd been enough power in that swing to bruise down to his guts.

Trayson whirled, dropping the trowel and lunging to the edge of the garage, grabbing a chainsaw.

Beau struggled to his feet. "Power's out," he grunted.

Trayson grinned, too wide for his face, taking it over with that humorless mocking look that only one being Beau could think of could pull off.

"He's possessed," Beau said. "The demon knocking got him."

The demon wearing Trayson locked his eyes on Beau, and the chainsaw roared to life in his hands, the cord dangling in midair.

The guys screamed and scattered as Trayson lunged with the demonically charged chainsaw. Beau looked over at Skylar, taking his scapular off from around his neck and holding it up. Skylar caught on and took off his cross, holding it up too.

They rushed the demon from behind, slamming him to the ground, Beau taking out his knees as Skylar swung his saw-wielding arm into the wall. The saw ground to a stop the moment the demon dropped it.

The demon faceplanted with Beau on his legs. Beau pushed his scapular to the back of the damned thing's neck, praying. It shrieked with a high, unholy voice, the rotting meat stench spilling around them.

Nate and Judd ran from opposite ends. Nate slammed down on the possessed man's back, pulling his arms back and holding him in an elbow lock.

"It's a demon," Beau snapped. "You ain't gonna be able to hold him."

"Demon?" Judd said as Trayson bucked under Nate. Nate scrambled to keep his hold on the thing. "Fuck me, man. No girl could be this cr... Never mind. They totally could."

"Anything to tie him up with?" Nate grunted, the effort of holding the demon obviously wearing on him.

Beau knew. He'd wrestled with his possessed friend last September, and she'd been easily twice as strong as him. The only advantage Nate had right now was leverage, and that'd go out the window if the demon managed to buck him off.

"Duct tape," Judd said, running across the garage, grabbing a giant roll off its hook on the wall.

"Will that hold it?" Skylar asked, blinking over and over again as Judd ran back, like that'd clear the unholy scene in front of him away.

"Not for long," Beau said, grabbing the edge of the tape and winding it around the demon's hands. "I got holy water in my truck though. Nate, I got him. Finish that bomb."

Nate let the wriggling demon go, and Judd sat on the back of the fucking thing's knees. It wouldn't stop a demon. It could break every bone in Trayson's body and keep the loose bag of bones and torn tendons moving, but even demons had their limits when it came to physics, and this fucker wasn't getting up from this position without a lot of effort.

Beau twined the duct tape around Trayson's arms all the way up to his elbows, probably damaging Trayson's shoulders, but it was better than being a demon's bitch. Beau ripped off the edge with his teeth, cursing leaving his knife in the truck as he secured the edge. He turned, keeping his weight firmly on Trayson's knees, and grabbed the man's feet, wrapping them from shoes to knees.

"How's the bomb coming?" Beau called, easing off the demon.

"I think… No, I can smash in some more. More's better; more pressure."

"You ever done this?"

"Bombs? Yes. But we always had at least det cord, and usually C4. This… this is my redneck coming out."

"We all got it, buddy," Judd said. "The laces are soaked."

"Okay," Beau said. "We'll tape the canister to the garage door, and have the plywood over it, direct the blast as much as possible."

"You're all going to die," Trayson cackled under him, his voice light and high, like a woman's.

"We talking to the demon in there, or the witch?" Beau asked.

"What do you think, handsome?" he purred.

"That's… disturbing," Skylar said.

"Demon," Beau said, "I know you're a demon. How does it feel to be some puny human's bitch? You going to take that from her? Letting a pathetic human you would wipe off your shoes boss you around like that?"

Neither Trayson, nor the things riding shotgun in his soul, said a word.

Beau risked a glance to the side where the guys secured the can with tape and were taping plywood to the garage door. Judd propped it all up with a few of the two by fours. Beau nodded, that'd help with a little extra stability.

They'd gotten one end of the lace secured in the coffee can through what looked like a poked-out hole in the bottom, and dragged the jar back slowly, letting the sloshing shoelaces pull out on their own.

"No," Beau said as the last bit came out and Judd lowered it to the ground. "We should have it stretched between the can and something else, so it's in the air. It'll burn better with oxygen on all sides."

They looked around.

"The hooks," Judd said, pointing behind Beau and his prisoner. "We tie one end to a hook." He did it, and Beau got off Trayson, grabbing him by his bound legs and hauling him back across the floor.

"Y'all, I'd recommend praying," Beau said as Judd pulled a lighter from his pocket. He crossed himself. The demon possessed man on the ground growled and spit on Beau's boots.

"Shouldn't we have him next to the explosion?" Nate asked. "It might not kill him, but it-"

"No," Beau said. "Nate, your friend's still in there. We're looking at an exorcism if this thing is able to stay after we break the witch's control over it, but he can still be saved."

Judd flicked the lighter, and they pulled Trayson's prone body up the short steps to the door and through it. Beau kept it open a crack to watch the flame. It crept along the shoelace, so slight he only saw it flicker here and there on fatter parts of the laces and where he'd tied the two together.

The slight smoke and heavy corn scent of good ol' fashioned backyard brew hit Beau's nose, and the flame lit up bright at the knot just under the coffee can.

Beau slammed the door shut, scrambling up a few stairs to where Judd and Nate held tight to Trayson's tied up body to keep him from sliding down.

Boom.

The blast shook the door and rang Beau's bell, making him see stars as his right ear buzzed. His left ear was a complete blank, and he tilted to the side as he lurched forward to get the door.

The smoke rushed in, sending them all into coughing fits. Beau's eyes burned as he ran to the fiery mass, and he teared up. It could've been from the smoke or relief. He didn't really give a damn, because a hole big enough for even him to get through was in the aluminum door.

"It's open!" he yelled after a quick cough, climbing out.

Beau stayed low, eyeing the sprawling land behind the bar leading to the lake. His left ear didn't seem to be working, and his right felt like it was hearing underwater. If anything wanted to sneak up on him, it could. His truck sat in the parking lot just to the left, along with Judd's truck, and what must've been the Yanks' rental car.

Beau pulled his gun again and ran to his truck, keeping low to the ground and struggling to stay straight with his balance so off. A witch wanting vengeance from a safe distance might still be watching what she'd wrought from the outside, and she would've noticed that blast.

Beau got to his truck, unlocking the back quickly to keep from having to jump over it and expose himself more. He grabbed his bugout bag and ran low back to the guys standing next to the garage.

Trayson lay in the garage on the other side of the hole, a smile too wide to be natural stretching his face.

"Get down," Beau hissed. "The witch could be nearby."

"We're out," Skylar whispered as he and the guys squatted down. "Now what?"

Beau froze. *Now what?* He'd been so focused on getting out of the trap, he couldn't remember what to do now.

"Drag him through." Beau jerked his chin over towards the hole in the door. "We'll put him in my truck with binding agents and take him to the church."

"Does the Church even do exorcisms anymore?" Skylar said. "There hasn't been one approved in the U.S. in…"

"Years," Beau said. "Not officially. They can't risk the press in America. But now? The Church is training exorcists again.

They aren't making it public, because most westerners wouldn't believe these days that demons exist."

"Or there'd be some kind of group arguing for the ethical treatment of demons, and how they had a right to possess people," Judd said, the joke falling flat.

Beau crossed himself, eyes constantly scanning the world around them, his nerves stretched tight. He'd faced one demon. It'd taken a group of them, including a priest, to exorcise it, and that was with Sarah fighting from within. Someone who didn't *know* to fight, who probably didn't realize when he'd been taken over, and then was just asleep in his mind, wouldn't stand a chance.

This wasn't a demon driving people subtly towards evil to damn their souls. This was a demon planted in someone to do evil through his body. The first was far worse in the long run, but a demon doing a witch's bidding was more dangerous in the short run.

"We should be able to save him if we can destroy whatever the witch is using to direct the demon," Beau said, mind dragging something up from the depths of his memory. "If I remember correctly, it's usually a dark altar with the demon's name or something of his tying him to the witch."

"So, we find a crazy witch's altar, which could be anywhere, and destroy it, cool," Judd drawled, yanking out his phone.

"Easier than exorcising a demon," Beau said.

Judd looked at him, then his expression softened. "Baby," he said into the phone, "are you okay?"

She said something and Judd sighed, saying, "Sorry, Scarlet. I'm in trouble, and I was thinking whoever it was went after you. Stay there, okay? Stay in public. I'll explain later."

He hung up, flinching. "How am I going to explain this to her?"

"Live now, lie later," Nate said. "Beau, any way to track a witch?"

Beau shook his head. "You'd have to have powers yourself, and... Judd, names of women who'd be capable of this?"

"I'm supposed to pick one?" Judd asked, continuously scanning their surroundings just like Beau.

"No. Tell me all who come to mind."

Judd closed his eyes. "Off the top of my head, the crazies were Liz McBryde, Stephanie Harrison, and Shelly Jory."

Beau nodded and pulled out his phone, calling Sarah. He gave her the names and asked her to pull up background checks, still scanning around them.

The air was still, the earth deathly quiet after the boom of the explosion. The fire licking the edges of the garage door had quickly burned themselves out without real fuel to keep going, and lightly popped in the background.

Judd and Nate looked around, guns up, while Skylar kept an eye on Trayson.

"Found them," Sarah said after a beat. Beau turned on the speaker. "Oh, I think we got a winner. This Stephanie girl has a restraining order against her... filed by, I'm guessing her ex-fiancé from what it says in the affidavit, and it was just filed last month."

"Knew that bitch was crazy," Judd muttered.

Beau shook his head. "I don't think it's her. Sounds like she had someone else to go crazy over."

"One sec," Sarah said, the keyboard clicking in the background. "Okay, according to her Instagram, she's smashed in New Orleans, and has been for the past few days. Can't be her, unless she planned on this and posted pictures to say they went up now when they were posted a bit ago. Nah, she's got a few girlfriends with her, and one just posted a pic of all of them trying on masks."

"You found that in like two minutes," Nate said. "Are you a hacker?"

Sarah and Beau laughed.

"Not even close," Sarah said. "I can barely make Excel work. I'm just looking through databases. You'd be surprised how easy this stuff is to find if you have someone's name and approximately where they live. Speaking of, I've got addresses for the other two."

She gave them, and Judd put them into his phone.

"Shelly still lives in the same place," Judd said as Beau hung up with Sarah.

"Try her first?" Beau said.

They hauled Trayson into the back of Judd's truck, secured him with rope, holy water and more duct tape, and Beau sat in the back with his gun drawn, scanning their surroundings as the guys got in the cab and fired up the truck.

It sputtered and died.

Judd jumped out.

"I just gave her a full checkup," he said. "She was purring this morning."

"Witch," Beau said, jumping down as the guys piled out. "At least that's some good news."

"What is?" Nate asked.

"If she's hexing it, she's gotta be close enough to do it, and she'd have to have her altar with her too. Assuming she needs it to work this level of magic."

"Why are we assuming that?" Skylar asked.

"It's a feeling," Beau said, scanning the woods around them. "This doesn't feel like a pro. It's too sloppy."

He pulled a cross necklace out of his bugout bag and slung it over his head to lay with his scapular, then stuffed his rosary beads in his pocket, and held his pack out in front of them. "Guns, knives, scapulars, holy water, rosary beads, my Bible, crosses, and other stuff I can't remember right now."

"I can't believe I'm about to say this," Judd said. "Y'all arm up. We're going on a witch hunt."

Skylar was given a crash course in use of a Glock, told to keep Trayson down, and to shoot anyone who came in. We left them with plenty of bottles of holy water and crosses in the maintenance shed.

Judd, Nate, and Beau armed up with some more stuff from the maintenance shed, then slogged to the line of woods just behind the bar, moving quieter than Beau ever had while hunting, but then again, they were after much more dangerous prey today.

With the rain in these parts, they figured the witch had to keep her altar inside, like a car or something with protection from the elements. There was only one other structure remotely close to the bar, Judd's Aunt May's trailer that had sat abandoned since she'd died a few months ago.

Fire rushed past Beau's head a second after he spotted the clearing with the trailer, and he hit the ground, scrambling behind a thick tree on instinct, yelling at the others. They dropped and took cover before he was done screaming a warning.

A woman cackled. Not laughed. *Cackled.*

"Shelly," Judd hissed. "Shelly!" he yelled after a moment. "Shelly, is that you?"

The witch cackled again, a scornful sound. "Knowing my name won't help you. I'm not a demon."

"No!" Beau yelled. "But you called one. It's going to be mad at you."

She laughed a more normal laugh, like she honestly thought that was funny. "He's my pet. I conjured him. I have him on a leash. I can make him do anything."

"A demon isn't a pet!" Beau's heart raced. He was right about this being some amateur. "It's a *fallen angel*, with all the power that comes with. You don't have an Army dog ready to follow commands. You have an angry being with nothing but contempt for humans and packing about a thousand times the punch of one of us, on a very thin leash. It will come after you once it breaks free. Let us help you."

The tree against Beau's back crackled, and he combat rolled behind another as the first went up in flames.

"I don't like mansplaining," Shelly said deadpan. "Nothing against y'all, you're free to leave. Judd's the only one who needs a lesson here."

"Shelly," Nate called, "it's Nate. You know me and Beau. We all went to high school together. I'm telling you, this isn't a game. This isn't getting back at an ex. This isn't even life and death. The whole demons being fallen angels thing is real, and you're risking your soul. Let us destroy your altar, get that thing away from us, and take you to someone who can help."

She answered with another fireball that sailed through the trees and crashed on the wet grass near Judd's truck.

Beau peeked around the tree. She was a young woman, his age at the most, with dyed blonde hair and a face like a milkmaid, complete with round cheeks and bright blue eyes. She stood in the doorway of the trailer, arms crossed over her chest, looking like any other Southern girl shouting at rowdy boys, crazy and not at all worried.

She really had no clue what she'd done.

"Fuck this," Nate whispered, pulling up his gun and ducking out from behind his tree, keeping low and shooting.

Beau covered his ears in time, but the blasts still made them ping. What was Nate trying to do? The bullets bounced off the air in front of Shelly and the trailer.

"Shit," Nate hissed.

"What were you going to do?" Beau whispered. "Kill her?"

"I was trying to scare her away."

Beau looked between his friends and the trailer. Most trailers like that had backdoors.

He pulled out his phone and texted his friends he was going around back, and they should keep shooting, keep her distracted.

Nate and Judd gave him quick nods after glancing at their phones. Beau dropped to his belly, squirming back to the next bunch of trees without getting above the undergrowth between him and the witch.

Bullets flew through the air as loud as anything, but Beau's ears were numb to it by now. He stood once he was out of sight of the clearing, and ran through the woods in a wide arc, coming up behind the trailer.

The witch's altar stood on the trailer's makeshift patio. It had an awning over it and drop-down edges on the sides, leaving the front covered by a mosquito net.

The bullets rang out on the other side of the trailer, and Beau's stomach dropped. That shield was probably harder to break through than the best backstop, but he was still downrange from shooting.

It's a battle, not a hunting trip or a day at the range, he reminded himself, grabbing a thick rock and throwing it at the altar as hard as he could.

It bounced off the back, and Beau nodded. He'd been expecting as much. Theoretically, if they pounded the shield with enough force, it'd eventually break down, because nothing had infinite energy. But the guys would run out of bullets soon, and they had to get this done before the demon broke free and took Skylar.

The bullets still flew, but only here and there, and Nate screamed from his cover, trying to talk sense into Shelly.

Beau inched forward, keeping low as he could on his feet. If the witch turned around in the doorway, she'd see him if he was too high up, still could probably. Beau reached the tented structure and slowly raised a finger, pushing it forward. It hit mosquito net and he breathed a sigh of relief.

Zzzzzzz, sang out. Beau yelped, falling on his ass as the fingers that hit the shield burned.

The witch screamed something. Beau jumped to his feet, going into a dead run faster than he had since he'd been a high school wide receiver, slicing between trees as zapping filled the air.

He dropped to his knees, gasping air as the trees blocked whatever the witch was throwing his way now, pulled out his phone, and texted one word to Judd.

Napalm.

They hadn't used Styrofoam dunked in gasoline to burn shit since they were kids, but Judd'd had both in the maintenance shed and brought them in his backpack. Maybe it'd work against this shield.

"Fuck!" echoed through the woods a moment later.

Beau's blood ran cold, and his zapped fingers went numb.

"No! Nate, get her out of here!" Judd yelled.

The witch let out a scream that made the hairs on Beau's body stand straight up. The wail of a broken and cursed woman with nothing left to lose or to live for.

He lurched to his feet just in time to see Shelly running full out towards the bar's parking lot to a red SUV that hadn't been there before.

Red hair swished in the sunlight as a tall woman jumped out of the SUV, and Beau ran for the witch before he realized what he was doing.

Nate and Judd jumped out of their cover and ran as the witch passed them, screaming war cries as they went.

Judd's girlfriend Scarlet screamed and ducked back into the SUV, leaving her back vulnerable and open.

Fire shot from Shelly's hand, and Scarlet dropped, rolling to the side in a move similar to Beau's combat roll, something black and long secured against her chest. She popped up and whipped the sawed-off shotgun she must've grabbed from the vehicle, pointing it directly at the witch.

She didn't so much as blink at the obvious magic going on in front of her face.

"I'm doing you a favor," Shelly snarled as she slowed to a walk, her sweet looking face twisted with hatred as fire grew in her hands. "He's-"

"Bitch, please," Scarlet snapped, racking the shotgun and shooting Shelly in the chest.

The witch flew backwards, her shield obviously taking the brunt of the hit.

Shield!

She had two shields going now!

Beau turned and ran for the trailer as screams and shots echoed behind him. He slammed into the mosquito net covered doorway with his shoulder at full speed.

His arm, shoulder, and head screamed and burned like he'd run into a solid wall of fire...

But the air gave, and he fell into the tent, flopping against the heavy wooden altar. He grabbed the long table with his good hand and heaved with everything he had in him as he stood, pouring the pain into action, and flipped it over, sending bowls, candles, cloths, and only God knew what else, crashing to the ground.

A candle flipped into the side of the tent, and it went up like an inferno.

Beau backed out quickly. He half jogged, half limped back to the parking lot, every muscle on his right side burning or numb even though it all looked normal. Shelly sat on the gravel with her hands up, glaring at the people and guns surrounding her. She gasped, eyes shifting over their heads as her glare melted into a look of pure horror.

Beau followed her gaze.

Skylar was at the edge of the lot, his mouth hanging open. A smear hung over him, making the air sour and marking it with evil so pure only the truly blind to the supernatural wouldn't feel it.

Beau crossed himself as the smear rushed across the parking lot and dropped next to Shelly. Pulling off his cross and throwing it over her head, grabbing her as he prayed to God to save her, protect her long enough to give her a chance at redemption.

He didn't dare look, just kept hold of the shaking girl, staring into her eyes as he prayed until the smear on reality dissipated.

The girl's mouth worked, and Beau nodded as he stood up.

He had to have been protecting Shelly for a while, because Skylar and Trayson were out in the parking lot, and the others had backed up and put away their guns at some point.

"I... I didn't know," Shelly choked out.

Beau shook his head. "Doesn't matter. You called it. You promised it something, and it wants to collect."

She burst into tears, saying over and over again that she didn't know.

Beau stood. "We need to get her to the Church."

Scarlet raised a thin red eyebrow at him, her brown eyes sharp and angry behind her glasses as she and Judd held each other.

"Her soul is damned," Beau said. Shelly sobbed, a short, soul wrenching sound. "She was an angry girl who was taken advantage of by a demon looking for the weak and broken. She at least deserves a chance to work for her salvation."

Scarlet's glare melted, and she turned into Judd's arms. He hugged her close, his girl so tall any one of them could've held her like that without needing to bend over.

"I agree," Trayson rasped.

Heads snapped around to look at him.

He shook his head, eyes holding a fear Beau recognized all too well. "That... thing." Trayson shook his head and licked his lips. "I never believed in Hell. I do now, and no one deserves that."

He met Beau's eyes, and they nodded together.

Trayson didn't want someone to go through what he went through, even the person who'd set him up for it in the first place. That was something to respect.

"Okay," Judd said. "Y'all take her, but I gotta do this now."

He dropped to one knee and pulled a box out of his jean's pocket. Scarlet's eyes popped, and her mouth fell open.

"I was gonna do this all fancy on our anniversary, like bar full of flowers, and your friends and family singing 'Redneck Woman,' because that's your favorite song. But I can't think of a more perfect time than this, because you saved my bacon, and you are fucking hot with a gun."

He opened the box with a click. "Scarlet Hoyt, love of my life, woman I never want to settle down with, but I want to go on every adventure with until we're worm food, will you be my wife?"

She made a small sound, then grabbed his free hand, pulling him to his feet and kissing him deep enough to make Beau blush.

She grinned and slung her arms around her man's neck. "You bet your redneck, crazy, roadhouse ass I will."

Hell, Hath No Fury

By Michael K. Falciani

It was a hot summer night in Alabama when I found out demons were real.

I should have known—that whole week was riddled with problems. First world problems, Dec would say. Dec, short for Decland—that's my boyfriend, or ex-boyfriend. I'm not rightly sure, since I break up with him every other week. Not his fault, mind you. He loves me proper, like a man should. I'm the crazy one. Still, can't find no peace around him—but that's a story for another time.

Like I said, the day started with problems. I flew home to Alabama to see my daddy in Mobile. I needed a place to think. Can't gather my thoughts to save my life in San Francisco. Everybody's in a rush all the time, and everything's a competition.

It's all, "My daughter is the first chair for the piccolo in the middle school orchestra." Or it's, "My son just made the varsity football team, and he's only 14 years old."

I mean, whoopty do, right? So, your daughter beat out the one other piccolo player in school? Did you know your husband's sleeping with that piccolo tutor you pay for? She told her hairdresser, so now it's all over town.

You say your son made the varsity football team? Course he did. We all know his daddy is a former NFL tight end. Well, all of us cept your husband.

Lord howdy those people drive me insane. I had to get otta there.

I'm Maria, by the way. Maria Addison Donnelli. Used to be Maria Shank, until I had enough of being ignored by my now ex-husband. He was a looker, I'll give him that, but Lord Jesus, a more arrogant man I've never met. Good riddance to him.

Anyway, back to the demons.

Now, I'm a god-fearing woman, always have been. I sleep with the good book right next to me every night. I read from it, too. I'm not just one of those pretenders who goes around spouting the word of God like they are one of his disciples back in the days of fire and brimstone. I try to walk the walk, if you take my meaning.

Still, nothing in that book prepared me for what I saw last night.

I apologize, here I am starting at the end of the story when I reckon, I should bring you up to speed. I warn you though, best fasten your seatbelt, because it's a hell of a ride.

On my third day home, I got word one of my old high school friends, Jeanna, had lost her parents. She was living up in Coffeeville, some eighty miles north of Mobile.

Coffeeville was a small town, so small there wasn't a single traffic light. Hell, you had to drive nearly an hour to get to the nearest Piggly Wiggly. Fewer than four hundred people lived here now, as times were tough. Despite that, there were three churches and two Dollar Stores within walking distance. That might seem excessive, but many folks here were poor and found comfort in the house of the Lord, Jesus Christ.

"Go visit your friend," my daddy said to me, waving me off with a smile. After fifty years of living in Mobile, he still speaks with an Italian accent. He emigrated here from Rome back in the sixties. He's lived here ever since. Used to own a chain of restaurants up and down Mobile. I spent my entire life growing up in them. Good food and good company, he used to say.

He took every Sunday off though. Called it, "family time." That's my daddy for you.

On my drive to Coffeeville, I heard my phone vibrate.

Decland

I hate to admit this, but my heart does a little flip in my chest every time he calls. He's the best man, outside my daddy, I've ever known. You know those great guys you see on Netflix or Amazon Prime, the ones you know are going to end up with the girl in the end because of how great they are? He's like that, only better, because he's real.

"Hello," I answered, knowing exactly what he was gonna say.

"How's the most beautiful girl on the planet?" he asked.

You see what I mean?

"Thank you for saying that, but you know it's not true," I say back, trying not to gush.

I hear him laugh on the other end. "A blind man could sense your beauty, my love."

"What do you want?" I ask, before he turned my good sense into mush.

"Why did you up and leave?" he asked. "I mean, I had to contact your work to find out what happened to you."

"I needed to get out of town," I answered, a bit too defensively. "I just need a few days away from…everything."

"You mean away from me," he said, reading my thoughts.

"I don't know what you see in me," I tell him for the millionth time. "I keep telling you; I'm no good for you."

He laughed again. It's irritating how nothing gets him down.

"Think what you want Alabama, but I'm going to marry you as soon as you figure your life out."

"No, you're not," I practically shouted. "I'm never getting married again."

"Ok," he replied affably. "We'll just live together for the rest of our lives. That's perfectly fine with me."

He's so infuriating.

"What are you doing anyway? Your dad said you left town?"

"You called my father?" I asked, more than a little annoyed.

"Well, you don't pick up your phone half the time, and when you do, you're Miss Grumpy Pants, so yes, I called your dad. We had a good talk."

"Maybe you can call him back and ask him where I went!" I yelled, growing angry. "Stop calling me. We are done!"

"Will you calm…"

I pushed the end call button before he could say more.

Yes, I'm temperamental, but I'm never going to be stuck in a relationship with another person again. I'd be lying if I said there weren't times when I wanted to be with Decland. Other times…I just don't understand what he sees in me. I'm a simple girl. I'm an assistant manager of the local grocery outlet, nobody of importance. Decland, he's this big shot college professor, who teaches ancient history over at the university where the college girls all *swoon* over him.

One day I'm at work, and he just walks up to me out of the blue and says, "You have the face of Aphrodite," and gives me this beautiful smile, full of kindness.

Of course, I thought he said, 'Hermaphrodite,' so I cold-cocked him in the jaw.

As he's lying there on the ground, a big hunk of top sirloin on his face, he's laughing himself silly. I knew he was a good fit for me.

I put him out of my mind, once I got close to my destination.

I got off the interstate and turned onto highway 69. A quarter mile later, I took a left on Hickory and pulled into the second house on the right. I got out of my car and heard the front door of the house swing open.

A woman of color, medium sized in height and build, came outside and gave me a bear hug. Jeanna had been my best friend since high school. I hadn't seen her in over ten years. She had a few more wrinkles than I remembered and had become a bit weightier, but her dark eyes were the same.

"God, it's been too long girl," she said to me, stepping back and taking a look. She shook her head and smiled. "How do you do it Maria? You haven't aged at all. Still the same dark-haired beauty you were in school. You don't look a day over thirty."

"I'm forty-four love, same as you," I responded. "But thank you for saying that."

Clasping her hand tightly in mine, I dropped my voice. "I am sorry to hear about your folks. They were good people, always kind to me."

Jeanna glanced around and took me by the hand. "Best you come inside. We've got a few things to discuss. I'll send one of the boys out to fetch your things."

I was led into the living room and sat on a second-hand couch of brown suede. It was comfortable enough, though it smelled of cigarettes. I met Jeanna's two sons, Matt and Jason, neither of whom took after their mother. Both were lighter of skin on account of their daddy, and both looked to be in their early twenties. The older of the two, Matt, carried in my duffle bag, while Jason handed me a glass of ice-cold sweet tea.

"Thank you," I said, watching him sit on his chair, polishing a shotgun. He glanced from time to time at a green camouflage walkie talkie laying upright on the table.

Matt dropped the bag on the floor, took out a six-inch hunting knife and began to sharpen it.

"Ya'll expecten a war?" I joked, grinning at them both.

Neither smiled back. They just looked up at their momma.

"I'm sorry Maria, don't mind them," Jeanna said, lighting a Camel. "They're just worried about their sister."

"Sierra?" I guessed, trying to remember her name. "She's got to be, what? Ten by now?"

"Eleven last Sunday," Jeanna corrected, exhaling smoke out the side of her mouth.

"Why the concern?" I asked, curious.

All three looked at me without speaking. After a moment, the boys went back to their weapons while Jeanna leaned forward.

"Well, you've come to the heart of the matter. The boys and I didn't want to involve anyone else, but you came all the way up here from Mobile, and I could use the help."

"You know I'll do whatever I can."

I saw Jeanna tense up as she took another drag of her cigarette.

"You should go," said a deep voice. I was shocked to hear it come from Matt, as he was lean and wiry and slighter of build.

"We need her," argued Jason, frowning at his brother.

"We talked about this," Jeanna snapped, looking at both of them. "It's her choice. She can leave or stay, but I will not lose help, when we can use it."

"Is Sierra ok?" I asked, starting to worry.

"She's fine," Jeanna answered, looking weary. "Tell her," she said, nodding to Matt. "Tell her everything."

The older child nodded, while continuing to sharpen his knife.

"It started a week ago," he began. "A new preacher came to town, Matthias."

"There's a fourth church now?" I asked, surprised.

"I wouldn't say that," Jason snorted.

Jeanna swatted him on the leg. "Hush now, let your brother talk."

"Matthias brought two followers with him," Matt continued, "a man and a woman. Went to the town hall last Thursday and were awarded rights to start their services the very next day."

Matt paused, licking his lips. "I saw the woman from a ways off. Something about her, it was, I don't know, magnetic, like I was drawn to her."

I took a drink of sweet tea from my glass. It felt like heaven on the way down my throat. "Nothing wrong with being drawn to an attractive woman," I said. "Your mother turned more than a few heads in her day."

Matt looked down, and blushed. "I don't much care for women," he muttered.

Feeling like an idiot, I reached out and touched his hand. "I'm sorry Matt, I forgot."

"S'ok," he shrugged. "It don't matter. We have other concerns."

"Keep going," Jeanna said, nodding at him.

Matt took a deep breath and continued. "Ain't right what I felt toward her, but it was nothin compared to Jason's reaction. He damn near ran across the road trying to get to her."

Jason, the younger, stockier brother, was nodding in affirmation. "I never felt anything like it before," he said. "If Matt hadn't clamped on to me, lord knows what would have happened."

I took another drink and set the tea on the coffee table. "I still don't see the problem boys."

"You will," Jason said quietly.

Setting aside his knife, Matt continued. "At first we didn't think much of it. Hormones runnin' wild and such. On Sunday, after folks attended service at the new church, people started to go missing."

"What do you mean, they went missing?" I asked.

"He means they're dead," Jason cut in harshly.

"Dammit Jay, we don't know that," Jeanna snapped, looking at her younger son angrily.

"Sierra said…"

"I don't give a rat's ass what she said," Jeanna continued. "They may still be alive!"

"Calm down the both of you," Matt ordered, looking at them in frustration. "We don't know anything for certain."

He turned and stared at me. "That's why we need you."

I frowned at Jeanna. I didn't understand a lick of what was going on. "What do you need me for?"

Matt sighed. "She's never going to believe us," he muttered again.

"Just tell her," Jeanna insisted. "She's smarter than all of us put together."

Matt scratched at his chin and shook his head. "We think the followers with Matthias are some kind of supernatural beings."

The house went quiet for ten of the longest seconds of my life.

"Ya'll are messing with me," I laughed, looking straight at Jeanna.

"I know it sounds crazy," she answered, the smoke from her cigarette dancing in the air in front of her. "But hear the boys out."

"You know how I went crazy with lust when I saw that girl?" Jason asked, putting aside his gun. "Sierra says that Widow Pickens had that same look on her face when she was talking to the man Matthias brought with him."

"That doesn't mean…"

"Widow Pickens is ninety-eight years old," Jeanna cut in. "She hasn't lusted after a man in nearly a half century. When she saw him, it was like her hoo-ha had been slapped by a wet sponge! Sierra said she damn near jumped his bones at the service."

"She's one of the folks that's come up missing," Jason chimed in. "No one's seen her since Sunday."

I looked carefully at each. All three were deadly serious. I took another drink of sweet tea, swirling the information in my mind.

"Sierra?" I asked.

It was Matt who answered. "Sierra's only eleven years old. She—well, she hasn't gone through puberty yet. I figured she'd have the best chance at resisting Matthias's followers."

"So far it has worked," Matt continued. "She's outside the church now, hiding in a tree with her walkie talkie, giving us updates."

I exhaled deeply. "Let's say I believe you for a second," I offered. "What is it you want me to do?"

"Well," Jeanna said, taking a last drag of her cigarette, "I thought, you being so smart and all, you might know something about this stuff. Didn't you ever hear about this in Sunday School or anything?"

The crazy thing was, I *had* heard about this kind of thing, though it hadn't been at Sunday School.

"Well shoot," I swore under my breath.

"What's the matter?" Jeanna asked.

I shook my head, annoyed as all get out. "I don't know much myself, but…"

They all looked at me, waiting to hear what I was going to say.

"I know someone who does."

Jeanna leaned her head forward. "Who is it?"

Lord Jesus I did not want to call him back, not for this. "Well, Christ in a handbasket," I snapped, annoyed as all get out. "I must love you girl—I wouldn't call for anyone else."

I whipped out my phone and pressed Decland's number. As I clicked the speaker button and set the phone down on the arm of the couch, he answered.

"I was just thinking about you, beautiful," I heard his voice say sarcastically. "Still mad at me for loving you?"

"Decland, shut up," I hissed, looking at Jeanna. "I have you on speaker, and I need your help."

There was a moment of silence on the other end. "Why am I on speaker? Who's in the room with you?"

Sweat began to drip down my face. "I'm with my friend Jeanna, and her two sons Matt and Jason."

"Ahh, the infamous Jeanna," he replied in his suave voice. "It's a pleasure to make your acquaintance."

"Are…are you her boyfriend?" Jeanna asked, giving me a small smile.

"Well, we've been seeing one another for almost a year…"

"Shut up Dec, no one is interested in my love life."

"I am," Jeanna said, her smile widening.

I covered the speaker with my hand. "Do you want my help or not?"

"He said he was in love with you," she replied, raising her eyebrows.

"He is not in love with me. He just likes too…," I stopped, nearly saying too much.

Jason leaned forward. "Likes to what?" he asked.

"I enjoy everything about her," Decland's voice said loudly over the phone. "She loves me too—though she won't admit it. She's the most incredible…"

"Decland, shut up!" I screamed, cutting him off.

"What? It's true. I love you, and you love me. No matter what you…"

"Dec, I swear to God if you say one more word, I'm going to stab you in the neck," I threatened, sweat beading down my face.

There was silence on the other end. "Dammit Dec, did you hear me?" I shrieked.

"You just told me not to speak, or you'd stab me in the neck," he answered. "How am I supposed to answer with that kind of threat hanging over me?"

Jeanna began to laugh. "I like him."

"Ask him," commented Matt, who still looked focused.

"Look Dec, we can talk later. Right now, I need your help."

"I'm listening."

I took a deep breath. "This is gonna sound crazy, but I want you to answer my questions, ok?"

"Fire away."

"You used to play that Dungeons and Dragons game, right?"

"Sure did, that's how I got interested in ancient cultures."

"Did you ever hear about any supernatural creatures that could seduce men and women?"

There was a pause before he answered. "There's all kinds. The ancient Greeks believed in sea creatures called Sirens. They would lull sailors in with their songs. There are nymphs, and fairies, too, all rumored…"

"What about a type of being that uses lust to lure in their prey?" Matt asked.

Another pause. "There is one," Dec said. "It's called a succubus. They often work with powerful demons to lure men to their deaths with a single kiss. They were said to take the form of voluptuous, beautiful women."

"Could they make a man go crazy? Like a dog in heat?" Jason asked.

"Yes—but, what's this about?"

"Are there boy, succ-u-buses?" Matt asked, stumbling over the word.

"Succubi—yes, a male is called an incubus. Are you playing a game or something?"

All of us sat there quietly.

"Hello? Are you still there?" Decland asked.

"I have to go baby, I…" I hesitated, glancing at Jeanna. "I love you, Decland. I'll call you later."

"Wait, what? You love me? What the hell is wron…"

I pressed the end call button.

Each of us sat, blinking at one another.

"Do ya'll have Wi-Fi here?" I asked.

"You believe me, don't you?" Jeanna asked.

"I don't know," I said honestly. "But it won't hurt to do some research, see what we might be up against."

"Why didn't you ask your boyfriend?" Jason asked. "He seemed to know all about them."

I couldn't tell them why. The answer was terrifying. As sure as I know Decland, I knew if he suspected I was in trouble, no force on earth could keep him from me. I couldn't take the risk of losing him.

"You love him," Jeanna said. It was not a question.

"Let's get to work," I replied, ignoring my old friend.

We decided the best thing to do was go to the new church and see for ourselves. After some fierce negotiations, I talked Jeanna and her sons into letting me go with Sierra. All of us were vulnerable in some way, but not her.

Jason contacted Sierra on the walkie talkie and let her know I was coming.

"What's she look like?" I heard Sierra ask her brother.

"A short woman, with light skin and black hair. She has a kind face and," I saw him glance over at me, but I pretended not to notice, "she's a stunner Double C. Like something out of a movie. Even Matt thinks so."

There was a pause on the other end. "Well maybe she's a succubus too," Sierra said harshly. "Fooled you all with her womanly wiles. Not me, I'm hard core, unlike you milksops."

The walkie talkie went dead on the other end, evidence that Sierra was done talking.

"Sorry about that," Matt said, shuffling over. "Sierra can be...difficult sometimes."

"She can be a pain in the ass, is what she can be," Jason said, shaking his head. "But she's smart and tough. Last year she chased after me with a shovel when I touched her science project. Damn near knocked me unconscious."

"Don't worry about her," Jeanna said, crushing her latest cigarette in an ashtray. "You'll get on just fine. What is it exactly that I'm supposed to be looking for?"

"See if these things have a weakness," I answered. "In case they are what you think, we'd best know how to fight them."

"Take this," Jason said, handing me a four-inch knife.

I smiled at him. "What kind of girl do you think I am?" I asked. Raising up my white pastel dress, I showed him the small, but powerful handgun I kept strapped against my thigh.

"You can take a girl out of the South," I began.

"But you can't take the South of the girl," Jeanna finished with me, whooping up a laugh.

"Decland know about that?" Jeanna asked quietly.

I gave her the naughtiest smile I could. "He knows every inch of my body, inside and out."

It Came from the Trailer Park

The plan was to drop me a block away from the church, and have Sierra meet me outside. I'd go in, pay my respects, pretending like I was new in town. Sierra would use that time to see if she could sneak in the back and find out what was happening at the new church.

Jason let me out of the car a quarter of a mile away across from Greer's Food Tiger. I started to walk north along Back Street till I saw the church. It was a small building with a faded red exterior. Outside on the street was a white sign with bold black lettering that read, "Church of Orphanim, and the Lord's Philosophy."

Giving a sideways glance, I saw a tall gangly girl with skin the color of coconut rum walking next to me.

"I don't think you're that pretty," she said, looking me up and down, a sour expression on her face.

I almost laughed. I could smell the jealousy oozing off of her. "I think you're beautiful," I replied kindly. It was the last thing she expected to hear.

I was being honest. Yes, she was a tomboy, with scuffed up knees and elbows. Her hair was a virtual rat's nest, and she was a bit awkward with those long legs. Underneath all that, I could see flawless skin, the kind folks pay a heap of money to get back in San Francisco. Her face was that of her mother, before the weariness of the world wore it down. Any fool could see she would grow to be a beautiful young woman.

"Hmmph," she snorted, unsure of how to respond.

She unclipped her walkie talkie from the side of her belt. "Big Jay, this is double C, you read me? Over."

There was a moment of quiet before her brother responded. "This is Big Jay, I copy, over."

"I've made contact with the movie star, over."

"Very funny C, just be safe. Over."

"Ya ya, I'll be fine, over and out."

I looked over at her with one of my eyebrows cocked.

"Double C?"

"He couldn't say my name proper when he was young," she explained, "called me CC."

She frowned at me.

"How do you do that?" she asked, nodding at my eye. "Raise just one brow?"

"We pull this off, and I'll teach you," I answered with a wink. "Now, how about you tell me your plan?"

She gave me a long look. "You want to know *my* plan?"

I shrugged. "It's your town. You're the one keeping eyes on things. I think it best I listen to you."

I could tell what I'd said meant something to her. She tried not to let on, but I could see she was pleased.

Sierra leaned over and spoke quietly. "I haven't seen the life suckers," she said. "They left more than an hour ago. Matthias was out front before you got here singing a hymn I ain't never heard. After that, he went back inside."

"I'll go in the front door," I said, nodding at her. "Wait a minute or so, and you can sneak in the back."

Sierra nodded and slipped off an old ratty backpack. Tucking her hand inside, I saw her pull out a canister of honey.

"What's that for?"

"Never you mind," she answered crossly. "I got plans you don't need to know about."

I couldn't help but smile at her bravado.

She slipped into the woods next to the church and waited for me to go in. I took a deep breath, walked past the sign, and opened the church door.

You know that old sayin, don't judge a book by its cover? I don't know who came up with that, but they were dead wrong. That dilapidated little building on the outside looked brand spanking new compared to the inside. There were three rows of pews, six in each, running from the front of the room to the back. The pews were all worn with time, barely holding together.

At the front of the room was an arched ceiling, a podium of pure white underneath. On the front of the podium was a wooden carving. It depicted a soldier wearing a ducal crown, riding atop a griffon.

I know from experience most holy places give a body a sense of peace. This one most certainly did not.

I took a few steps forward, wondering where Matthias had gone.

"Welcome," came a voice from behind me.

I think it's safe to say I nearly jumped out of my skin. I turned around and laid my eyes on a kindly older man. He had frosted red hair and the greenest eyes I'd ever seen. His face turned with a smile.

"I must apologize," he began. "I didn't mean to frighten you." He spoke with the voice of a saint, a learned man, for certain.

"That's alright," I gasped, trying to get my heart under control. "You startled me."

He raised his hands in apology and his smile widened. "I was tending to our prayer candles," he said, stretching his hand to the back of the room.

There was a small alcove to the right, next to the door. It was lined with two tiers of votive prayer candles. The place smelled of cinnamon, though I could detect a hint of *something* underneath it, a smell I couldn't put my finger on.

"I'm Matthias," he said, declining his head, placing a hand to his heart. "What brings you in today?" he asked pleasantly.

I took a deep breath. I don't care for lying in the house of God as a general principle, but today was an exception.

"I don't rightly know," I began. "I'm new to the area, thinking of moving to Coffeeville. I heard there was a new church in town, and it just sort of called to me."

Mattias smiled again. "I see," he said.

I frowned at him. "You don't believe in divine inspiration?" I asked.

He laughed aloud. "Oh, I've *seen* divine inspiration," he answered. "But not today."

Nothing about this felt right. I needed to get out of there. "If I'm not welcome here," I began, starting for the door.

His hand shot up, faster than I would have believed possible, and grabbed onto my wrist.

"On the contrary," he said, his red hair beginning to smoke. "I've been expecting you—Maria Donnelli."

My heart lurched in my chest. "Let me go," I yelled, trying to rip away from him.

"Oh no, my dear," he replied, his voice becoming deeper, more monstrous. "Your corrupt heart will burn for the sins committed against the Erinye."

He blinked once and his eyes changed from deep green, to a ghostly white.

"Get off of me!" I screamed, kicking out, landing a sharp blow against his shin.

Normally a shot like that would drop a person to the ground. Not him. Matthias's smile vanished, and his hair burst into flames.

"Rabid animal," he hissed, releasing his hold. "Run if you will. You cannot hide from me. Even the protection of *Origen* cannot save you."

I didn't know what he was talking about, but I came to recognize what I'd been smelling. Sulphur and brimstone—coming from Matthias. I needed to get out of that church.

I tore past him, opened the door, and walked straight into the hands of the most beautiful man I'd ever seen.

"She's yours, Salem," Matthias said from behind me. "Feed if you like but make it slow. I want her to suffer."

"It would be a pleasure," the man replied, his eyes an icy blue.

I could feel it, a warm rush of physical desire building in my chest. I knew this creature, the incubus, was using his power on me. A picture of Decland flashed in my mind, and I managed to look away.

"She is strong," another voice said, stepping into view.

A woman, with curves a Kardashian would envy, stepped forward and touched my face. "She is in love," the woman smiled, with soft, pouty lips.

"She is protected by the Oathbreaker," Matthias warned. I could hear him close behind me, the smell of brimstone overwhelming. "Leave your brother Valais—her will cannot hold against an immortal."

I hate to admit this, but he was right. Every second Salem held me in his grip, I could feel my will to fight against him weaken. If I looked back into those eyes, it was all over. Thankfully, it never came to that.

I heard something buzz past my ear. A crossbow bolt buried itself in Salem's eye.

"What the hell?" I heard Matthias curse from behind me.

"Eat this devil spawn!" Sierra shouted from the front of the room. She ran up the aisle throwing a balloon filled with a liquid at Matthias. He reached his hand out to catch it, and the balloon burst open, drenching him in a sticky, golden substance.

Honey.

"We need to get out of here!" Sierra screamed, grabbing onto my hand.

"Not so fast," Valais snarled, drawing a wicked looking knife from under her dress.

"Your wiles won't work on me succu-bitch," Sierra threatened, drawing a knife of her own.

"I don't need them to," Valais hissed back.

I'd had enough. I pulled out my gun and fired. Three shots to the chest knocked Valais to the ground, her dress smoking from the nearly point-blank gunpowder burns.

I turned back and saw Matthias staring at us, hatred etched on his face. "Your assault will avail you nothing, little girl. I command legions of…"

He stopped and yelped in pain, slapping at his neck.

"We need to run," Sierra urged, tugging at my arm.

"What did you do?" I asked, glancing down at her.

"I command legions…" Matthias said again, before stopping to slap himself on the head.

"I kicked a hive of hornets in the back of the church and doused him in honey-water," Sierra explained. "Let's go!"

I didn't resist her pull on my hand, and both of us lit out of there. I looked back only once as we were tearing down the street. I caught a glimpse of Matthias unceremoniously whacking away at himself as an entire hive of angry insects extracted vengeance for the attack on their hive. It might have been funny, except for two things. Valais was sitting up, looking angry. Next to her Salem did the same, furiously ripping the bolt from his eye.

Knowing we'd quite literally stirred up a hornet's nest, Sierra and I raced home.

It was twilight when we skidded to a halt in front of Jeanna's home. Matt and Jason were sitting out on the porch.

"What happened?" Matt asked, his eyes wide at the sight of my gun.

"They…knew who…I was," I panted, out of breath from the half mile run.

"I…saved her," Sierra panted next to me.

"Girl, where'd you get that crossbow from?" Jason asked, stepping toward his sister. "Did you…you used my credit card last month, didn't you? Goddammit, I knew it!" he stormed.

"Don't," I said, raising my hand, still trying to catch my breath. "She…saved my life."

"What did you mean when you said they knew who you were?" Matt asked.

I shook my head, my hands on my hips. Lord almighty, it was a good thing I'd been taking spinning classes this past month, otherwise I would have collapsed on the way back.

"I don't rightly know," I answered honestly. "Something about *Origen's* protection, and I'd committed a sin against something called the Erinye."

He looked to say more but Sierra waved him off. "We don't have time for this Q and A," she said. "I reckon we've about five minutes till they come here after us. We done gone and pissed them off."

Matt looked at his sister and nodded. "Alright, best we get inside. Jason, keep a lookout."

Jason, never taking his eyes from Sierra, nodded once and sat back down. "Drunk purchase my ass," he muttered as she walked by. "You owe me fifty-one dollars for that crossbow little girl."

"I'll pay for it," I offered, thankful to be alive.

Once inside, Jeanna took one look at me and bade us to sit down. "What happened?" she asked. "Are you alright?"

"I met Matthias and his underlings," I started, with a shiver.

"And?"

"The incubus took a bolt to the eye and got up like he'd been bit by a mosquito," I answered. "I put three 9 mm rounds in the woman's chest from my Smith and Wesson, and she brushed it off like it was nothing."

Jeanna blinked in disbelief. "I'm glad you're ok," she said at last, reaching out and clasping hold of my hand tightly.

"I'm fine, by the way," Sierra groused, annoyed at being ignored.

Jeanna frowned. "You'd be as fine as a fox in a hen house," her mother said. "No matter what you were up against."

"She saved me," I offered, knowing it was important to Sierra that her momma knew. "Otherwise, I'd be dead."

Jeanna's face softened somewhat. "Alright then, that's fine. Thank you, child."

"Hmmph," Sierra snorted, crossing her arms over her chest defiantly.

"Did you make any headway finding their weaknesses?" I asked, changing the subject.

Matt scratched his head. "Well, yes and no," he answered. "The bad news is, they don't have much in the way of weaknesses. They suck life from humans and feed off sexual energy. There's plenty of that here in Coffeeville and lots of humans around to sustain their appetites."

I glanced outside and then back to Matt.

"You said there was good news?"

He nodded, grimly. "According to supernatural-being.com, they *can* be killed."

"How?"

He paused before answering. "Decapitation and ripping out the heart."

I looked at him, uncertain if he was serious.

"Well, that sounds pleasant," Sierra muttered under her breath. "Speaking of unpleasant, I saw what was going on behind that church."

"What was it?" I asked, forgetting her objective in all the excitement.

"It was bad," she explained. "Them town folk that are missing. They ain't dead. He's got them all in the back. I went to rouse Granny and…"

The door banged open, and Jason backed in, eyes wide with shock. "Ya'll better come see this," he said, beckoning to the rest of us. "Matty, get your shotgun."

"The Weatherby?"

Jason shook his head. "The 590."

Matt blinked twice in surprise before he ducked into the back of the house. The rest of us stepped onto the porch and gaped.

Hovering above the yard against the darkness of the night sky was a demon. There's no other way to put it. It was big too, nearly seven feet tall as close as I could figure. It glowed with fire smoldering all along its wings and torso. It wore some kind of armor made of ivory white bone. In its hand was a curved sword, flames all along the blade. It would have been cool as all get out if it hadn't been there to kill us. With a roar it dove, its sword leading the way.

"MOVE!" bellowed Jason, who blasted at it with his shotgun.

I jumped down the steps, rolling to my feet, gun in hand. I saw Jason's buckshot tear into the demon, knocking it from the sky, but caused no lasting damage.

Jason, looking grimly determined, pumped his shotgun again as he strode down the stairs. He blasted at it, but this time the creature rolled to the side, dodging the blast. Before he could get a third volley off, the demon leapt to its feet and grabbed the gun out of Jason's hands, tossing it aside. Cool as a winter wind, Jason slid his knife out of its sheath and stabbed the demon through the heart. The demon looked down at the knife and glowered in rage.

"What the fu…" Jason began, until the monster tossed him aside like a rag doll. He came to rest twenty feet away, crying out in pain.

"Double C!" Jeanna barked. "See to your brother."

My old friend whipped out two ivory handled colts and opened fire. I squeezed the trigger of my own gun and emptied the magazine.

Whatever this thing was, it wasn't stupid. It folded its wings around its body in a shield of protection. Every single shot we fired was deflected by its armor-like wings.

"Damn," I cursed, knowing my extra magazines were still in my car.

"Double C!" Jeanna screamed, trying desperately to reload her guns. "Get a move on."

I tried to make for the house, but the demon cut me off. I backed up, until I could feel the solid wall of the house behind me.

Sierra tried. Staggering as she was under the weight of her older brother, she snapped off a shot with her crossbow. The demon didn't even look her way and caught the bolt out of the air.

The demon reached out, mere inches away. A gun blast sounded from the porch, jolting the creature away from me.

I took the opportunity and sprinted over to Sierra, lifting Jason under the armpit.

"Everybody inside," Matt said calmly.

The demon stepped forward again, and Matt sent another shot toward it. This time the creature fell to the ground.

"I can't kill it, not at this range," he said. "Get in the house. We'll force it to use the door, and I'll hit him when he comes in."

With Jeanna helping us, we managed to get Jason inside on the couch. He was dazed more than anything, though he was bleeding from the temple.

Sierra ran into the bedroom and grabbed a can that read, "Big Sexy Hair," along with her momma's lighter. Determined, Sierra held the can up, ready to immolate the demon as soon as it came in the room.

I picked up a kitchen knife laying on the dinner table as Matt backed through the front door.

"Stay behind me," Matt said, licking his lips nervously.

The demon leapt up to the porch, roaring at us once again. It stabbed its blade at Matt, who backed away reflexively. Then, quite unexpectedly, the demon stopped its advance. It half turned its head in confusion, before being thrown out of the doorway to slam onto the ground outside.

We all looked at one another wordlessly before moving to the porch. It was a sight I'll never forget.

There was a man, clean cut and handsome, with a sword in his hand, fighting the demon.

"Who is that?" Sierra asked, awed.

Decland. I don't know why, but somehow, someway, Decland was here. Not just here but fighting like mad to save our lives.

"Is this the best he could do?" Dec was saying. "A Hell Knight? I've killed scores of your kind."

In answer, the demon swung its fiery blade at Dec's head. Like a cat on a hot tin roof, Decland blocked the strike with his sword and danced to the side. Before that supernatural fiery hell spawn knew what had happened, my boyfriend slashed it across the neck. The demon let out an earth-shattering scream as molten blood poured from the cut. Unlike when Jason had stabbed the demon, this time the creature fell to the ground and turned to ash.

Decland spun around to look at me and flashed one of his crooked smiles. "Hi gorgeous. I'd have been here sooner, but, you know, traffic."

"What, in the mother of all that is holy in this world, are you doing here?" I asked, both thrilled and annoyed to see Decland.

"I've been in Alabama since this morning," he answered, cool as a cucumber.

"Why?"

"Who cares?" Sierra asked, looking at him dreamily. "If I had a boyfriend that looked like that, I'd marry him twice."

"Hush now," Jeanna said absently, brushing at her hair.

"I'm just sayin I wouldn't kick him otta bed for getting crumbs on the sheets," Sierra continued.

Apparently, Matt and his mother were of the same mind as Sierra—none of them could take their eyes off Decland.

"Have you all lost your cotton pickin minds?" Jason asked, holding a bag of ice on the back of his head. "We just got our asses whooped by a demon! Why is it me and the movie star are the only ones who give two shits about that?"

Jason was right, of course, but the others were right, too. I forget sometimes that I live in San Francisco. Big city like that has gorgeous folk all over the place. In Coffeeville, well, men that look like Dec are a mite less common. Plus, I'd been seeing the man for some time now. They were just getting their first dose of him.

"Jason is right," Dec said, nodding at him. "We have much to discuss."

"Hold on just a minute," I said, narrowing my eyes. "How did you know where to find me?"

"I tracked your phone," Decland answered simply. "It's no great mystery. We've been tracking each other since you thought I was cheating on you with that English professor at the university, remember?"

"You cheated on Maria?" Jason asked, glowering at Decland.

Decland shook his head with a chuckle. "Of course not. I love Maria more than I've ever loved anyone. It would take a force beyond this world to tear me away from her."

Decland moved closer to Jason. "I understand you were the first to fight the Hell Knight. You managed to stab it in the heart. That's no easy feat, son. If your knife had been blessed like my sword, you'd have killed it without me."

Just like that, silver tongued as he is, Decland won over his last objector.

"How is it that you know so much about this?" I asked, rather pointedly. "Did you teach a class on demons or something?"

Dec became serious. "There's not time to explain it all, but you're all in danger. A powerful demon lord has come to Earth."

"You mean Matthias?" Sierra scoffed. "He's just an old man."

Decland shook his head. "Matthias was his name in heaven. In hell, he is known as Murmur—once the foremost of the Orphanim, angels that carried the throne of God. Now he's a duke of hell." Dec paused, looking at each of us. "He knows I am here, and he will be coming for us all."

"How do you know who it is?" I asked.

"I just do," he answered evasively.

"Can't you walk down to the church and kill him?" Matt asked.

Decland shrugged his shoulders. "Maybe, but this goes beyond him. Murmur can open a portal to hell without using human life force."

"That's what he's doing!" Sierra cut in. "I've seen it with my own eyes. The townsfolk, they ain't dead, but I think—I think he's draining their energy, or life force, or whatever you call it."

Decland looked at her sharply. "Why do you say that?" he asked.

"Because that's what I saw behind that church," she explained. "Thirteen people, all laying there, exhausted as all get out. I tried to rouse Granny, but she glossed over me like I wasn't there."

"He said something strange to me, something I didn't understand," I said, looking at Dec. "That the protection of *Origen* couldn't save me—that I'd committed a sin against the Erinye."

For the first time since I'd known him, Decland looked worried.

"The Erinye?" he asked quietly.

"Ya, what's he talking about?"

Decland sighed. "The Erinyes are the goddesses of vengeance and retribution," he said. "Also known as Furies."

"Dec?" I asked, suspecting there was more.

"There are three," he continued. "The first is Alecto, known for her endless anger. The second is Tisiphone, whose name means 'vengeful destruction.'"

"The third?" I asked, sweat dripping down my face.

Decland did not speak for the span of a few heartbeats. "The last is Megaera."

"What was she known for?" Jeanna asked.

"Jealous Rage."

I wiped the sweat from my forehead. "What does she want with me?" I asked.

Decland sat there, flush with guilt. "I am sorry my love. I have put you all in danger."

"What are you talking about?" I asked, reaching out, taking his hand.

"Maybe I should have told you from the start, but—I didn't think you'd believe me."

"It's ok," I replied, squeezing his hand tightly.

"No, it isn't," he muttered as he stood.

He ran his hand through his hair. "I never thought it would come to this. All of you should run. Get away from here as fast as you can."

"Hey," I said, standing up next to him. "That's enough. You've stood by me through everything, my divorce, my kids— I'm not about to throw away the only man I'd ever consider marrying again."

A small smile crept onto his face. "You'd marry me? After all the times you've refused?"

"Maybe," I countered. "But only if you tell us what's going on."

He pressed his lips together, making his decision. "Megaera is angry with me," he began. "I—well, I spurned her a long time ago."

"The Furies are ancient," Matt said. "They've been around for millennia."

"Yes, dating back to the earliest days of Greece," Decland agreed. "I was called Origen back then. It means 'Of the Mountain.'"

"Wait a minute," Sierra said. "Are you saying you're thousands of years old?"

"Yes," he answered. "When I broke it off with Megaera, she cursed me to walk the Earth for eternity, never to find love again."

He paused and looked at me. "I never did, until I met you."

I started walking toward the door.

"Wait, where are you going?" asked Jeanna.

"Some immortal from thousands of years ago has it in for my man?" I clucked over my shoulder. "I'm fixin to get my gun. I'm not going down without a fight."

There was no leaving the rest behind, as Matthias, or Murmur, whatever the hell he's called, wasn't about to let Jeanna's folks go free. Having Decland was a huge help. I found out he was stronger than I thought. Course I figured as much when he tossed the Hell Knight off the porch with one hand. Still, it was nice to go into a fight with a heavy hitter on your side.

Decland confirmed that Matt was right about the life stealers; decapitation and heart ripping would do just fine.

The demons from hell were another matter. He said only fire, distilled from a pure source, could harm them. Jason, God bless his soul, got out a bottle of the purest moonshine in the county and filled up a bunch of bottles to make Molotov cocktails. Sierra was designated as the fire starter of those explosions.

Most important were the blessed weapons. In addition to his sword, Dec handed over a pair of knives. He gave one each to the brothers. Finally, he handed me a sawed-off shotgun. "Consecrated by the Archbishop of San Francisco," he said.

"Cordileone?" I asked, admiring its walnut stock.

"Some years before him," Dec confessed, giving me a brief smile.

We came up with a makeshift plan, based on Sierra's intel of the place. Jeanna would drive her pick up and rescue her folks and the others behind the church. Sierra, Jason, Matt and I were going to go with Dec and see how much hell we could raise; pun intended.

"What about those life suckers?" Jason pointed out.

"I have an idea," Sierra said, a rapacious look in her eyes.

"By all means," Dec smiled. "It's your show."

We all huddled round to listen to her plan.

"Here they come," Valais whispered to her brother.

"I want the child," he hissed, rubbing at his ruined eye.

"There," Valais said, pointing at two humans approaching from the left. "They think they can flank us." Her eyes narrowed. She could see long, dark hair flowing from underneath Maria's hood.

"Pity the girl is with the Oathbreaker," Salem whispered. "I know how much you wanted her blood."

"Kill her for me brother," Valais answered, steel in her voice.

"Go, both of you," Murmur stated, staring coldly at the warrior with the sword walking directly toward them. "Kill the others but leave Origen for the Fury. I will take him to her in chains."

With inhuman speed, Salem and Valais raced to their prospective marks.

Both Sierra and her companion halted, as Salem stopped in front of them. "Let me deal with your friend first, child," he hissed, grabbing Maria in his hands. "Then you are mine."

Salem reached out with his power. "Come to me, woman. I will drink your life force until all that is left is a withered husk."

Salem's eyes widened. He was met with a wall of fury that could come from only one source.

"You're dead," Sierra said, a malicious smile on her face.

Shaking off the hood, Salem was stunned to see Jason, a long black wig on his head. Moving quickly, he rammed his blessed knife deep into the chest of the incubus.

"Rot in hell," Sierra quipped, wiggling her fingers at Salem, as Jason cut out the creature's heart.

A moment later the incubus turned to dust, a look of disbelief on his face. Valais felt an echo of loss at the death of her brother. Impossible! No mortal woman could resist him.

Turning around she saw Jason take off the wig he'd been wearing and throw it to the ground. If that wasn't Maria, then that meant..."

"Hey there sugar pie," the figure in front of Valais said, removing the hood from her head. "Looks like brother done gone and got himself killed." Standing next to Maria was Matt, a blessed knife in his hand.

Valais grabbed onto his arms. She reached out with her powers—and was met with a dark look of anger in the man's eyes.

"You're barking up the wrong tree there sweetie," Maria said. "Matty here likes men. Don't take it personal; it's a matter of choice."

Valais was in shock. She barely felt the cold steel of the man's knife slice its way along her throat, all the way through her neck. The succubus fell to the ground, her head rolling clear.

"Thank you for visiting the great state of Alabama," I continued, stepping over her body. "Don't let the gates of hell hit your ass on the way out."

I'm not going to lie to you—I took great satisfaction in ridding the earth of that life stealing prima donna. Things, however, were about to get interesting.

"Come, my children," Murmur shouted. "Come forth and drink your fill!" From behind the church, a dozen demons came a-calling. Two, one with the face of a toad and the other a goat, shot straight for Decland. He cut them down like a hot knife through warm butter.

"You fight well, mortal," Murmur said respectfully, "but the lost blade of Durandal will not save you."

"We shall see," Decland replied grimly.

Murmur transformed. One moment he was an old man with graying red hair, the next he was a flame haired soldier wearing a ducal crown who carried a spear of fire.

The two shot forward, their weapons ringing like a clarion bell as they clashed time and time again on that unholy ground.

"We've got company," Matt stated in his calm voice.

Ten other demons from Murmur's legion came charging at us. I readied my sanctified shotgun, as Matt drew his 590. Before they got too close, one of Jason's Molotov cocktails bombed them.

"Burn you bastards!" Sierra screamed in delight. That got their attention, as two of the creatures went up in blue flames. Four of the demons peeled off and raced toward Jason and his sister.

That left the last four to us. I levelled my shotgun and went to work.

Fighting demons is a nasty business. Don't let some soldier of fortune tell you different. Matty blasted the first one to dust, and I shot a second one to where it spun out of control and landed off to my left, dead as a doornail. The other two were on us faster than Charlie Daniels could sing "Chicken in the bread pan pickin out dough."

One with a reptilian head jumped on me, knocking me to the ground. I jammed my shotgun lengthwise in its mouth, else that hell spawn would have killed me right there. We rolled around in the dirt for a few seconds, as I fought to keep alive. I knew I couldn't keep him away from me for much longer.

An explosion of sound echoed next to me. The demon on top of me ceased its struggling. I shifted its weight off of me and saw a hand covered in blood floating in front of my face. I took it, as Matt helped me to my feet.

"Thanks," I said, meaning it.

"Look there," he said in answer.

Decland was bleeding from wounds on his hip and bicep. However, Murmur looked to have taken the worst of it, as he bled deeply from a cut on his chest, near the heart.

"How," Murmur asked, looking at his bleeding torso in disbelief.

"Because I'm better than you," Decland panted, triumphantly. "Now, summon her so we can end this."

Despite his imminent demise, Murmur smiled. "She doesn't love you anymore, Origen. She will bathe in your blood."

The demon lord tilted his head back and screamed a single name. "Megaera!"

Decland swept his blade across Murmur's neck, sending him back to hell. An instant later, the Fury appeared.

I wish I could tell you she was as ugly as a three headed dog, but that would be a lie. Megaera was tall, with an athletic build. Reminded me of an amazon princess if the truth be told. With hair as black as mine and a face of unearthly beauty, she was an inspiring figure. I was more than a little jealous.

"That is enough," Decland said, looking at her in fury. "Your jealous rage has gone on for too long."

Megaera walked past him, right up to me.

"This is the creature you've chosen?" she shrieked in rage. "A subspecies, barely able to speak?"

"Immortal or not," I snarled, gathering an anger of my own. "I'm ten times the woman you are, honey. You best get on out of here while you're still in one piece."

Matt strode up next to me, his 590 ready to rock.

The Fury turned to Decland. "I cursed you for the sins you caused me. We could have lived together forever. We could have loved for all eternity!"

"Hey psycho," Sierra called from behind Megaera. "It's been thirty seconds, and I already hate you. How'd you expect Origen to deal with your crazy ass for all eternity?"

The Fury, apparently, wasn't used to hearing insults, because she lost her mind after that.

"Infidel!" she screamed. Megaera raised her hands and two curved swords, pulsing with darkness, appeared in them.

"Get back, all of you!" Decland yelled, rushing to the attack. He ran forward, and she swatted him aside like he was a horsefly. Dec slammed into the church wall, his sword flying wide.

"Matty, give me a leg up," I shouted, getting an idea. Matt crouched down as I ran toward him.

"Double C," I screamed, "light the last salvo!" I jumped on Matt's back, and he threw me forward, right toward Megaera. Sierra, understanding my idea instantly, lit the last Molotov cocktail, and Jason heaved it at the Fury. I waited till it was directly in front of her face and fired my blessed shotgun.

An explosion like I'd never seen erupted, blasting us all backward. I covered my eyes with my arm as best I could just as the explosion went off. Between the fire of the purest moonshine in Alabama and my blessed shotgun, Megaera and that pretty face of hers exploded in a ball of fire.

I landed some thirty feet away, and rolled, my back to the explosion. When I looked up, I turned in time to see Megaera crash to the ground, her face nearly gone.

A scream, full of anguish and loss, roared out of her mouth and shook the very air around us. "Noooooooo!" Then, there was a huge implosion, and Megaera was gone.

I ran over to check on Decland. He was groaning like a man does when they get so much as the smallest scratch. "You ok baby?" I asked.

"Yes, I'll be right as rain once I heal," he answered, touching the side of my face. Looking past me, he saw the others all walk toward us.

"Everybody alright?" Matt asked, looking carefully at his siblings.

Jason smiled, the first such look I'd seen from him. "Just a normal Tuesday night," he said. "Slaying demons and such."

"I knew what you was thinking," Sierra said, nodding at me with excitement. "Light the bomb and WHAM, kill a bitch! Did you see what happened Matty?"

"Yes, I was standing right there," the elder sibling said, chuckling at his sister.

Jeanna honked her truck's horn at us from the back of the church. "If ya'll are done congratulating yourselves, we've got folks to rescue.'

Sierra looked over. "Granny and Pappy?"

Jeanna smiled. "They're fine." Jeanna paused a moment. "Proud of you girl, proud of you all."

"Well, we'd best go lend a hand," Matt said, nodding at his brother.

"Come along when you're ready," Jason said, reloading his shotgun. "Come on, Double C."

Decland looked at me and stroked my face. "You ok, Love?"

"I'm alright," I answered. "But—do you have any more ex-girlfriends I should know about? If I'm gonna marry you, I need to know about that shit."

Not a Keeper

By RJ Ladon

Tarzan lay on the back of the couch, his orange fur catching the light through the trailer window. The old tomcat had a scar that went from the corner of his lip to his ear. It still looked like an earthworm, even though the wound was well over ten years old.

TJ poked at the scar with his finger. "Did Tarzan really beat up a pit bull?"

"There were two. They chased him up a telephone pole and kept him there for a day. Tarzan must have gone crazy from hunger and thirst 'cause he came down with an attitude bigger than both of them dogs. He tore 'em to shreds and sent them yipping back to the Johnson's trailer. To this day, those dogs are still scared of him." I scratched Tarzan's forehead. "That was an amazing fight I won't ever forget." I leaned back into the couch and studied Timmy Junior. "Didn't you come over to make a racecar today?" I pointed at the pile of Legos the boy had pulled out earlier.

TJ nodded, but soon his gaze left the Legos. "What's that, Grampa?" He pointed at the stiff green fin mounted on a plaque of oak. The humongous fish fin was all that was left of the critter me and Bobby destroyed last week.

"That, my boy, is the only proof of Avon Bottoms Swamp Monster. I fully expect Ripley's to be callin' at any moment." I ruffled his hair. TJ was a boy of nine who seemed to have difficulty losing his baby fat.

The boy's eyes glistened with the proper excitement. "Oh, yea?" He paused and looked at me sideways with one eye, like a chicken right before they peck ya. "Really? You ain't feeding me no line, are you Grampa?" He sat on the floor, hunched over a mass of Legos. His little fingers snapped pieces together while he talked as if his hands or the Legos had a mind of their own.

I was affronted by that little squirt. "You listen to me, TJ, and I'll tell you the whole story." I craned my neck to look into the kitchen and cleared my throat. "Woman! Bring me a beer!"

"Git it yerself! I'm cooking dinner." Gracelyn shouted from the kitchen table while turning a page of The Enquirer.

"You ain't cookin nothing. I can see you reading that damn magazine." I huffed. Who did she think she was? I rounded on TJ, pointing at his round face. "You! Get me a beer."

TJ jumped to his feet, wobbled, and then dashed out the front door of our double-wide. He let the door close, but I could hear him getting into the fridge through the wall. The clinking of the bottles and the thud of the door made my mouth water. TJ fumbled with the door, pulled it open, and stumbled inside with three bottles in his arms. He carefully set them on the side table and pulled up his pants before sitting among his Legos.

"Why did you bring three?" I eyed the boy suspiciously.

"Welp," he said while prying two Legos apart. "If your story is long, you'd ask me to get you another beer. If that happens, you tend to forget where you were, and I don't get to hear the whole story." The Legos popped apart. TJ held them up triumphantly, smiling. "And, if you've drunk enough and I'm lucky, you'll let me have some." The boy gave me chicken-eye again. "Maybe you'd even let me have a whole one?"

"Gosh darn, boy. You sure have a weighty pair." I knew he was up to no good. But then he went and admitted it. I shook my head with amazement. This boy is gonna go far. I took a bottle off the table and twisted the cap free. I swallowed deeply, leaned forward in my recliner, and handed the half-empty beer to the boy. "You can have half."

TJ looked up at me and grinned. His two front teeth were so much larger than the others. "Awesome. Thanks, Grampa." He took a sip, then set the beer aside and continued working on the race car. The tires were knobby, not a good racing slick. I wondered if Lego knew what a race car needed. "Grampa?" I looked back to TJ. "Are you gonna tell your story or watch me play?" His voice was a little whiny, as if he really wanted to hear about the swamp monster, and the chance of getting beer was just gravy.

"Alright." I picked up another beer and opened it. Where to start? I leaned back and rubbed my chin. "It was the beginning of bass harvest, and for May, it was warm. I wore my shorts, you know, so I could use my tattoo." I pointed down at my shin to indicate the tape measure tattoo I used to make sure my catch is within limits. TJ nodded without looking up from his Legos. How could he not appreciate this artwork? It was lovely. "Okay, so you don't like tattoos."

TJ's shoulders slumped. "It's not that, Grampa," he whined. "I've seen it before." His eyes glistened as if he might cry at any minute. "Aw, come on. It's beautiful, really it is. I just wanna hear about the swamp monster." TJ wiped his nose and inhaled, sniffling.

As if on cue, the magazine in the kitchen slapped the table. My eyes rolled. I leaned back in the recliner. Good Lord here comes the yelling. "Darryl, don't you dare tease that boy with a story, and you not give him one." Gracelyn chided, but she didn't scream. She tromped into the TV room, causing the double-wide to tremble under her ample weight. She stopped next to TJ then turned to face me, hands on hips. The fat on her upper arms wobbled in a pleasing manner. "My eyes are up here, Darryl," she snapped. I licked my lips, surprised that she wasn't going on a tirade. I chanced a smile. "We want TJ to tell his mum that he had a good time. And tell her he wants to come back. Don't we?" Gracelyn bent over to ruffle the boy's hair. My eyes widened at the peep show her low-cut shirt gave me.

I cleared my throat and quickly gulped some beer. "Yes, darling." I nodded numbly, not knowing where my luck came from and not caring. "We definitely want TJ to visit again." *Especially if he can tone down your temper.*

She met my eye and winked. "I'll make some samwiches for my men. Is bologna good?"

"With ketchup. On white bread," TJ requested.

I nodded in agreement, knowing better than to look a gift horse in the mouth.

Gracelyn waddled back into the kitchen. I heard the fridge door open and close. Within minutes we men had our samwiches on pristine floral paper plates. Gracelyn trilled, "kitty, kitty." Then she and Tarzan left us in peace.

I nodded to TJ over my plate. "Your gramma only brings out the good plates for important occasions." TJ smiled, his eyes glittering. I was sure the boy felt important. He picked up his crust-free samwich and took a bite. We ate in silence.

Gracelyn threw open the kitchen door. "Damn it, Cindy, put that chicken down. Don't start with your sass child. I will call your mother." The door closed, and I heard her sit and return to reading.

I cleared my throat and washed the remains of my samwich down with a gulp of beer. The boy was right. I needed more than one. "Okay. Now, where was I?" I thought back to the recent scare with Gracelyn. "Oh, yes, shorts and my tattoo."

TJ nodded. He took his time eating his samwich, nibbling like a mouse.

"Bobby came and picked me up in his El Camino. Did you see his new camouflage paint job?

TJ vigorously shook his head. "Did he really? I'm glad he did. White is so boring."

"He did a good job with nothing but a three-inch brush and a couple gallons from Ace." The truck had cattails and swamp grass painted on the lower half and leaves and branches on the upper. The camouflage would not do well in the depths of winter. Maybe Bobby would repaint it later in the year. "You'll see it tonight when Bobby comes by. Bobby had his flat-bottomed aluminum boat hitched to his El Camino. I tossed my fishing supplies…."

"Beer?" TJ asked.

I nodded. "A case or two. But I brought my fishing pole and my tackle box too. We really planned on fishing."

TJ flashed a grin as if to say, *sure, Grampa, sure.*

I cleared my throat. "Anyway. We drove to the Sugar River Boat Launch. We saw boats and cars from all over. Fancy cars and boats that had matching paint, decals, and pinstriping. Can you believe that?"

TJ had pushed his empty plate aside and held his beer in his hands. He nodded in agreement at my disapproval. Whoever had enough money to buy a matching car and boat set had more money than brains. What a bunch of idiots. TJ opened his mouth, then closed it, thinking. "Go on, Grampa, then what happened? Did you have to wait long to launch your boat?"

"Naw. We weren't going to wait for those idiots. Besides, we had a secret launch site." I grinned at TJ's stunned expression. "That's right, I'll show you when you're old enough." I took a swallow of beer. "Down the road from the boat launch is a gravel road. Now it ain't just any old road. This one has a gate marked 'DNR ONLY,' and it's locked with chains."

"Whoa." TJ nodded appreciatively. "Did you bust through with Bobby's car?"

"Don't be daft boy, this ain't the *Dukes of Hazzard*." I grinned, holding my secret for a second or two, then I leaned in and whispered to him. "We'd been here before. We cut the padlock off months ago then secured it with some wire. You know, to make it look like it was still locked."

TJ's mouth hung open in amazement. "You could've gotten caught."

I nodded. "I suppose. But we were careful." I sat up and peered into the kitchen. Gracelyn was reading again. "Don't tell yer gramma. She'd have kittens."

The boy shook his head. "I'll never tell."

"Good." I sat back and smiled.

"So, then what happened?"

"After we went through the fence, we made it look all proper like. Wiring the chain links back together and whatnot. We even put some branches over the fence to make it really look unused." I drank some more beer and set it on the side table. "When we drove off, I thought I saw something in the woods. I swear something was watchin us. But I paid it no heed, which was to my detriment."

"What do you mean, Grampa?"

"I should have said something to Bobby." I shook my head. "It's like my Pa used to say, 'No use crying over spilled milk.' What's done is done."

TJ stared at me as if I had spouted off the wisest saying in history. His mind blown, I continued with the story. "We reached the launch site and put in the boat. Then we had to camouflage the El Camino and trailer. With its new paint job, it was easy to hide. Bobby drove it into some brambles, and we threw some branches on top."

Someone ran onto our porch and pounded on the door. I stopped recounting my adventure.

"Oh, for cryin out loud." Gracelyn hurried to the door, rattling the trailer with every angry step. She pointed at me. "Keep on telling TJ the story. I've got this."

The door opened, and I saw a flash of a figure, and then Gracelyn pushed whoever it was out the door. It didn't matter. The trailer had thin walls. "Damn it, Bobby. Can't you see Darryl is entertaining TJ with a fishing story?"

"But that's why I came, I found...."

"I don't care what you found. Now go. Come back in an hour."

"Bobby?" TJ climbed to his feet and stumbled to the door. "Gramma!" The boy's whine was ear-splitting. "Don't make him go. I wanna hear his side of the story, too. Then I'll know what Grampa said was true."

I was heartbroken. *Did TJ think I told lies?*

All three of them walked in. TJ sat among his Legos, Bobby sat next to me on the couch, and Gracelyn went back into the kitchen. Tarzan followed her, mewing. "TJ, do you really think my stories are lies?"

The boy frowned and shook his head. "Not lies, Grampa. Mom calls them exasterbations."

Bobby laughed, then punched me in the shoulder. "TJ's not wrong. You do exaggerate. Your twenty-inch fish suddenly turned into thirty inches with the second telling."

"Aw hell, TJ, I wouldn't lie about the swamp monster. That is real. There's proof there on the wall."

"And in my El Camino," Bobby added.

"Hush now, Bobby. I was in the middle of telling TJ the story. Where was I?"

"You and Bobby hid the trailer and El Camino." TJ supplied.

"That's right. We got into the boat and attached the trolling motor...."

"Can I get a beer?"

"You have got to be kidding me. Did you hafta wait until I had started again?" This was getting ridiculous.

Bobby shrugged his shoulders then tilted his head to the side. His lazy eye rolled around like it was floating in a stream, or perhaps a toilet. Damn him. I can't stay mad at Bobby and his stupid elephant ears.

"Alright, go get a beer." Bobby was on his feet before I finished my sentence. "Bring back five, two for me, two for you, and one for TJ."

Bobby was out to the beer fridge and back. He quickly passed around the beer and got comfortable on the couch. "Okay, Darryl. I won't say another word."

I looked at TJ, and the boy rolled his eyes. He didn't believe Bobby either.

"Okay, we are in the boat, and we've got the trolling motor going. It was then that we saw a huge V-shaped trail in the water. And that's when Bobby said…."

"Whoa, that's one big catfish," Bobby said. "Wanna do some noodling instead of bass fishing?" Bobby grinned at me then seemed flustered. "What? Why you mean muggin me, Darryl? I'm adding to the ambiance." He waved his fingers about. "A good story needs a good narrator, and frankly, you suck."

"Bobby!" I yelled at him, "It's my story."

"Well, then tell it already."

TJ laughed long and hard, falling into his Legos and rolling around. He finally came up for air, gasping like a fish. "Don't stop now." TJ wiped his eyes and sniffled. "Well? What happened next?" The little shit had the nerve to point first to me, then to Bobby.

Bobby grinned. "Your grampa said, let's go noodling."

"That's not what I said." I cuffed Bobby on the back of his head. "I told you how I didn't want to compete with a bunch of rich idiots. Those rich types have all the new fang-dangled fish finders and specialized equipment. With all their noise and big motors, they'd scare off most of the big fish. You know the big ones are big because they're smart. But I'd be lying if I said that V-shaped trail didn't have my fingers twitching. I love noodling. Wrestling a catfish outa their holla with nothing but your hands is a whole lot of fun. Man versus beast, there's nothing better. You just feel alive when you're that close to death. Am I right, Bobby?"

Bobby was still rubbing the back of his head. "Yea, I suppose."

"Can a catfish kill you?" TJ's jaw hung open.

Bobby's maniacal grin returned. "A channel cat can hold you underwater until you drown. Heck, boy, there are some catfish big enough to swallow you whole. But the meanest cat is a mama. They will protect their eggs to the death. Nothing will stop them. I hear tell they're as tough as a gator who's sitting on eggs. Don't ever mess with a mama."

"Or a Gramma!" Gracelyn hollered from the kitchen.

"Especially that Gramma," I said while hiking my thumb in Gracelyn's direction. "Tougher than a bear, that one. Prolly angrier too."

"I heard that, Darryl." She sounded like she was smiling, but I was not about to look.

TJ covered his mouth, but I saw a grin from under his fingers.

I drank half a beer and set it down. "So, there we were getting ready to noodle. I had duct tape in my tackle box. It's kinda like armor, see? You wrap some on your hands before you go after a catfish. Their bite hurts otherwise."

"Whoa. Is it true that you let them bite your hands?" TJ leaned in closer.

Bobby slapped his leg. "Heck, yea. Those mama cats are not gonna go for bait on a hook, but they will go for you because they think you're a threat to their babies."

TJ frowned. "But wait, what happened to the swamp monster?"

I held up my hand. "Don't get ahead of the story. We had duct tape, and we followed the direction of the V."

"Don't forget the other stuff in your tackle box." Bobby chuckled, and his lazy eye rolled.

"I know what Grampa has in his tackle box. He showed me." TJ snapped a Lego in place.

I tapped my foot until TJ looked up. I jerked my head toward the kitchen and held my finger to my lips. TJ nodded and continued snapping Legos together. "Anyway, we followed what was left of the V-shaped wake until it disappeared. The swamp in that area was thick with trees, which is good because mama catfish love to hide in sunken logs. We thought for sure we were in a great place for noodling."

"Boy, were we wrong!" Bobby punched me in the shoulder.

"Damn it, Bobby. You're gonna ruin the story."

"It's okay Grampa, I already know it's a swamp monster."

"See, I didn't ruin nothing." Bobby leaned back and sulked.

"Anyway." I glared at Bobby, hoping he would keep quiet for ten minutes. "We saw the round curve of a huge tree trunk. I jumped in and reached under the water, but it took a while to find an opening. Once I did, I leaned my chin on the edge of the trunk and reached into the hole. I must have looked like a vet checking a cow." Bobby laughed and slapped his knee.

TJ looked at me sideways with a curled lip. "What?"

Bobby winked at the boy. "It's okay. You'll understand when you're older."

"I didn't get a bite. I tried another hole, still nothing. The next hole, I got a bite all right. Nasty sharp little teeth."

"Yea, you did, screaming like a little girl."

"You would scream too. That monster has sharp teeth." I wrung my right hand thinking about it. I had five band-aids covering the tiny punctures. "On top of it, all that bite seemed to affect me in a weird way. My hand went numb, and my arm started to feel tingly. I could feel the weirdness climbing closer to my head and heart."

"I got him back in the boat." Bobby hit his chest like a proud ape. "And thinking it was a cottonmouth, I started to suck out the poison."

"I told ya before there ain't no cottonmouths in Wisconsin."

"It was poison!" Bobby pawed at his tongue. "My mouth went numb, and I couldn't talk."

"That was the only blessing of the day." I chuckled. "The poison was from the swamp monster." I pointed at Bobby. "Not a snake."

Bobby narrowed his eyes. "It was poison." He pouted a bit as if I would argue.

"I can agree to that." We stared at each other, not wanting to say anything more.

TJ was not satisfied. "What did it look like? How big was it? How'd you kill it?"

"It was tall and thin, covered in scales like a fish. It even had fins, like that one," I pointed to the fin on the wall, "on different parts of its body. It was blue, green, and gray in a striped pattern, like a tiger. I took it out with a stick of dynamite." I smiled, remembering the toss. I watched as it landed right next to the creature before it exploded. When the smoke cleared, the swamp monster was gone, evaporated by the power of dynamite.

"Whoa! I wish I was there." TJ whined.

"Wanna see it?" Bobby was hanging off the edge of the sofa, leaning towards TJ.

I stammered. "Wait, what?" There's no way. He wouldn't have.

"That's why I came over. I've got it in the back of the El Camino." Bobby grinned. "You're welcome."

He did it. He really did. He picked up the carcass and put it in his truck. And now he's inviting TJ, to see the bloody, gut dripping mess. Is he out of his mind?

TJ pumped his chubby little arms and hollered with excitement. "Yes!"

"Oh, hell no. You are not showing that child a bloody carcass." The trailer shook under Gracelyn's thunderous proclamation. "I've seen you boys bring back deer for processing. TJ is too young to be traumatized in such a manner." She stood on the threshold between the living room and kitchen, hands on her hips, luscious arm fat swinging.

Bobby stood, hands up as if holding back Gracelyn. "It's not like that. There's no blood, no missing limbs, no guts pooling out. It's just a body."

TJ's bottom lip protruded dangerously. "I wanna see blood and guts!" His little fists were balled tight. "I want blood and guts!"

Gracelyn waddled over to the boy still sitting among his Legos. She patted him on the head like a pup. "I'll go look, and if it's safe, you can come see too." Gracelyn tried to be soothing but seemed to miss that TJ wanted to see all the blood and guts. He didn't want *safe*. His scowling face said as much. She moved to the front door and went outside.

Bobby and I waited on the couch. We watched TJ become redder and redder. If he kept going, his face would explode. His mouth opened, but I didn't know if he were about to hurl or scream.

Gracelyn returned, frowning. "Is this some kind of joke, Bobby? You ain't got nothing in your El Camino. Nothing swamp monster anyway. You need to toss some of that junk."

Sheet white, Bobby jumped from the couch and ran to the door. I've never seen him move that fast before. TJ's face stopped turning colors. He closed his mouth and stood. The boy rushed after Bobby, and Gracelyn didn't stop him. Well, I wasn't about to get left behind. I zipped past Gracelyn and went to the front porch railing. I noticed Bobby lying on the ground. "What ya doing?"

Bobby's finger shot into the air, pointing at me. "Shut it, A-hole." A puff of dust pipped because his face was pressed to the gravel. He sat up and pointed. "Look at that."

TJ was at Bobby's side in a flash. "What?"

"See the track there? Flat and almost duck-ish?" Our lawn, which was mostly dirt and very little grass, was perfect for collecting footprints and Tarzan droppings.

TJ stomped around as only children can. "Where?"

"No, not there, there. In the dirt by the clump of dandelions. Hell, boy, don't go stepping on it. What's wrong with you?" Bobby scolded.

The print was flat and triangular shaped, which I suppose looked similar to a duck foot. But this foot was well over a size fifteen double-wide, which in my book isn't very duck-like. "I saw it before TJ stomped on it." TJ shot me a squinty accusatory stare.

"Which way was it headed?"

"Not sure. Wait, I see another." I pointed, and Bobby followed my direction.

"Looks like it's going toward the pool." Bobby ran back to his El Camino. "We're gonna need some weapons."

The trailer park where I lived had a pavilion and a pool for all the members to use. It was awfully nice of Betsy and Tom, who owned the land. But it would have been better if they added chlorine from time to time. The pool tended to turn green for six months out of the year. Not that anyone here cared. Plus, there was the added benefit of getting frogs and tadpoles early in the season, like now, when the pool was forgotten. Bass love frogs, and I love bass.

I joined Bobby and TJ as they went through the junk in the back of the El Camino. Bobby pulled out an enormous old clamshell dog crate. The front metal door was bent like a taco. "Did you put the swamp monster in there?" I asked. Bobby's old dog Pepper had chewed up sections of the crate, making it almost worthless.

"Well, yea, I thought it was dead. It stank like fish and earthworms, and I didn't want it to get chewed on by Tarzan or some rabid raccoon. I wanted to protect it." Bobby kicked at the limestone rocks that made up the driveway. Something he did when he was a kid and felt ashamed.

"Look, Bobby, we need to catch or kill that thing before something bad happens."

"We could just go out for supper. You know, just leave for a few hours. And by the time we get back, the cops will have cleaned it up." Bobby sunk his hands in his pockets. "Or maybe you and Gracelyn and TJ can stay with me for a little while."

"Are you suggesting we run?" I asked.

Bobby snorted. "Well, yea. Nobody knows it was me who brought it over."

"I do, Gracelyn does," I indicated TJ. "Can't forget TJ. One of us might accidentally say something."

"Well, don't." Bobby smiled, and his lazy eye flopped. "Besides, it could slink back to the swamp without anyone seeing it, and we're getting worked up over nothing."

"What if it moves into the trailer park? What if it takes over the pool?" TJ asked. "I'm not sure that would be so bad. Maybe I can keep it?"

"This ain't no pet. Weren't you listening to my story? Remember the poison bite?" Were they both out of their minds?

"Well, of course, I remember Grampa. But what if it was protecting its babies? A catfish doesn't mean to kill. It's just protecting."

I disagreed. The boy had never put his hands in the mouth of a catfish. Those mother fish have every intent to kill who or whatever is after their young. Wait a minute, what if TJ is right? What if that was a mother swamp monster? Catfish lay thousands of eggs. Would a swamp monster do the same? A rustle of wind tugged at a receipt protruding from a plastic bag. Something on the paper caught my eye. I pulled it free, then scanned the rest of his vehicle. "Bobby, how long was that swamp monster in the back of your truck?"

Bobby shrugged his shoulders. His lazy eye turned to the left. "I don't know."

"Damn it, Bobby. Think." I thumped him on the forehead.

Bobby frowned. "I had to leave Sweet Savannah in the park overnight." Bobby caressed the side of his painted El Camino. "So, the monster was there for ten hours at least."

"Ten hours? Ten fucking hours?" My hand rubbed my face. I think a headache was moving in. "There was more than one in the back of your truck." I held up the receipt for him to see what looked like a tiny handprint.

"A baby? You're worried about a baby?" Bobby held the paper, measuring the print with his fingers, holding them a couple inches apart. "It ain't gonna be taller than two feet."

"Don't be stupid, Bobby." Anger flared up. He didn't understand. "How many eggs does a catfish lay?"

Bobby's mouth dropped open as he thought. "But this is only one handprint."

"Look in the bed of your truck." I couldn't bring myself to call it Sweet Savannah, no matter how many times he asked me to. Who the hell names their truck anyway?

Bobby and TJ looked over the side. Each one pointed to a different section and claimed that they saw another print.

I nodded. "More than one. We haveta take them all out."

"All of them?" TJ squeaked. I could see the wheels turning in the boy's brainpan. He wanted a pet.

I sighed. "If you're not up to this mission, you should stay inside with your Gramma."

"No, no, I wanna come." TJ's puppy eyes flashed, and he pouted.

"Knock it off, TJ. You're with men now. Time to act the part." I was sick of pampering this child. He needed to grow a set like earlier when he asked for a beer. "No more pouting. No more begging. Got it?"

The boy looked around as if Gracelyn might stick up for him and force us to take him. But she was still inside. His face hardened, and TJ nodded.

"Good." I looked through the rest of the junk in Bobby's El Camino. "Where are the weapons?"

Bobby reached in and grabbed a crowbar, a baseball bat, and a metal ammunition case. "I didn't bring my 12 gauge, but I have dragon's breath rounds in here."

Dragon's breath was an incendiary round. It doesn't have pellets or a ball to back up the fire it belches. "We're going to the pool. I don't think that round is going to help. Plus, who the hell will clean my gun afterward. Since you didn't bring your own. Those damn rounds will gum it up with magnesium."

Bobby shrugged. "I guess I'd clean it."

"Just leave them here. Come on, TJ, let's get some real weapons." I left Bobby at his truck, and we went to the shed. I unlocked the door, then leaned down and whispered to TJ, "You can't tell your Ma or Gramma what I have in here. Understand?" I held the door closed until the boy nodded. Bobby joined us by then, with the bat and crowbar.

Inside my small shed was an old fridge that I converted to a gun safe. It sealed out the moisture and kept my guns safe and Gracelyn none the wiser. Wrapped around the outside were towing chains and locks. Above, in the rafters, was a wooden box of dynamite. If one stick of dynamite wasn't enough to take the creature out, maybe four or five might do it. I pulled the box down and looked inside. Four sticks wrapped up in duct tape and a disposable Bic lighter were left. I pocketed everything. I had worked open the combination locks when we heard a scream.

"Sounded like Mrs. Smith," Bobby said. "She's got all those chickens. You don't suppose...." He trailed off.

Gracelyn's phone sounded. She had "My Achy Breaky Heart" at the highest setting. That awful song ended when she answered. I hoped one of her friends in another part of the park wasn't calling her for help. My fingers moved as fast as I could will them, and the final lock opened. I pushed off the chain and opened the fridge. Inside was my ax, machete, chainsaw, thirty-thirty rifle, and shotgun.

"What the hell Darryl? All that protection for this?" Bobby pointed at my weapons then snorted with disbelief.

I grabbed my 12 gauge and a box of shells, shoving them into Bobby's hands. "I'll pretend you didn't say that."

More screams and hollers rolled across the trailer park. I looked over the remaining weapons. I gave the ax and machete to TJ. "The machete is sharp, the ax not so much. Both will do damage."

Bobby looked at me like I was insane. I explained, "If the kid is in hand-to-hand combat, we're all fucked. Might as well give him a fighting chance." Bobby frowned but nodded.

I pulled the thirty-thirty rifle for myself, slinging it over my shoulder. I stuffed all the shells I owned into my pockets, but there probably wasn't enough. I pulled the chainsaw off its pegs. Bruce would have been proud. "Let's roll!" We left the shed with the fridge wide open and empty.

A car tore down the blacktop road outside my trailer. A head and body hung out the window. The long hair made it impossible to tell if they were male or female. Whoever they were, the handgun they held was beautiful. A Colt forty-four, the most powerful handgun in the world, according to Dirty Harry. They fired round after round as they sped away from some kind of madness. They disappeared, then we heard them burn rubber down county highway MM. They were either headed into town or the freeway.

A small child-like thing ran down the blacktop as if it could catch the squealing car. The blue-green child stopped and slowly turned to face us. Its mouth appeared way too big for its face. Its jaw opened, and we could see rows upon rows of teeth, like a walking shark. The creature made a sound like insane, unabandoned laughter. I felt my blood run like ice.

TJ mumbled, "Mama," then dropped his weapons. It's possible that the boy wet himself.

The creature advanced slowly at first, then it ran towards TJ. I grabbed a shell, put it into the thirty-thirty, pointed, and shot. I missed. The creature was too close to ready another round. I jumped in front of TJ and held up the rifle as a partial shield. The monster jumped. I deflected it from my face.

The swing from Bobby's bat connected the side of the creature's face. Time slowed, and I watched as the monster collapsed around the bat. The sound of breaking bones and soft tissues was music to my ears. The creature flew a couple feet before striking Bobby's truck, sliding off the cattails painted on the fender and into a swamp monster puddle.

I looked at TJ. The boy was staring off into space, shocked into stillness and silence. "TJ, do you want to wait inside with Gramma? Bobby and I got this."

"We do?" Bobby blinked a few times. "You got any spikes or barbed wire in your shed? I think my bat needs an upgrade."

"Yea, nails and a hammer. My shed is your shed." I turned away from Bobby and touched TJ. The boy screamed, then fell to the earth in a heap of tears and whimpering. "TJ, we don't have time for you to fall apart. Let's get you into Gramma." I knelt and picked him up.

TJ stiffened and screamed, "No! I will help you." He sniffled and wiped his nose. "I hafta." The last came out in a whimper. "I hafta. Otherwise, Dad is right, and I'll be nuttin but a mama's boy." He wiped at his nose again, a grim determination on his face. TJ picked up the ax and machete and held them to his chest.

"I'm ready." Bobby returned with a smug grin. His bat was crisscrossed with nails, turning it into a knight's Morningstar.

"Are you ready to break that in?" I nodded to the freshly armored baseball bat.

"Hell yea! Oh, sorry, TJ. I thought you were in the trailer with Gracelyn."

"He's coming along. Don't look at me like that. He has to. It's a matter of honor."

TJ nodded vigorously. "I don't wanna be a mama's boy." Tears poured down his pudgy face.

"You," Bobby thrust the head of the bat at me. "You're an ass. I'll have nothing to do with explaining nothing to nobody. You're gonna hafta."

I didn't understand a word Bobby said. I nodded and smiled. "Yea, sure, Bobby."

Bobby slung the shotgun over his shoulder and walked toward the edge of my trailer. He crept and peeked around the corner. "It's clear." Then he disappeared.

TJ looked up at me, then jerked his head in the direction Bobby went. He followed Bobby's path, and I was right behind. I checked my six, but it was quiet. As I came around the corner, I watched Bobby walk the center road. He'd stop and look around trailers before continuing. It was slow going, but Bobby was being smart—for once.

A donkey and some chickens were in the road, not far from Mrs. Smith's trailer. There was a squeal, and a pig quickly joined the other farm animals. "Get out, foul beast!" came a shrill cry from Mrs. Smith's trailer, but it didn't sound like Mrs. Smith. The cry preceded a loud metal "thunk." A small blue-green body flew out the door, across the porch, striking the neighbor's trailer, and falling to the ground. Gracelynn stomped onto the porch with the air of a lioness. The fat of her upper arms swung with every stride, stirring my loins. In her hand was a ten-pound cast iron frying pan. "And stay out!"

Mrs. Smith ran to Gracelynn's side. "Thank-you. That monster ate all the eggs." The tall thin blonde hugged my wife, then turned away and began to call her pets. "Here chick, chick, chick, chick." The chickens and donkey wandered up the porch stairs and into the trailer. "Come on, pig, what do you need a separate invitation? Come on, pig, pig, pig, pig." The spotted pig snorted then trotted after the other animals. Mrs. Smith pointed at us. "You be careful out there." She entered her trailer and closed the door.

After a few seconds, the door opened again, and out trotted Tarzan. In his mouth was something small and blue-green. It might have been a leg. He dropped it at Gracelynn's feet then looked up at her like an obedient dog. My wife tapped her shoulder, and the orange tabby jumped up gracefully.

"Ain't Tarzan your cat?" Bobby elbowed me in the ribs.

I shrugged. "Gracelyn feeds him."

Gracelyn stomped down the stairs, pointing at TJ with the cast iron pan. "What is he doing here? Why isn't he in the trailer where it is safe?"

The three of us swallowed in unison. I opened my mouth to speak, but TJ got to her first. "Gramma, soon I'll be a man. I need to learn to act like one."

Gracelyn snorted. "Well, you ain't gonna learn from these two." She looked over the weapons we all carried. Her eyes narrowed. "Maybe."

Tarzan growled then jumped from my wife's shoulder. He padded along toward the pool. Without a word, Gracelyn turned and followed the orange tabby, pan held high, ready to put it to use.

Is this what we've come to, following a woman and a cat into battle? We looked at each other. TJ wiped his nose with his forearm. The boy stepped forward as if to follow Gracelyn and Tarzan, but then he stopped and looked at us.

"Get it!" Gracelyn told Tarzan. The cat ran under the skirting of a trailer. A moment later hissing, and strange screaming came from under the thin steel. There was a thud, and the skirting bowed out. Two small blue-green critters came through, with Tarzan herding them toward his mistress. Claws and nips kept the swamp monster babies on target. At the last moment, the orange tabby pounced on one, shoving its face into the ground and biting it hard at the nape. Gracelyn took out the other by swinging the pan with prejudice. My wife sent the creature flying high and into a tree, where it hung lifeless. Tarzan carried his prize to his mistress and dropped it at her feet.

Bobby grunted. "Welp, we ain't got dressed up for nothing. Can't let Gracelyn and Tarzan have all the fun." He sucked at his teeth, refusing to look at me. "We've gotta take this cat hunting." Bobby stepped forward, keeping a pace or two behind Gracelyn and Tarzan as they checked other trailers. TJ was quick to chase after them. I grunted, then followed.

No longer taking the time to investigate every trailer, Tarzan and Gracelyn trotted towards the pool. I joined Bobby and TJ and asked, "Why did they stop looking for the critters under trailers?"

"Gracelyn said there were only a few egg snatchers. She thinks that they got 'em all. Mostly, she's trusting Tarzan to lead her to the next one." Bobby nodded to the raised orange tail as it disappeared behind the upturned and stacked picnic tables that were in the pavilion near the pool.

Tarzan hissed and growled. We heard something huge fall over, and then an orange object was tossed into the pool. Gracelyn screamed, "Tarzan!" She pushed Bobby aside and rushed to find the cat, if he was still alive.

"I don't think so, asshole, that's my cat too!" I rushed forward with Bobby hot on my heels. I started the chainsaw, revving it loud, hoping the noise would bother the creatures. If it did irritate the monsters, it didn't cause them to run away like I expected. In fact, it was strangely quiet. All I could hear was the *bub, bub,*

bub of the chainsaw idling. Nothing moved among the picnic tables.

Bobby twitched; he saw something. He raised his bat and dropped it. When he raised the bat again, a little body came up too, entangled and impaled in the huge nails. The little body screamed and writhed in agony. Bobby seemed startled then smashed the bat into a picnic table to either knock the thing loose or put it out of its misery.

A block of wood whipped past my head. I jerked, realizing Bobby's antics had distracted me. The mama swamp monster stood behind an overturned table and was preparing to toss another. I screamed and charged the creature. The creature threw the chunk of wood, hitting me in the shoulder. I swung the chainsaw and struck the tabletop. The chain dug in, eating hungrily. The creature moved aside as if it expected the attack. It pushed the table, causing the wood to pinch the blade, disabling my weapon. Then came around the table to my side. How the hell did it know about chainsaws? I jerked the chainsaw a few times but couldn't get it to budge. "Son of a bitch." I let it go and backed up. I had other weapons.

I rolled the thirty-thirty rifle around the strap and held it ready. I kept an eye on the monster as I worked the shells out of my pockets. Why didn't I have the damn weapon prepared to go? One shell loaded, two, three.

TJ yelled, "Grampa, help."

I looked away for a second and saw TJ fighting a baby monster near Gracelyn, who was lying on the ground. I fired a shot at the creature then levered another shell into place. The beast seemed to have moved, or I missed. I shot at it again then ran to TJ and Gracelyn.

I stood over Gracelyn, who had a wet Tarzan in her arms. Both of them were quiet and limp. I looked back at the pavilion. The monster wasn't in sight. "What happened, TJ?"

"Gramma pulled Tarzan out of the pool, but he was hurt bad. One of the monsters bit him. The little monsters started to surround us. Gramma smashed the ones who got close. I think I was in the way." TJ sniffled. "She hit one near me, but then she got bit on the leg." The boy frowned. "Then I got mad and cut its head off." TJ held the blade up, showing me the blood on it. "But now Gramma isn't moving. Tarzan neither. Are they dead?"

"I don't think so." I shook my head. "Remember I got bit too, and I'm still here."

"That's cuz Bobby sucked it out."

I forgot about him. "Where is Bobby."

"Are you gonna ask him to suck out the poison?" TJ sounded hopeful.

"Actually, no, I want to gather our forces." *And make sure Bobby was alright too.* "We need to end this and get an ambulance." I saw a lone picnic table nearby. "TJ, help me move that table. It will help protect Gracelyn and Tarzan." As we pulled the table over, I kept an eye on the pavilion. Where the hell did that monster go?

"There's Bobby." TJ pointed.

I whistled, and Bobby trotted over to us. "I found a nest of the little fuckers in that hollow tree." Bobby hiked his thumb over his shoulder. "Whoa, what happened here?" He looked over Gracelyn and Tarzan.

"They got bit. I don't want them to die." TJ whimpered.

Bobby checked Gracelyn and Tarzan. "They're breathing. When your Grampa got bit, he slept for a little while before he woke up."

"Damn it, Bobby."

"Look at him Daryl, the boy is scared."

A deep bellowing growl seemed to shake the earth. The filthy pool sloshed and jiggled like jelly.

"What's that?" TJ squeaked.

"I don't know." I heard something move in the brush nearby. Three of the little ones rushed past and into the pavilion. "I think mama was calling the little ones."

"What for?" TJ asked.

"I think it's calling for help," Bobby said, slapping the crowbar into his hand. He dropped the crowbar, swung the shotgun into his hands, cocked it, and fired. The birdshot took out two that were headed to their mother. Another three ran into the pavilion.

"You'll run out of ammo too fast. I've got a better idea. They're all in the pavilion, right?" I pulled the bundle of dynamite free. I patted myself until I found the Bic lighter. There was liquid in the blue see-through container. I flicked my thumb across the brass dial of the lighter. Nothing happened, no spark. I shook the container and tried again. Failure.

Bobby pointed. "How old is that thing? Could be water in there."

"Shut up," I growled.

"Throw it at her. We'll light it another way."

"What if she throws it back? That one is smart. It disabled my chainsaw."

Bobby took the dynamite from my hands and cut the wicks short. "Make it, so it don't matter. Let her pick it up now." Bobby snickered.

"How are you planning on lighting it from here?" I scowled at him.

Bobby pulled a few incendiary rounds from his pocket. They read *dragon's breath* on the side. "I brought my lighter." He grinned, and his lazy eye flopped. "Their ad says it can spray fire up to three hundred feet. All I need is fifty."

"You're a crazy bastard."

"Maybe so." Bobby poked the dynamite in my hand. "Throw it. Let's make sure we kill her real good."

"You're cleaning my rifle."

"If I survive." Bobby stood and shot off a regular round at the pavilion. "The next one is dragon's breath. Toss it."

"TJ, stay low with Gramma." I joined Bobby, and jumping sideways, I threw the bundle of dynamite like a football. A few moments later, the creature appeared. It picked up the dynamite, then sniffed and licked it.

Bobby fired.

The round was like nothing I ever saw. It was more firework than bullet, more sparks and noise than I expected. I was so bedazzled that I forgot to duck and cover. The dynamite exploded in a flash of light, and I was thrown hard to the ground. I know I was dazed, but for how long? I remember chunks of wood falling all around me. I remember my head pounding, and my ears made a high-pitched squeal.

I sat up. Smoke from the pavilion and the chunks of wood around me made it difficult to see. I coughed and hacked. "Bobby?" I couldn't hear myself over the ringing in my ears and the pain in my head. "Gracelyn? TJ?" The more I moved, the more my body hurt. I tried to stand, but the ground was unsteady under my feet. I fell back to the ground. The ringing in my ears began to subside, and I thought I could hear people talking. It sounded like bees buzzing. "Hello?"

There, I heard something again. I crawled to where TJ and Gracelyn should have been. I didn't dare try to stand yet. The world kept tipping to the right and wouldn't straighten out. I passed the picnic table, and there was TJ. He appeared safe. I touched his leg.

The boy jumped then sat up. "I thought you died." Tears ran down his face. His eyes were swollen and red. TJ pushed his way into my arms, rubbing his face on my chest.

I held him close, feeling him tremble, and it dawned on me how little he was. I saw Gracelyn and Tarzan nearby, and they appeared to be in the same position as before the dynamite, except for light debris covering them. I reached over and removed a shingle from my wife's back. Gracelyn moved. Slowly at first and then, she pulled Tarzan closer to her chest. The tomcat meowed.

TJ jerked from my arms and stared at Gracelyn. He blinked at me and then looked back at his Gramma. The boy leaned on top of her and the orange cat. "Being a Gramma's boy ain't so bad! Right Tarzan?" TJ scooped up the tomcat and hugged him separately. Tarzan accepted the indignity in stride. Maybe he was too tired to fight. The boy set the cat on his feet, but Tarzan was still too tipsy to walk straight. He flopped onto the ground and proceeded to groom his fur.

"Bobby," I shouted. "Bobby. You dead?"

"Yes," came a muffled call from a pile of debris.

I tried standing again, pleased that the world was much steadier. I pushed part of the pavilion roof off the pile, and Bobby came into sight. He was cut up and dirty but didn't seem too worse for wear, all things considered.

Multiple sirens approached the trailer park. Bobby laughed and then sighed. "So, you reckon we ought to find the carcass as proof of a swamp monster? Or should we just hide, back at your trailer, and deny the whole thing?"

It Came from the Trailer Park

Jimmy's Good Homebrew

By Charity Ayres

The low hum that danced across the baked air shifted into a wail followed by a long chittering sound. The mournful sound of the cicada cut through the otherwise silent world and created an exclamation to the heat that sizzled skin and caused sweat to flow in long rivulets down overheated bodies.

Smack!

"Fucking bugs, fucking heat," Jimmy flicked the now-dead mosquito off of his arm from where he'd slapped it into a bloody inkblot.

"Yep," Cyan nodded like a slow-moving bobblehead, her eyes closed. Her skin had the mottled color of a harsh sunburn, and her freckles looked dark against the pinkness. She scraped a nail across her skin to pull a lock of cotton candy pink hair away from her face.

"That all ya got to say?" Jimmy shifted to push at Cyan's leg with the tip of his dirty toe. She swatted him without opening her eyes.

"Depends. You gonna say anything else? All you've said for the past two days is, 'Fucking bugs, fucking heat.'"

"Well, if the damned power weren't out-"

"You mean if you'd paid the bill," she cut in.

"I paid the bill, Cyan. Ain't like you got room to talk, anyhow," Jimmy reached down and scooped up the jar of mostly-clear liquid to take a long draught. His throat worked as he tilted his head back to pour it in before swallowing and giving a full-body shiver. He scratched at thistle-bare whiskers on his chin. They were almost invisible due to sparsity and the pale color of his hair.

"You know I ain't had power for almost two months now, Jimmy," Cyan opened her eyes to give him a long roll before shutting them again. She leaned her head back against the wall of Jimmy's trailer, the old seat creaking underneath her in warning.

"But you almost never pay your bill. I pay mine every month," Jimmy nudged her with the jar, and Cyan took it. She opened one eye to look at the drink before she curled her lip and took a gulp. She swallowed and coughed.

"Damn, that's some rough shit. Worse for being warm."

Jimmy just grinned and reached for the jar. "You just don't appreciate good 'shine."

Cyan snorted. "I *make* good 'shine, Jimmy. You make fucking rotgut that's burning us from the inside while the heat's cooking us from the outside."

The low whine of a horsefly zipped around their heads for a moment before landing on Jimmy's arm. He downed the rest of his drink before bothering to swat it.

"Fucking bugs, fucking-"

"Not this again!" Cyan cut in and gave him a wide-eyed death glare. Jimmy shrugged and walked inside his trailer. She heard him puttering around inside before he came out with a full jar. She shook her head and opened her mouth, but a loud hum sounded in the distance and stopped her.

Cyan and Jimmy leaned forward, putting a hand to their brows as they looked down the winding dirt road leading away from the trailer park. Dust rose in the distance on the road.

Jimmy frowned and looked at Cyan with one eyebrow raised. The park they lived in was barely that and rarely saw any kind of visitors. Cyan had a trailer a few spots behind Jimmy's. The only other inhabitant was an old-timer named Moses, who lived in the very back of the lot, almost up against the river. The only other thing in the park was an abandoned, rusted-through trailer. Jimmy's rig was the closest to the road and where they often sat.

"Maybe they're coming to fix the power," Jimmy said softly as they both watched the smoke-like rise of dust on the horizon. He knew there was a chance that he hadn't gotten his bill in on time or with enough money to keep them from cutting him off. The likelihood that it was the power company coming down the road was pretty slim.

Suddenly a big truck came into view that was hauling ass. Behind it, the duo could see another vehicle.

"Think he's running from the police?" Cyan cocked her head. The truck had the gas floored and hit every rut as it bounced up and down in the air above the road.

"Maybe...wait, there's another car...."

And then there was another and another. The line of cars increased as it spread like thin wings behind the truck and across the fields like a motorized stampede.

"Where the fuck do they all think they're going?" Cyan looked at the line and then behind them into the trailer park, which dead-ended at Moses' rig. "The only roads past us are deer trails."

"Dunno," Jimmy wondered for a brief moment if the stash of "antiques" his grandfather gave him that was hidden under his bed could account for a full-scale police show-down. Cyan wondered if there was time to grab her shotgun before the vehicles reached the trailer park.

Both watched as the invasion of cars and trucks reached the front of the trailer park and slammed to a stop. A tall man in a dirty wifebeater over expensive, if torn, slacks and ridiculous wingtips climbed out of the cab and walked toward them.

Jimmy looked the man up and down for a moment. His eyes snagged on the expensive watch, and his eyebrow quirked at the stains of black and green on the man's forearm. As he got closer, they caught the scent of expensive cologne overlaid with the reek of fire, diesel, and sweat.

"Want to buy some 'shine? Made it meself," Jimmy held out the jar. The tall stranger arched an eyebrow at him, reached in his pocket, and threw his wallet at Jimmy's feet. He took the mason jar and downing it. He sputtered when he finished and handed Jimmy back the jar.

"What's the fastest way around the river?"

"Go back the way you came and-"

"They've taken the city; we can't go back," the man cut him off.

"Who's taken the city," Cyan leaned forward and looked at the tall man. Jimmy saw a gleam in her eyes. The man was attractive, but that didn't mean she had to look at him with such excitement.

"The aliens."

Jimmy and Cyan stared at the man and said nothing. Someone in one of the cars at the entrance to the park leaned on the horn, and the man blinked.

"The aliens that landed two days ago and started destroying the cities?"

Jimmy and Cyan continued to stare at the man.

"Look, I don't know what rock you've been living under, but the city is gone, as are most of the largest cities around the world, last we heard. The government tried to nuke them, but they crawled right through like it was nothing. We tried to fight them with guns and bombs, but it rolls right over that damned hard shell on their backs. We've got no choice but to run, now. Word is that the military's got a few bunkers down near the coast, so we're headed there. I recommend you pack your...."

He looked at the trailer behind them, and his left eye twitched for a moment.

"House?" Jimmy prompted with narrowed eyes at the condescension in Mr. Fancy Watch's eyes.

"Right. Pack what you can and get out," Fancy ran a hand down his face and turned his head to survey the park. "Get anyone who might be left here out, now. Do you have a car or truck? I might be able to find someone with room to take you."

Horns honked behind him, belying the theory that someone might wait for them to pack and climb aboard the retreat train. Cyan lifted her butt just above the seat and stared at the group behind the man before slowly lowering herself back down.

"Huh," Jimmy grunted. "We'll check to see if old Moses can go."

There was a long moment where no one moved or spoke before the man cleared his throat.

"Um, great. Now, about getting around the river...."

"You're gonna have to off-road it but follow the tree line until you get to an old burnt-out house with a tree growing out of it," Cyan gestured over Jimmy with her left arm. Jim stood and went inside his rig. "Follow what's left of the drive to a deer trail. Gonna have to be single-file, or you won't fit. Keep on, and you'll find a beat-up covered bridge they used to use for cattle and shit. Might cave in if you go across too many at once, but it's shallow, so you can drive the taller vehicles over if ya need. Old highway's about a mile east as the crow flies."

Jim came out and handed the man a jug of moonshine and nodded.

"Thanks," the guy hesitated once more, opened his mouth, shut it, and then opened it again. "Don't wait too long to leave.

I don't know how many alien foot soldiers saw us hightail it out of the city, but they move fast and eat everything in their path. You've got a day, maybe two at best before they spread to the outskirts."

"Noted. We're gonna go rouse Moses now," Cyan nodded.

"Enjoy the 'shine," Jimmy nodded and jerked his chin at the man in good-bye.

As the man walked away, he turned to Cyan and cocked his head.

"Whatcha think?"

"They're scared. That city boy looked like he'd been through hellfire and brimstone fo sho," Cyan shook her head. "Thinking we better brave crazy Moses and load the truck up some just in case."

"You first. Moses damn near shot my foot off last time I tried to be neighborly."

"Pissing a hello on his front lawn when you're drunk as a skunk is not neighborly, Jimmy."

"It needed watering. I was tryin' ta help."

Cyan rolled her eyes and stood. Her shirt clung to her doughy back, and Jimmy heard several pops as she moved. He reached over and grabbed a ripped tee to pull over his skinny chest. They walked down the steps to the hard-packed dirt that served as a walkway to Jimmy's door. It didn't take them long to hit the dried grass barrier that was Moses' lot, but it felt like a slow walk through hell in the burning heat. Waves of heat rose off of the packed earth around them and in the dried grass that was the front yard. It was as though they could see the grass burning.

Jimmy paused at the line of grass and rolled back and forth on his feet. Cyan turned to arch an eyebrow at him.

"You gonna go knock or what?"

"How 'bout we just yell for him from here?" Jimmy tucked a hand in the pocket of his dirty jeans and pursed his lips before taking a sip from the jar he brought with him.

"Chicken shit," Cyan muttered and shoved him forward with both hands, keeping pace behind to shove him every step or two. "He ain't gonna shoot you."

"You don't know that. You know he don't trust no one other than those kooks he talks to on the radio," Jimmy muttered as they reached the door. He lifted his fist and rapped on the loose screen door before stepping to the side of the doorway.

"What, you think he's going to blast through his door just for you? Like he'd waste the ammo that way," Cyan rolled her watery blue eyes and pushed her hair out of her face. She leaned toward the door. "Moses! Moses, open up! It's Cyan and Jimmy."

"Get your dirty hick ass off my porch before I let my double-barrel give you a kiss, Jimmy." His voice rasped out in a low growl from their left. Both of them spun to see his gun lifted and aimed squarely at Jimmy's chest. The old coot was fully dressed in army fatigues with black paint smeared under his eyes. The sun glared off of the white pate of his bald head. "Hope you emptied your bladder before coming over here."

Jimmy put his hands above his head, dribbling some moonshine on his shirt in his haste. "It was one damn time, Moses! I apologized."

"Don't recall *that* ever happening," Moses chewed at something and looked them both up and down. "Besides, how do I know you two ain't the aliens come to claim me?"

"Apparently, they're bigger, badder, and more bug-like from what we hear," Cyan lifted one shoulder and pursed her mouth. "Plus, I'm thinking they probably wouldn't bother trying to talk to you before killing you."

"Fair 'nough." Moses lowered his gun. "Radios went silent yesterday from my city friends. The only ones still online are the other park pirates in the state. It seems like the aliens ain't reached out to us poor trailer folk as of yet."

Jimmy nodded, his arms still frozen above his head.

"Put your damn fool arms down, Jimmy," Cyan hissed and turned back to Moses. "So, you knew about this shit and didn't bother to tell us."

"I told y'all weeks ago that something was coming, and you didn't listen. Why would now be any different?"

"You also told me Santa Claus was a construct from the government so that they could take over kids' brains to turn them into some kind of mini military," Cyan drawled.

"And that all garden gnomes have trackers and are made of powdered C4 in case the government needs to kill off a neighborhood," Jimmy added.

"All true but kind of moot right now," Moses turned away and motioned them to follow over his shoulder. "Though if we could get the signals for the gnomes, we might be able to use it against the alien fuckers."

"According to the fancy city boy who came past a bit ago, they tried bombing the aliens, and it didn't faze them," Jimmy called from where he followed behind Cyan. "They're headed to some military base or bunker or something to the east."

"Yeah, my buddy at Riverside Park said it's about an hour southeast of him. They were headed that way, too."

"My truck is mostly full if you want to grab some stuff, and we'll head out," Cyan said as they rounded the rig and went in the back door.

As he stepped through, Jimmy let out a low whistle. Wall to ceiling of the rig was covered with boards, lights, and technology that Jimmy had never seen before. The interior looked like the inside of the computer he'd found in the dumpster at his last job, except it was all on instead of dead and powerless. Three visible computer monitors showed nothing, but blue screens and headphones hung over a massive office chair.

"You two grab your shit and bring it back here. We're taking the whole rig," Moses looked them over for a long moment before leaning over to type something on a keyboard. "I was just about to raise the rig a bit and release the clamps when you two came wandering over."

"We can't drive this bucket through the trail! It won't fit on the old Smith property or through the bridge," Jimmy motioned around the room at the various equipment filling the room. It was the master bedroom of the rig, so no telling what additional weight existed in the rest of the rig.

"This rig could double as a bunker," Moses sighed and leveled Jimmy with a look. "The wheels are tripled up underneath, and I do regular maintenance on the whole thing. My truck could haul a big rig if I chose. Shut your mouth about things you know nothing about, you damn hick. If you hadn't walked over here with Cyan, I'd have left your dumbass here when I pulled out."

Jimmy's mouth would have made an excellent trap for bugs as he stared at the old man.

"Guess your paranoid ass is good for us," Cyan let out a low, whispery laugh. "Okay, so what do we need to do, Moses?"

The old coot looked from them to the equipment; his eyes narrowed. Jimmy knew that look from when Bobo Cooper tricked him into handing over his favorite truck in the first grade.

"You'll drive, Cyan. That way, I can stay in the rig," he nodded to himself before tossing an annoyed look at Jimmy. Jimmy knew Moses was trying to figure out a way to uninvite him.

"First, go grab whatever you have to take and be back here in ten minutes," Moses jerked his head toward the door behind them in dismissal.

Cyan tugged Jimmy out behind her, and he half stumbled down the steps. Moses came out behind them and climbed under the rig with a speed that surprised them both.

"Jimmy, go," Cyan shoved him ahead of her. "Only get what you absolutely need and get your ass back over here, like he said."

Jimmy stumbled once and then set off at a jog. He stepped into the disaster that was his rig. Wrappers littered the table alongside pillars of beer cans and empty mason jars. He ran into his bedroom, scooped up the "antiques" his grandpa left him: a shotgun, handgun, and all of the ammo he could find. Beside his kitchen counter sat five jugs of his homemade moonshine. His gaze flitted between the jugs and his guns.

"City boy said that weapons are useless against the bastards," Jimmy scratched at his chin as his pale eyes flitted back and forth between the weapons and his 'shine. "Seems like we might need some end of the world party fuel. Plus, we run out of gas. We can add a bit in as a back-up."

He wasn't sure moonshine would work as fuel, though he'd heard someone say they'd done it once. Either way, it was a pretty good argument for taking his moonshine over the guns.

Jimmy scooped up his handgun, tucked it into the waistband of his jeans, and filled his pockets with bullets. He reached for the first jug and, finding it light, downed the contents. A full-body shudder ran through him as it hit his gut with a vengeance. His moonshine was for sipping; he'd always said that. He scooped up the remaining four jugs and headed out of his rig.

He stumbled to Moses' rig due to the combined weight of the jugs and the lightheadedness from downing a good amount of moonshine. The old man's front doors were open, and Jimmy walked in to set the pitchers down.

The living room was clean and sparse, with built-in cabinetry and furnishings. The old man hadn't been lying when he said his rig was set up for travel if need be. It looked more like the interior of a camper than a trailer home. He noticed it was narrower than his rig and wondered if it wasn't some kind of converted fifth wheel instead of a trailer.

He wandered further in and found the kitchen. It had a basic hotplate and a tiny microwave over the sink with a dish rack. Inside the cabinets were rations stacked neatly and carefully, filling each cabinet to the brim. It was truly a bunker with military survival rations and a narrow water filtration beside what looked to be an angular water storage. Jimmy shook his head and closed the cabinet.

He wandered back to the door to see Cyan carrying a couple of large duffels toward him. He hopped out and took both from her, putting them inside the rig. Both were so full that they wouldn't zip. One was filled with weapons and clothes, while the other was full of food and water.

"Where's your stuff?" Cyan asked as he set down the bags. Jimmy motioned at the jugs, and she slapped herself in the forehead. "Are you shitting me, Jimmy? What about food? Clothes? Family heirlooms? Something?"

"Oh! Right!" Jimmy jumped down out of the rig and set off at a near-sprint to his trailer. He shoved clothes from his pile on the floor into a backpack before reaching inside his closet. Inside was the hammered copper pot that was the original still his grandfather had given him. Still and bag in hand, he ran to the open doorway of Moses' trailer under the glaring gaze of Cyan.

"I hope that bag at least has clothes or something in it?" She stared at the copper pot in Jimmy's arms with a look of disgust.

"Yep."

"Time to go!" Moses paused as he stepped into the rig as though he sensed the tension in the room but didn't care what it was about. "Cyan, the truck is hooked up and ready. She's a little temperamental to anyone but me, so just be kind to her, and she'll get us where we want to go." He looked at Jimmy. "Can you follow a paper map, dumbass?"

"He's destroyed almost every phone he's ever had and doesn't have a clue about map apps," Cyan cut in with an eye roll. "A paper map is *all* he knows."

"Good. I marked the path on the map so clearly that even that idiot should be able to help you navigate. There's a radio in the truck that I'll use to tell you if we need to change course." He stared at them for a long moment while they stared back blankly. "Well? Get your asses in the truck. This damn rig ain't gonna drive itself to Riverside or that damned government pit everyone's headed to."

Jimmy and Cyan jumped out the door. Moses had knocked the porch loose when he came in, and it sat on its side on the ground. He pulled the door shut and latched it behind them. Jimmy looked up at the door. It looked a good deal higher than it had when he'd gone in a moment ago.

Under the rig, he could see a bed of massive wheels holding the trailer aloft. The tires looked like something he'd seen on a monster truck with their ridges. Cyan shoved him, and they ran the length of the trailer to a large truck that Jimmy was sure he'd never seen before.

"Where's he been hiding this thing?" Cyan whistled and ran around the front of the truck to get in on the driver's side.

Jimmy reached up for the handle and hauled himself into the truck. It wasn't quite as big as a big rig, but it was bigger than his old pickup truck. He dropped into the seat and pulled the open map off of the dashboard. Cyan buckled in and gave him a look until Jimmy pulled the seatbelt across his chest and clicked it in place.

"Aliens have destroyed most of the world, and you're worried about a seatbelt," Jimmy grumbled as he spread the map out on his lap.

"Why the hell am I fastening in all this damn moonshine!" The radio roared with Moses' ire, and Cyan cut Jimmy a glance.

"At least it will be a party," Cyan replied into the handset of the radio with an eye roll.

"Tell that asshole not to get us lost," Moses called back.

"He can hear you," Cyan snorted before throwing the truck into gear and accelerating.

"I know," Moses replied. "Now, radio silence unless absolutely necessary. You never know who's listening."

"Old bastard was the one who started it," Jimmy huffed and then looked back at the map. They'd follow a similar path that they'd given the travelers from earlier but needed to follow the shore of the river for a bit further. Moses had a railroad bridge marked as their turning point.

"Did you know there were tracks near here?"

Cyan nodded once as she mowed over the edge of the fence at the entrance to the trailer park. The truck was a bit wide and didn't turn easily. "It hasn't been used in about fifty years, but the bridge is still there and in pretty good shape. Forgot about it."

Jimmy looked in the side view mirror and watched the trailer park disappear behind them in a cloud of dust. He stared for a good while until he couldn't make out anything that looked familiar behind them.

"It was just a place, Jimmy," Cyan cocked her head at him. "You always complained about your rig and being in the middle of nowhere as it was."

"Guess I shouldn't have," Jimmy admitted.

"Why's that?" Cyan tilted her head toward him but kept her eyes on the road.

"If I'd lived in the city, I'd prolly be dead," Jimmy shrugged.

They were both silent as the truck mowed on through fields of grass and tall weeds. The silence stretched for a moment as they both thought about how the day had changed. The moment broke when Cyan drove over a particularly hilly part of the trail.

"I don't feel most of these bumps," she commented. "This is a damn fine truck."

They shifted into comfortable jabber about which truck brands were the best as they drove on. The railroad bridge showed up so fast that they almost went right over the sunken tracks and past it. Cyan paused the truck and looked out over the decrepit bridge. She picked up the radio.

"You sure about this bridge, Moses?"

"Drive a little closer and let me look," he called back. Cyan pushed forward and stopped about a quarter of a football field away. They heard some kind of humming. They both looked around the inside of the cab to try to pinpoint it.

"I still can't quite tell. Drive forward a bit more so the camera can pick it up," Moses grumbled.

"You could come out and look, you know," Cyan replied but cut the distance in half. Jimmy knew she didn't want to get too close in case she needed to back up.

"It's a little old, but it'll hold us," Moses snapped through the radio, and Cyan sighed with a slow shake of her head. The man's belief that he was never wrong was likely to get them all killed.

Cyan pushed down on the accelerator and drove forward onto the bridge. Unlike the earlier part of the drive, they felt the beams and gaps on the bridge as they drove. Jimmy tried to distract himself by looking for patterns in the rust, but all it did was show him that the whole damn bridge was covered in it.

"Less impressed with the truck right about now. A smaller one would be nice," Jimmy muttered.

"You're just worried the weight will break through and send us falling to our deaths like when you shot that squirrel out of the tree," Cyan said without looking up. Her hands had a death grip on the wheel, and she locked her eyes forward.

"I didn't know it would land head-first," Jimmy's voice rose, and his cheeks flushed. They'd had this argument before.

"Pinging a squirrel in the head when it was that high in the tree...."

"I weren't aiming for that one!" Jimmy snarled. Cyan opened her mouth to comment when they heard a loud grinding noise, and the truck stopped. The radio snarled out Moses' discontent.

"Why'd we stop?"

"We're fixin to check it. Keep your wig on," Cyan yelled into the radio and then dropped it back down. She eyed Jimmy, who shrugged, and they both climbed out of the truck. One of the front sets of wheels on the trailer was dropped down between broken beams on the bridge.

"Force of the other wheels shoulda pushed it through, I'd think," Jimmy scratched his head. He walked over and kicked it.

"What the hell did you think that would do?" Cyan slapped him on the back of the head. Jimmy shrugged, shuffling his feet like a small boy. "Stay here while I go see if I can't back her up and pull her forward to clear it."

"Yes, ma'am."

"Don't sass me," she yelled over her shoulder.

Jimmy tucked his hands in his pocket and watched as Cyan pushed the rig back and forth or tried to. The wheels looked truly stuck. A few moments later, Cyan cut the engine and came to stand by Jimmy. They heard the back door open up, and Moses came wandering out of the rig to look.

"I can't rock it loose because it's stuck," Cyan said in a voice that told Jimmy it was something she'd already said to Moses a few times.

"Need a jack and a spare cross-beam," Jimmy said, his head angled to look at the tires. Cyan and Moses stared at him for nearly a minute without responding. Problem-solving had never been one of Jimmy's strong suits, and they both knew it.

"I'll get the jack," Moses got moving back toward the rig.

"I saw a loose section we can haul over," Cyan jumped over the gap and ran back down the bridge.

Jimmy watched her go, shrugged, and walked over to pull open the front door of Moses' trailer. Just inside, he could see his jugs of moonshine strapped to one of the immovable cabinets. He also saw his way in: a rolled-up ladder. He jumped and swatted at it until he got it close enough to pull open. Jimmy climbed in, filled a jar he'd used as a lid on the jug with booze, and climbed back down, flinging the ladder up before he closed the door.

"Are you going to pick daisies all day or come help me?" Cyan yelled from a little way down the bridge. Jimmy took a quick sip before he jogged toward her with his drink in hand.

"James McCobb, you ain't got the sense God gave a billy goat. Put down that shine and help me!" Cyan tugged at a loose beam that had broken near where the train tracks ran over the bridge. It wasn't a full beam, but it was at least a 150 pound or so section.

Jimmy took a good swig and put the jar down near where the beam jutted out. They worked to wiggle it back and forth, grunting and growling as they tried to pull it free from whatever had it pinned in place.

Jimmy paused to wipe sweat from his brow and took another drink. It was getting closer to evening, but the heat hadn't abated. The sound of the cicadas lifted around them. As Jimmy drank and Cyan shifted around on the bridge in an attempt to find a better way to tug out the beam, the sound grew louder.

"Fucking heat, fucking-"

"Hush your mouth!" Cyan suddenly slapped a hand over his face and turned to look down the bridge. Jimmy turned to look and saw movement.

At first, it looked like a large dog running in a combination of hops and sprints, but the noise of the cicada grew with it. Jimmy stuck a finger in his ear and shook it, but the sound didn't decrease. It got painfully loud the closer the creature got.

"Cyan, d'you think-"

"Shit!"

A shotgun blast cracked through the air, and Moses was suddenly beside them, shooting at the thing running toward them. It was unclear whether or not the shot even touched on the creature, but it seemed to speed up. A low whine joined the clicking rattle of sound that Jimmy'd thought was a cicada. Cyan howled as she put both palms over her ears and dropped to her knees on the bridge.

Jimmy pulled out his handgun and fired. It was just close enough that he saw the bullet hit and bounce off of something that looked half like the bug it sounded like and half like a massive cockroach.

"That dog won't hunt! Run!" Moses yelled.

Jimmy looked down at a crouching Cyan who still had her hands over her ears and turned to see Moses' backside as he hightailed it as fast as his old body would take him. In one of Jimmy's hands, he held the gun, and in the other was his jar of moonshine. Time slowed for a moment as he contemplated his longtime friend on her ass, a gun, and his moonshine. He shook his head just as Cyan's leg flailed out and sent the jar flying from his hand. Jimmy reached down, grabbed Cyan's elbow, and pulled her up to run.

He dragged Cyan a couple of steps when a shriek rent the air, shattering the sounds of the alien's pursuit. Cyan dropped her hands from her ears as they both turned back. The creature had stopped its run down the bridge and seemed to be erupting.

"Tell me that thing isn't giving birth," Cyan breathed.

They watched as the creature stumbled a few more steps with glowing innards liquifying and spouting up from its body like a strange, destructive fountain. It bubbled, made an odd warbling noise as it stuttered to a stop, and just seemed to ooze into the beams around the railroad ties.

"What the hell just happened?" Moses was suddenly beside them, peeking between their heads to stare.

"I don't know," Cyan shook her head. "The sound it was making...I couldn't think, and then Jimmy...."

She turned and looked Jimmy up and down as though she hadn't been his neighbor for nearly ten years. Jimmy reached his hand up, still holding the gun, and used the back of it to wipe sweat from his brow.

"You shot at it, right?" Cyan asked.

"Yup. Bounced off it like a bad check," Jimmy shrugged.

"Then what?" Moses leaned close to look into Jimmy's eyes. He could smell that the man had recently eaten jerky and felt his neck slowly retract his face away.

"Helped up Cyan and tried to run," he twitched his nose before he took a step back from the old man.

Cyan looked at the gun in his hand. She frowned and looked around. "Where's the jar of shine you were drinking?"

Jimmy's pale, bloodshot gaze darted between the others. He chewed his response for a long time before answering.

"Threw it when I picked you up. I couldn't carry it, the gun, and you. 'Shine had ta go," he nodded and saw Cyan's eyes light up. She reached over and punched him on the shoulder, her mouth set in a wide grin.

All three of them slowly turned to the still-bubbling mass that was the alien.

"Well, butter my butt and call me a biscuit," Moses reached over and slapped Jimmy hard on the back. "We need to get the trailer loose, and I need to contact everyone I can."

"Could be a fluke," Cyan cocked her head and stared down the tracks.

"But it sounds like nothing else has worked so far, so it's something," Moses muttered and walked with them down the bridge to the chunk of wood they'd been trying to pry loose.

The three of them heaved and pushed until it slid free from where it was wedged. The broken end looked shattered and rotted, but it otherwise seemed intact. Moses ran to the rig and tapped on a section at the back. A compartment that had been entirely invisible popped open. He pulled out a small chainsaw and goggles. In no time, he had the beam cut to a long angle.

The man worked faster than they would have expected at his age. He quickly set the jack and had Cyan and Jimmy place the shaved-down plank under the wheel. It was less than an hour before they got the rig free and were again moving along the bridge at a steady pace. Cyan drove a little faster, hoping that the momentum would keep them moving if they found any other large gaps. Moses was inside the rig calling anyone he could to explain their discovery.

After crossing the bridge, Moses gave them a couple of updates on the course but was otherwise radio silent. Cyan glanced at Jimmy several times as he sipped from a new jar of moonshine.

"Something to say?" Jimmy grunted and took a good swig of his drink.

"Nope," she grinned and turned back to the road. "It's just-"

"Change of course. There's a road about three miles ahead on the right. It leads to the Heavenly Hills trailer park. We're stopping there," Moses cut in.

"Roger dodger," Cyan called back on the radio. They'd transitioned onto a decently level road and picked up speed. They'd reach their new destination quickly, but Moses started chatting on the radio about what he'd found out.

It seemed several of the trailer park occupants had been gathering near Heavenly Hills because the nearby military bunker had stopped letting anyone come inside. Some of Moses' friends said they thought the aliens could detect heat signatures or something, and the military didn't want to lure them in. He also said a buddy of his had a massive still at the trailer park, and they wanted to pump out as much moonshine as possible. Moses had tried the military bandwidths, but no one would respond to his calls.

"Bastards are all about controlling us but not helping us," he growled just as they were turning down the road he'd directed them to.

Ahead of them was a steep incline, and Cyan shifted gears to haul the massive rig up the hill. It leveled out at the top, and then they were at the gates of Heavenly Hills. Though, if you read the sign with just the upright and not the hanging letters, it read "Hely Hills."

Jimmy snickered and raised his glass in salute as they went through the rusted gateway.

The park was alive with people walking all around, going in and out of trailers, and a line of old codgers in beat-up nylon lawn chairs with shotguns resting on their laps. One of them jutted his chin up at Jimmy as they came in, and he returned the gesture. Another old-timer waved a jug at them a few seats down, and Jimmy lifted his jar in return.

They made it about halfway into the park before Moses' voice came over the radio.

"Turn left at the orange trailer."

They couldn't have missed the orange caution cone trailer if they'd tried. Beyond it was a big roundabout that Cyan pulled into and angled back so they could get back out of the park when they needed. She parked, and they climbed out of the cab to find Moses already running cords to a nearby plug.

"You Charlie?"

Jimmy and Cyan spun to see a scrawny shirtless guy wearing jeans that'd seen better days and no shoes.

"Who?" Jimmy asked.

"He's over there," Cyan motioned toward Moses and gave Jimmy a look.

"His name's Charlie?"

Cyan clapped him upside the head and gave him a shove toward the man they knew as Moses.

"Jimmy, there's the one who figured it out," Moses pointed, and the skinny guy looked him up and down with disbelief.

"It don't amount to a hill a beans if we can't prove it," the guy turned back to Moses with a shake of his head. He looked back at Jimmy. "What made you put 'shine on the bastard?"

"He was saving my ass and needed a free hand," Cyan puffed up beside him, and Jimmy ducked his head. "Like a bona fide hero."

"How 'bout that," Scrawny looked Jimmy over again, then set off, motioning them to follow. "We gots another hero here y'all should meet. Fought roundabouts, your neck of the woods and military pricks wouldn't let him or his crew in either."

Moses stepped forward and slapped a jug of shine into Jimmy's chest hard enough that it knocked some air out of his lungs. They rounded the orange trailer and found Mr. Fancy Watch talking to the old guard in their lawn chairs. It was a very heated discussion from the volume of Fancy's voice.

"I don't care how many damned shotguns you have. The blasts bounce right off of their shells!"

"You city folk think the sun comes up just to hear you crow, don't cha?" The old man laughed at his joke, and Fancy looked more annoyed.

"Charlie's friend Jimbo took one down," Scrawny called out over the crowd. They shut up and turned.

"Jimmy," he muttered, and Cyan gave him a shove and jerked her chin at him with a glare at his low pitch. "My name's Jimmy," he said louder.

"Jimmy melted the one chasing us," Moses called out.

"Like with a blow torch?" Voices started calling out questions from all around.

"Nope," Jimmy rocked back and forth on his heels. "I gave it some shine."

Night birds and crickets punctuated the silence for a long moment before they broke out in laughter, except for Mr. Fancy Watch.

"Wait, what do you mean? Like shoe polish?"

The old codger he'd been arguing with started choking on his laughter, and several of his buddies leaned over to smack him hard between the shoulder blades.

"You gave it firewater? Like what, you set down and passed the jar around?" A young woman called from the edge of the circle, a fussing baby perched on her hip.

"Naw. Tossed it at 'em," Jimmy shrugged, and Cyan stepped forward.

"One of the buggers came running after us as we were crossing the bridge, and it made these horrible sounds. I fell, and Jimmy ran over and faced it, a gun in one hand and his family's recipe in the other. He saw me down and tossed the drink at the creature while keeping his gun leveled at it as he pulled me to safety."

Jimmy felt his chest puff up. He did sound like a hero when she said it like that. She didn't need to know that he'd paused when he realized he couldn't help her, hold a gun, and carry his drink at the same time. He'd planned to run for the trailer with her where the rest of his store was.

A couple of hands slapped him on the back, and Cyan gave him a broad, warm smile. She rarely smiled at him other than a grin or snickering when he did something stupid. Jimmy puffed up a bit more and smiled back.

Questions started to fly about Jimmy's recipe. His was a traditional recipe without frills, similar to what the other homebrewers made, so they started pulling out mash, jugs and setting up various sized stills. Several people brought out jars, and Cyan swatted Jimmy away when he tried to go in and fill up his glass.

"How much did you hit the alien with?" Fancy asked Jimmy, taking a jar and filling it. Jimmy tapped the jar in his hand with a dirty fingernail.

"I'd drunk about half," he nodded, his mouth scrunched up in what he assumed was a serious expression but looked more like he was trying to release swamp gas.

"And you threw it at the alien? Was it a direct hit or partial? We need to figure out how to hit the monsters," Fancy motioned at Jimmy, his bright watch glowing in the sunlight.

"Didn't see."

Cyan jumped in, "He was busy helping me try to get away. We turned back when it started making a strange noise and bubbling."

"We have to test it, then," Fancy nodded slowly and dragged one hand down the stubble on his chiseled jawline. Jimmy saw Cyan watch the movement and grunted.

"I'll go," he cut in. Fancy looked him up and down again and looked around at the raggedy group in the trailer park.

"We'll set up a small group to head out and try to find one of the scouts like you all faced off against on the bridge. They seem to work in a military-style with single creatures heading out ahead of the masses to seek out groups of us," he explained, taking a few steps to circle back, his gaze on something only he saw. "We can't head into one of the more populated areas, but they're likely already reaching for the outskirts. We heard some of the military in the city mention something about heat signatures, so it seems like that's what they thought the aliens honed in on to find us. It sure as hell seemed like there was never anyplace anyone could hide."

Jimmy lifted his hand and dragged it down his peach fuzz stubble. Thirty-odd years old, and he'd never managed to get more, but he mirrored the serious look on Fancy's face.

Yells came from the northern section of the park, and the group turned en masse. A few people came running past, away from the disruption.

"They're here! They've found us!"

The group looked at each other for a moment before grabbing whatever artillery they could find. Jimmy tapped Fancy on the arm, and the man looked at the jar held toward him as though it was his last rites before nodding once and taking it. Jimmy reached down and grabbed a few more jars, filling them and handing them out to anyone nearby. Cyan took one, drank a swig, and made a face before taking a rifle from a lady that looked like Aunt Bea from The Andy Griffith show.

Guns and shine in hand, the group pushed forward through terrified people running almost blindly toward them and away. Ahead of them, a glow rose, and they heard the sound of rending metal, and a few shots blasted off over the loud chittering that seemed to be the creatures' endless war cry.

Jimmy followed the group's movements as they ran in a low, rough formation with Fancy at the tip. More people streamed past, and Jimmy paused to wonder exactly how many people were housed in the motorhomes and mobile units of the park.

When they rounded a precarious mobile home that seemed to be listing to one side, they saw one of the creatures feeding on something that looked like little more than raw meat as it chittered away. They halted, and someone took a small drink from their jar in what was likely meant to steel their nerve but ended up with the drinker sputtering from the rough brew.

The creature's head popped up from its meal, and it let out a shriek. Cyan and a couple of others dropped to their knees and tried to cover their ears, but the rest of the group charged forward, laying down fire as they went. The creature just watched them come as though they'd been formally invited.

Jimmy watched as Fancy brought his arm back and launched it over his head like a human catapult. The glass jar seemed to hold itself stubbornly upright as though affronted by the fact that it was being used so poorly as it arched in the light of the nearby burning mobile home.

A loud crack sounded as the jar hit the hard shell of the creature before it tipped and spilled its contents all over the alien. The creature screamed and was echoed by those on the ground as its body began to bubble and boil. It tried to pull itself toward them as though it planned to take them within its wicked witch of the west impression, but the moonshine dribbled down its legs, and they began to boil and burst as well. The group was silent as the creature became little more than bubbling ooze and lost its ability to shriek.

Jimmy blinked a couple of times, took a sip of his brew, and turned to find Cyan who was crouched on the ground a few feet behind him. He tucked his gun away and reached down to pull her to her feet. She staggered and wrapped her arms around his waist. He wasn't sure if it was for stability or not, but he puffed out his thin chest in response.

"Well fuck me, that worked," Fancy turned a wide-eyed gaze on Jimmy before striding forward to where the creature ooze had settled. Several people shuffled forward to poke at the remains and converse in low tones with Fancy, who didn't say much but shook his head as he surveyed the scene.

"How much of this did you bring, again?" Fancy called out to Jimmy.

"About three big jugs of it," Cyan called out in response. "But we can make more."

"Any man worth his salt round here has some shine stored up," a big man with a mullet and bald top called from Jimmy's left.

"We'll have to try them all and make sure it isn't just a fluke," Fancy called back. "Spread out and gather any moonshine you can find. Hell, find any alcohol you can. We don't know what's causing this to work, but we need to get every possible weapon we can."

The group scattered. Cyan stepped away from Jimmy and they headed back toward the center of the trailer park. Fancy walked up and took a position on Jimmy's left.

"I'm going to need you to go with me to the military base. We need to try to make them see that there's an opportunity here. You made the discovery, so you need to tell them your story. I'll tell them about this success."

Jimmy gave a single nod.

"We can't give them your entire store of moonshine, though. If we do, they'll take it and we'll be stuck," Fancy tapped his right hand against his dirty dress pants. "We need to take as much of any brew we can get. If we're lucky, we'll find one of the monsters on the way there and we can test a few different types to see what works.

"As far as I know, the government hasn't figured out a way to trap and contain these things, so they won't likely have one to test on. Not that that's certain -- they aren't likely to tell us," Fancy shrugged and then ran a dirty hand through his hair. It barely moved despite the rough treatment.

"We'll do what we can to help," Cyan assured him.

Jimmy nodded again.

"We'll leave in ten," Fancy jerked his chin at them and then walked away.

Jimmy and Cyan went looking for Moses.

"I'm coming with," was the old man's immediate response.

"Taking that whole mobile home over to the base is going to be a slow bit of travel, Moses," Cyan said with a shake of her head.

"We move faster with that than most folk do," Moses shook his head. "Plus, my buddy Wave showed me something that he hacked into from the government. I don't know if that city fella's right that they can't contain the critters, but they sure have figured out a way to track 'em."

Cyan's eyes went wide, and they followed Moses into the back of his unit. He flipped on a screen, and they saw what looked like one of those inkblot tests a shrink gives you to try to make you believe you only see monsters or sex or something. This was in red and grey though.

"What's that?" Jimmy jutted his chin at the screen.

"The gray is people," Moses exhaled. Most of the screen was covered in a mass of red with a few dots seemingly at random near the tiny blobs of gray.

"They're everywhere," Cyan said tonelessly.

"And I can use this to track them while we move out," Moses rolled his shoulders once before typing something in his computer that zoomed in on the screen. "We can avoid them or find a few stragglers to test on as we go."

Jimmy nodded yes while Cyan's head went from side to side.

"This is insane," Cyan gripped Jimmy's arm as though he were planning to turn and run out to face the creatures on his own. "We can't face them like this."

"Someone's got to," Moses shrugged. "Might as well be this dimwit and his lucky throw."

Cyan's mouth curled into a snarl as she leaned forward into Moses' face.

"Jimmy's a damned hero, and you best remember that, old man."

Jimmy's pale eyebrows disappeared into his hairline at Cyan's aggressive reaction to Moses' words. He reached forward and patted her arm awkwardly, half-tempted to step outside of the home rather than be in the middle of whatever was going on.

Cyan closed her eyes for a moment, took a breath, and turned away. Moses looked at Jimmy with a good deal of side-eye but didn't say anything.

"You'll go along," Jimmy nodded at Moses. "We'll tell him," he pushed Cyan gently to exit. He knew Cyan believed he'd done something heroic and for a split second considered telling her the truth. Instead, he hurried to find their fearless leader.

They found Fancy talking to the old-timers again. He was giving directions on how to keep everyone safe. He also had two big jugs of liquid at his feet and a couple of bottles of cheap whiskey. He nodded as they walked up.

"We've got a truck parked near the entrance," he looked at their empty hands. "Where's your moonshine, Jimmy?"

"It's in Moses' trailer. We'll be taking it, and him, with us," Cyan explained.

"We don't have time for a full trailer-"

"He can track 'em," Jimmy cut in. Cyan stared. She could probably count the number of times Jimmy had ever cut someone off with one hand -- if it were missing a few fingers.

Fancy arched an eyebrow. It was likely few people had ever cut him off. Possibly fewer than Jimmy's count.

"That might help us find one to experiment on," Fancy mumbled and then gave a quick nod. "You win. Let's go."

They marched back to Moses' trailer where he was waiting outside for them.

"I'll navigate to the base if someone else can drive?"

"I'll drive," Cyan said with a nod. "Moses needs to be watching the buggers."

Fancy tossed a bag of something at Jimmy who missed and had to retrieve it from the ground. It was a big bag of water balloons. "It'll be easier to lob them, and we'll have a better chance of hitting one on the first try," Fancy explained. He lifted and passed Jimmy and Moses a few more jugs and some bottles he'd gathered.

"I have a funnel and some buckets," Moses nodded.

"Use different colors for the different types of 'shine, Jimmy," Cyan stepped forward and gave Jimmy a hug. He nodded and followed Moses into the trailer. They walked through a narrow doorway from the old man's electronics area into the main section of the trailer. Moses set down the jug he was carrying and then moved back into the other room. The old man settled into his chair, set the radio up, and motioned Jimmy in a shoo-in motion.

"Funnel's under the sink with the buckets," he called as Jimmy wandered in.

He grabbed a column as the trailer jolted forward and he heard Cyan's voice come across the radio. Moses replied to something about the direction they'd be going. Jimmy grabbed the items from under the sink and found a bolted seat near his moonshine and the other jugs and bottles. He chose the green balloons for his moonshine and red for the other shine with yellow for the piss-water whiskey. He filled up about a dozen of each balloon and then set them aside as he re-secured the jugs and bottles where they'd been beside the door. No sense in wasting good 'shine if he could help it. He took a drink and frowned. Whoever had made it used some fancy store-bought stuff.

"Jimmy, come in here," Moses called out as he was getting a small sample of one of the other homebrews to try. He carried his jar and sat in a chair near the old man. It might be awful, but no sense in wasting it.

"Grab the radio. I'm going to pinpoint the location of that dot and read it off to you."

Jimmy picked it up and squeezed the button once. There was static and then nothing.

"You have to hold it down but be careful. It sticks. We won't be able to hear them if the button gets stuck," Moses waved his hand around impatiently. Jimmy nodded and put the handset up to his mouth.

"Tell them to stay on 91 south for another few miles…"

"Stay 91 south," Jimmy repeated.

"Then turn on 48 west to Briartown," he continued.

"To 48 to Briartown," Jimmy said.

"Roger," Fancy called back. "Is there a creature in Briartown?"

"Just beyond the town, there's a red dot near a group of gray," Moses nodded. "I'm hoping we'll get there in time to help."

"Just past," Jimmy said and set the handset back near the speaker.

"I cannot believe your dumbass found a solution to something like this," Moses gave Jimmy a surprised smile. "Granted, it's luck, but the fact that you put yourself in front of Cyan…"

Jimmy fidgeted and looked around the room.

"You didn't, did you?" Moses breathed a slow sigh. "What happened? Cyan says you tossed that jar like it was a holy hand grenade and then swooped over to save her. I was running my ass off and didn't see."

"I hesitated," Jimmy lifted one shoulder. He released a long breath as he let the truth pour out. "I knew I couldn't help and hold my drink. Cyan kicked it out of my hand. I was going to run for the trailer."

"You almost kept your drink over Cyan?" Moses let out a low whistle. "You really are the dumbass prick I always thought you were. Sheer luck, I guess. Well, even a blind squirrel can find a nut sometimes."

Jimmy shrugged, and they felt the trailer shift and come to a stop.

"Grab that bucket, boy. We got some monsters to kill."

Jimmy handed one of the buckets to Moses and grabbed the second one that held the balloons just with his recipe of homebrew in it. They hurried out the back door to find Dave and Cyan waiting.

"Which is which?" Dave asked as he stepped forward and looked into the buckets.

"Green is mine," Jimmy held forward his bucket of green and red balloons. "Red is the other 'shine, yellow is piss whiskey."

Fancy grabbed a few of each. Behind them, in the distance, they could hear yelling and the ratatat of gunfire. After each of them had a few balloons, they took off at a run toward the sound.

They found a Piggly Wiggly parking lot for the apocalypse. Bent and broken carts were knocked everywhere, there were several cars that looked like they'd been run over by monster trucks, and one tall pick-up was parked in the center of it all with a flag-waving from the back window. The truck was the source of the gunfire.

At the entrance of the store were two of the creatures, chittering madly at the men in the truck. It looked like they'd been in the process of ripping the front portion of the store away when the redneck vigilantes showed up.

Fancy ran up to the truck and shouted something at one of the men firing a semi-automatic rifle at the creatures. The side of the gun had, "Deer killer" written across it in block lettering. The vigilante nodded and yelled something at the driver who leaned on his horn and then put the metal monster in gear. They charged near the creatures and then veered away, drawing them out from the store entrance. The monsters ran forward, and Jimmy swallowed hard at the image of the bridge replaying in his head.

The four of them ran forward with Fancy in the lead. He tossed a yellow balloon at the nearest creature, and it broke but poured off the beast's shell-like water. They all dropped the yellow balloons and shifted to red and green. It would be a holiday-themed throwdown.

Cyan and Moses chucked red balloons at the creature. One broke and had the same effect as the yellow, but the other split open and the creature screamed. Its body began to boil and twitch and both creatures turned to face the four.

Dave threw another red, but it did nothing. They all dropped the remaining red and started hurling green balloons at the monsters. They shrieked and screamed as their bodies melted from Jimmy's good homebrew.

As the bodies became a bastardization of Jell-O shots on the pavement of the Piggly Wiggly, the four moved closer together and the truck squealed around to park near them.

"What the hell did you toss at those bastards?" One of the men called out as they walked near. Jimmy recognized the passenger of the truck and then saw the resemblance between him and the much older driver. Father and son bonding, it seemed.

"Several things, but mostly moonshine," Fancy answered and turned to Jimmy. "Did you use different kinds of the brew in the red balloons?"

"Yep. Two different bottles," he nodded.

"So, yours and one other work against these things. We have to figure out why," he started walking back toward the trailer and they all followed, including the two men from the truck.

Jimmy looked and found Cyan walking near Moses. She made no move to walk by him despite her earlier affection. He frowned but hustled after Fancy.

They all climbed into the living room area of the trailer where Fancy'd pulled the jugs free. He popped open the tops, two cork, and one screw top, and took a sniff of each. He held up one jug.

"This is one of yours, right?" he asked, and Jimmy nodded. "So why does yours and one other work and not the third one? They all smell the same and are made the same, right?"

"Hell no," Jimmy shook his head and the two men that had followed let out hearty laughs.

"Can always tell a city boy with good 'shine," the older of the two laughed and slapped his son on the back.

"What's the difference?" He arched an eyebrow while the two men continued to chuckle.

"You gotta have good corn mash or it don't work," Jimmy said as he walked over and pulled a jar from Moses' cupboard. "If you buy mash that's made, it has other stuff in it to help it keep. If you make your own, it doesn't have that dog shit in it."

He took one of the jugs from Fancy and poured. It was the same one he'd drunk from earlier. The man took it like a shot and the father-son team cheered at him. Jimmy poured from his own jug and handed the man that one as well. He downed that one too but came up sputtering.

"It's rough, but it's made, not bought," Jimmy lifted his chin as though daring the city dweller to say something about his brew. He jerked his head at the last jug. "That one's homebrew, too. Not some fancy-ass piss water shit."

"Okay, so we know which ones will work and which won't." Two drinks in and the fella looked a little light-headed. He turned to the father and son. "Find anyone you know that makes homebrew like this and tell them to pull all of it that they have if they want to survive against these things. Have them put it in water balloons or water guns or whatever they can find, but it only takes about a cup of the stuff to completely destroy one of the monsters. Tell everyone.

"Moses, get online and start spreading that any way you can. Make sure they know not to use..."

"Dog shit store-bought mash," Jimmy supplied.

"...that stuff in their brew because it won't work. Cyan, if you'll drive, I'll navigate to the base. Jimmy, keep filling balloons, but only with the two good brews that we have. Leave a little in the jugs to give to the government when we get there."

The group split to follow directions. Jimmy could hear Moses calling out on multiple channels with few responses coming back. It wasn't long before Jimmy had filled as many balloons as he could and moved to sit beside Moses. The old man looked like someone had kicked his dog every time he called out and didn't get a response.

It wasn't more than an hour of driving before the trailer slowed to a stop.

"Why didn't they tell us we were here? What's the damn point of this radio if they can't let us know?" Moses slapped the handset, and it squawked once before giving a steady hum. He frowned at it, picked up the handset, and swore. "Damn thing was stuck. They couldn't call back because they were stuck listening to me try to call every damn person I know with no response."

Jimmy and Moses turned to leave. The open door brought in the smell of fire, gunpowder, and something rotten. The world outside was a red blaze of light with black clouds that obscured the night sky.

"It's destroyed," Fancy said as he moved to stand beside them. "The whole base is gone."

Creatures skittered toward them from the fiery remains and all four of them yelled. Jimmy and Cyan dove for the trailer to get the bucket of red balloons. They heard a yell and chanced a look back to see both Fancy and Moses being dragged away by the creatures. Cyan slammed the door shut and they moved into the main area of the trailer which rocked around them as the monsters climbed over the top.

Cyan ran further into the trailer to the tiny bathroom and banged around for a moment before coming out with what looked like two tiny yellow pills. She shoved one in either ear, and then slowly walked over toward Jimmy. Her face was calm despite the shaking of the trailer.

She leaned across him, grabbed a balloon from the bucket, and sat in one of the chairs before pulling a gun from her back.

"Weapons won't work on 'em," Jimmy felt uncomfortable as Cyan watched him.

"It has a different purpose," she cocked her head to the side. The shriek of bending metal and scrape of claws echoed around them but Cyan didn't move or seem shaken by it. "Your damn moonshine was almost more important than my life, hmm?"

"What?"

"The handset was jammed on when you admitted that to Moses, earlier. Did you know? Damn fool doesn't even come close. Selfish, stupid, human is more accurate. I thought you'd really shown that you cared when you tossed the 'shine and turned to carry me away. It was like a damned romance novel and shit."

Jimmy swallowed hard and his mouth popped open, but he said nothing.

"I was going to spare you. I was going to save you for your heroics and selflessness instead of seeing you as a waste of space on this planet."

Jimmy leaned away from her, his mouth lax and eyes wide. "You're one of them?"

"Giant fucking bugs? Hell no. My race has been here since before your piddly-ass human evolution put you upright. We were few and changed to blend in, thinking we could grow with your race until you started destroying the world so selfishly. Then, our plan changed. We might be few, but we need this planet to survive. Those bugs out there? They can't defeat us, only weaken us through that shrieking they do. Not that it matters now that you've shown us how to defeat them with your damned backwater brew."

Jimmy stared. Beside him, there was a noise and the door ripped off of the trailer. One of the creatures stuck its head in and Cyan softly lobbed the water balloon at it. Jimmy watched her as it fell and shrieked behind him, slowly turning into a bubbling mass of goo. Cyan didn't react. She waited until the noise subsided and smiled at Jimmy.

"But, why Cyan?"

"Simple Jimmy. We were here first. Humanity is a blight that those creatures have almost completely wiped out for us. It's time to take back our planet. It's just too bad you chose so poorly, Jimmy. Feels like I should be askin' you for your last words?"

Jimmy looked at her for a long moment and said, "Fucking bugs, fucking-"

Cyan lifted the gun, pointed it at Jimmy, and fired.

Gimme Some Lovin'

By William Joseph Roberts

"**O**h, no you don't! Get your little ass back here. You aren't squirming away that easily. Hey now! No biting!"

My earpiece crackled to life and Mandy's voice came through crystal clear, "Everything OK, Brax?"

"Yeah. These little bastards are biters, especially the red ones."

Mandy let out a muffled giggle. "Redheads always were your downfall."

"Oh, ha, ha, ha," I laughed. Red hair was probably the only thing my business partner didn't have going for her. God she was beautiful. Part African American, part Korean, five two with this big pair of golden almond shaped eyes.

"Just hurry up and be careful," she said with a tone of caring annoyance. "The sooner you get the crazy lady dropped off with the feds, the sooner we can get paid, and you can get back home."

"Will do, Mandy," I mumbled before returning to the task at hand. I held the large reddish-gray rabbit by the ears against the blood splattered wall of the weather aged barn. "Hold still for one more second and I promise it'll be over with quick."

The machete cut through easily in one swing and embedded into the blood-soaked wooden wall. I picked up the rabbit's thrashing carcass and tossed both it and the severed head onto the pile just inside the barn doors.

"You, sick sadistic son of a bitch!" the old woman shouted. "Those were my babies! You killed them! Murderer! Murderer!"

I glanced back over my shoulder at the front porch of the rustic farmhouse. "You call me sadistic? You seriously think that I'm sadistic?! You were going to release your mutant Veloci-bunnies of doom to destroy the entire Midwest! People like you are the sadistic sickos of the world," I shouted as I jabbed a bloody finger at her. "People like you cause regular folks to suffer!"

That's when I noticed my blood caked arm. The thick layer of dried blood nearly hid the dragon tattoo on my right forearm. The thought of what I had just done, job or not turned my stomach. I struggled to gulp down a breath then I swallowed hard and forced my lunch back down.

"No one would take my organic soy sprout research seriously! They wouldn't have had a choice after my babies ate their way across the country!"

"Brax," Mandy shouted through his earpiece, "Just gag the crazy lady and let's go!"

"I hear ya, Mandy," I said and let out a long sigh as I looked at the ground around me. Scooping the remainder of rabbit parts into a bucket I walked into the barn and stared with dismay at the heap of bodies.

"Sometimes I really hate my job."

I tossed the contents of the bucket onto the pile then doused it with two large cans of gasoline. "I'm sorry about this, fuzzy buddies." The thought of my cats in a similar situation left a lump in my throat. I poured a trail of gasoline out of the barn and shut the doors behind me.

"You'll burn in hell for this," the woman shrieked.

"Shut UP!" I exploded, glaring at the woman. My ears rang from the rage that began to build deep inside as I stomped toward the farmhouse. A deep growl escaped from between my clenched teeth. "Because YOU created them, I was called! Because of YOU, the government men called me! Because of your insane plan I was sent here! Because of you, they had to die!"

"Noooo," she moaned as I stepped onto the porch. "No, no, no!"

"Because of you, my hands are covered in innocent blood!" I leaned down and forcefully grasped the arms of the wooden rocking chair. Spittle flew from between my clenched teeth as I fought to control the rage building in me. I brought myself nose to nose with the terrified woman. The arms of the rocking chair creaked and groaned under the strain of my grip.

"*You* created them, and I had to destroy them!"

The woman suddenly went limp and slumped in the chair, her head falling to her chest.

I closed my eyes and straightened, taking slow, deep breaths.

"One....two....three....four....." I mouthed quietly then stared at the unconscious woman for a long moment, questioning why I was even here.

"I really need a vacation."

A vacation was exactly what I needed. Even Mandy thought I could use a break after the last couple of weird jobs I'd taken on. Since I was in the neighborhood of Watts Bar Lake, I decided to take up an offer from my buddy, Leo Daniels. He always said to drop in anytime if I wanted to do some fishing and drinking. More drinking than fishing I'm willing to bet, but that still counts, doesn't it?

I'd met Leo shortly after being stationed at Seymour Johnson Air Force Base. He had originally been a Crew Dawg on the F-4 Phantoms and one of the best damned mechanics on the airframe from what I'd been told. Once the Air Force had begun phasing out the F-4's in favor of the sleek new F-15 Eagles, Leo had been transferred over and landed in the 335th fighter squadron. I'd gotten to know him on swing shift while turning wrenches till the wee hours of the morning. He retired shortly after I'd arrived on base, but we stayed in contact over the years. I had stopped in once or twice before, but it had been a few years since my last visit.

The summer evening was more than comfortable when I rolled into the Bayside Marina and Resort RV Park. Fireflies flashed and danced about as the sweet smell of barbeque lazily hung in the air. The place was just like I remembered it. Dirty, run down, and overly decorated with pink flamingos.

I rolled up and parked outside one of the newest looking RV's in the park. A twenty-eight foot long dark brown and grey number with several slide out sections. Careful not to rev Valerie, my Kawasaki Vulcan 800, I shut off the engine and dismounted. No sooner had I knocked on the door of the RV than a low growl came from inside. RV rocked side to side with heavy footed steps as someone made their way from one end to the other. After a few long moments of fiddling with the locks the door flung open, and a massive red-faced beast emerged. Her look of anger quickly shifted to a glowing smile. She leaned against the door frame and shifted as to show off some naked thigh from beneath her pizza sauce-stained nightgown.

"Hey big boy, looking for some fun?"

"No, I was looking for Leo Daniels."

The anger returned to her overly plump cherubic face. "Leo don't live here no more. He's down at the docks. Slip sixteen in Henry Danielson's old houseboat," she said with a snarl. The camper shifted as she leaned out of the door pointing a chubby finger in my direction. "And if Bobby is down there with him, you tell him he still owes me a bottle of Mad Dog. An if he don't bring it like he promised, you tell him me and him's gonna have words the next time I see him."

I started to back away slowly, half afraid that she was about to pounce on me from her doorway perch.

After moving Valerie to the marina parking area, I made my way to the docks. On one side was the main marina area, complete with bar, grill, bait, tackle, gas and fishing licenses. Someone was setting up to play live music at the far end of the dock near to where a guy was mixing drinks in a small dockside tiki hut. What looked like a small river barge sat half beached and sunken on the marina's boat ramp. I continued along the shoreline another fifty feet to the gangplank that led to the marina's docking slips. The metal awning structure that covered the docking area creaked and groaned with my every step. Several of the support posts looked as if they had collapsed and broken multiple times in the past before being repaired in the cheapest manner possible without the use of duct tape. The underside of the dock looked like a veritable forest. Weeds and small trees had taken root in every available crack and cranny possible across the structure.

I found slip sixteen at the far end of the dock, occupied by a houseboat that looked like a left over from the fifties, miraculously still afloat. I picked up a piece of metal tubing I'd found lying on the walkway and tapped at the awning frame. "Leo! Hey Leo, you in there?"

Mumbled curses accompanied the sound of someone stumbling and fumbling with the door. The cabin door at the front of the boat opened and Leo popped his head out of the half-opened door.

"Who the hell is beating..."

I dropped the tubing and smiled wide. "Permission to come aboard?"

Leo rubbed his eyes and blinked to clear his vision and just stared at me for a long moment. "Well, I'll be damned, you dirty son of a bitch. What the hell brings you out to slum with the likes of me?" He motioned for me to come aboard, then stepped back into the cabin and returned with a pair of beers in hand. He twisted off the top of one, flicked the bottle cap into the water with a snap of his fingers, then offered the bottle to me.

"My pleasure." I took the beer and took a long swig. After a long day on the road, the ice-cold barley goodness was soothing to my parched throat.

Leo grabbed a cooler from inside then led the way to the sun deck of the houseboat. He promptly twisted off the top of his beer and snapped the cap off the side. Kicking off his flip flops Leo propped his feet up onto the side rail, relaxing back into one of the dry rotted deck chairs.

I gently sat back in one of the other chairs and stretched. "So, what's with your lady friend up on the hill? You lose the camper in a divorce or something? You must have had your hands full with her cause she sure is a whole lotta woman."

Leo choked on the swig of amber goodness, shooting a golden stream out of both nostrils. "Who? Deloris? Oh, good lord no! We just traded up. Between the boat being on the water and the waterbed on board it was enough to make her seasick. Otherwise, she's mostly harmless as long as you stay out of reach of those sausage fingers of hers."

"Alright," I conceded. "Then who's Bobby? Cause she was sure interested in knowing where he was."

Leo leaned up and pointed toward the marina bar. "She should know where he is. He runs Rum and Rednecks, the marina bar and grill." He took another swig then chin nodded at me. "So, what brings you around these parts?"

"Been doing some contract work for the government and I just happened to be passing through."

"Good pay?"

"Yup."

"I probably can't ask what it is, can I?"

"Nope," I said, then took another long drink from the beer, finishing it.

Leo finished his then tossed the empty bottle overboard and reached into the cooler for another. "Dammit, man."

"What's wrong?"

"If you want another beer, we'll have to go over to the marina. Got nothing but ice left in here."

"Fine by me." I stood carefully, not wanting to fall through the dry rotted fabric of the chair.

We strolled over to the main pier just as one of the musicians strummed the chords for Margaritaville. I took a dark Maduro cigar from my vest pocket as we took a seat at one of the outside tables after placing our order at the bar. I struck a match and puffed, enjoying the smooth sweet flavor of the mature tobacco.

"I didn't expect to see you this evening, Leo," a short pudgy man said as he approached. "You don't get out and socialize much."

Leo laughed. "It happens from time to time. This time it's because I have company and we ran out of beer."

I stood and offered my hand. "Braxton Hicks."

The pudgy man looked me over for a long minute, then took my hand and shook. "Bobby Raker."

I looked to Leo who gave a slow nod. "One and the same." Bobby flashed a look of confused concern from me to Leo and back again.

"Deloris expects that bottle of Mad Dog that you promised her," I said as I took my seat.

Bobby sat, propping his elbows on the table as he leaned forward. He took off his hat and rubbed vigorously at his face. He slicked back his long greasy looking, dirty blond hair then pulled the hat back on.

"I swear to God that woman is about to get on my last nerve." He pulled a crumpled pack of menthol cigarettes from his pocket and lit up.

A waitress dropped a beer and shot of whiskey in front of Leo and me before Bobby snatched one of the other bottles from her tray meant for another table. He took a long drink then hotboxed most of his cigarette.

Leo laughed then slammed back his shot and took a swig of beer. "What's wrong?"

Bobby glanced from me to Leo like a paranoid ferret on crack. He turned up his beer then let out a long sigh of resignation. "There's just no pleasing that woman. You'd think she'd be appreciative of an affectionate man such as myself. Especially when I'm all the time bringing her little gifts and something specials, like picking up a plate of her favorite barbeque or those twice deep-fried pork rinds that she loves so much. You'd think the least she could do when I come over to give her some sweet lovin' is to keep her kids put up and out of my way. And ya know what? I'm an adult. I can be the bigger man and keep my mouth shut about how rude and unchristian she's being. But the one time she catches wind that I went hoggin out of town she just won't let it go. Enough's enough ya know." Bobby lit a new smoke from the stub of the last one and sucked down half of the menthol stick in one draw.

Trying my best to hold in my laughter, I dipped the unlit end of my cigar into the shot of whiskey and took several long puffs. I glanced over at Leo who wasn't much help. He just shrugged and looked away as he nursed his own beer.

"You ever thought about maybe apologizing to her?" I asked.

Bobby stared at me with that unmistakenly angry look of *are you crazy* painted across his face. "Why the hell would I ever do that? It's not like I'm married to her or anything. We just have a fun rough and tumble whenever I'm in the mood for some meaty pork chops. I swear to God," he fumed then took another slug from his beer.

I could tell that no matter what I said, nothing would ever change Bobby's mind on the subject. I waved at the waitress and held up two fingers, then downed the rest of my beer. Doing my best to ignore Bobby's trailer park nonsense, I focused my attention on a small group of dancers gathering near the stage. They started a line dance to the tune of some country song I didn't recognize. It was an enjoyable enough show. Ample cleavage and ass cheeks peaked out from low-cut shirts and shorty shorts of the dancers as they bobbed and jiggled in time with the song. Lake princesses every one of them. The best mix of that dirty country girl you could never have and a leathery tanned bleach blonde beach bunny.

A blood curdling scream from the RV park broke my focus from this particularly fine pair of legs I'd just been watching. The music stopped just as suddenly as the next scream resounded across the still surface of the lake and reverberated off the opposite shore of the cove.

A gunshot broke the eerie silence that had settled over the marina. Frightened screams arose from the gathered crowd on the dock.

"What in the hell is going on over there," Bobby muttered as the three of us stood and gawked in the direction of the RV park.

"Die spawn of Satan!" a gruff male voice shouted followed by the pop and flash of two more gunshots.

"That sounded like Mason," Leo said.

"It sure as hell did. And he just signed his eviction order. He knows better than to discharge a weapon in the RV park. I swear to God," he said with an exasperated sigh. "Some people's kids."

Another scream followed by a pair of muzzle flashes that erupted from behind Deloris's RV just as a young woman appeared from the left of the trailer. She stumbled and nearly rolled her ankle several times as she sprinted across the dusty gravel road and onto the pier. The messenger bag slung over her shoulder slapped heavily against her thigh as she ran to the heavy clomp of her military style boots across the weathered wood planks of the dock.

"Isn't that Lucy Mae?" Leo asked, squinting to get his eyes to focus.

"Lucinda," Bobby corrected. "Remember? She identifies as Lucinda the ancient succubi now."

I looked over at Bobby with what must have been a contorted look of confusion because he shook his head and shrugged.

"Don't look at me. I don't get it either, dude. Kids these days, I swear to God."

Lucy collided with Leo and buried her face into his chest. "Those things!"

"What things? What's going on, Lucy?"

Motion drew my attention back to the RV park. An older man with a cane in one hand and a pistol in the other hobbled around from behind Deloris's camper.

Bobby cupped his hands and shouted at the man. "I swear to God, you know better than to fire that thing off in the trailer park, Mason!"

There was a sudden mix of confused gasps and frightened screams from the crowd gathered on the dock as we all spotted the things chasing Mason. More of the things suddenly appeared, clamoring their way from the water and onto the dock.

The things looked like something right out of a bad horror movie. They were humanoid but bloated in that way a body does after it's been in the river for a few days before the state troopers fish them out. They were a slime greenish color with bits of lake grass and twigs clinging to their matted mops of hair. Some of them were missing sections of flesh, as if something had been chewing at them or maybe it had sloughed away off of the bone.

One of the lake princesses standing near me fainted and her old man caught her, then unceremoniously dropped her, and sprinted for an expensive looking speedboat tied off to the far end of the dock. Screams of absolute terror overshadowed the gurgling roar of the creatures as they swarmed over the dock. People scattered in all directions. Most ran for their docked boats while some sprinted across the ramp to shore or lept into the water to what they thought was safety.

One of the creatures quickly snatched up the lake princess that had just fainted and dove back into the water, taking her to the depths with it.

Bobby snapped out of his stupor and did one of the most awkward fat man shuffles I'd ever seen as he sprinted for the door to the bar. "Everyone! Get inside," he yelled then disappeared into the building.

Leo shoved Lucy in the direction of the door then drew a blacked out 1911 from the pit of his back under his baggy shirt and fired at the creature nearest to him. I picked up the plastic patio chair I had been sitting in and threw it at the next nearest creature then drew my Taurus Judge revolver and fired. The one quarter ounce rifled .410-gauge slug easily penetrated the creature's head and blew out a sizable chunk from the opposite side.

Leo fired at two more of the creatures then kicked one of the patio tables into the path of another. "What the hell are these things?"

"A pain in the ass is what!" I stepped forward and put the muzzle of my revolver against the side of another creature's head as it climbed out of the water and pulled the trigger. It fell back with a hard belly-flop slap against the water. "All I wanted to do was relax and maybe fish a little bit, but nooo. I get to deal with blob things from radiation lake instead."

"There isn't any radiation in this lake," Leo argued.

I laughed. "Really? Then what the hell are these things?"

"Okay, that's fair."

A dozen more of the creatures swarmed onto the dock and ambled our way. I fired the last of the shotgun slugs and reholstered my revolver.

Leo let out a roar. "Dammit!"

I glanced over to see Leo fumbling in his pockets and the slide of his 1911 locked back.

I grabbed a long-handled gaff hook that hung from the side of the bar as a decoration and charged at the creature nearest to Leo. The spiked tip of the gaff sunk into the creature's torso with a sloppy wet pop.

It opened its mouth and let out a gurgling hiss, then pulled itself toward me, further onto the gaff and over the hook. Using the pole as leverage I pulled the creature toward me then swung it into two more of the things.

"Banzai!"

A small Asian man in a chef's hat suddenly charged from the entrance of the bar and decapitated one of the creatures with a comically oversized meat cleaver.

"Koichi-San! Don't let them things bite you," Bobby shouted as he reappeared from the entrance. "I don't want to have to find another sushi chef on short notice before the summer rush, I swear to God."

Bobby charged from the bar's entrance and swung one of the most back yard engineering abominations I have ever witnessed. It was a battery powered side grinder that had been heavily modified. Fitted with what looked like a three-foot-long chainsaw bar and chain crossed with the hilt of a great sword. He depressed the trigger a split second before the blade contacted the creature. The chain sword chewed its way through the thing's torso like a hot knife through butter.

"Yea, freaking haw!" Bobby shouted. "Didn't I tell you this thing would come in handy one day, Koichi-San?"

The sushi chef gave Bobby a baleful glance then hacked another of the things in two with his meat cleaver.

I stomped on the thing's chest after forcing it to the dock, then twisted and pried the gaff loose. It clawed at my steel-toed boots, trying to squirm from underfoot. I brought the tip of the gaff down with all my might through the creature's left eye, pinning its head to the dock.

Between the four of us, we made short work of the remaining creatures. Body parts littered the dock and several of the dismembered chunks continued to quiver and squirm.

I slammed down a shot of whiskey from a nearby table then drew my revolver. Opening the cylinder, I tipped the revolver up letting the five spent shotgun shells slide out and clatter to the dock. "So, when did y'all start having these pest problems around here?" I asked as I reloaded then holstered the Judge.

"Chū ni ikou. Anzen." Koichi-San said, then hurried back into the bar.

Bobby flicked at a piece of flesh that clung to the chain sword. "Come on y'all, Koichi-San has a good point."

Leo managed to fish his spare magazine out of his pocket and reloaded the 1911. "I didn't know you could speak Japanese, Bobby."

"I can't."

"Then how did you know what he just said?"

"I didn't. But he's heading inside and that sounds like a good enough plan to me for now," Bobby said then slipped into the bar.

Leo shrugged. "At least this is better than listening to Deloris bitch at the neighbors," he said as he followed Bobby into the bar.

I followed behind Leo and we both made a beeline for the bar. Bobby was already behind the taps pouring a fresh round for everyone.

"So, anyone going to tell me what the hell is going on around here?"

"Well, bless your heart," Bobby said with a hissing laugh. "Do you think we know what that was?

Leo sucked the froth from the top of the beer. "You've got me. I'm just glad the rest of you could see them. That's when I knew it wasn't a flashback."

I looked at Leo and shook my head in confusion. "You've seen those things before?"

"No. Just had a few bad acid trips before that come back to haunt me every now and then."

Koichi-San reappeared from the kitchen area and placed a platter of sushi on the bar top. "Eat." He nodded with a grunt then disappeared back into the kitchen.

"Well, hello there, darlin's." Bobby snagged a handful of sushi rolls from the platter and popped one in his mouth. He let out giggled moans I'd only heard come from a lady in the heat of passion. "I swear to God, you don't get any better than this."

Leo picked up one of the rolls and stared at it. "What is it?"

"Koichi-San's special curried catfish roll." Bobby's eyes rolled into the back of his head after popping another roll into his mouth.

"So, what the hell are we supposed to do about all of those bodies out there?" Leo asked.

Bobby just continued his mouth breather chewing as he swayed side to side, drunk on the trailer park goodness of Koichi-San's catfish sushi.

I raked my hand across my face from frustration. "You know this isn't anything natural, right?"

Leo laughed then took another sip of his beer. "I kinda figured as much."

"Well, I've dealt with a lot of strange stuff in my line of work. Just not mutant lake monsters."

"Well, I will tell y'all this. Ain't no one at the Sheriff's office going to believe any of this. If anyone mentions that Mason shot first, they'll just run him in for all of the bodies and the dead tourists so they can go and sit on their fat asses back at the jailhouse."

That's when I heard a sobbing wince come from the bathroom. Leo must have heard it too, because he looked at me at the same time I looked at him.

I quietly stood and drew my revolver. Leo slid from his seat and stepped ahead of me.

"I swear to God, ya'll."

Both me and Leo glared back at Bobby, motioning for him to be quiet. We continued toward the bathrooms. Leo stopped and listened at the women's restroom door for a moment then nodded. He drew his pistol and grabbed the door handle then mouthed the word one. Leo yanked open the door on the count of three and Lucy let out an ear-piercing scream. She had crouched and tucked herself into the corner of the room between the sink and the wall.

"I'm sorry! I didn't mean to do it!" she said between breathy sobs.

Me and Leo looked at each other again with that *what the fuck* look.

"Dammit Lucy! I almost shot you full of holes," Leo grumped as he made his way back to the bar.

I holstered the Judge and held out my hand to her. She was a cute little thing. Thick hair, the shade of midnight that hung down past her shoulders in little spiral curls framed a face as pale as the dead with heavy mascara and black lipstick. Black leather pants, spiked leather collar with pentacle, combat boots and her Marilyn Manson t-shirt tied in a knot just under her ample breasts rounded out the overall goth chick look.

"Come on. Let's get you a drink or something." I said as she took my hand and pulled herself upright. Clutching her messenger bag to her chest, she avoided eye contact and headed straight for the bar.

I closed the restroom door and followed behind her. "Bobby, pour her a drink."

"I don't know who you think you are, mister stranger," Bobby said with a sideways bob of his head, "but I would like to keep my liquor license." He leaned up on the bar and cupped his hand away from Lucy then whispered, "she ain't legal."

I turned to Lucy, and she just gave me that shrugging smirk look. She sure could have fooled me.

"Legal to drink," she said. "I'll be twenty next month."

Leo slammed his empty beer bottle onto the bar. "Just give her a drink and put it on my tab, Bobby! After what she just went through, she deserves it. And give me another one. I ain't seen shit that weird since Vietnam."

He threw up his hands and backed away from the bar. "No sir I will not. I cannot legally serve a minor in my establishment."

Leo walked around the end of the bar then grabbed three shot glasses and the first bourbon on the shelf. "And just because some bureaucrat in Washington says it's alright, she can fight and die for her country at the age of seventeen," Leo said with a growl. "Piss on them and piss on you, Bobby Raker." He poured the three shots then picked up one for himself and saluted us. "Cheers."

I took my shot and leaned against the bar, facing Lucy. "So, what did you mean earlier when you said that you didn't mean to do it?"

She pulled her messenger bag tighter against her chest and stared at the bar top.

Leo grabbed Lucy's shot glass and set it behind the bar. "That's the exact look my daughter used to get when I'd catch her red handed in something she knew she wasn't supposed to be doing."

Tears began to darken the canvas bag that she cradled.

"Lucy, honey," Bobby said in a caring tone. "It's alright. You can tell us whatever it is."

She sobbed for a moment longer before sucking in a shaky breath and looking up at the rest of us. "I just wanted to change my fate and get out of this trashy trailer park."

"Hey, now!" Bobby threw a bar towel at her. "There ain't nothing trashy about this place." He hummed in thought, shifting his weight from one foot to the other. "Eccentric maybe, but definitely not trashy."

Leo laughed and took another shot of whiskey. "She's right, Bobby. It's trashy." He leaned toward her and then spoke in a soft, fatherly voice. "Go ahead, Lucy. Tell us what happened?"

Chewing on her lower lip, she let out a reluctant sigh. "I might have raised a powerful necromancer from the dead."

That's just perfect, I thought. "I step away from the weird shit for a little break, and it just happens to hunt me down like a crazy ex-girlfriend." I poured myself another shot and slammed back the dark amber liquid. "Alright, are we talking about an ancient necromantic practitioner or some man bun wearing dead dabbler?"

Bobby slapped the bar top, so flustered to find the words as he stumbled over himself to get anything coherent out. "I swear to God, you people are crazy."

Leo nodded at me with a grumble. "This the weird government contract work?"

"Yup."

"Fair enough," Leo said with an unsure nod then poured another round for each of us.

I turned back to Lucy. "Alright, Lucy. Give me all of the details of what happened and exactly what you think you did to cause all of this."

"I just wanted to change my fate." Her voice was as soft as a kitten's purr. She glanced at each of us and continued. "Necromancy had interested me for a while and while doing some research online I came across a story about the rise and fall of America's most powerful necromancer. Her name was Annette McCallie, the wife of Colonel Gerald McCallie, a wealthy landowner and businessman from Rhea Springs during the early 1800's.

Just after his death in 1840, Miles, Gerald McCallie's right-hand man on the plantation, found Annette McCallie in the family mausoleum, speaking in tongues over the disinterred body of her dead husband while under the guard of her manservant, Claudius, who was said to be a mountain of a man.

Supposedly Miles convinced the other slaves on the plantation that she had become the devil's concubine and that she was doing his evil work. They overwhelmed Claudius after the loss of dozens of men. When they entered the mausoleum, they found Annette in the necrotic embrace of her late husband, chanting and screaming in an unknown language as the undead fiend writhed atop her in the throes of passion.

The slaves decapitated both the fiend and the witch, then placed them in their respective vaults. A silver stake was driven through each of their hearts, and their bodies covered in wreaths of garlic and bathed in holy water.

The slaves attempted to burn Annette McCallie's book of spells, but nothing would so much as smudge the pages, so they placed her book of evil in the vault with her corpse and sealed the vault lids in place."

"Honey," Bobby interrupted, "did you hit your head on something, because that's one hell of a tall tell. Rhea Springs has been at the bottom of this lake since the early '40s."

"I'm not lying!" Lucy opened her messenger bag and produced a leather-bound book. The faded black dye of the cracked leather showed years of wear and weathering. She gently caressed the lines of the embossed Celtic knot that decorated the face of the book before jerking her hands away.

I turned the book around and opened the two brass latches that held the cover closed. "What's this?"

"Annette McCallie's spellbook," she said sheepishly.

Leo let out a hearty laugh and turned up the whiskey bottle. "I thought you said her book was buried with her."

"It…was." Lucy glanced up at each of us with sad doe eyes.

I flipped through the pages. Beautifully flowing handwritten script danced across the yellowed rough-cut sheets of paper. The opening line read:

Maireann an chraobh ar an bhfál ach ní mhaireann an lámh do chuir

I couldn't understand a word of it, but page after page was the same sort of script meshed with sketches of plants and archaic symbols.

Leo slid the book away from me and leaned back to get his eyes to focus. "That's Gaelic," he said, then shoved the book back to me.

"Irish Gaelic to be specific," Lucy added. "It really isn't that hard to learn once you understand the basis of the language."

I leafed through more of the pages then latched it closed. "If this was buried with Annette McCallie, and Rhea Springs has been under water since the '40s, then how did you manage to get your hands on it?"

"The McCallie family graveyard was located on the top of a hill, which has since become known as Cemetery Island near the south end of the lake."

I wiped my hand over my face out of frustration. "Okay, so you stole the dead witch's book. Was it cursed or something? Is that what caused the bodies from the black lagoon to come after everyone?"

"Um...," she trailed off for a moment in thought. "Everything was fine until I read a particular passage out loud." She opened the book and flipped to a page near the back then turned the book so we could see it.

"Alright, but what does it say? I can't read any of it."

"I thought it was a channeling spell, but I must have translated it wrong." Lucy looked away and started to mumble. "I think it's actually a...resurrection spell."

I snatched the bottle from Leo and downed a mighty gulp. "And let me guess. You meant to channel the witch's powers but instead you managed to resurrect the evil witch of the east, who's pissed and wants her book back."

"That's…yeah, that's pretty much it."

"Dear, God, Lucy," Bobby huffed. "Have you lost your ever-lovin' mind? How did you even get out there in the first place?"

"I kinda stole one of the boats from the marina when you were out of town." She shrugged innocently.

Leo stole the bottle back from me. "We're about to do something stupid, aren't we?"

I shrugged. "Maybe."

He took another swig from the bottle then passed it off to Bobby. "Does that book of yours say anything about how to kill the witch?"

"No, but I did see a binding spell that might slow her down. And if I had to guess, we can stop her by putting this back into her chest," Lucy said as she produced a tarnished silver spike from her bag.

I took the spike and bounced it in my hand. "I'll be damned if it isn't solid."

"I bet it's worth a small fortune," Bobby said, licking his lips.

Leo laughed. "No shit."

I placed the spike and spellbook back into the bag and slung it over Lucy's shoulder. "If this is what will put that witchy bitch back in her grave, then I'm gonna shove this thing where the sun don't shine."

We scrounged around Leo's and geared up before climbing into one of Bobby's rental boats. I snatched Bobby's brand-new Mossberg 590, complete with red dot sight and mounted tactical flashlight from behind the bar. Leo strapped on a pair of .45 Long Colt six shooters that looked like they were right out of an old spaghetti western while Bobby looked like a military surplus store. He'd gotten decked out in flak vest and Kevlar helmet with two shotguns crossed in holsters on his back, dual Desert Eagles in hip holsters and his great chain sword, fully charged with a backup battery in each cargo pocket of his Bermuda shorts.

It was sometime after midnight with the moon full and high in the sky when Bobby idled the massive pontoon boat up to the rocky beach of Cemetery Island. I grabbed the mooring rope tied to the bow of the boat and jumped to the rocky beach. A hiss like the sound of steam escaping met me on the ground.

"Someone shine a light down here."

Leo appeared at the front of the boat, shining a Maglite down at me. "Whatever you do, Brax, don't move."

Following the light to the ground I found three massive orange and black water moccasins. Their coiled bodies looked as thick as a baseball bat.

"Don't you hurt those beauties," Bobby shouted. He fumbled in a side compartment under one of the seats.

Lucy quietly shushed him. "Do you want to let the witch know that we're here?"

"Honey, if you only knew what Koichi-San could do with water moccasin meat, you wouldn't be complaining."

No sooner had Bobby reached over the bow of the boat with a pair of mechanical grippers than a bloated figure charged out of the water toward me. Leo drew and fired both of his revolvers, shooting from the hip before the ghoul could even clear the water.

I was at a complete loss for words. I'd never seen anyone move that fast in my life, let alone with a pair of six shooters that splattered the creature's brains across this side of the lake.

Leo shrugged and holstered his guns. "Retirement left me with a lot of free time."

Remembering the snakes, I looked down to find they had slithered away at some point amid the commotion. I took Leo's Maglite and tied the boat off to one of the many scrub trees that covered the island.

Bobby lept to the shore in an amazing three-point superhero landing with his chain sword in hand. He knelt and held the monstrosity out like it was some legendary sword of power. "Oh, holy trinity of the trailer park and Mason's bathtub Madonna! I call upon y'all to bless this here weapon of purity and vengeance! And to protect us from the evil we are about to kill."

Leo dropped from the front of the boat to the shore. "You've been playing Dungeons and Dragons with Donnie and Earl again, haven't you?"

Bobby shrugged. "Maybe."

"Let's get this over with..." I had started to say before Lucy cut me off, screaming. I spun, scanning the overgrowth of the island behind me. Between the trees and brush, malformed figures had appeared from the darkness of the undergrowth.

"Brax, get back!" Leo's six shooters rang out again amid the buzz of Bobby's chain sword.

I unslung the Mossberg and with the soul satisfying sound of the shotgun's pump action, I chambered a round.

Six of the watery ghouls charged onto the beach at us from the underbrush. Bobby charged forward to meet them head on. The chain sword chewed into the bloated corpses with ease. I fired, cycled the pump action and slam fired the next three rounds, shredding the torsos of things charging at me. Leo fired round after round into the creatures, dropping three more by the time I put a final round into the back of a ghoul's head.

"Alright," I said, turning to face Lucy. "Where's the crypt?"

"Mausoleum," Lucy corrected.

"Doesn't matter," Leo grumbled. "Let's just take care of this thing."

She pointed directly ahead. "It's just a few hundred feet ahead through those trees."

I slung the shotgun and fished an aluminum baseball bat from the boat that I had brought along just in case ammo got scarce. I held out my hand to help Lucy down from the boat. "Let's get this over with."

She let out a whimpering sob. "I don't know that I can do this. I've never killed anything before. I don't even know for sure how I brought the witch back to life."

"You're the only one that can read the spells in that book," I reminded her. "Anything you can do to slow those things down so we can put that stake back through the witch's black heart will be helpful. It doesn't matter if you know how you did it before or not. The fact is, you're a natural magician whether you want to admit it or not, and you've already done it once."

"But you're a wizard, Lucy...," Bobby whispered in a cryptic voice.

She glared down at Bobby and sucked in a composing breath before taking my hand to steady herself as she slid down from the bow of the boat. "Yeah...maybe, but I'm not a very good one."

"That's beside the point."

"Just stay close and be ready to cast that binding spell that you found. I've got no doubt that you can do it," I reassured her. "We're going to need all the help we can get."

Bobby took point as we pressed forward into the underbrush. The light of the full moon filtered through fog enshrouded branches of scrub oaks and privets that covered the island. The McCallie family cemetery which was the namesake of the island quickly came into view. Wrought iron barriers embedded in stacked stone pillars encircled the site. Simple headstones and intricately carved stone monuments seemed to glow beneath the light of the full moon. The beautifully forged gate hung open, one side slumped to the ground, its hinges relenting to time and corrosion. The other was swung inwardly enough for a person to easily pass between the two.

Lucy hunkered up against me, clinging to the back of my arm. "That's the mausoleum," Lucy said, pointing at a large marble structure that stood out at the back of the clearing. It looked like a miniature gothic temple of sorts. Ornately carved white marble that towered over the other monuments of the small graveyard.

Bobby whimpered. "I swear to God this place gives me the heebie-jeebies." Bobby turned to Lucy with a contemplative glare. "Bless your heart, girl. You were either really desperate or stupidly brave to come out here on your own like that. I sure couldn't have done it," he admitted as he continued forward.

Lucy slapped a hand over her own mouth and let out a muffled scream. Her panic-flooded eyes bulged as she pointed ahead of us into the graveyard. Following her stare, I easily spotted the cause of her distress. A petite figure emerged from behind one of the many monuments. She danced to a silent song as she crossed the clearing. Her long blond locks floated softly about her face like a glowing halo. The flowing white silks of her gown hovered around her and drifted slowly like heavy smoke.

Bobby crossed himself as he muttered quietly. "Blessed mother of the great trinity."

"Let's get this shindig on the road already," Leo said in a low cautious tone then stepped through the open gate.

The night had gone eerily silent after our beach landing. It was so quiet that I could hear the beating of my own heart. That was, until Leo passed through the gate, crossing the threshold of the graveyard. No sooner had he entered that every shadow seemed to come to life. Bloated, misshapen forms skulked out from the foggy darkness throughout the graveyard.

Muzzle flashes accompanied the cacophony of Leo's six shooters. In a split second he had dropped two of the charging ghouls.

I brushed Lucy away from my arm and charged into the fray. "Keep her safe, Bobby!"

"But who's going to keep me safe?"

Baseball bat reared back at the ready I charged for the closest creature, connecting with a solid thunk with the thing's skull. One more solid whack crushed in the side of its face as it slumped to the ground.

The unmistakably strange buzz of the chain sword meeting flesh resonated throughout the clearing amid the discharge of Leo's .45 Long Colt rounds.

"Braxton!" Lucy shouted. "She's getting away!"

I put my full body weight into an uppercut swing that connected with a sicky snap of bone under the chin of the next creature. Its neck snapped back awkwardly as it spun in a reverse somersault. Continuing, I skull checked one after another of the advancing ghouls. It was like shooting fish in a barrel. If the zombie apocalypse were to ever actually happen, the shambling type like these guys would hands-down be more preferable to the freaky fast sprinting type.

I stole a glance in the direction of the witchy apparition and caught a glimpse of her as she disappeared through the entrance of the mausoleum. "Get ready to cast that spell!" I looked back over my shoulder to see Lucy heading my way, fumbling in her bag for the book. Ribs cracked and broke as I struck another creature across the chest. Swinging my bat in a wide, overhead arc, I crushed in the back of the creature's head.

This just seems way too easy, I thought as I took down the next ghoul to charge at me.

"I swear to God!" Bobby shouted.

That's what I get for thinking. The gods of dumbassery must have been watching with riveted amusement or I just jinxed the hell out of myself, because a swarm of the things overran Bobby as he swapped out battery packs. Skidding to a halt I fought for traction in the damp grass.

Leo charged in, shouldering his way through the pack of ghouls surrounding Bobby. "Chase down the bitch and put this shit to rest! I've got Bobby!"

I got my feet back under myself and grabbed Lucy by the wrist. "Stay close." Lucy fought to keep up with me as we sprinted for the mausoleum. Three of the creatures appeared from behind the building just as I reached the opening. The first one snatched the bat right out of my hand and backhanded me, knocking me to the ground. The thing fell on top of me and let out a gurgling roar that bathed me in the stink of fetid flesh and rotten fish. The ghoul lunged, latching itself to my chest. Its black teeth gnashed down on my left pectoral. I couldn't get a grip around the creatures' neck no matter how hard I tried. Its bloated skin was as slick and slimy as it looked. I punched and clawed, pounding my elbow into the side of the thing's head. It was like it didn't feel pain, which made sense if it was undead. Arching my back, I rolled to one side and drew my revolver then sent a four-ounce slug soaring through the ghoul's rotten skull. Pushing the corpse off of me, I fired three rounds into the other creatures that loomed over me, poised to pounce on their prey.

I pulled up my shirt to check the wound. It was mostly superficial. No worse than a few bite marks I'd willingly earned with much better looking wrestling partners, except for the single tooth that had been left embedded in my skin. I gripped the slime covered enamel and wiggled it loose. Squeezing the wound caused blood to run freely, flushing the wound of any other debris.

Lucy rushed to my side. "We have to hurry, Braxton. I have no idea what she is capable of right now. But the longer she has, the more chance she'll have to build her power up."

Getting back to my feet, I dusted myself off and holstered the empty revolver. A quick glance around didn't reveal where the baseball bat had been dropped, but I couldn't waste any more time. I adjusted the straps on the shotgun, flipped on the mounted tactical flashlight and brought it up to the ready position before stepping over the threshold of the mausoleum.

Aged marble steps led down into the musty darkness of the crypt. Mischievous giggles echoed up from the underground chamber on an icy cold breeze. Fog formed in front of me from my next exhaled breath. Gooseflesh suddenly rose with the hairs on the back of my neck. Lucy moved in so close that she should have easily melded with me if that were possible. If Lucy could have gripped my arm any harder, I'd swear she would tear the flesh from the back of my arm with little effort.

"I welcome thee, valiant warrior," the sweetly sinister voice said. Rusted hinges creaked as the iron doors of the mausoleum clanged shut behind us. I suddenly felt like a fly in a spider's web, being politely welcomed to the dinner table.

"I reward those who serve me well."

Reaching the bottom of the stairwell we entered the burial chamber. Two large, ornately carved marble vaults took up most of the available space in the room. An alcove, complete with stone altar and braziers that burned an ethereal blue flame were set in the opposite wall.

"Don't be afraid, warrior," the voice said in a soothingly smooth tone.

Without pulling my eyes away from the altar, I blindly reached into Lucy's bag and retrieved the silver spike. Leaning close to her ear I whispered, "Get your spell ready."

"I promise," the voice said with a sultry hiss. "Return my book and I will reward you with an eternity of whatever your heart desires."

The apparition reappeared, laying nude across the marble altar. Smokey white tendrils formed from the discarded gown beneath her. The ghostly appendages cupped her ample bosom while writhing about. The witch let out a soothing moan as the other worldly tentacles caressed and undulated across her body.

"Come to me, my brave warrior."

Everything around me blurred. Blues became reds and greys shifted to greens as the world distorted around me. The witch arched her back and let out another low moan before spinning where she sat my direction.

She softly cooed with a sly smile then opened herself to me. "You can have all that I am and all that I will be."

I stepped forward, unable to stop myself.

"Be mine." She motioned slowly with a slender finger. "Become one with me."

The witch's pale flesh glowed with golden radiance. I could feel the pulsating warmth of her building the closer I got. She was peace; she was warmth; she was happiness; she was pleasure.

"Cluinn mi, o spioradan Uisge, Talamh, Teine, agus Adhair. Aoighean nèamhaidh, Deamhain nan rìoghachdan ìochdaranach Agus spioradan nan sinnsirean. Tha mi a 'gairm ort, Gus a cheangal…"

The words that floated into the warmth that surrounded me sound so familiar. Like something I had heard before. Like

Scot's Gaelic…Lucy…That sounded like Lucy reciting the spell.

I blinked then shook my head to clear the fog of whatever the she bitch had done to me. I looked back, finding Lucy reciting from the open spell book. Her black hair floated about her head like an evil spider about to pounce. She suddenly flew backward, smacking against the stone wall of the crypt then limply fell to the floor.

"Time to finish this," I growled and turned to face the witch. Something with the grip of a steel vice pinned my arms against my sides, forcing the breath from me.

"A pity," the witch sighed. "You could have had it all."

I flexed my arms, gasping for the slightest breath I could get.

"I could let Claudius crush you like the husk that you are…" She slinked down from the altar and began prowling across the stone floor like a hunting cat. A loud laughing grunt filled my ears. Looking down I found two massive ebony arms the size of my thighs wrapped around my chest. My ribs felt like they were about to shatter every time the muscles flexed in the slightest.

"Or perhaps I could have some fun of my own…" she leaned back, kneeling before me. A self-satisfied grin stretched across her pallid face. Claudius loosened his grip just enough that I was able to take a quick breath and laugh. The witch jerked her head back in an unsure glower.

I fumbled for the grip of the shotgun with my right hand. "Gimme some lovin', baby," I growled, then raised the shotgun and forced the tip down her gaping maw and pulled the trigger.

Her head snapped back and limply fell backward to the stone floor. Pulses of ethereal flames erupted from the gaping hole in her head. Claudius convulsed with each pulse of energy, then released his grip and fell backwards. I collapsed to the floor and sucked in a gasping breath.

The witch's body wriggled and squirmed with each pulse, wrapped and encircled by the smokey tendrils of her gown. A sudden motion caught my eye. Chunks of the witch's skull vibrated and moved like an amoeba in search of its next meal, making their way back to the body.

"Shit!"

Pain shot through my left side when I tried to stand. Her muscle-bound servant must have cracked a few of my ribs after all. Holding my elbow close, I let the shotgun drop to the sling and swapped the spike to my right hand. The silver spike plunged easily into her soft flesh. Blue flames licked out from the spike, transmogrifying the soft pale skin to the desiccated husk of a long dead corpse.

"Yup. This was the perfect getaway from all the weird shit." I forced myself to my feet and stumbled over to where Claudius's remains lay. I'm not sure that I could ever eat another piece of jerky after a night like this. His skin had drawn and sunken in, pulling tight over his massive frame.

Lucy let out a low moan and started to stir.

"Don't try to get up too quick. You hit the wall pretty hard."

She jerked upright, looking around for the witch.

"She's dead…," I started, "again."

I slid down against the wall next to Lucy and picked up the book. "Let me catch my breath and we'll get out of here."

Lucy brushed the hair out of her face and stared over at me in the dim glow of the flashlight. "What do we do about the book? The legend says that it can't be destroyed. And what about the witch? That silver spike is the only thing containing her."

"Nothing to worry about. I happen to know a guy that will help me put both her and the book in a safe place where no one will bother them."

"I sure hope so."

I grunted, pushing myself upright. "It's O'beer thirty somewhere, and I think we earned a few drinks tonight."

Lucy helped me to straighten myself, and we limped our way out of the McCallie family mausoleum.

Von Neumann's Cyclone

By Michael Gants

Terrance Jones was tired and running a lot later into Huntsville than he'd originally planned. He hated driving through Atlanta; unfortunately, there was no better route to get home when coming from Savannah. Thanks to a four-hour traffic jam, his rig had only moved about half a mile. The lost time meant that he wouldn't arrive at the construction dealership before they closed for the long holiday weekend. He needed somewhere to keep the flatbed trailer and big-wheeled crane until they opened, and alongside his mobile home was the best, and safest, place he knew.

The sun was low in the partly cloudy sky, throwing long shadows from the pines surrounding Rocket City Estates. The mobile home park currently housed two dozen trailers and prefabs along a single oblong loop of paved road. Most of the residents were on the wrong side of middle income but the neighborhood had pride. Most of the residents maintained their grass-covered yards and homes in good repair. The occasional one or two did sport a vehicle (or several) on blocks. Most had working vehicles in their driveway. The neighborhood population consisted of the usual mixture of people in Huntsville, with no one group making up a significant portion of the population.

Terrance slowly pulled his rig halfway down the north side of the southern leg of the loop, keeping an eye out for playing children and unleashed pets. His wife's battered white sedan was absent, which meant that Tanisha had gone out to grab groceries for dinner and tomorrow's grilling extravaganza. He thanked the heavens for her; she was the best thing to happen in his life.

A quick look was enough to ensure that he had room to park the rig beside the house. Carefully, he backed the trailer into the grassy space between his single wide and the Munzoz's prefab home. He relied less on his mirrors than his years of experience to ensure he kept the trailer closer to his place than theirs. There was no way insurance would cover damage to the house if he put part of a crane or trailer through a wall, not to mention what Tanisha would do to him.

Once he was certain the flatbed trailer was safely parked, Terrance shut off his truck and hopped down. He walked to the front of the Munzoz's house, glancing at the azalea bush's fuchsia and purple flowers. Mrs. Munzoz had planted them near the door to liven up the walkway, and they were a welcome bright contrast to the pale beige siding. The house did not have a doorbell, so Terrance knocked loudly on the metal frame. A short, rounded woman with straight black hair, caramel-colored skin, and bright brown eyes opened the door. He smiled at her.

"Good evening, Terrance," Mrs. Munzoz said. She and her husband had moved from somewhere south of Mexico two decades earlier and her melodious accent tinged her words. "What can I do for you?"

"Hey Elena. I needed to let you know I had to bring work home tonight. I parked it between the houses for the weekend. It's a crane and is going to look to certain children like a great jungle gym. I know it's a lot to ask, and I won't be upset if it doesn't work, but could you tell Enrique and Louisa not to play on it? I can't deliver the crane until Tuesday morning, so it's going to be here until then."

Elena's smile grew wide. "Yes, I can see where that will be a terrible temptation for them. I'll make sure they understand that no matter what it looks like, the crane isn't a jungle gym for them to climb all over. Or do anything else," she completed with a laugh.

Terrance wiped the beaded sweat from his brow with a huge flourish. "Whew! That takes a load off my mind." His smile softened. "Seriously, thanks. I'd hate for either of your kids to get hurt."

Elena nodded sagely. "I know you would, and I appreciate you informing me about it ahead of time. They're at vacation Bible school right now, but they'll be back soon. This way I can prevent the little *gamberros* from surprising me with their antics. Are we still good for the cookout tomorrow?"

Terrance gestured toward the park. It was a small community space built on a lot where the ground was too soft for mobile homes to be parked. Several years earlier the residents had collected enough money to purchase the land for the neighborhood. Since then, they had worked to improve the open space by adding a set of swings, a climbing structure with a slide, a pair of horseshoe pits, picnic tables, and a section of smooth sand for people to safely set up their grills. On big holidays, it was used for neighborhood parties and cookouts.

"Oh yeah. The annual Rocket City Estates Fourth of July Jamboree is a go for launch. I'll set up my two grills and fire them up around eleven, so the meat is ready by lunch."

"Good. We are all looking forward to it. The party always reminds me of the gatherings back in El Gaucho, back before we moved here. Only with more neighbors and less family. I'm going to be bringing a corn salad, pineapple salsa, and homemade tamales."

Terrance's eyes grew larger. "That's a fair amount of food. Those sound amazing as always. That pineapple salsa goes great with the chicken." He mimed rubbing his belly.

Elena laughed again at the sight. Her smile widened, and she waved pleasantly. "I will see you and your wife tomorrow."

"Tomorrow, then," Terrance said and turned to leave. Elena continued to wave as she closed the door. As he walked back to his trailer, he glanced across the road toward the houses at the end of the turn. Roger Billings sat inside a wire-covered frame made of two-by-fours and tapped away at his computer.

Roger was always pursuing some oddball hobby, just like his father, William. Terrance stared for a moment at the two large electrical towers that stood guard on a gravel patch in the Billings' back yard. He knew that Roger's newest passion was filming videos for YouTube but had never spoken with the young man about them, so he was not sure what the machines were for. Roger waved, and Terrance returned the motion.

Roger had watched with envy as Terrance had pulled in. He was always amazed at how smoothly the older man could maneuver the big 18-wheel rig and trailer. Roger had problems backing his dad's subcompact into the driveway; he could not imagine trying the same thing in a truck that was three times higher and had a huge trailer attached. Terrance made it look effortless, which was probably why Roger always felt a bit inexperienced and silly around the man.

He opened a browser window and took a quick look at his last video's comments. Based on what his viewers had typed and the likes, his subscribers enjoyed the various music pieces he used the coils to play. The game theme was one of the most requested pieces, not only in that video but also in several others he had released recently. Roger knew enough about social media to keep his finger on the pulse of his subscribers. He wanted to branch out and try a few different pieces of music in the future, things like classic 1970's guitar rock and early 1990's country. For right now, though, he would continue following the suggestions in the comments, which meant continuing to program themes from video games or movies, with an occasional piece of techno. On the other hand, changing up the type of music would force him to learn more electrical theory. He hoped it would be more interesting than his professors at the University of Alabama Huntsville made the subject.

He sighed and flipped a switch in the cage, killing the primary power leads to the Tesla coils. A look at the multimeter confirmed that the coils were no longer powered. Roger waited to ensure there were no further discharges, then stepped out of the Faraday cage. His current test session, using the theme music from a popular video game series, seemed to be working out and it appeared there were a good number of bright discharges. It was always a little difficult to measure the full effect of the discharges during the day though. He was not completely happy with how the session had gone and wanted to tweak a few notes on the computer to change the charge rate of the coils and see if he could synchronize the electrical discharges a bit better.

Roger opened the main breaker and then turned the ignition switch off to shut down the generator. His dad had managed to find a broken military 100 kW diesel generator for sale at a surplus sale and purchased it for pennies on the dollar.

While Roger and his dad had not been close before, they had bonded last fall repairing the machine. It had taken them several months of troubleshooting and a couple of hundred dollars in parts, but they had finally restored the generator to working order. He was thrilled that his father had found the old monster. Even now, it cost him less in diesel to run than what the electric utility would charge him for the power. All of it added up to savings he needed with tuition coming due for the upcoming fall semester.

Satisfied all the machines were safe after a final dead check, Roger rolled the two Tesla coils back to the shed, shut the door, and locked it. He took a quick look at the sky, then checked his phone's weather app. The weather forecast on the NOAA app gave a one hundred percent chance of clear skies during the night, with the chance of clouds increasing to 90 percent both tomorrow night and Sunday morning. The precipitation forecast projected a 70 percent chance of thunderstorms tomorrow afternoon, but the chance of rain dropped to 15 percent by nine p.m. in the evening. The coil discharges always looked better in the dark, and the cloud cover could give a nice background to the arcs. Roger glanced at his watch and gulped. Right now, he needed to get changed and head out to his job.

As expected, the annual Fourth of July get-together and cookout was going amazingly well. Tables nearly groaned under the weight of the dishes the neighborhood had brought. The dishes ranged from Latin America cuisine to foods from Germany, Thailand, North Africa, and the United States of America. Kimchi shared space with Chicago-style hot dogs, challah bread sat next to brats, and over on the dessert table, banana pudding and date-filled phyllo dough awaited. An international feast for a wholly American holiday. Terrance could not help but grin at the nature of the spread.

Children ran about holding pinwheels, laughing, and screaming in joy while the adults grilled, talked, battled over cards, or tossed horseshoes. Too often anymore, all he heard on the news was how people were at each other's throats, how people could not get along, and that the color of their skin or where they were from automatically made them less. Here in Rocket City Estates, at least today, all of that seemed far from true. Terrance watched everyone at play as he tended the grill, keeping an eye on the chicken he was grilling. Not that his neighbors were perfect. He knew he was not. Today though, it appeared that no one worried whose kids played with whom, or what their neighbor's beliefs were. It was about coming together as a community and celebrating the birth of the nation. He gave a brief thanks to the powers above.

It was almost one in the afternoon and some of the adults glanced concernedly at the growing dark gray clouds on the horizon. The weather report predicted the rain would not start until after four or five, but everyone had lived in the South long enough to know the weather people only had the slightest idea of what the weather was really going to do. If the storms rolled in and stayed past dark, there would be no fireworks, which would disappoint more than just the kids. Several of the adults were looking forward to the display as well since last year drought and wildfire concerns had prevented the use of fireworks. The wind was still just a light breeze, with no trace of the gust front that would come before a storm. Most people decided there was still plenty of time for the festivities and went back to whatever they were enjoying.

The screen on the house three doors down from the edge of the park popped open with enough force to slap the aluminum-sided trailer with a loud tinny sound. Terrance looked up from the grill in time to see Roger running pell-mell down the street toward the park, waving his hands to get attention.

"Juan, would you keep an eye on these? Roger looks like he's gonna hurt himself running that way." He wiped his hands and put down the brush and bowl he was holding. "They're almost ready for another brushing of the sauce."

"Sí, Terrance. I will take over." Juan Munzoz's accent gave the words a lyrical quality. He stepped up to the propane-fired grill, set his beer on the built-in metal counter, and took the basting brush in his right hand. Terrance wiped his hands and quickly stepped through the crowd, reaching the edge of the park where it met the street just as Roger skidded to a halt.

"Holy sh...smokes," Roger corrected himself when he noticed a couple of the younger kids had drifted over when they saw him running up. "It's headed our way. The news says that no one can stop it. Not the cops or the Army. Went right through them. We're gonna need to get everyone out of here. Get somewhere safe!"

Terrance stared down at the young man, gathering his thoughts. "What are you babbling about? It what? Please tell me you ain't decided to start taking recreational drugs and are on some sort of trip."

"What? No, you know I've never done drugs, and I'm sober. Didn't you hear what I said?" Roger stared at Terrance, perplexed that the big man was doing nothing. Terrance was not a person to sit idly by while things went weird. He was a decision-maker and a thinker, unlike Roger's father who was more a fly by the seat of your pants kind of man. That was the whole reason Roger had told Terrance first.

"I heard what you said," Terrance stated, crossing his arms and sighing in exasperation. "I just don't get what you're talking about. Start at the beginning. What is the 'it' you saw on the news?"

"I didn't tell you?" Roger asked. He shook his head in self-disbelief. "The news report says that a bunch of experimental robots are tearing their way through the city. They put up a map of Huntsville, and based on the projection, those things are headed straight for us. These machines eat all the metal they can touch, and then they reproduce. Faster'n rabbits or mice according to the scientist they were interviewing."

The whole story caught Terrance off-guard. He looked hard at Roger. "This is a joke, right? You've been watching something on YouTube or a sci-fi movie. Metal eating robots?" Terrance guffawed. "This is Huntsville, Alabama. They are just getting back into building rocket engines again. This isn't home to some high-tech laboratory where mad scientists develop super robots, especially not ones that can reproduce."

Roger held up a hand, stopping Terrance's tirade. "According to the report, they broke out of some lab out on the outskirts of the city. The robots have been slowly moving in our direction since. The group of scientists and computer programmers from the company think something has gone wrong with their programming. The shutdown command only worked for most of them. A fair number are still working. I watched a video of these things demolishing a tank! It took them less than seven minutes, and no one could prevent it. This isn't science fiction, it's real. Based on what the scientists are projecting using the rate these things are moving, if something isn't done, this whole place is gonna be robot chow in about three hours." Terrance continued staring at Roger, trying to process the absurdity of what the young man had told him.

With a screech of tires, a single police car turned into the neighborhood, its siren wailing full blast and all its lights were running. Between the strobes and the flashers, the whole car looked like a last-minute firework display. The officer drove down the road to the park. Everyone at the cookout, children included, stopped what they were doing and turned toward the sounds and lights. People who had not joined the festivities stepped out of their trailers or manufactured homes to stare as the vehicle came to a hard stop. Tanisha walked up beside Terrance and put a hand on his arm nervously, waiting to see why the police were here.

There was an electronic squeal as the officer turned on the car's announcing system. "This is not a drill. This is a city-mandated emergency evacuation notice. All persons living in, eh." There was a pause as the police officer checked her display. She spoke again, this time her inflection flat as she read from the unseen notice. "All persons living in Rocket City Estates must leave not later than two and a half hours from this notice. Evacuation routes will be clearly marked. Please bring no more than a single vehicle per family unless the number of members is greater than the capacity of the vehicle. Again, this is an emergency evacuation notice. Your evacuation time is no later than three forty-one p.m. Central time."

The police car drove around the loop, making the same announcement twice more before the officer pulled out of the park. Its siren wail continued unabated, diminishing somewhat as the pines lining the road blocked some of the sharp sounds. Now that the group had quieted, they could hear other sirens around them and distant muffled announcements. Several people jumped as their phones buzzed or alert tones sounded. The message from the alert system was almost identical to what the police had been announcing. It boiled down to "Get out now."

Now that the excitement of the police car was over, the younger children began drifting away, returning to their running around and playing. All the adults and several of the older teens remained behind, waiting for someone to talk. Terrance found himself and Roger the center of attention unexpectedly; Roger was looking at him.

"Look guys. The best idea is probably to listen to the police and get out of here. From what Roger just told me that he saw on the news, this is going to be bad. Tornado F5 type natural disaster bad." The crowd began pushing inward, closing the space around Terrance and Roger, everyone beginning to talk at once.

"I don't have the money to just leave here," one of the neighbors burst out. "Everything I own and love is right here."

"Yah," shouted another. "I can't just leave my home. There's nowhere for me to go."

"Come on kids, we've got to go *now*!" shouted a woman as she grabbed the hands of two little boys and started hurrying toward her house.

"What are we supposed to do? My homeowner's insurance ain't gonna cover this." The man began to laugh slightly hysterically.

The words became a jumble, and Terrance could sense panic setting in.

He raised his hands and shouted, "Wait, wait, wait! Back up and give me some room. Look, this is the same as if we had a tornado or fire headed this way. We get out and rebuild when we come back. We help each other. Y'all know that we can't stop a tornado or change its course. You can just get out of the path and hope the damage isn't too severe."

People grimaced. Most of them had lived in the South long enough to recognize what Terrance was saying had merit.

"Let's gather up the food, grab the children, and begin loading people into vehicles to get them evacuated."

Roger looked around at the faces, seeing the despair at losing their homes but understanding the reality of the situation. No one in his or her right mind stood in the path of a tornado.

Being young and somewhat scattered in his focus, many of the adults of the trailer park did not consider Roger to be bright. They were wrong, it was simply too many ideas running around in his head. An idea began forming. The news report had surprised and scared him. The robots were not exactly like a tornado. Terrance had been right when he mentioned a wildfire. Wildfires, unlike tornadoes, could be fought if you had the right equipment.

He looked around while thinking hard. What did they have here in the neighborhood different from what the Army and scientists were using to combat the robots? His gaze drifted across the houses until it came to rest on the bright blue and white crane sitting placidly on the flatbed trailer next to Terrance and Tanisha's home. Unconsciously he snapped his fingers.

"What if we could fight them off? The robots I mean," Roger said with a distant look on his face.

"What are you talking about son?" asked William Billings, Roger's father. He had stepped out of the crowd when Roger had run out of the house. "I thought you said the news people said that nothing was working against them."

Roger ignored the question and asked one instead. "Terrance, what's that crane's boom made of?"

Terrance glanced across the road at the pristine blue and white construction vehicle. He shrugged. "Metal I expect."

"What kind?" Roger asked a bit exasperatedly.

"I don't know...steel? I didn't think to check it with a magnet or anything when I picked it up, just verified that it was properly on the trailer. Then I hooked the trailer up and drove back here for delivery. Why?" Terrance's voice had taken on a sarcastic tone as he spoke. He stared at Roger, trying to understand where the kid's head was right then, asking about the crane.

Roger glanced over at his father, once again failing to answer any of the questions thrown in his direction. "Dad, do you still have those rolls of heavy gauge electrical wire you bought back when you wanted to build an underground bunker? And the metal plates and pipes?"

William blinked at the apparent non sequitur. He thought furiously for a moment. "Uh, yeah. At least I think I do. Don't remember moving them down into the hole or selling them off."

"Great!" Roger spun around, looking over the remaining crowd. He spotted a familiar face. "Mr. Munzoz, you're a welder, right?"

"Sí," Juan answered, "I weld for Teledyne Brown, down near your university." He gazed questioningly at the young man. "Why are you asking?"

"Do you have your welding machine here?"

Juan shook his head and shrugged. "No, I don't own one. I use the machines in the shop. I do not have a portable welding rig."

Roger frowned.

Terrance put a hand on the young man's shoulder and shook him gently. "What are you asking all these questions for? I haven't heard you explain what this plan of yours is for fighting off these robots. Might help if we all understood what you are planning to do."

"I haven't?" Roger looked down in confusion for a moment and then grinned as he looked back up. "Alright. The plan is pretty simple. We use the electromagnet."

The crowd continued to stare at him. Looks of confusion and disbelief crossed most of the faces. Terrance just kept a neutral expression and waited for Roger to finish. "I figure since the crane is steel, we can turn it into a giant electromagnet. Turn it on and we can suck the entire swarm toward the boom. We'll weld my Tesla coils onto the end of it and use them to blast the robots with the plasma arcs. BAM! No more robots! I've got a whole bunch of music that produces a serious amount of plasma arcs per second."

"You want to..." Unbidden, a chortle slipped out of Terrance's mouth. "You want to use a giant magnet and lightning bolts to destroy a robot swarm? Do you think we're part of some sort of science fiction show?"

Roger placatingly held up his hands. "They are plasma bolts, not lightning. I know it sounds a bit off."

"A bit?" Terrance asked sternly, one eyebrow climbing in surprise.

"Okay, it probably sounds completely bonkers. Plasma arcs can destroy objects. I've watched a few YouTube videos showing that part off. Electromagnets work in real life just fine and are powerful. They use them in junkyards all the time to lift cars, which are way heavier than these little robots. We've got everything here we need to build this. I've got the coils and a generator, Dad's got the wire and plates, and you have the crane. All the pieces and parts are right here except the welding rig."

"I've got one," shouted an older woman from the back row of the crowd. She pushed forward through the people to talk without shouting. He recognized Sally McAllen, a hatchet-faced woman with a screechy voice who worked as a cashier at the nearby supermarket. "It belonged to my no-good husband. That bast..." Sally paused and surveyed the group. Clearing her throat, she started again. "Anyway, the useless idiot left me and ran off with a peroxide bimbo from that bar he was always hanging out in. I've still got all the junk he left behind in my shed. Y'all are welcome to use any of it; including the welding whatever it is, if y'all need it."

No one said anything for several seconds. Then Juan laughed out loud, the sound echoing faintly from the houses. "Why not? What do we have to lose that we wouldn't lose if we evacuate? No one has said these robots are dangerous to people. I'll help in any way I can."

"You guys are nuts," one of the members of the crowd said. He turned and hustled his wife and children away. "We're getting out of here. You stay and play heroes; I'm getting my family to safety." Several other people left, some grabbing food to take with them, others simply heading for their homes to pack up a few items before evacuating.

Terrance glanced down at Tanisha. She was his rock, and whatever she decided, he would follow through with. If that meant leaving, they would leave. She looked up at him and smiled. "Roger's right. If we can do something about this threat, we need to. I'm not waiting around for the government to figure out how to do something. Last time my mom did that, we ended up stuck in the Astrodome waiting for some agency to get us the money to fix our house. Which we could have done ourselves. I say we stay."

He smiled down at her and kissed her forehead. "I love you. If that's your decision, then that's what we'll do."

Roger's smile grew. "This is going to be AWESOME!" he shouted and pumped a fist into the air.

The first order of business was getting the crane off the trailer and set up. That would take at least twenty minutes. While Terrance worked on getting that done, Roger and a group of others would get the cable spools, Tesla coils, and metal plates.

Finally, Juan would go with Sally to get the portable welding rig and the necessary equipment to use it.

With the trailer next to the house, there was not enough room to get the crane off the flatbed trailer. Terrance would need to pull onto the main street to unhook it. He carefully maneuvered the entire vehicle out from the side of his house and onto the blacktop, checking to make sure he had plenty of room both ahead and behind. He shifted the truck to neutral and set the parking brake. Since he was the only one in the group who knew how to unhook the trailer safely, he hopped down from the idling truck and walked back to the remaining group.

"Alright, I need two people to help with unhooking the rig. I can't be here since I've got to pull the rig out of the way to drive the crane off the trailer" he said.

"Why not just leave it right there?" asked Richard Garcia.

"Because we have no idea which way these things are going to come into the Estates from. It'll also be easier to wrap the cables around the boom if I lower it closer to the ground. Which I can't safely do if the crane is still sitting on the trailer. Which brings us back to the need to get it off said trailer," said Terrance angrily.

Richard gulped and nodded.

Terrance took Richard and another volunteer, showing them how to remove the large metal connector pins holding the transfer section of the trailer to the carry section. He disengaged the clutch on the trailer's connector, unlatching the grips. Pulling the truck and front section of the trailer away released the tension on the pins. As soon as the front section of the trailer was clear, the two men darted forward and removed all four pins. Terrance waved them back and reconnected the transfer section to the carry. He stuck his head out of the window.

"Everyone clear?"

Richard and the other man performed a fast walk around, then Richard gave a thumbs-up sign. "All clear," he shouted.

Terrance eased the truck forward, checking his mirrors every few seconds to ensure that the trailer's front section had fully disengaged. As soon as he could see that everything had been done right, he pulled the truck all the way to the curve and onto the grass. He shut down the engine and ran back to where the trailer sat.

"Anyone here ever work a crane?" he asked, swiveling his head to check the crowd's reactions. No one nodded, raised a hand, or said yes. "Great. I guess that means I get to do it. I'll need Richard and Vince as spotters," he said, pointing at the two men. "The rest of you go over to the park so that I can see you. If I can see you, I won't accidentally hit you with this monster." The crowd laughed nervously and moved away.

Together the men walked around the trailer, unhooking the safety chains, and putting them in the storage compartment. After this was all over, he would have to still deliver the crane. Terrance was not looking forward to explaining what had happened to it. Once that was completed, he climbed onto the trailer and into the crane's cabin. A large plastic envelope was taped to the seat.

Inside the envelope were the keys and a thick Operator's Manual. He flipped through the pages, reading how to start the machine and drive it. He started the engine, then after a brief recheck of the Operator's Manual, raised and stowed the hydraulic leveling jacks. Watching his spotters, he backed the crane off the trailer and continued for several yards. Terrance cautiously turned the crane in a circle trying to get a feel for the steering. He winced when he accidentally crushed one of his neighbor's mailboxes in the process. Tanisha would not be happy that they were going to have to pay for a replacement.

Now that the crane was facing toward the trailer park's entrance, he lowered the boom down as far as it would go, then shut off the engine. He sat there a moment, watching several cars and trucks, packed with fleeing neighbors and their possessions, turn out of the Estates and drive away. One drove around the crane, honking in frustration. He sighed and stepped out of the cabin. When he turned around, he saw William's group. They were rolling the spool of heavy cable down the road toward where the crane was parked. The remaining people followed.

"Roger, what do we need to do now?" William asked as they arrived at the crane.

"Wrap the cabling around the boom, as near to the top as we can get it. After that, we can weld the Tesla coils on. If we do it in that order, I can be sure the wraps won't interfere with the welding." Roger pointed back toward his house. "Then we'll move the generator over here to hook up the wires and power everything up."

"How long will it take?" asked one of the crowd members.

Roger shrugged. "I hope less time than it takes for the robots to get here."

Wrapping the wires around the crane boom proved to be harder than Roger had made it sound. The heavily insulated cabling weighed almost six pounds per foot, and it took nearly everybody left in the Estates to move it around. People stood in line from tallest to shortest and drug the wire around the boom arm. The entire spool of cable had to be lifted and over the boom, a painstakingly slow process that took nearly ten minutes for the first loop to be completed. The subsequent loops went a bit faster, as Juan figured out a way to get three people looping the boom at the same time. With the boom nearly to the ground, starting near the top made the most sense. However, each wrap raised the level of the coil a bit, making it that much harder to maintain the wire straight. After twelve wraps, the youngest children dropped out as they ran out of energy. Other people began cycling out of the work pool as they reached their personnel limits. They would rest, then trade with someone who needed to rest.

After nearly an hour and a half of backbreaking work, the upper quarter of the crane boom was completely wrapped in rubber-coated heavy grade electrical cabling. With a sigh of hydraulics, Terrance raised the boom to what Juan had dubbed 'the matador position.' This was what Roger and Terrance had decided would be the optimal height to fight the robots from. The top of the crane boom hovered about five feet above the roadway.

Roger took the cable's two free ends and worked them past the cab to the rear of the crane where he intended to attach the generator. He discovered that the cable from the lower section of the boom was too short. This required lowering the boom again and unrolling one loop of cable, raising it again, and checking the length. The cable run was still too short. Terrance grumbled and lowered the boom again. Juan and Roger, plus two other adults removed a second looped portion of the cable. This time with the boom in position, the cable was long enough to reach the generator.

Roger rubbed his hands together. The plan seemed to be working. Now they needed to power the magnet. First Juan needed to weld the Tesla coils and stands to the crane boom.

Terrance rotated the crane and lowered the boom until the hook rested on the ground on the grass on the side of the road.

Two women and Victor carefully undid the massive bolting arrangement that held the several hundred-pound hook to the pulley cables. Removing the hook ensured when the coils were activated, the plasma arcs would impact the robots rather than the huge piece of metal swinging at the end of the boom.

While the three people worked on the hook, Juan used an electric grinder to speedily remove the slick white coating and buff the metal clean. Filling material would not adhere properly to the paint, and as the paint burned from the heat of the weld, it would give off fumes that could make a person sick or even kill them.

Next, he used another wheel to roughen up the metal, ensuring a good surface for the welding. With bare metal showing, he finally checked the surface with a heavy-duty magnet. The magnet jumped from his hand to the metal. The boom was made with high iron steel, meaning the two flat plates William brought over could be welded to it.

While Juan was preparing the weld area, Roger and William hooked the generator's tow arm to William's old subcompact. The generator pressed down on the hitch, compressing the suspension, and lifting the front end. Terrance watched the process and hoped the car would have enough traction to move the generator the few yards needed.

It did. William towed the generator behind the crane. Then they unhitched it and physically pulled it around until the tow arm faced the right way. Using a set of heavy bolts and drag chains passed through the generator's tow bar, Roger, Terrance, and William attached it to the tow rope bar on the crane's bumper. This setup would allow the crane to move while keeping everything powered, Roger hoped.

Now that the metal was prepared, Juan tacked the large flat plates with several well-placed spot welds. He turned to

Terrance. "Lift the boom up about half a meter, por favor. I need to see how much flex the plates are getting by themselves. Then I will figure out what supports I need to add. There is no way these plates will hold the coils without help."

Terrance flashed a thumbs-up sign, climbed in, and lifted the crane boom. The left plate bowed immediately, snapping two of the tacks. The right held, not flexing as much. Juan contemplated the situation as Terrance lowered the boom back to the ground.

"William," Juan began, still looking at the plates and scratching his chin. "I am going to need those steel pipes you spoke about. Can you get them for me? They need to be at least a meter and three-quarters long."

Seeing the puzzled look on William's face, Juan smiled. "Lo siento, I still think in metric. About five feet long. I would prefer them to be at least two centi-, er, about an inch in diameter." He thought for a second. "We might be able to use as small as half an inch."

William nodded and turned to his son. "You heard the man. Check the right side of the shed, in the big round bin. If you can't find the pipes in the right size, grab some of the angle irons near the back wall. Hell, just grab the angle irons anyway."

Roger grabbed two of the teenagers in the group and took off at a sprint, grass blades spraying out from his feet as he ran, the two others following him. Minutes later the trio returned with an armful of piping and several pieces of angle iron of varying lengths. They dropped them on the ground and smiled. Juan looked at the pieces arrayed on the ground, then chose two of the pipes and tacked them to the far corners of the left plate. He and Victor pushed them together to form a V shape. Juan joined the tubes quickly and welded the pair against the flat arm of the boom and the plate. He welded a piece of angle iron about halfway up the V.

"That should keep the pipes from buckling under the load." He pointed to the angle iron. "That helps distribute the weight evenly between them." Roger nodded. He knew almost nothing about welding and was surprised at how much engineering was needed to figure out how something should be constructed to prevent it from breaking the welds.

Juan used a similar build on the right-hand side, though only one tubular support went as far as he needed. He added two additional angle irons back to the plate to prevent twisting.

"All right, raise the boom. It is time to see if these welds can hold themselves and the plates."

Everyone backed away as Terrance slowly lifted the crane's boom to nearly its full height. The plates did not even wobble on the way up.

"They look good from here," shouted Terrance over the diesel engine's noisy exhaust.

"Same here," replied Roger, shading his eyes as he started upward.

Juan waved his hand toward the ground. "Bring it back down. I need to figure out how to mount the Tesla coils. Those are going to be a bit harder to do since the center of gravity has to be right. I do not think we can afford for one of them to fall, or all of this work will be wasted."

Roger and his friends crossed the road again and began shimmying the first coil across to the mount. Once the coil was next to the boom, Roger recognized the major issue.

"Juan, how are you going to mount these so they're upright? The plates are facing us so we're gonna need to tip the coils over and hold them in place while you weld. That's gonna be tough to do."

Elena looked doubtful for a moment, then clicked her tongue against the roof of her mouth. "That's going to be dangerous.

We need more than just the four of you." She turned and called out to the remaining crowd. "We need people here. At least another three. If you have rested enough, come help. These men are trying to save all our homes. Don't just stand there and ignore the need. This is America. We stand together." Her voice boomed across the group. Moments later, most of the crowd surged forward, each remaining man and woman clamoring to help.

"Hold on, hold on!" shouted Roger. "We can only fit about five of us around one of these things at a time. Plus, we gotta be delicate. We break anything, and there's no replacement parts. Then we will be out one which means less chance to actually kill these robots."

People shuffled about until Roger and four others were in place. They carefully lifted the first coil upward, tilting it so the base lined up with the plate. Groans, grunts, and blowing breath could be heard from the group.

Juan struck an arc, the white-blue light was harsh in the late afternoon haze. He fed the rod into the groove and watched through the tinted lenses as the metal pooled and ran under the glowing tip. He tacked in several spots, then began laying his first bead in between the upper tacks. He worked his way down, ensuring that everyone's hands were clear of the area, and they were looking away with closed eyes.

Once the first bead was down, Juan started over and ran a second, then the third bead, pausing to make sure the material was cooling properly and not cracking. Partway through the fourth pass, two of the men changed out. Juan paused, watching the rapidly cooling material to see if it flexed or cracked during the changeover. The men moved carefully and switched out for rested people. The Tesla coil stayed steady the entire maneuver. Once everyone was back in place, Juan restarted the torch and continued. Six full passes and he shut down the welding rig and stepped back.

"Alright, side people, slowly release your holds and step back. Three of the five people released their grips and gingerly stepped back. Roger and Juan stared at the coil, watching for any motion. Nothing moved.

"Next, the two of you underneath, slide to the side, and keep a grip." The last two did so, pushing upward against the unyielding Tesla coil.

Roger swallowed. "Time for the real test." He waved to the two men. "Let it go and get back."

The men released the coil and quickly stepped back two full strides. The coil sat motionless, pointed out toward the horizon at an eighty-degree angle.

"Whew," Terrance said as he wiped the perspiration from his brow. "I wasn't sure that would hold. Or if it did, would the plate or struts bend?"

"No, I am pretty good at eyeballing these things," said Juan as he put down the welding gun and put his hands on his hips. "Pretty good job."

"Now we need to get the other one in place and welded."

Victor's son Adam hustled over and spoke. "Looks like things might be getting worse. We're now under a tornado warning as well as the robot invasion. This is beginning to sound even more like a bad science fiction movie."

Everyone looked up at the clouds covering the sky. While they had been working, the color had changed from light gray to an angry yellow green. The scent of ozone tinged the air, and a few lonely raindrops spattered the ground, darkening the asphalt where they hit.

"The perfect color for a tornado or two," whispered Tanisha.

The group glanced to the west when they heard a buzzing sound like a swarm of ground hornets. A thin finger of dust and smoke whirled around above the tree line marking the progress of the sound. They watched in confusion and fear as an oily cloud of gray-black motes slowly slid through the tree line. The buzzing rose as the mass of objects cleared the undergrowth. The chain-link fence that marked the neighborhood's boundary shivered under the assault from the robots, seeming to collapse in on itself as the swarm destroyed it. The crowd gasped and split up, running for shelters, and getting out of the way of the incoming objects.

Terrance gaped as he saw the swarm envelope a parked Taurus near the fence. The car began to disintegrate, the windows and rubber lining dropping to the ground as the metal was consumed. Black bug-like objects crawled over the sedan's surface, and he could see flashes of tiny lightning all over the vehicle.

"What are the chances?" asked Roger when he noticed the damage happening to the car. "The robots have formed a tornado-like structure. I mean it's inverted, with the large part of the funnel on the ground and then it shrinks to a bit of a point at the top. A robot tornado tearing through our trailer park. Should we call it Robotnado or Twisted Metal Twister?" said Roger, a grin creeping across his face.

"This isn't the time for those kinds of jokes, not when this whole place is in line to get destroyed by those same robots you're making jokes about." Terrance jumped into the crane's cab and started it up, leaving the door open so he could still talk to Roger. "Get that generator running."

Roger turned a key and pressed the start button. The diesel engine turned over, belching black smoke that was ripped away by the rising wind. He flipped the main breaker. Needles on several dials jumped, pegged, then settled down to a point with only tiny variations in motion. Roger pressed two more buttons and a row of lights illuminated. The crane's boom seemed to vibrate. "You've got power to the coils. The entire boom's now a magnet."

"If the coils have power, why aren't they discharging?" Terrance shouted back as he began driving the crane toward the mass of robots oozing across the Estates.

"Starting the program now!" shouted Roger, tapping his phone's screen. A music app appeared, and he scrolled through the songs. "No, no, maybe, no, YES!" He touched his finger to one of the listings. "Close the door!" he warned.

Terrance quickly grabbed the door and latched it shut. A moment later the coils began humming audibly as they warmed up. Suddenly, a bluish arc of electricity shot out from the left side of the boom, followed by a second and a third. It took only a few discharges for Terrance to recognize the music as Lynyrd Skynyrd's unofficial anthem for their state. When the second coil began firing, he couldn't help but sing along to the odd-sounding music.

"Sweet home Alabama," he belted out off-key. Thankfully no one could hear him over the sounds of the two diesel engines and the buzzing of the robot swarm. He slowed the crane as he drove onto the grass, making sure with a quick glance back the generator remained attached to the tow bar.

Still singing, Terrance extended the boom to its full length while the crane bounced through the grass. As he passed between a row of houses, Juan could not help laughing. The situation made Terrance look like a modern-day Don Quixote, charging the robot swarm with a magnetized crane boom for a lance. Three children's bicycles leapt from the ground and clanged into the boom as the vehicle passed one house. The house itself leaned slightly, then slipped back onto its slab as the magnetic field sped past. The jury-rigged electromagnet worked perfectly.

Terrance made small adjustments as he drove, ensuring he kept the boom aimed at the center of the writhing mass. He slowed by downshifting as it pierced the heart of the robotic cyclone. He turned the wheel to keep the crane moving with the robots' chaotic motions. He could see the tiny black metal carapaces hurtling around, then getting caught by the magnetic field and sucked to the boom with barely audible clangs. He watched the arcs lash out, oftentimes playing over several robots both still in the air as well as on the boom. None of the robots seemed to be affected by the micro strikes of lightning. They continued swarming, flitting around, and destroying any metal they touched.

He fumbled his phone out of his pocket and speed-dialed a number, then hit the speaker button. "Yeah Terrance?" asked William from the other end of the call.

"The arcs aren't working," he said as he rotated the crane to follow the path as the swarm attempted to dodge around the boom. "The robots are being pulled to the boom, and I think they are starting to attack the crane. I see a bigger problem though. None of them are being hurt by the arcs. I thought these things were supposed to get fried by these coils."

"That's what Roger said would happen."

"Well, it looks like he was wrong." Terrance thought quickly. He swept the boom through the funnel rapidly, moving it up and down as well as side to side. The mass thinned with each sweep until he could not see a single robot flying about. "I think I've gotten all of the bots. They're stuck to the magnet and can hardly move. I think it's time to kill them with fire. Like a fire ant nest."

"What?" asked William.

"Grab a propane tank. Open the valve and toss them at the robots. We'll try and fry them that way."

"Won't the tanks explode?"

"Propane tanks don't explode easily. We just need to get the gas burning." Terrance said.

William ran from the shelter of the trees out to the park, making sure his Bluetooth earbud was firmly in place. There were tanks of propane connected to some of the grills. He verified the valve was shut on one and began unhooking the line. For a moment he was stymied until he reversed his motion, having forgotten that the threads were reversed for pressure tanks. The hose popped free, and he hefted the bottle. It felt about three-quarters filled. Hopefully, that would be enough. He ran toward the crane.

"Terrance, I've got a bottle of propane. I'm going to toss it into the magnet's attraction area. That should give us the fire you want."

"Hope it works," said Terrance.

"I know." William paused and set the bottle down. The crane was only about thirty feet away and no longer moving. He turned the valve, listening to the hiss of the compressed gas and catching a whiff of the skunk-tainted vapors. He grabbed the bottle, ran a few feet, and threw the bottle as hard as he could toward the boom.

The bottle bounced twice, then rolled. It came to rest just in front of the wheels. Terrance rolled the crane back a few feet. For a second or two, the off-white bottle sat, spewing the contents out. Then the magnetic field intersected with the bottle. It slid sideways, then jumped up to clang loudly on the cabling. William could no longer hear the gas escaping.

The arcs from the Tesla coils continued, having now segued into a piece William recognized from an older Disney pirate movie. Pulses of ionized plasma danced through the winds, striking the robots. He could see the lower portion of the tank was covered in robots. The random micro bolts of lightning struck the cylinder as the robots breached the pressure vessel. The gas began burning, spewing flame from the holes. Robots crisped and blackened, but others continued their attacks. Fire was not enough.

"Burning is good, but we need to knock these things apart as well. Fire plus explosion would be better," William said as he ran back to the park, calling for Roger.

"What did you say?" asked Terrance.

"Don't worry. Trust me," replied William.

Roger met him at the grills. "Get me tape. Duct tape would be best if you can find it." He flipped open a blue Igloo cooler and pulled out several red cylinders with fuses. Roger raced over to their car and popped the trunk. He rummaged about for a few moments, then shut the lid and ran back.

"Here," he said, holding out a roll of silver tape.

William unhooked a second tank and then bundled the M-80 fireworks with tape. Carefully he wrapped more tape around the bottle and hooked the bundle to it with the fuses pointing down.

"Dad, what are you doing?" Roger asked concerned.

"Killing those things with more bang." William lifted the nearly empty bottle and shook it as he ran toward the crane again. He set it down, lit the fuses with a lighter, then opened the valve.

Without waiting he tossed the propane tank as hard as he could at the crane's boom. This time the tank was grabbed by the field immediately and slammed into the boom.

The fireworks detonated a second later. Propane gas spewing from the tank burned and the fire raced in through the valve, causing the vapor inside the tank to ignite. The pressure vessel walls exploded outward, bits of metal and robot innards flying out in all directions.

Without any memory of what had happened, William found himself flat on his back. Tilting his head, he could see that several of the nearby houses' windows had been blown out by the pressure wave. In the sky, an expanding ring of smoke blew out from around the crane's boom. Charred wood, leaves, metal, and robots began raining down. Metallic pings sounded as the bits hit metal roofs.

In his earpiece, William faintly heard a sound. He reached up and pressed the headset more firmly into his ear. "William, can you hear me?" the voice asked distantly.

He nodded, then realized that no one could see him over the phone connection. "I'm phone," he croaked as he ran a hand over his body to confirm the statement. "Fine. I mean I'm fine. Phone still works."

"Great, because the crane boom is on fire, one of the coils is busted, and I think I've got a piece of metal or two in my thigh from your brilliant idea."

William stood shakily and looked over at the crane. On the upper portion of the boom, there were spots of fire, and he could see where the explosion had stripped insulation from the cabling. A circle around the base of the crane had been blown out, now a rough patch of dirt and clay sat exposed. Small fires burned in the grass while thick black smoke rose in a column and was driven westward by heavy winds. Terrance raised the boom upward to prevent the fire or any of the exposed wiring from coming into contact with the ground. Without further warning, the heavens opened up. Torrential rain fell in sheets so thick William partially lost sight of the crane. He was soaked in moments.

"Terrance, I'm going to grab Roger and shut everything down. How bad are you bleeding?"

"It's not horrible. I can keep pressure on it. Good thing the rain started. Looks like it's put out all of the fires on the boom and ground."

William turned and walked unsteadily through the downpour to where Roger ran toward him. Roger stopped when he got to William and checked his father over for injuries. Both Juan and Victor also came over. "Roger, I'm fine. I need you to go and shut down the generator. We've got to get Terrance out of the crane. He got injured during the explosion. The cables got damaged too, so the entire metal body might be energized. I think that your coils are broken too."

Roger nodded. "I brought gloves in case. Not too worried though. The generator's grounded, so even if the crane is energized, the switch will be safe." He ran to the generator, making sure not to get any nearer to the crane than necessary. He flipped the switch for the main breaker, de-energizing the cable runs and the Tesla coils simultaneously. Then he turned the key to shut down the entire generator. The diesel engine clunked a moment before stopping.

Cautiously Roger pulled the heavy-duty multimeter from the storage box on the machine and plugged in the probes. He pulled on the leather and rubber gloves, reached out, and touched the

Michael Gants

the grass while thick black smoke rose in a column and was driven westward by heavy winds. Terrance raised the boom upward to prevent the fire or any of the exposed wiring from coming into contact with the ground. Without further warning, the heavens opened up. Torrential rain fell in sheets so thick William partially lost sight of the crane. He was soaked in moments.

"Terrance, I'm going to grab Roger and shut everything down. How bad are you bleeding?"

"It's not horrible. I can keep pressure on it. Good thing the rain started. Looks like it's put out all of the fires on the boom and ground."

William turned and walked unsteadily through the downpour to where Roger ran toward him. Roger stopped when he got to William and checked his father over for injuries. Both Juan and Victor also came over. "Roger, I'm fine. I need you to go and shut down the generator. We've got to get Terrance out of the crane. He got injured during the explosion. The cables got damaged too, so the entire metal body might be energized. I think that your coils are broken too."

Roger nodded. "I brought gloves in case. Not too worried though. The generator's grounded, so even if the crane is energized, the switch will be safe." He ran to the generator, making sure not to get any nearer to the crane than necessary. He flipped the switch for the main breaker, de-energizing the cable runs and the Tesla coils simultaneously. Then he turned the key to shut down the entire generator. The diesel engine clunked a moment before stopping.

Cautiously Roger pulled the heavy-duty multimeter from the storage box on the machine and plugged in the probes. He pulled on the leather and rubber gloves, reached out, and touched the

483 | Page

exposed body of the crane with the probe. The meter indicated zero voltage. The crane was safe.

He hurried to the side of the crane's cab and waved to Terrance through the starred window. He could see blood staining Terrance's leg and hand. "Go ahead and shut down the crane. I've stopped the generator and verified the crane isn't electrified."

Terrance reached over, shut down the engine, and popped the door open. He sagged visibly in the seat. "Did we get them all?" he asked as Tanisha arrived.

She looked in and blanched at the blood. Nodding, she said "As far as we can tell. Not your worry now. Now you need to get fixed up."

"I think I'm going to need to see a doctor. This is—" The large man slumped forward, and half slid out of the cab.

Roger jumped up and grabbed Terrance's shoulders before he slipped off the machine completely. "Dad!" Roger called out. "Call nine one one. We need an ambulance." He helped the large man down, Tanisha keeping pressure on the wounds.

Terrance's eyes opened, and he smiled. "I guess country boys can survive. Even through robot apocalypses." The group around him laughed and waited for the ambulance to arrive.

Halloween Surprise

By J. L. Curtis

Grady Hart, twenty-six, browned by the sun, wiry, and needing a haircut, pulled into the little north Texas rodeo arena late on Friday afternoon and backed his old Chevy and trailer in between two brand new rigs. *Must be nice. Hell, I bet those are nicer than my damn house.* He sniffed the air. *Ah the aroma of the rodeo…*

Ed Fuller ambled over. "Bout damn time you got here. I was wondering if you were going to make it," he said with a grin.

Looking up at Ed's six feet two, Grady sighed. "Got tied up trying to get a couple of damn cows back in. They pushed the fence down to get at the grass on the other side…again." He walked to the back of the trailer and carefully opened it. "Better get out of the way. Rocky's in one of his moods."

Ed stepped quickly to the side of the trailer, holding one side of the butterfly gate open. "Oh hell. That's all we need. If he's…I hope he'll be okay to work tonight."

Grady untied Rocky and slowly coaxed him to back out of the trailer, whispering to him the whole time. Rocky humped his back, and Ed could have sworn the hair on the lineback dun's spine stood up as Rocky made a try at Grady's hat. "Lemme know when you're ready to make a practice throw or two. They got us up early in the schedule tonight."

"Gimme a few to get him calmed down. Where you parked?"

"I got here early, so I'm in the back," Ed said with a smile as he walked off.

"Asshole," Grady said, but smiled. "Alright, Rocky, you over your little mad?" He reached up and caressed Rocky's forehead, making sure to stay well above his nose and lips. Rocky blew softly and sidled toward Grady as he tied the hackamore off to the side of the trailer. "Oh no you don't!"

Twenty minutes later, he rode Rocky around to the back of the arena and found Ed sitting on the tailgate of his truck. "You ready?"

Two runs later, Ed looked over at Grady as they rode out of the arena. "Got a bee in your bonnet tonight? Two runs in the low fives! We keep that up, we'll be in the money tonight!"

Grady shrugged. "Just concentrating, and Rocky's on a roll. I'm gonna go rack out for a bit. He loosened Rocky's saddle and replaced the bridle with a hackamore, tying him loosely enough that he could crop the grass at the back of the trailer and settled down for a nap, safely out of Rocky's range.

A high pitched "Horsieee!" woke him up, and he saw a determined little blonde girl racing by him to embrace Rocky's head, much to Rocky's surprise. Grady bolted up as he heard a frustrated female drawl. "Patti, come here right now. That's *not* your horsie horse."

He almost knocked the petite blonde over and grabbed her arm to keep her from falling as he turned toward Rocky, afraid of what he would see. To his amazement, Rocky was standing stock still and not reacting to the little girl who was petting him on his nose. He blew softly, and she giggled, then let go of him. Just as he went to reach for the hackamore, Rocky softly lipped the little girl's hair and whinnied gently, setting her to laughing again.

She toddled back to the blonde he now realized was standing behind him. "Sorry, ma'am. I didn't mean to—"

The blonde picked up the little girl and started apologizing, "I'm *so* sorry. She...got away from me when she saw your horse. I hope she didn't hurt anything!"

Grady blew out a relieved breath now that the little girl was safely out of range. "Rocky's rough around the edges, I was more worried about your...charge there than anything else."

The blonde made a moue. "She's my daughter. Patti's four and loves all animals."

Grady let his mouth run away. "You don't look old enough to have a four-year-old daughter!" When he realized what he'd said, he blushed and started trying to apologize.

She laughed bitterly, "You sound like my parents, just before they disowned me."

"I'm sorry. I..."

Patti, picking up her mother's bitterness, piped up, "I sorry, Mommy! I no mean to do bad."

She patted her daughter. "Oh honey, you didn't do bad. Well, you shouldn't have touched his horse without his permission. Next time please ask me, okay?"

Patti glanced at Grady, "Me ask him?"

Grady chuckled. "Yes, ask me first, okay little one?" He impulsively stuck out his hand. "Grady Hart."

She took his hand. "Sandy Riley, and this is my PITA, Patti."

"We get pizza, Mommy?" Both of them laughed at that as Ed rode up.

"You ready, partner?"

"Gimme a sec. Let me get the bridle on, and we'll go do it."

Sandy asked, "You a team roper?"

Ed said, "We try."

She smiled. "Who's the header and heeler?"

Grady replied, "I'm the header. Ed's just bringing up the rear as usual."

Ed snorted at that and said, "I'll meet you at the back."

Trading the hackamore for Rocky's bridle, he quickly mounted. "You going to watch?"

She shrugged. "For a little while. Patti needs her sleep, so we'll probably leave pretty early."

Rocky shoved his nose at Patti and whuffed as she gently petted his nose, scaring the hell out of Grady. "Rocky, stop that! If y'all will excuse me—"

Sandy stepped back. "Good luck!"

Twenty minutes later, Grady and Ed sat behind the gate with two runs under their belts, both right at five seconds each. "One more good run is all we need," Ed mumbled.

Grady sat relaxed in the saddle, idly looping and shaking out his lasso. They were finally waved into the chutes, and they bumped fists as they went into them. Grady reached up and made sure his hat was tight on his head, glanced at Ed, checked the arena, and nodded to the cowboy releasing the cow. "Let 'er rip."

The steer broke from the gate, the barrier dropped, and Rocky charged out of the chute. Grady got a quick loop on the steer, pulling its head to the left until his foot slipped through the stirrup. He got it back out, but his motions confused Rocky, who didn't finish heading up the steer as Grady catapulted off of him. The announcer was saying, "And some bad luck there for Hart. I don't know what happened, but they're done for the night. It is a shame because they were in the lead!"

Grady got up, spitting arena dirt and limping. He walked around Rocky and searched until he found the miscreant heel of his boot. He started to throw it, but just gripped it as he remounted, shook the loop loose and waved to the crowd as he and Ed trotted out of the arena. "What happened, Grady?"

Holding up his boot heel, he grumped, "Damn heel came off just as I pulled the steer."

"You alright?"

"I think so. I'm gonna hurt in the morning, but…ain't a damn thing I can do about that."

"Yeah. Might as well go home. We're out of the money and everything else."

"Sorry, man."

Ed shrugged. "Nothing you could do about it. We gonna enter the rodeo in Lubbock next month?"

"Yeah, I'll get the entry fee in. I owe you one after tonight." Ed turned toward his truck as Grady rode back around to where he parked. It surprised him to see Sandy and Patti standing at the hood of his truck. He got off Rocky, tied him to the trailer and limped toward his pickup as Patti started toward the trailer.

She stopped and looked up at him. "Horsie okay?"

He chuckled as Rocky whinnied and lowered his head. "Horsie is fine." He held out his hand. "Let me introduce you to him." She took his hand, and he led her to the horse. "Rocky, this is Patti, Patti, this is Rocky." Rocky gently lipped her hair, causing her to laugh and pet his nose.

He blew in her hand, and she giggled. "Horsie like me!" She threw her arms around his head and kissed him. Grady limped to the bed of his truck and threw the errant heel in the bed, pulled his muck boots out from between the bed and cab, and sat down to take his boots off.

Sandy asked, "Are you okay? You took a helluva fall out there."

He started to shrug and winced. "I'm going to hurt in the morning, but I'll live." He tried to brush some of the dirt off his shirt and pants but gave up.

Without the heel on his boot, he couldn't get enough leverage to get it off and she said impatiently, "Give me your leg." She straddled it, giving him a marvelous view of her posterior as she tugged until the boot finally came free. "What do you want to do with it?"

He pulled on his other boots and stood, stamping his feet into them. "Throw it in the bed. I'm not sure if they can salvage those old things again."

She smiled and said, "I hope you feel better. Patti, say goodbye to Grady and Rocky. We have to get home now."

Patti pouted but hugged Rocky's face again and trilled, "Bye, Rocky!" She trotted over to where he stood and hugged his legs. "Bye, Grady." She looked up at him and added, "You keep Rocky safe!" Running to Sandy, she grabbed her hand and pulled. "We go now, Momma."

Sandy shook her head and said, "It was a pleasure to meet you, and I hope you have better luck next rodeo. Take care of yourself, too!" She smiled as Patti tugged on her hand impatiently. "We are going, young lady!"

Grady chuckled. "It was nice to meet y'all, and good luck with her," he said, pointing at Patti. "She's gotta be a handful!"

Sandy smiled ruefully as they turned to go. "She is. She *definitely* is, but I love her anyway. Bye."

Once they had left, he loaded up Rocky, slipped his revolver back on his belt, and slid the speed strip in his weak side pocket, then patted his chest, ensuring his medicine bag was still there.

Ten minutes later, Grady pulled onto the county road and headed for the ranch. Almost a mile down the road, he saw a figure walking on the side of the road, then a second smaller figure. *Is that…That's Sandy and…Patti! What the hell are they doing walking out here?* He flipped on his flashers and pulled over ahead of them. He hopped out of the truck and made sure his pistol was safely under his vest as he walked back. "Sandy? It's Grady. What are y'all doing walking down the road?"

Sandy and Patti's faces were highlighted in the flashing red warning lights as she walked up. "We're walking home. My car…wouldn't start. We don't have too far to go, just to the trailer park on the other side of the freeway."

Grady looked down the road and could see the freeway in the distance. "Y'all want a ride? It's…not a good idea to be out here walking when the drunks start leaving the rodeo. I'm going that way, if that means anything." He sighed. "But I don't have a car seat for Patti."

She smiled. "It's not far, but…yes, we would appreciate a ride. I don't really…like walking out here, but Patti really wanted to see the rodeo." He led them around and helped them into his old Chevy, moving some things to the floorboard to make room for Patti in the middle. Between them, they got the center seat belt around Patti as she squirmed, and he finally got behind the wheel with a sigh.

"And here we go," he said as he carefully checked his mirrors before he pulled back onto the road.

As they passed under the freeway, he saw a Waffle House at the end of the off ramp and Patti started singsonging, "Awful House. Mommy, want Awful House!"

Sandy looked ruefully at him. "She likes Waffle House. I…can't afford it often, but…"

On impulse, he pulled in. "I can afford to buy you and her something. Ain't no biggie."

"Yaay! Awful House!" Patti squealed.

It Came from the Trailer Park

Grady winced at the pitch and tone but laughed as Sandy shook her head. "Sorry," she said. "Excitement makes her forget her *inside* voice."

Patti immediately quieted down, saying softly, "Sorry, Momma." She drooped in the seat as Grady maneuvered the truck and trailer so that he was facing back out and wouldn't be blocked in. They got out and strolled to the door, with Patti singsonging softly under her breath. As soon as they were inside, Patti ran to the back booth and hopped up on the seat. Grady let Sandy go first and happily watched her walk back to the booth. He appreciated the fact that she left the side of the booth facing the door open for him as she got Patti in a booster chair she'd grabbed on the way by.

Patti was looking around and squealed again. "Joseph! Mommy!"

Grady watched as the fry cook looked sharply at them, then dropped the spatula on the grill and walked back to the booth. *This dude…pale as a ghost, and sunglasses at night? What the hell?*

Sandy glanced back and said, "I'm sorry, Jozef."

Grady could tell the man was staring at him as he bent over. "Ah, *copilul meu*, what are you doing?" He bent over and gracefully kissed Patti on the head, causing her to giggle. Grady didn't understand what he'd said, because of his thick accent. Then the man smiled, and he saw the large canines, which made him wonder. "Sandy, you grace us with your presence. To what do we owe the honor? *Slavic accent? Definitely central European…he knows them. What…is that the daddy?*

Sandy laughed. "Stop it, Jozef. Grady, Jozef is my neighbor. He…sometimes watches Patti when I work late."

Jozef stood up, bowed, and extended a pale hand. "Jozef Tomáz. It is my good fortune to be this gracious lady's neighbor." His grip was surprisingly strong, considering that he didn't look that muscular at all.

Grady shook his hand carefully. "Grady Hart, I'm just giving them a ride home and buying them...food."

Jozef nodded. "You were in the rodeo tonight, yes?" Grady nodded and Jozef continued, "I will prepare their normal meal. What would you like?"

Surprised, Grady stuttered, "Uh, whatever Sandy is having is fine with me."

Jozef nodded and walked back to the grill as Sandy grinned at him. "Jozef is a...bit...different. He's been here for a while, some kind of issue with his eyes. He can't be out in the sunlight, so he's the night cook here. Usually, he doesn't come in this early though." She lowered her voice. "I think he might be in that Witness Protection Program, too. He's...from somewhere in central Europe, but he's...evasive about where."

Grady smiled at her. "Anything's possible. I...was..."

Sandy shook her head sadly. "No, he's not the daddy. That...sumbitch is long gone."

Jozef delivered their waffles with bacon, presenting the one with a smiley face in whipped cream to Patti. "Here you go *copilul meu*, enjoy. More coffee?"

Grady nodded. "Please." As Jozef walked back to get the coffee pot he asked softly, "What does...whatever he said to Patti mean?"

Sandy laughed softly. "He calls her my baby in...I think it's Romanian."

"Oh." Jozef poured more coffee, and Grady added, "Thank you." He topped up Sandy's cup and went back to the grill as one of the waitresses yelled an order from the far end of the restaurant.

They finished their meals, with Patti nodding off and Sandy said, "Well, time to get this one home and in bed." She reached for the bill, but Grady quickly snagged it.

"I said I was buying."

"Okay, I'll leave the tip. That's kinda Dutch, right?"

Grady chuckled. "More or less." After they got back in the truck, he asked, "The trailer park to the right?"

"Yes, please. You can just drop us at the gate."

He pulled out of the parking lot, drove down to the entrance to the trailer park, then swung in. "It's pretty dark in there. I'd rather see you safely home."

Sandy cocked her head as she looked at him. "Well, I guess. It is kinda dark in the new section. You can circle around and not have to back up, if that works for you?" He nodded, and she directed him to the back of the property. It was definitely dark back there, and he felt the hair on the back of his neck rising.

"Why no lights back here?"

She shrugged as she unbelted Patti. "They're working on putting them in. We've only been back here…a month or so. It's a nicer trailer than I was living in up front." She sighed. "It's a little more expensive, but it's got more room for Patti and two bathrooms, which is great."

Grady hopped out of the truck, pulled his pocket light out and flipped it on, lighting the way to the door of the trailer as Sandy carried Patti up the steps. She deftly manipulated the key and door, then flipped the inside light on. "Dammit, that's another light bulb burned out. I swear, I've already put two in that…lamp outside the door."

Patti woke up and mumbled, "I go bed now, Momma." She tottered down the hall as Sandy smiled ear to ear.

"She thinks she's old enough to go to bed by herself. I'm glad she is finally sleeping in her own bed; she kicks like hell!"

He laughed as they stood awkwardly at the door. "Well, I'm glad you're home safe and I—"

Patti's scream echoed down the hallway, and Grady didn't hesitate. Stepping around Sandy, he hissed, "Stay behind me," as he drew his revolver and sprinted down the hall. She screamed again, and it startled him to find cold air coming out of Patti's room as he stepped in.

He glanced up to see if the lights were on, as the room seemed dim and Sandy pushed by him, scooping Patti up off the bed and retreating to the door. "What's the matter, honey?"

Through her sobs, Patti replied, "Meanie is…" she pointed to the bed, "under there!" She turned back, hiding her face in Sandy's shoulder as Grady dropped down to his knee and looked under the bed. As he did so, he felt a tingle from the medicine bag around his neck.

It was even darker under there, and he pulled his pocket flashlight out, flipped it on, and shone it under the bed. He could see *something* under there, but couldn't really make it out in the darkness. Getting down prone, he extended the light and revolver. "Come outta there, you sumbitch!"

He cocked the hammer, and suddenly the darkness disappeared. The lights came back to full illumination, and the room started warming up. He quickly decocked the revolver, got to his knees, holstered it, and groaned as he finally straightened up. Sandy asked, "What…did you see?"

Grady turned to her, a bewildered expression on his face. "I'm not sure. I…it was dark. Real dark, like my light wasn't working. Was it my imagination, or did the lights get brighter in here, and it is getting warmer?"

She cocked her head. "You didn't see *anything* under there?"

"Not really. It just disappeared, like a shadow." He reached up and touched his medicine bag, and it felt a tad warm. *That's different. Did I imagine that?* He shook his head. "Sandy, I don't know what to tell you." He looked at Patti. "Is the meanie gone now?"

Patti nodded, still clutching Sandy's neck. "Him gone."

Sandy bit her lip. "Guess I'll put this one to bed with me, again. And it's late." She turned down the hall and added, "I don't know what the...heck is going on, but I don't like it. I...thought she was just having nightmares, but now..."

Taking the hint, Grady replied, "Yeah, I need to go, too. Today was a long day. I'm just glad I could help, if that's what you want to call it."

A quirky smile flashed across Sandy's face. "Well, whatever you did scared it off. I thank you for that. At least I have a gun. I can and *will* shoot the sumbitch, whatever it is." She stepped out of the room, and Grady followed her to the door. She gave him a peck on the cheek and added, "I do appreciate it. All in all, I...we had fun. Good night."

He nodded. "I did too, well, except for the last bit." Stepping out of the trailer, he blew out a breath as he heard her lock the door behind him. *I need to talk to Grandpa Hart and Grandma. There is something weird here. Really weird...*

Grady turned into Grandpa Hart's driveway outside Medicine Creek just before lunch. *Made good time. I wonder...* Grandma Topsannah stood on the front porch, just as she did any time he came to see them. *How the hell does she know? I know they don't have the gate alarmed. She's as beautiful as always...Prairie Flower is right...* He pulled under the trees and noted that both vehicles were in the garage as he got out and stretched before he walked up the steps and hugged her. "It brings joy to my heart to see you, Grady," she said as she hugged him back, smelling faintly of honeysuckle. "George is down at the pond, as usual." Her tinkling laugh took the sting out of the words, and he could only shake his head as she pulled him toward the front door.

"Grandma, I…need to talk to…maybe both of you."

She cocked her head as she led him through the house. "Go get your grandfather. He forgets the time and forgets to eat as he challenges the wily bass in the pond. You know that. We will talk after we eat. Never discuss trouble on an empty stomach."

Feeling like he was twelve again, he replied, "Yes, ma'am." Walking down the path to the pond, he took a deep breath, smelling the evergreens and listening to the birds chirping in the trees. As usual, his grandfather was sitting at the end of the dock on his broken-down old chair he'd salvaged from the barn. "Any luck, Papa?"

His grandfather snorted. "You know better than that, boy. I swear the damn fish have all been netted and moved!" Reeling the bait in, he stuck his rod in the PVC pipe he'd mounted to the piling. Getting to his feet, he turned and held out his arms. "Come, my boy. What troubles you?"

Grady hugged him, feeling the wiry muscles in the old man as he laughed. "Grandma says we can't talk until after we eat." Grady started to step back and realized his watch was caught in his grandfather's hair. "Dammit, I'm caught, Papa! Hold still. Why do you still wear braids?"

He finally got untangled and his grandfather pulled the offending greying braid over his shoulder and inspected it. "Traditions, Grady. Traditions. I must keep my hair long as a priest of the Chippewa." Expertly re-braiding it, he flipped it back over his shoulder as they walked up the path.

Topsannah had three plates covered with napkins sitting on the back porch table, iced teas at each plate, and something covered by a pie carrier sitting off to the side. "Sit, let us break bread. Ham and cheese, macaroni salad, and pecan pie. How was the drive, Grady?"

A half hour later, he realized he'd been grilled better than any interrogator he'd encountered in any of his military training. *Thank the Lord that Grandma had no inclination to join the military. I'd hate to think what else she would have picked up! And not one word about why I'm here.*

Grady helped her clear the plates and poured three coffees, carrying them back outside as she quickly washed the empty plates. She came back out and sat beside George, casually holding his hand as she asked, "What did you want to talk to us about?"

"Well, I don't know how to describe what happened. I…was at a girl, no a woman's trailer when her little girl in her bedroom screamed. I went running in there with the mother and… it was dark and cold. The little girl said Meanie was under the bed."

He stopped for a few seconds to gather his thoughts and took a sip of coffee. "I got down on my knees and shined my light under the bed. There was…I don't know how to describe it. Something *dark*." He reached up and touched his medicine bag. "And it felt like my medicine bag was…tingling. I don't know any other—"

George sat up sharply when he said that. "Tingling?", He looked at Topsannah. "Tingling, how?"

Grady shrugged. "I don't know. I've never felt anything like that before. It…just *tingled*. And it was warm."

George and Topsannah looked at each other for a few seconds and she leaned forward, touching the medicine bag around his neck, singsonging under her breath in Comanche. Moments later, he felt the medicine bag grow warm and said, "Warm like that, yes. But…it didn't tingle!"

Topsannah dropped it back against his chest and sat back, staring at him. She shook her head and turned to George, then said something in Comanche that was too fast for him to follow. The two of them went back and forth for a couple of minutes, until his grandfather finally said, "An evil spirit. Where exactly is the place where this happened?"

"It's a trailer park that backs up on the Pease River just down from Mule Creek. It's…a couple of hundred yards off One-ninety-three." He reached up and put his bag back in his shirt. "What did you sense, Grandma?"

She turned back to him. "Evil. Hateful." She cocked her head. "But a very specific hatred. Almost…" She glanced at George and another fast spate of Comanche followed. He nodded, and she added in English, "An Indian hatred. Like a warrior hating an enemy. Grady, you must be careful. I need to…consult with some people."

Grady glanced at his watch. "Well, I do need to be heading back. I…don't know how to contact her, and I don't want to just show up. It might not be taken the right way."

George laughed. "So, you like her is what you do not say."

Grady blushed as he got up. "I don't know, Papa. I only met her once."

Topsannah rose gracefully. "You will meet her again. We may need to visit to…prevent a worse evil." She kissed him on the cheek. "Drive safely. You are all we have left."

George got up and said, "I will walk out with you. I need to go get my pole I left at the pond." Topsannah chuckled and rolled her eyes behind his back, causing Grady to smile and shake his head as he followed George out of the house. At the truck he said, "You listen to your grandmother. She knows what she is talking about. You know you are always welcome here."

Grady hugged him and said, "I'll be up more regularly. Thank you." He got in the truck and waved as he turned around, heading down the driveway. He looked in his rearview mirror to see the two of them standing on the porch, arm in arm.

Grady woke Monday morning to his personal radio squawking his name as he came out of the shower in his line cabin/mini house. Grabbing it, he said, "Go for Grady."

A man's voice said, "Come by the main house before you do anything else."

"Be there in fifteen." He quickly finished dressing, thought about grabbing a piece of toast or something, grimaced and slipped his pistol on his belt then pulled on a vest to cover it. Grabbing his hat off the stand, he was out the door in five minutes and trotted over to the little stable to check on Rocky. He had plenty of water and hay, and was ignoring Grady, so he got in the truck and headed down the highway to the main house.

The old man greeted him as he walked in. "Grady, I need you to take this paperwork to my lawyer, Mike Beckman. He's expecting it." He handed over two manila envelopes and smiled. "There's a cute little lady receptionist there you need to get to know."

Grady laughed. "I'll take this in for you, but…I'm…well, if she's pretty, maybe…" He blushed slightly as the old man laughed at him and pushed him toward the door.

A half hour later, he pulled up in front of one of the older buildings in town and hopped out of his truck, taking the envelopes with him. *I'm not dressed for this*, he thought as he looked down at his clothes. He scrubbed his boots against his pant legs, trying to make them look at least a little bit better, and was reminded that he'd taken a pretty good fall on Friday night. He sighed and stomped into the building.

He finally found the right office by the small brass plaque next to a door near the back of the building. *Now to drop this and get out of here. I gotta figure out how...* Opening it, he stopped suddenly. Sandy looked up as the door opened and smiled at him. "Grady? What are you doing here?"

He mutely held up the two envelopes and finally said, "Uh, hi, Sandy. Uh, these are supposed to go to Mr. Beckman."

A young man came out of one of the offices and came to the front. "I'll take those," he said peremptorily, reaching for the envelopes.

Grady's hackles rose at his tone of voice, and he said, "Are *you* Mr. Beckman?"

"Well, no. But Mr. Beckman doesn't see just anybody, I handle—"

"I was told by Mr. Cartright to deliver these to Mr. Beckman personally," Grady snapped.

Sandy got up. "Rocking C? I'll see if Mr. Beckman is available." She winked at Grady as she brushed by him, a little smile on her face. Moments later, she came back. "Mr. Beckman will see you now. If you'll follow me." Grady followed her toward the back of the office. *She looks nice all dressed up. What was that wink for?* She opened a door and said, "Mr. Beckman, Grady Hart from the Rocking C."

He heard a deep voice say, "Come in, come in. Sandy, would you bring us some coffee please?"

"Yes, sir." She backed out and Grady stepped into an old school law office, all dark wood and bookshelf after bookshelf ringing the room. But a modern computer sat on the desk the spare white-haired man was getting up from.

"Come in, Grady," he said as he walked around the desk. "Let's sit over here where it's comfortable. What has that grouchy old bastard got for me this time?"

Grady inadvertently laughed, to his horror. "Um, I don't know, sir." He held out the two envelopes and added, "I'm not privy to—"

A half hour and two cups of coffee later, he walked back up front, passing the young man in the hallway. Sandy looked up and cocked her head at him. "How did it go?"

He shrugged. "I'm not sure. But," he rushed on, "Ah, I talked to my grandparents about what happened at your trailer."

"What?"

"They are…full blood Indians. My grandfather is a…like a high priest of the Chippewa, and my grandmother is a Comanche medicine woman. They think, no they *know* something is wrong. They were saying it sounds like…something out of a bad dream, but they want to come down and check around your trailer."

She looked up at him in consternation. "What do they think it is? What did they call it?"

He sighed. "They said something like a wraith that…wants to steal Patti's soul."

"Oh, *hell* no. That ain't happening!" She bristled and continued, "When do they want to come? I'll make damn sure I'm there. Do I…shit. I don't have any place safe for Patti."

"Do you have any…self-protection?"

She nodded. "I've got a shotgun, well, a couple of them, and an old thirty-eight that I usually have in my purse." She bit her lip. "Can they come soon? I don't want Patti hurt!"

"I'll call them as soon as I leave here." He turned toward the door, then stopped. "Uh, can I have your phone number? I don't have any way to get in touch with you."

She laughed softly, "Of course." She quickly scribbled it on a pad, ripped it off, and handed it to him.

"Thank you. I'll...let you know as soon as I talk to them." He stood there for a few moments, and she got up, came around the desk and put her hand on his arm.

"No, thank you," she whispered, giving him a peck on the cheek. "Now go, before Mr. Beckman catches us."

Grady snorted. "Yes, dear." He opened the door and stepped out into the hallway, hearing her laughter as he walked away.

Topsannah picked up the phone on the second ring. "Yes, Grady?"

"I spoke to...Sandy about y'all coming down. She wants to do it sooner rather than later."

"George is going to look around down there this evening. I am still doing research. I...may have found something, depending on what he finds or doesn't find."

"How soon?"

She sighed. "As soon as we finish what we are doing. We do not rush things, Grady."

"Yes, ma'am," he said quietly. "I will wait for you to call me back." He could almost see Topsannah shaking her head at him as he waited for her response.

"Do you like this woman?"

That wasn't the question he expected, and he had to think about it. He finally said, "I…find I am attracted to her. I…like her and her little girl."

"That is good. We will call you." He realized he was listening to a dial tone and slowly slipped the phone back in the holster on his belt. *Why does she always make me feel like I'm twelve?*

Three days of hard work on the ranch cured him of any moping around, and he'd talked to Sandy twice, but nothing untoward had happened. They both laughed when Patti had gotten on the phone and wanted to speak to horsie before wandering off.

Friday morning, he finally got a call from his grandfather. "Tomorrow night. If the lady agrees. There is much evil there. Old graves were disturbed."

"What should I tell Sandy, Papa?"

"Tell her we would like to come meet with her about dark. Topsannah feels that the evil will come with the moon. Say nothing about the…*other*."

"Okay, Papa. I will call her this evening. She doesn't like to be called at work."

"That is fine. We will see you tomorrow."

He realized he was once again listening to a dial tone. *They just…don't get phone etiquette. Never have, never will. Of course, they don't just make conversation for the sake of hearing themselves talk. I wonder how many words they actually say to each other in a day?*

Grady had loaded Rocky and was heading for Lubbock, chatting with Sandy on her way home. "So, they are coming down tomorrow afternoon. I'm guessing they'll want to be there about five thirty or six as the sun sets."

"Will they want to eat? I can fix supper if you'd like."

"I can bring some steaks, if you have a grill—" His phone beeped, and he glanced down. "Uh, hang on Grandpa is calling me. Uh, let me call you back."

"Okay, I need to pick Patti up from daycare anyway. Call me later, okay?"

"I will." He clicked over and said, "What's up, Papa?"

"We are on the way. Be there in an hour. Topsannah found that tonight is apparently the anniversary of the battle that took place there. She now thinks something may happen tonight."

"Battle?"

"Rangers against the Nokoni band of Comanches. They killed women and children, along with warriors and one medicine man. They were buried in a common grave. I saw bones on the surface behind the trailer park."

"Oh shit. I'm…was on my way to Lubbock. I'm turning around now. It'll take me at least an hour to get back."

"Tell her to stay in her trailer with the lights on and her daughter with her."

He disconnected, jumped on the brakes as hard as he dared. *Please don't go down, Rocky!* He pulled off the road, and after a quick look, swung across to the northbound lane. In his mirror he saw Rocky's head up and breathed a sigh of relief as he stepped on the gas. Dialing Sandy again, he quickly said, "Grandpa and Grandma are on the way. Something they found. I'm turning around. I'll be there in an hour. They want you to stay in your trailer with the lights on and Patti next to you. Get out your pistol and your shotgun."

"What…what is coming, Grady?"

"They didn't say, but…something evil."

"Should we leave?"

"I…don't know. Do what you think is right. I'll be there as soon as I can."

"Drive safe. I'll…we'll be here."

Grady started to put the phone up, then realized he needed to call Ed and let him know he wouldn't be in Lubbock. Ed hadn't left yet, and wanted to help, but Grady told him to standby.

Forty-five minutes later, just as the sun was setting, he pulled into the trailer park. As he turned the corner, he saw his grandmother pull out and follow him to the back section where Sandy's trailer was. He jumped out of the truck and bolted up the steps to her door. He knocked and said loudly, "Sandy! It's me! Are you—"

She jerked the door open and hissed, "Shush! Patti is asleep on the couch!" She looked behind him and asked, "That your grandparents?"

He looked around, nodded, and waved them up. "This is George Hart, and this is my grandma Topsannah."

Sandy shook hands with both of them and said, "Please come in. Can I offer you tea or water?"

Topsannah replied, "Thank you, water would be fine." She glanced over, saw Patti asleep on the couch, and smiled. "And the precious one." Sandy came back with four glasses of water and Topsannah pulled out a small medicine bag with a leather thong. "Would you object if I give you this for your daughter?"

Sandy took the little bag gingerly. "What is in it?"

"Some traditional charms and blessings. We felt it appropriate to make this for her, based on what Grady has told us."

Sandy nodded. "Thank you. Anything that will stop the nightmares and whatever the hell else is going on around here…"

George held up his hand. "May I?" When Sandy nodded, he went on quietly, "This," pointing to the floor, "is sitting on what was an Indian burial ground. I found bones between the back of the park and the river. We believe what you are encountering are the spirits of the dead, who are angry, and want to strike out at those who disturbed them."

"But we didn't do anything!" Sandy exclaimed.

Topsannah said, "No, *you and the little one* didn't do anything, but you are here. The evil is striking at you."

Sandy started to reply when the lights flickered and went out. George was up like a shot. "Outside! Everybody outside. Evil comes!" Sandy darted toward the couch and scooped up Patti, shepherded by Grady, his pistol already drawn. George and Topsannah were conversing in Comanche as they led the way down the steps into the bright moonlight.

Jozef walked toward them from his trailer, cursing in some foreign language until he noticed Grady's pistol at low ready. "Are there problems?"

George replied, "Evil comes, *Not Man*. Are you of them or us?"

Drawing himself up, he replied, "Jozef Tomáz, late in Romania. The little one is my *copilul meu*, my child to protect, if you will."

"Do you have a weap—"

Patti's scream chopped off any conversation as she yelled, "Meanie!" and pointed to a darker spot at the end of the trailer. Jozef disappeared, seemingly into thin air, and returned seconds later, even as Grady stepped in front of Sandy and Patti and fired a shot in that direction, knowing there was only a field and the river behind the trailer. George and Topsannah both started chanting, almost harmonizing as a blue glow formed.

Jozef held two swords in his hands and looked at Grady. "Give your pistol to Sandy. Do you know how to use a sword?"

He handed it to her and said, "There is a box of ammo under the seat." He looked at Jozef and added, "No, why?" as he took the sword.

"Easier to kill with sword." He handed a Katana to Grady. "You play baseball?"

"Uh, yeah."

"Swing like bat. Singing Wind is sharp."

Sandy pointed at the other end of the trailer. "What is *that*?"

A greyish being shambled toward them and Jozef spat. "Strigoi!"

"What?" Grady asked.

"Undead. You must...take head from body."

"Oh hell."

Sandy stepped up beside them. "How the hell do we do that?"

"Where's Patti?"

"She's sitting on Rocky." She pointed behind them as Grady turned to see Rocky standing stock still, ears back, with Patti gripping his mane and hugging his neck. *Oh shit, oh dear. Rocky please be good. How the hell did you get out of the trailer? And how did she get up there?*

The air started getting colder and darkness seemed to boil out from behind the trailer as Jozef cursed. Sandy glared at the approaching darkness and muttered, "Really? You are *not* taking my daughter!" She raised the pistol and looked for a target as the blue glow increased. More undead shambled between the trailers at them.

"Did you put Patti on Rocky?" Sandy nodded without taking her eyes from the encroaching darkness. *But who let him out of the trailer? I'll...*

A bear with a blue nimbus surrounding it suddenly roared and came from behind them, tearing into the encroaching darkness at the far end of the trailer as Jozef *flowed* up and lopped the head off the first undead with almost no apparent effort. The body collapsed and bones rattled on the ground as the 'flesh' turned to dust.

Time seemed to stand still as Grady's combat awareness kicked in and he strode forward, gripping the katana like a baseball bat. *Swing it like a baseball bat. Right. I got this. Step and swing...*

The first undead he stepped in front of wore the remnants of buckskins, a knife in hand, and Grady almost shivered looking at the dead face. He cocked back, stepped, and swung, and almost lost the katana as it passed through the neck of the undead, bouncing its head from its shoulders. Stepping to the side, he confronted the next one, tomahawk raised and swung more carefully. *Ah, that's how it's done.* He didn't know how long they fought, or how many undead he'd *killed* again as he and Jozef stood at the end of the trailer, but he was blowing hard and sweating in the cool night as he remembered Topsannah's chanting, flashes of gunfire, the bear snapping and growling as it attacked the *darkness* at the far end of the trailer, and Jozef seeming *flowing* from undead to undead. *Bear, there aren't any bears around here...* when Topsannah's voice finally penetrated his consciousness. "Grady! Grady! It is over!"

He sagged as he turned to survey the scene. Sandy was standing by Rocky, gun in hand, Patti still perched on his back. *Thank God for that.*

George sagged against the steps of the trailer, panting. Topsannah was hoarse and sweating, and Jozef had disappeared again. The lights in the trailer blinked and came back on, illuminating the area covered in 'dust', bones, various weapons, and remnants of clothing.

Sandy asked wonderingly, "Where did all the bones come from?"

Topsannah replied, "The…undead. We…must recover them and bury them tonight."

George groaned as he got up slowly. "Too old for this." He scrubbed his face and almost staggered as he walked toward Topsannah as she chanted one last time and a soft wind seemed to pick up the dust and carry it beyond the trailers.

They hugged and sagged against each other as Jozef appeared out of the darkness. Something mangy with one buffalo horn dangling from the tip of his sword. "Vat is dis?" He asked disgustedly. "One who hid in the dark wore it."

Topsannah grimaced. "Medicine man's headdress. His bones we *must* bury."

Jozef spat. "Lich. There were more who collapsed when I behead him."

Grady's head snapped around when Rocky squealed, pitched, and suddenly stomped with both front feet. "Easy boy. Easy…" Rocky sidled around, keeping one eye on a patch of ground as Sandy pointed the pistol and pulled the trigger.

The hammer clicked on a fired cylinder and Grady walked over swinging the sword like he was warming up with a bat. There was one spot that looked darker than the surrounding area, and he gingerly poked it with the sword. There seemed to be a pop, and Patti singsonged, "All gone, now! Mommy, all gone! Me love horsie!" She hugged Rocky as he tossed his head.

Sandy said, "I've got some trash bags inside. I guess that will work for cleanup."

Grady handed Singing Wind back to Jozef and said, "Thank you. That's a nice little sword."

Jozef snorted. "It should be. It is a twelfth century Katana by a master sword smith." He contemplated it for a couple of seconds. "Owned by a friend of mine for many years. He gave it to me before he died."

Topsannah said, "I will watch the little one. Three trash bags please."

Jozef spat again. "Make it four. I will help. I do not want to do this again."

George laughed tiredly. "Nor me. I'm too old. This is stuff for kids."

Rocky neighed and shook his head, causing Grady to laugh. "I don't think Rocky wants to do it again either…maybe he's got his mad out for a while though."

Two hours later, bones and the rags of cloth and buckskin picked up, a hole dug down by the river, and the bones reburied. Grady was loading Rocky back into the trailer. "How the hell did you get out of the trailer? Did you open it yourself?" Rocky neighed and he chuckled. "I know. You think it's funny don't you, Rocky?"

George and Topsannah had left as soon as they completed the burial, and Jozef had gone to work, grumping about evil in America. Sandy stood on the steps as he finished up and walked over. "How is Patti?"

Sandy grinned tiredly. "Sound asleep. I can't thank you enough for…everything. Well, except for the nightmares I'm going to have."

"Sorry." Grady cocked his head. "Uh, would you like to go to dinner sometime?"

A corner of her mouth crooked up. "I think I might like that. Of course, we'd have to bring Patti."

"I can live with that," he replied as he hugged her.

It Came from the Trailer Park

The end

That's a Little Weird, Even for a Trailer Park.

By LawDog

I sipped my coffee and glared at my front yard, or rather at the patch of crabgrass that simulated a lawn at Hidden Haven Trailer Park, and at the item still steaming gently in the morning air. That's it. Enough.

I paused just long enough to snag my "Do Not Meddle In The Affairs Of Wizards" coffee mug, grabbed my cane, and stomped down the gravel street on the way to the office, absently waved my coffee mug at Bob in the (quite frankly nasty) pool, and was brought up by an altogether too-cheerful greeting: "Good morning, Mr. Phil! How are you?"

I'd like to hate Rupert, but it's hard to hate someone that damned cheerful – even at crack-of-dawn in the morning.

"Morning, Rupert. Could you leave a message for Doug to come by and see me when he gets in?"

Rupert sashayed out from behind the counter and topped off my coffee mug. "Sure," he chirped, "Is there something I can help you with?"

I sipped. Ah, Kona. Rupert always has the best blends. "It's the Clarks." He grimaced, "Oh. Buddy again?"

I nodded. He sighed, dramatically, "I'm so, so sorry. As soon as Iggy gets here, I'll send him by with a baggie." There was a pause, while Rupert fluttered his fingers, gently.

My turn to sigh, "Yes?"

"Could you do me a favor, Mr. Phil? We had a new tenant move into 15B last night, and Doug hasn't had a chance to check him out yet, and I'm … well, I'm not sure he's really a good … fit."

"No, problem. I'll go talk to Frank, and then check on the new guy."

The mild worry cleared from Rupert's visage like storm clouds. "Thank you, Mr. Phil! Give my love to Viv! Don't set anything on fire!"

I glared at the spotless doublewide in 37A. Nothing in a trailer park should be immaculate, but the actual grass was clipped to a regulation height, the deck was freshly painted, and the lawn decoration was tasteful, unfaded, and appropriate to the season. I would swear that each piece of gravel in the drive had been hand-scrubbed to a pristine white.

Gawd.

Acutely conscious of my ratty bathrobe, tartan flannel lounge pants, hostile koala t-shirt, and comfortable bunny slippers, I knocked gently on the hardwood door and stepped back.

Moments later, Frank Clark opened the door and squinted at me dozily. Even in boxer shorts, the man looked like a cologne commercial, and I sighed. "Phil?"

"Morning, Frank."

Behind him, I heard a murmur, and his wife Vivian slipped up beside him, wearing one of his shirts, to lean against him, blinking sleepily. Goodness, someone was out late last night.

"Morning, Phil."

"Morning, Viv."

"What's up, Phil?"

I tapped my cane gently on the probably hand-woven doormat which announced "HELLO" in some classic, understated font. "Buddy got out last night. Again."

More blinking, as the information wended its way through the muzziness, then Vivian's pretty eyes opened wide, "Oh! Phil, I'm so sorry!"

Frank took a little while longer, then it dawned, "We'll take care of it! Promise! Sorry!"

Privately, I doubted it. Buddy was a spoiled rotten little shit, but I did like Frank and Vivian, so I nodded gently, and let them get back to their bed, before I stalked off, muttering to myself.

In contrast to the Clark residence, the trailer in 15B was a battered Airstream with what looked like several decades of road grime and hard use. On the door, next to a stencil of a flying saucer inside of a circle-slash 'NO' symbol, were the hand-painted words "FUCK OFF" in rattle-can orange. I approved.

At my knock, the door flew open, revealing a slender, agitated man with half a roll of Reynolds Wrap around his head, and another full roll wrapped around his BDU trousers like a miniskirt.

"Are you one of them?"

Oh, boy. Keeping my voice gentle, I replied, "Depends. Who's 'them'?"

He produced a battery-powered drill with an egg-beater in the chuck, and waved it at me. "Zeta Reticulans."

I shrugged, carefully, showing my hands. "Not that I know of." The eggbeater spun, and little strands of LED lights whirled around the beaters, flashing in different colors. He moved it carefully towards my coffee cup, "Grays. Is that a probe?"

I moved my cup out of range, "Uh, it's for holding coffee, and I'm not gray at all."

He squinted at me, put the drill/egg beater/LED light thingie on something inside the trailer, and came out with a kazoo to which he attached a can of compressed air. Moving like it was a tube of nitroglycerine, he waved it up and down my cane, each push of the button making a god-awful noise, "Is that cane actually a probe in disguise? Are you aligned with, allied with, bound to, part of a treaty, or otherwise beholden to any alien race, whether Grays, or any other species?"

I pushed the auto-kazoo away, firmly. "No."

He sighed. "Good. I fucking hate those god-damned probes. Want to come in?"

Behind him, I could see that the walls of the Airstream were covered in copper mesh, and the windows wrapped in multiple layers of aluminum foil, and I'm pretty sure I've seen this movie on Court TV, "No, thanks, I'm good."

"You'd think that someone who can come across interstellar space, faster than the speed of light could do that sort of thing non-invasively." His slight frame vibrated like a chihuahua on crack. He leaned forward and whispered, "Honestly, I think they *like* doing the probulating thing."

Okie-dokie. "Well, I just stopped by to welcome you to the neighborhood…"

"Oh, I won't be here too long. They always catch up, and then …" I had thought the vibrating was bad, but incredibly it got worse. I tapped my cane gently, backing up. "Ok, you have a good day …" He seized my hand, shook it briskly, then brought the drill-eggbeater out again and waved it in front of my chest, squinted suspiciously at the LEDs and sighed in relief. I gently extracted my hand and continued my retreat, waving, until I made my escape around the front of the Airstream.

Later that evening, I contemplated the setting sun, added some finishing touches to a new addition to my front patch of crabgrass, then went inside to open two bottles of beer.

About 20 minutes after the sun went below the horizon, someone knocked gently on my door, which I opened to reveal a surfer dude staring with some amusement at my "Come Back With A Warrant" doormat. I handed him one of the bottles as I stepped out onto the deck, closing the door behind me.

"Doug," I said, clinking the necks of the bottles together, "How are you?"

He grinned at me, took a sip of the Scotch ale, and sighed happily, "Evening, Phil. Rupert said you needed to talk to me?"

I sipped mine. Nectar of the gods. "Yeah, the Clarks ..."

He waved his bottle, "Is Buddy getting out at night again?"

"Yeah, and the little twerp ..."

"Crapped on your lawn again?"

"You damned betcha ..." My tirade was interrupted by a baritone *crump* from the front of my lot, followed immediately by the squalling of a startled puppy and the skattling sounds of a five-pound dog hauling ass down a gravel street.

Doug gave me an exasperated look. "Phil. What did you do?"

I took a sip of beer, swallowed. "It'll wear off."

"Oh, God. Frank and Viv are going to tear you a whole new asshole."

"Speaking of, have you met the fruit loop in 15B?"

"Don't change the subject, Phil. Although he is a little out there ... Well, shit, there's Frank and Viv. Don't let me get in the way."

"What the fuck, Phil!?" Around the corner of my trailer came Frank Clark, followed closely by his wife, who was cradling something in her arms.

I waved at the couple, "Evening, Frank. Evening, Viv. It'll wear off."

"Wear off?! *Wear off?!* This is not fucking cool, Phil!" Vivian came to a stop next to her husband, and in her arms was a Yorkshire Terrier with an absolutely gobsmacked look on its little face. Kind of adorable, actually. The dog, not Vivian, who maybe looked a bit homicidal.

I tapped my cane, gently, "If he hadn't been crapping in my yard, nothing would have happened."

"Seriously?!"

And then the world buzzed and went kind of ... dull.

When I surfaced, I couldn't think. The world was black-and-white, and I was ... numb. In front of me were ... people? And there was movement. From between ... Frank? and ... Doug?

came a small ... person? Gray skinned, big black eyes, long little digits. Behind it, several more were poking around. Poking things with their skinny little fingers. Poking Vivian, and Buddy, and me. In the back of my mind, something was yelling, but I just couldn't think.

"Hah! HAH! I figured it out, you little motherfuckers!"

All of the little gray dudes turned to look in the direction of 15B, and something deep down inside of me tried screaming. But it was the roar of the ten-gauge shotgun fired by Mr. Tin-Foil Fruit-Bat that cleared the brain fog away like mist in the teeth of a howling gale.

I shook myself as the world came up to speed and grinned at the alien. "Oh, you poor dumb bastards. You came to the wrong trailer park." I reached for the eldritch power I had spent a lifetime studying, spoke Words and slammed my cane into the deck at my feet. In front of me, a lightning bolt hammered down out of a cloudless sky and blew the little gray pervert into smoking bits. The clap of thunder that accompanied the lightning made sure that everyone in the Hidden Haven Trailer Park who hadn't been roused by the shotgun was now alert.

I'll give the second one props, he started towards me, waving a silver cylinder with bits and lights all over it, before Frank the Werewolf hit him like a furry tan Buick. Beside me, Doug moved incredibly fast, fangs erupting from his gums, as he grabbed an alien, and picked it up like a cob of corn; past him Vivian -- in full snarling fury -- tried to fast pitch another one through my trailer. Several times.

I gathered fire into my hands and looked around. At the pool, hundreds of tentacles erupted from the depths and yanked two more Grays into the water as Bob woke up, and I was vaguely aware of yet another one running in circles with five pounds of enraged Buddy clamped firmly on its left ham. Down the street, one of the aliens staggered out of the herb patch belonging to the goblin commune in 22A, dragging two of the tie-dye wearing kobolds who were gnawing like rabid beavers on alien ankles. A third was on the being's shoulders, vigorously realigning extraterrestrial chakras with what looked for all the world like a Himalayan salt lamp in a hemp pillowcase.

Then I noticed the silver saucer hovering overhead. Well, well, well.

Drawing on the nearest of several ley lines, I created an exit portal just in front of my hand. The entry portal? Somewhere out around the asteroid belt, and when the marble-sized chunk of nickel-iron came out it was traveling at interstellar speeds. The brief flash as it ignited part of the atmosphere on the way through the open hatch in the bottom of the UFO was really kind of pretty. The plasma glow of the dozen or so of its buddies following could have been thought of as romantic, although probably not to the crew of the spaceship.

The saucer lurched, slightly, then righted, as a rotating glow began to spin around the bottom. Down here on the dirt, the Gray with Buddy attached to his left butt-cheek was making laps around the trailer, fluting little distress noises. Up above, the saucer made a sub-harmonic, bone-rattling hum interrupted by a grinding noise, flickered, and vanished.

Beside me, Doug grabbed up his beer, and took a big mouthful, gargled, spit, and swigged again. "You ok, Doug?"

He waved a tiny gray arm at me -- just the arm -- and spat again, "God. Ugh. They taste like a high school boys' locker room smells. God. Yuck."

Over by the pool, one of Bob's Grays crawled out of the water, and began scrambling for the hedge, before Bob's tentacles swarmed out and dragged it back in. Doug winced. "Dude, Bob watches a lot of Japanese porn."

"Yup."

"A lot. Of the really weird -- and we're talking Japanese here -- porn."

"Yup."

"Don't you think we should go, I don't know, save him?"

I used my toe to nudge the silver cylinder that Frank's first victim had dropped. It thrummed like a single-cylinder diesel engine, and several pointy, spinny, flashy things snapped out of the surface, before the crackle of sparks made us both jump. I shrugged, "Nope."

Doug looked at the probe for a moment, his fangs showing, "Good point."

In the street, Buddy's Gray was spinning in circles trying to pry Buddy loose. I sighed, snapped my fingers, and manifested a walnut-sized part of the Earth's core inside the alien's little gray skull. It made a wonderful 'Pop' noise, and ET was abruptly a head shorter. Buddy barked madly, then cocked a leg on the alien. I frowned at him as he side-eyed me the entire time, kicked gravel on the corpse, and trotted over to Frank, where he barked and growled.

"I saw, Buddy," Frank said encouragingly, as he bent and scooped up the five-pound hound, "Very cool!"

Vivian appeared from the alien-shaped hole she had created in my trailer. Although being a werewolf is apparently very hard on clothes; it's also apparently very good on developing … lungs, which caused Doug and I to abruptly turn around and start surveying the landscape. I shrugged out of my bathrobe and held it behind me.

There was an exasperated feminine snort, as Viv took it from my hand. "It's not like you haven't seen boobs before, gentlemen."

Doug sounded pained, "Yes, Vivian, but there are rules. Rules are important. They keep civilization civilized."

"Speaking of civilized," Frank passed Buddy off to his wife, who immediately cuddled him, "My son is a were*wolf,* not a were*yorkie.*"

I folded my arms as Buddy gave me a teacup-sized glare, and I cocked an eyebrow at Frank and Viv. "Yes, but yorkie crap is easier to pick up out of the yard than wolf crap."

Buddy had the grace to look a bit abashed.

"And hamster crap would be even easier."

Buddy blinked at me in startlement. His mom half-turned, hiding him from me, as his father ran his fingers through his fur and sighed. I wasn't sure he thought I was serious, so I squinted at him, "The spell will wear off in a couple of days. And it's better than waking up in a vet's office. Or any other number of other things I could have done."

Frank held up both hands, err, paws, "It won't happen again, Phil. Swear to God."

I sighed. "Ok, Frank. I'll be there in the morning to get my robe back. I'll fix the hex then. Go home." Frank smiled at me, well, as close to a smile as you could get with a muzzle full of fangs, put his arm around his wife, and they trotted off down the street; Buddy eye-fucking me over his mother's shoulder the entire time. Oh, well.

Down the gravel street, two figures wandered towards us, one carrying an enormous double-barreled shotgun over his shoulder, the other pushing a rolling dumpster.

"Good evening, Master Douglas," said Igor, immaculate in his tweeds, "Magus Phillip."

"Evening, Iggy," I replied, as Igor imperturbably used a reach extender to pick up what looked like a separated gray drumstick and dropped it into the dumpster. "Sorry about the mess."

"Nonsense," Igor said, as he got the headless alien into a fireman's carry and chucked him into the dumpster, "I thought I'd show Master Eustace around the park and might as well kill two birds with one stone."

Tin-Foil Fruit-Bat winced at the "Eustace", switched the shotgun to his other shoulder, carefully wiped his hand on his orange hunting vest, and held it out to me, "Jack".

I shook the offered hand, gently, "It's not usually this festive around here. I guess the excitement will have you moving on?"

Igor gave me a level look, "Magus Phillip is quite the comedian." He picked up the alien probe, weighed it carefully, and gave me a Significant Look. "It conceals the inner kindness we all know is there."

Hmm. "Like I said earlier … Jack, did you say? Welcome to Hidden Haven Trailer Park."

He smiled, like it had been a while, and carefully adjusted his tin-foil fez. "Thanks. I think I like it here. Yeah. I like it here. Good folks. Yeah, I like it here."

I hoped the twitch wasn't too obvious. Jack nodded heavily, and walked back to his Airstream, carefully smoothing his aluminum miniskirt on the way.

"Master Douglas. I set your breakfast on the porch. You should eat it before it coagulates."

"Noodge, noodge, noodge."

"Breakfast is the most important meal of the day, Master Douglas. Magus Phillip, will you be repairing your trailer, or should I call the contractor?"

"Thanks, Iggy. I've got it."

"Very good, sir. Now I must contact the city for an extra trash pickup." Iggy touched the brim of his flat cap, and marched off in the direction of the office, the overloaded dumpster crunching through the gravel.

I grinned, in spite of myself. It's not always quiet, but damn I loved this place.

END

It Came to the Trailer Park

By Christopher Woods

I pushed the accelerator with my right foot, and my truck jerked before the motor rumbled and picked up speed.

"I guess it's time to take it up to Dan's," I said under my breath.

It wasn't like anyone could have heard it over the radio anyway. I tended to play my radio much louder than I should. I was already hard of hearing without assaulting my ears with Five Finger Death Punch. Years of construction and the use of power tools had made that a matter of everyday life for me.

Sadly, the economy was in the crapper, and work was hard to come by in east Tennessee. The truck jerked again as the motor missed a stroke.

"Thank god Dan is cheap enough."

Dan Hoffner was a local backyard mechanic who could fix almost any issue on a vehicle. He had reasonable prices and was a decent fellow.

I topped the hill and turned my truck into the lot in front of Reba's Deli and shut it off.

Reba's was the best food you could get in the Chapel.

"As long as you ain't in a hurry," I muttered with a grin and pushed the door open.

Laughter came from the long table near the coolers that had a sign saying Bullshitters' Table. I grinned and waved at the crowd of locals seated around the table.

"Hey, Sam!" Gerald Crow said and waved.

Several of the others waved as I made my way to the back corner booth and slid into the seat.

Laughter continued for a few minutes and tapered off.

"Did you guys hear about Ben Daniels?" Harley Welliver asked.

"No, what is it?"

"They said he died last night. Overdose."

"Hell you say!" Red Kronin looked at Harley in surprise.

"Isn't that Jeff's boy?" Crow asked.

"Yep," Harley replied.

"I'd like to say it surprises me," Mark Holland said. "Jeff's boy's been in trouble for years. They needed to get him off that shit."

I let the conversation fade and paid attention to the waitress who was making her rounds taking orders. The food must have been almost ready. Most of them get there shortly after Reba and sit around bullshitting until the food gets done.

"What can I get for you, Sam?" she asked as she stopped at my table. I was the last one to place my order.

"Western omelet, toast, and a bowl of gravy."

"No biscuits?"

"The gravy is for the omelet. Everything's better with gravy on it."

She laughed and headed back to the kitchen.

I sat back in the booth and just listened to the bullshitters tell stories. If there was one thing they were good at, it was telling stories.

My food came, and I dove into it with a gusto. It had been some time since I had been to Reba's. I moved out of the Salt's Chapel close to seven years ago, but my sister still lived there. I was up helping her build a porch on her house. I didn't make a lot of money when I did jobs for her, but she fed me well.

I thought about getting Reba to rent me one of her trailers for the month while I was here, but Milly wouldn't have it. She said I always had a place to stay when I was in the Chapel.

Reba had a large sprawl of land behind her restaurant that she had turned into a trailer park. She added new ones along the way, and the park had grown over the years. Twenty-five mobile homes dotted the ridge behind the store and stretched all the way back to the Morgan Salt Wildlife Management Area. Salt's Chapel was named for the same Morgan Salt.

I sat back and listened again as Crow was trying to explain just how big the catfish he hooked at the dam really was, when the door slammed open.

"I need a phone!" Harry Dodgins yelled. "We need to call nine-one-one! I think there was a bear attack!"

Reba picked up the phone beside her and called.

"A bear?" Harley asked. "In the Chapel?"

Dodge nodded his head frantically. "It killed Mary Ellen! It had to be a bear!"

"Mary Ellen?" Red asked. "Mary Ellen Blanton?"

I swallowed. I had known Mary Ellen for years. She went to the same school as I did, and we had even dated for a short time. I stood up and headed for the door.

"I'll be back to pay in a little bit," I said to Reba.

She nodded and kept talking to Freddy, the 911 operator. We only had a few of them in the county, and I knew Freddy was on duty. I didn't know he was working for the police department at all until I ran across a body one time on my way to work. Sarah Hawkins had a heart attack outside of her home, and I saw her body the next morning as we drove by. Gil, the guy who rode to work with me, had checked to see if she was dead as I called 911.

I exited the door and got in my truck. This was probably going to be unpleasant, but if there was a bear, it would need to be taken care of. My rifle was behind the seat. It was a Winchester

.45 long colt lever action. I was hoping that would be big enough for a bear.

I started the truck, drove behind the store, and turned into the drive of The Evening Star trailer park. Mary Ellen's trailer was all the way at the back of the park, which kind of made sense if this was a bear. Her place was backed by the Morgan Salt Wildlife Management Reserve. That was twenty-five thousand acres of woodland.

"Friggin' bear," I muttered as I drove through the park.

The odds were that the bear wouldn't even still be there, but I figured I should check. I saw old man Dennis step out of his trailer with a rifle that was almost as long as he was tall.

Old man Dennis was a fixture around the Chapel. He was just a little over five feet tall, and I wasn't even sure how old he was. His overalls were baggy, and his face was covered by a long white beard. The local news station had done a history piece on Salt's Chapel a few years back, and Dennis had been sitting in Reba's when they came through. I remembered the interview and when the reporter had asked him if he played the stock market, Dennis had just said, "Sure, I run a few head of cattle."

The reporter laughed and tried to explain what the stock market was to him. She finally gave up and went on with the interview. Dennis had just grinned as she left. Everyone considered us to be idiots out in the country. They were quite wrong. Some of the folks living out here were just as intelligent as anyone else. Hell, Greg Shapner lived about a half of a mile into the Chapel and worked in Oak Ridge at the nuclear facility. He was literally a rocket scientist.

I pulled the truck over and motioned for him to take the passenger seat.

"Reckon we had the same idea," I said as he climbed into the truck.

"Reckon so. Figgered that bear was gonna need shootin'," he said.

"What is that? An elephant gun?"

He patted the stock. "Reckon if I'm gonna shoot somethin', it ain't getting' back up."

"I think you may have that covered," I said. "That looks like a howitzer."

"It'll do the job."

We continued toward the back of the park. "Seems odd that a bear would come out this time of year, though," I said.

"Most of 'em are still hibernatin,' but if one was awake, it'd be hungry."

"That's what I figured too," I said. "I would have figured it might hit Dale's farm over there before attacking someone here."

Dale Windsor owned a couple of hundred acres on the right side of the trailer park where he had cattle, goats, chickens, and about any other kind of critter you could think of.

It was a larger version of my sister's place down in the Chapel. She had a couple of acres and had chickens, rabbits, Guinea pigs, three goats, a miniature horse, a couple of dogs, and two cats. At the rate she was collecting critters, she'd catch up to Dale soon.

I stopped the truck in front of the blue mobile home at the very back. "Did Dodge say where she was at?" I asked.

"Out back." Dennis opened the door and stepped out of the truck. He held the huge gun with the stock up at his shoulder and the barrel toward the ground. It would be quick and easy to just raise the rifle for a shot.

I drew the .45 from the scabbard behind my seat. It had been my father's gun, and the rifle scabbard had been a gift from me and my wife, Annie, several years before he passed away. I levered the rifle just enough to see if it had a shell in the chamber and removed the safety. Carrying it like Dennis was carrying his, I followed him around the corner of the trailer.

I felt my breakfast start to come back up, but I held it down. I'd seen a few dead bodies, but nothing like this. I'd seen deer carcasses and hogs being slaughtered, but what I saw in that small fenced in yard of Mary Ellen's trailer had me gasping for air to keep my stomach from spewing.

There was blood everywhere. It had turned almost black in the sunlight where it covered the wall of her home. The grass was coated, and there were spots all the way out to the gate.

Dennis stopped and raised his rifle to scan the woods behind Mary's and I tried to follow suit. There was no sign of an animal.

He glanced back into the yard and shook his head.

"What?"

"You don't even want to know, boy."

"What?"

He shook his head again. "Ain't no bear done that."

I was scanning the woods again. "Then what was it?"

"You won't believe me if I tell ya," he said and pulled a bag of chewing tobacco from his pocket.

"Coyotes?"

He took a huge pinch of the Redman and shoved it into his cheek. "Animals don't do that. They'd eat a person, sure 'nough. But they don't just rip 'em up for the hell of it. I reckon they'll find the only part of that girl that's missin' is her heart."

"Her heart?"

"That's right, boy. What we got here is a bit different than anything you boys have ever seen. What we got is only part animal. The other part is human."

"Oh horse shit!" I turned to look at Dennis. "You want me to believe this was a damn werewolf?"

Dennis didn't say any more after his claim, and we made an extra wide circle of the home. We were moving slowly along the tree line when the sirens from the police cars came within hearing.

The first cruiser pulled in beside my truck as we laid the rifles in the seat and stepped away from the truck.

"Sam," John Cole said as he stepped out of the car.

"John." I nodded in greeting. "Been a minute."

"Yeah. Wish it was under better circumstances."

"It's ugly, John."

"I have to go assess before the sheriff gets here. He's a stickler for reports."

"I don't remember Craig being that bad."

"Craig didn't run last year. We got a new sheriff. He was some kind of big city detective before he came here. Right out of New York City."

"How'd that even happen?"

"Our population doubled with the new subdivisions down in the Chapel. Lot of folks from up north moved in. Enough to swing the election. A lot of people liked the idea he was a detective too."

"Hmm."

"I really need to check out the scene."

I nodded and stepped back to the truck.

John walked around the corner, and I heard retching. I didn't feel quite as bad about almost losing my breakfast.

He came back around the corner as white as a sheet.

"I told you it was ugly," I said.

"Damnit, Sam."

"I know," I said. "I about lost my cookies."

"I almost can't believe that's Mary Ellen."

"It is," I said. "She had that tattoo."

"Damnit, Sam."

"Dennis says it's a werewolf."

John looked over at old man Dennis with an eyebrow arched.

"I didn't say it was a werewolf." He pointed at me. "He did."

"Really?" I asked.

"I reckon I just said this wasn't a bear. It ain't all animal, but it ain't all human, either. I suspect a person can't tear another person apart like that. Do you even know how much pressure it would take to pull someone's arms off?"

"I would prefer it if you kept that to yourself, Dennis," John said. "The sheriff already thinks we're just a bunch of dumbass hillbillies."

"Reckon I'll just go back home," Dennis said. "When you idjits are ready to talk about this, come see me."

He pulled the elephant gun from my truck seat and strode down the hill toward his trailer.

"What the hell is he carryin'?"

"If it had wheels, it'd be a cannon," I said.

"Hell, it'd send him to the ER if he actually shot it."

"I don't know," I said. "He's a tough old bird."

I turned as another cruiser drove past Dennis and stopped beside John's car. A tall blonde man I had never seen before stood up from the car looking back toward Dennis.

"That's Greg Iverson, our new sheriff."

Iverson was a little over six feet tall and built like a football player.

"Reckon he's a big dude," I said.

"Yep."

Iverson turned back toward us shaking his head. He reached back in the car and retrieved his hat.

"Still getting used to the fact that everyone has a gun down here," he said as he stopped beside John. "John, give me what you know."

"Mary Ellen Blanton was murdered, sir. She is behind the house. Something ripped her apart."

"You have a definite identification?"

"Yes, sir."

"And who is this gentleman?"

"Sam Colten," I said and held my hand out. "Good to meet you Sheriff. Not so good of circumstances to do it though."

"You found the victim?"

"Nope," I said. "I was down at Reba's when Dodge came in screamin' about a bear attack. I have my rifle in the truck, so I figured I'd come up and see if the bear was still up here. I ran into old man Dennis on the way, and we went out back to see if it was still around."

"And?"

"No sign of it."

He nodded. "We'll take it from here, Mister Colten. Leave your contact information with Deputy Cole in case I have questions."

The sheriff turned and strode around the corner of the trailer.

"You at Milly's"

"Yep."

"Alright."

I looked toward the bottom of the hill as three more cruisers and an ambulance turned into the drive.

"Reckon I better go." I stepped into my truck. "You'll let me know what they find out?"

"Sure thing, Sam."

I started the truck and drove slowly down the hill to keep a good clearance from the ambulance.

"Too late for an ambulance," I muttered.

One thing Dennis said really worried me. Animals killed to eat. I didn't see any parts of Mary Ellen that looked to be chewed on. Who or whatever had done this had done it for the pleasure of the kill. I hated to think it was a person, but...

They pronounced Mary Ellen's death an animal attack after a short investigation, and there was a three-day span where it was open season on any bears that could be found. The best way to get rid of something in Salt's Chapel was to open a hunting season on said something.

Twenty-one bears were shot and taken out of the Preserve over those three days. It was never firmly established if any of those bears were the culprit in Mary's death. I still had trouble with the whole thing. Old man Dennis said he would bet the only thing that was eaten was the girl's heart. I saw the chest cavity, and I was pretty sure it was gone.

I couldn't help but think he might have been right. A bear would have eaten all of her.

I shook my head as I pulled my truck into Reba's. What could I really do? The sheriff and his deputies swore it was a bear attack. I'd never seen a bear attack, so I really didn't have anything I could use to argue it was anything else.

"Hey, Sam!" Crow said with a smile as I walked in the door. "You about finished with that barn?"

"Almost," I answered and waved at the bullshitters' table. "Couple more days."

"Milly gonna put all them rabbits in there?" Harley asked.

"I reckon so."

Jill, the waitress, headed my direction.

"Would you like your usual?"

"Nope." I grinned. "Reckon I wanna live dangerous. How bout some country ham, eggs, and biscuits with gravy. I wanna see how high I can run my blood pressure."

I sat back in the booth and listened to the bullshitters. I was gonna miss that when I went home but being at home with my wife would make up for it.

"I reckon he just come back to life!"

I looked toward Harley who was holding his hands out.

"You're full of shit, Harley." Crow was shaking his finger in Harley's direction. "Three days ago, you're screamin' Ben died from an overdose. Now he's back alive?"

"It wasn't just me. Everybody said he died. Ask Reba!"

"I think you just fed us a line of bull shit. They don't call the table that for nothin'."

I laughed at Red's remark.

"I just told you what everybody told me! I swear, I just ain't talkin' to you people no more."

"Reckon we'd be a lot better off," Holland said around a mouthful of biscuit.

"I see how it's gonna be," Harley muttered. "Let's just change the damn subject."

"Who would've thought there were twenty bears in the chapel?" Crow asked.

"Where'd you get your information?" Red asked. "It wasn't from old Harley, there, was it?"

Harley sputtered and Crow shrugged.

"I tried, Harley."

Harley's shoulders slumped. "Some people are just hard to get along with. Them damn Kronins are some of the worst."

"Kronins ain't hard to get along with! I ain't never been hard to get along with!"

"Yeah, but there's a lot of you Kronins," Crow said. "What about Tommy?"

"Well now, I recon he's hard to get along with." Red nodded.

"Then there's Willy."

Holland snorted.

"Now you're just goin' straight for the rambunctious side of the family."

"Those are your brothers," Harley said.

"Well don't lump me in with them. I'm the black sheep of the family! Only it's more like the white sheep."

He sat back for a moment. "Maybe you're right. Some of them Kronins are hard to get along with."

I shook my head and moved my silverware as Jill brought out my plate.

"Jill, you reckon you can tell Reba I'd like to get about half a gallon of her coleslaw? We're goin' to a thing this afternoon, and I reckon she makes the best coleslaw around."

"Sure thing, Sam. It's the best I've seen yet."

I let the argument at the table fade away as I started eating.

I sat over in the corner of John Cole's new barn, John Cole Senior, that is. John Jr. was at the entrance talking to Milly. I was pretty sure he was sweet on my sister, and that wasn't really a bad thing. He was divorced and raising his kids. Milly always wanted kids, and I could see them as a pretty good match.

My thoughts were interrupted as I saw Johnny the Third step into the door with his hand in his pocket.

"Hey Johnny, what you doin'? You like that crab you was eatin' earlier?"

Davin Ford had been out in North Carolina and came back with a truck bed full of ice chests with fresh crabs and shrimp. So, of course, the low country boil had to happen the next day. The kid had dove into it once he saw he could crack the crab to pull the meat out.

"Yeah." He looked around to see if anyone was looking. "Look here." Johnny pulled his hand out of his pocket with something in it. "I got the claw."

I chuckled. "What you gonna do with that claw, little man?"

"Reckon I might stab Billy with it."

"Wait a minute, Johnny. You can't just go around stabbin' folks with a crab claw. What'd Billy do to deserve that?"

"He pulled Cybi's hair. I don't think that was right."

"It probably wasn't right, but you can't stab him for it. Reckon the best you can do is pull his hair and show him how it feels or somethin' along those lines."

Johnny nodded and slipped the claw back in his pocket. He stalked off in search of Billy Taggert.

Cybi Keck was John's neighbor's daughter. She was five years old and ran around the farm with Johnny all the time. She was Johnny's best friend, and he would do just about anything she said. By the looks of it, Billy might be in trouble.

I heard a squeal from outside of the barn. Then a kid's yell and a thud against the barn wall. I stood up and poked my head out the door to see Billy sitting against the barn with his hand over his left eye. John Jr. was pulling the Third away from the group of kids.

I let out a long sigh and returned to my seat. I really hoped he hadn't stabbed Billy in the eye with a crab claw. Maybe I should have taken the claw from him. Nobody had seemed overly worried about Billy, so I assumed he'd just been punched.

I took a sip of my drink. Someone had applied the liquor to the fruit punch with wild abandon. My eye twitched as I drank Jack's "Hunch Punch" as he liked to call it. I was almost finished with my glass of punch when John sat down in the chair beside me with a glass of his own.

He leaned back in the chair and took a long drink from his glass. "Sam, did you tell Johnny to punch Billy in the face?"

"Nope."

He looked sideways at me.

"I did tell him he couldn't stab Billy with a crab claw."

John almost choked on his drink. "What?"

"Well, his first plan was to stab him with a crab claw he's carryin' around in his pocket. See, Billy pulled Cybi's hair, and Johnny was a little put out about it. I told him the best he could do was pull Billy's hair to show him how it felt."

"Apparently, that's what he did. But then he pulled Billy's head forward by his hair and planted a good one right in the eye."

I chuckled. "That part he added on his own."

"What am I gonna do with that one?"

"Tell him he did what needed to be done as long as Billy knows what it was for. He'll not pull Cybi's hair again I'd wager."

John laughed. "I'd say he won't. Problem is, will Ned end up causin' a fuss?"

"He'd be a fool to cause a ruckus over somethin' so small, and I don't think Ned's a fool. The boy deserved it."

"Reckon he did."

We sat there in silence for a few minutes until we heard sirens coming from the other side of Weaver Ridge.

"That don't sound any too good," John said.

"No, it doesn't."

"I'll run to the house and call in. My cell ain't got service down here."

"You need anything, holler," I said.

I watched John run toward the house at the top of the hill. There were a lot of sirens, and I was more than a little worried.

A few minutes later, John came back down the hill with at least three guns hanging from his shoulder by straps. He was carrying a case of, judging by the strain he was under, ammunition.

I started toward him, but he shook his head and yelled, "Get your rifle!"

I scowled and ran for my truck.

"Get everyone inside!" I yelled to Milly as I passed her.

If John was arming up, something was coming.

I never considered myself a brave man. Everyone hopes they'll be brave when the time comes, but you never know if that's how it's going to go. In all honesty, I was terrified. My family was in the barn. Milly and Annie were the only family I had left, and I had seen what happened at Mary Ellen's. I knew in my soul that what John had learned was that there was another attack. Thank God Annie was still back home in middle Tennessee.

I pulled the Winchester from behind the seat and levered a shell into the chamber. Then I loaded another cartridge from the belt into the rifle. I carefully lowered the hammer so all I would need to do is cock it and put it into the holster which I strapped to my back with the harness. The Winchester was a saddle gun, so it was short enough to draw from the holster on my back. Then I pulled the other rifle I had put in the truck after the incident at Mary Ellen's.

It was another gun my dad had left me, a Marlin .444 lever action. When everyone was hunting bears, I figured the .444 would pack a lot bigger punch. The .45 used a standard .45 long colt bullet. The .444 was almost the same diameter but it was a lot longer. It would carry further and hit harder. I grabbed the sack of cartridges from the floorboard and closed the door.

John met me halfway back to the barn.

"Another attack?" I asked.

"It hit the Sands' place just over Weaver Ridge."

"Oh shit."

"Killed most of the family. Left little Jaimie alive."

"He's like two years old."

"Too young to give an accurate description. All he could do is point toward the woods."

There was a crash in the woods to our left, below the barn. We both spun toward the crash, and I levered the .444.

Three deer burst from the foliage and ran across the small clearing and past the barn.

"Was that blood on that last one?"

"Shit," I answered and turned the rifle back towards the woods.

There was another crash, and I saw something in the shadows. It was big. Whatever it was, it let out a roar that sent chills down my spine, and I fired the .444.

It roared again and came toward us. John fired his hunting rifle as I levered the action on the .444 and fired again. I know it was hit because it staggered when the bullets hit. I levered and shot again and again until the gun hammer dropped with a click.

John's rifle boomed again, and my ears were ringing. The bear or whatever it was stopped and roared again.

I dropped the .444 and drew the Winchester. Walking forward, I levered shot after shot into the thing. It got close enough to see some features, but all I could focus on were red glowing eyes and a lot of damned teeth. With a final roar, it turned and bolted into the woods. I was still levering the rifle when John laid his hand on my shoulder. The rifle wasn't firing, I was just levering and pulling the trigger.

My ears were ringing, but I could still hear him.

"You can stop now, Sam."

I shook my head to clear it and started pulling cartridges from the belt and feeding them into the Winchester.

"That was *not* a damn bear," I said.

"Nope."

"We need to talk to old man Dennis," I said and walked backwards with my eyes on the woods.

"Why?"

"Reckon he knows what it is." I picked up the Marlin and slipped it into the holster for the Winchester.

"Why didn't he tell the sheriff?"

"No one would believe him, John. That was a fuckin' werewolf."

He was quiet for a moment, but he didn't say I was wrong. He'd seen as much as I did.

"I gotta say, Sam," John said as we backed toward the barn with our eyes and guns trained on the woods. "Walkin' in on that thing shootin' might be the bravest thing I ever saw."

"Brave? I think I shit my pants."

"Well, if you did, at least you shit your pants walkin' toward it and not runnin' away."

"I guess there *is* that."

I heard sirens fire back up and figured we'd have company soon enough. I pulled the Marlin from the holster and put the Winchester back in its place. Opening the sack I had pulled from the truck, I started feeding the cartridges into the rifle.

"I need you to do this, Milly."

"What about the animals?"

"I'll feed your damn hamsters," I said. "Take your dog and go see Annie for a week or two."

"They're Guinee pigs, dumb ass."

"Whatever. I'll feed 'em and feed the rabbits and the chickens. I need you to go. I saw that thing last night, and I want you out of the area until we can take care of it."

"Just give me one of the guns," she said. "I can help."

"You've never shot anything in your life," I replied. "This ain't target practice."

"Then come with me. We'll pack all the animals up and leave this place."

"That thing killed Mary Ellen. It killed the whole Sands family except Jaimie. There's exactly two people who have seen it… three, if you count the two-year-old kid. No one's gonna believe what we saw, and they'll be after a bear again. Me and John have to go after this damn thing."

She shook her head and sighed. "Okay, I'll go see Annie next weekend."

"No. You pack it up and go today."

She looked at me for a moment and sighed again.

"You didn't see it, Milly. We shot that thing full of holes and it got up and ran away. Leave today."

She hugged me. "Be careful."
"I'll try."

"You ready for this?" I asked as John climbed into the passenger side of my truck.

"I reckon I'm as ready as I'll get. How'd Milly take the plan?"

"I helped her pack, and she's on her way to my place."

"I'm surprised she went."

"She loaded her trailer down with animals."

He chuckled. "Sounds about right."

"You sure you're wantin' to chase after a girl with all that?" I asked. His face turned a little red, and I laughed. "It's obvious you're a little sweet on her."

"Since Beck died, I ain't even looked for anyone."

John's wife had fought with cancer for several years before she passed away. It had been a hard time for John, Jr and it'd been hard on the Third as well. Johnny was young and didn't understand what was happening. I could see not looking after all that.

"Then I ran into Milly at the feed store."

"She likes you, too, John. Let's try not to get killed and see how that all works out."

"Good plan. So, what does Dennis know?"

"I don't know yet. He said it was part human and part animal when he saw what it did to Mary Ellen. Reckon we'll find out when we get there. Did you get your folks out of the area?"

"Dad took Johnny and headed south this mornin'."

"Good."

I pulled out from John's driveway and headed deeper into the Chapel toward Reba's.

"I'm havin' trouble reconcilin' what I saw last night," he said. "The longer I go the less I believe."

"I saw it fairly close up, John. Only thing I could call it is a werewolf. It stood like a human."

"I still have trouble."

"You didn't read a million books about things like this. I read a bunch. Thought it was all fiction 'til last night."

"How much do you think old man Dennis really knows?"

"Hard to say." I shrugged. "I know our bullets didn't do much but slow him down a little. Reckon silver works like it does in the movies?"

"I hope so," he said. "Or this sack of my grandma's silverware ain't gonna do any good. I thought I might melt it down and use it in my reloader."

"I'm down with that." I turned into the drive alongside Reba's. "We'll see what Dennis has to say."

We stopped at Dennis's trailer to find him sitting on his small porch with a shotgun across his knees.

"Wondered when you fellers were comin' by." He had a gap-toothed grin on his face. "Heard about last night. Did you see it?"

I nodded and stepped up on the porch.

He motioned to the other chair, and I sat down.

"I reckon you were right, Dennis. I can't call that thing anything but a werewolf."

"I figured when I saw that girl."

"So, what do you know 'bout werewolves?" John asked.

"I know you can kill 'em, but it takes a tolerable lot of killin' to do it. We ran across one of 'em in 'Nam."

"Really?"

He nodded. "See, we was sent to take out some folks that were based in this little village. Now, when we got there most of them people were dead. They looked a whole lot like Mary Ellen looked, all ripped apart, hearts missin'. There were only a couple of folks left, and this thing kept comin' back every three days and kill some more. All they would say was 'ma sói!' over and over. The sarge looked it up, and it was their word for werewolf."

"No shit?" John asked.

"We set a trap or two for that old wolf and waited for it to come back. We weren't sure what to believe from those villagers, so we figgered to ambush it."

"Did you get it?"

"Eventually. The first time it came back it got Reilly Dorn and dragged him off in the woods. Now it did that while fourteen men shot into him with M-14s. It just soaked up those bullets like a sponge and kept right on comin'. We heard Reilly screamin' for a long time out there in the night."

"Jesus." John shook his head. "Why did this one run last night?"

"He'd already ate that family's hearts."

"Jesus."

"You already said that," I said.

"I really meant it."

I chuckled for a second and turned back to Dennis. "You're here so I'm assuming you figured out how to kill it."

"We did. Burned it with gasoline after it stepped on a landmine." Dennis rocked a few times in his chair. "I ain't got no landmines anymore."

"Anymore?" John was wide eyed.

"After a while they get unstable. Had to get rid of 'em."

"You had landmines?"

"Maybe."

John shook his head. "Well, what else you got?"

"Reckon I could whip us up some napalm. Bait ain't gonna be a problem. It saw you boys, and it knows you saw it. It'll be comin' for ya."

"Napalm? You can make napalm?" I asked.

"You can't?"

"I never really thought I needed napalm, or I might have looked it up."

"Napalm was what you got from that statement? I was a bit more focused on the word bait," John said.

Dennis chuckled. "It ain't too hard to make. Dump some gas in a barrel and start feedin' Styrofoam into it. When it melts enough it makes a gel. Then all ya gotta do is make some Molotovs."

"Well ain't you just a font of psychotic skills?" John muttered.

"Useful skills when a damn werewolf comes a prowlin' around."

"True enough."

I turned to Dennis. "Well, I reckon it'll be comin' back to John's then. You wanna join us while we try to kill a, not as fictional as I thought, werewolf?"

"Damn skippy! Turn your truck around, and we'll load some supplies."

I nodded and went to the truck. I pulled my cell phone from my pocket and dialed a number.

"Dan?" I asked when the phone picked up. "What kind of guns do you have? I need you to pack every weapon you got and come down to John Cole's place."

"On my way."

That's the best thing about friends like Dan. He didn't even ask why.

We made it to John's after about thirty minutes of loading boxes from Dennis's back room. Anytime I asked what they held he just grinned. We stopped in at Reba's and bought all of her Styrofoam coolers and emptied the shelf of Styrofoam dishware. John already had about half a barrel of gasoline they used for the mower and small engines.

"How long you think we got?" I looked at Dennis as we stepped from the truck.

"I doubt we have long," he said.

I nodded and put on the harness that held my Winchester. I belted the bag of ammo on my side that held the bullets for the Marlin and grabbed as many packages of Styrofoam plates as I could carry.

John went straight for the house to get his rifle and a pair of colts he had bought a couple of years earlier. They were 1911s and packed a punch.

I entered the barn and dropped the plates. There was an old metal washtub in the corner, and I grabbed it. Outside of the back door was the barrel with a hand pump. I filled the tub about half full and dragged it inside of the barn with the smell of gasoline strong in my nostrils.

Ripping open the plates, I started feeding them into the gasoline. As they melted, I spied a gallon jug of used motor oil and dumped it into the mix.

I heard a vehicle in the drive, but it didn't sound like Dan's truck. I stepped out of the barn.

"Damnit, Milly!"

Then I looked closer and saw Annie behind the wheel.

"Shit."

I met Annie as she got out of the car. "What the—"

"Zip it, fat boy."

Milly got out of the passenger side and shrugged. She reached into the back seat and pulled the first of my shotguns out of the back seat. Annie turned and pulled the Shockwave from the other side.

I sighed and looked at Milly. "You remember how to shoot that thing?"

"Damn straight I do."

I turned to Annie. "You shoulda stayed home honey."

"I'm not staying home and letting you go to war with some mythical monster. I'll be right by your side."

"Damn, I love you," I said and kissed her. "So, let's go make some napalm."

Dennis was watching with a huge grin.

"What?" I asked.

"My Mary would have done the same thing," he said.

I nodded and reached into the car for the ammo box they'd brought with them. "We're fortifying the barn."

"I thought you were going crazy when Milly showed up. You're not, are you?"

"Nope. Me and John saw that thing when it came out of the woods. We shot it over fifteen times, and it got back up. It wasn't anything like I ever saw before."

"Then you'll need all the guns you can get."

I nodded. "You're probably right, but I still wish you were in middle Tennessee."

"You want me there; pack your stuff and go with me."

"I can't leave them to face this thing."

"Neither can I."

I chuckled. "Alright. Start feeding those plates into that tub as they melt. We want it thick and sticky."

She began dropping plates into the gasoline, and I shook my head. I would prefer her out of danger, but I knew she was solid. I didn't want anyone else at my back any more than her.

I heard the rumble of Dan's truck in the drive and looked out the door waving. His old Chevy rumbled to a stop in front of the barn, and he stepped out. Dan was a big guy, over six feet and five inches tall. He was built like a football player back in the day. Now he was a little rounder than he was then.

"You plan on shootin' much, you can expect the sheriff down here," he said. "He was parked a couple miles up the road."

"The sheriff? Or one of his deputies?"

"It was the sheriff. I don't like that guy."

"I'm not too fond of him either, but I feel better knowin' he's close enough to come help when this goes down."

"So... what is this? I brought a lot of weapons."

"Remember the party the other day. The attack on the Sands?"

"Yeah, they said you and John shot at a bear."

"It wasn't a bear. Now it's gonna be comin' for us cause we saw it," I said.

"What was it?"

"Believe it or not, I think it was a werewolf."

He nodded and reached into the back of his truck. "Reckon we'll need all these then."

I looked into the bed where he flipped back the tarp. "Is that a headsman's axe?"

"Maybe. I thought you would be happier about the two AK-47s."

"Oh, I am. It just struck me funny that you have a headsman's axe."

"I bought that some time back from old man Dennis." He glanced up to see Dennis toting another box from my truck. "Hey, he's here too? Good. I bet he has a plan."

"You don't have anything to say about it bein' a werewolf?"

"Not really. My pa told me about runnin' into all sorts of things over the years." He looked back up toward my truck. "So, what's the plan?"

"We're gonna burn that thing with napalm."

"Nice!"

I enjoyed his enthusiasm, but I really wished he had shared some of those stories from his dad over the years. I might have been better prepared for what we were doing. As it was, I was barely holding it together.

I nearly jumped out of my skin when a gunshot sounded from the house. I saw Dennis on the porch waving. I looked in the direction he had shot to see a deer down in the field.

"Friggin' deer huntin' while we're all waitin' to die," I muttered.

Dennis headed across the field with a sack and started doing something with the deer.

I shook my head and walked back into the barn. The fumes from the gas were strong.

"How's this?" Annie asked as she spooned the gelled liquid up from the tub.

"Looks good. Let's put it in those jars over there."

"How are we going to light these?" Annie asked. "The fumes are too strong to light them with rags like a Molotov."

"I didn't think of that," I said.

I went to the old part of the barn where John Senior kept his various piles of junk that hadn't been hung on the walls yet and started digging. I grinned as I found the roadside emergency kit.

Then there was another shot. And another.

"Oh shit!"

I ran from the supply room as I heard a roar from the woods.

"In the loft!" I yelled to Annie and Milly. "Take what you have jarred up!"

I ran out the front of the barn to see the werewolf stalking across the field. He wasn't running like he had been before when we saw him. He was boldly walking across the field. I was surprised at how accurate some of the movies I had seen came when designing their werewolves. But then again, werewolves were real. It stood close to seven feet tall if I was gauging it right. The wolf head was large, but the snout was a lot shorter than a wolf. The long arms ended in huge hands with claws.

It looked at the deer, and I could see its humanlike shoulders move with its laughter.

Another shot rang out as John fired from the right side of the barn. I saw the wolf jerk, and he looked in our direction, cocking his head to the side. I raised the Marlin and fired. The wolf jerked harder and snarled as he looked at me.

It loped toward me covering ground way faster than I was happy with. I levered the rifle and fired again. Someone stepped up beside me and that huge rifle of Dennis's fired.

How'd he get down here so fast? I wondered.

The slug from the elephant gun slammed into the wolf and knocked him down. It landed on its backside sliding toward us.

Dennis reloaded. "Didn't have time to make many of these."

The wolf roared and thrashed for a moment before it stood back up.

"Silver nitrate in the hollow points," Dennis said and fired again.

The wolf moved to the side incredibly fast, but the bullet still hit its shoulder. I fired the Marlin again wishing I had some of the silver nitrate. It seemed to hurt worse.

It started forward again and stopped as a quart jar hit it right in the snout.

"Shit!" I cursed as the jar dropped unbroken to the ground.

The wolf looked down and grinned.

The Marlin clicked as I pulled the trigger, and I dropped it to pull the Winchester from the holster. Then automatic gunfire erupted from the left side of the barn as Dan opened up with one of the AK-47s.

The wolf knew the AK was going to be more dangerous, so it turned toward Dan. I saw the shadow as Annie threw another jar.

We used to target practice with my dad. Someone would throw an oil can into the air, and we would shoot it. Typically, we used a shotgun. I raised my rifle and shot the jar just before it hit the wolf. The jar shattered and the gel splattered across the wolf's side.

Milly saw what I did and raised the shotgun.

"Throw!" she yelled, and Annie threw another.

I left it to Milly. She was good at targets.

I shot the wolf in the face.

It howled and turned toward me again. Two more jars shattered and splattered gel. It charged forward, so I reached toward the small of my back and pulled the flare gun I had taken from the emergency kit. The flare hit it right in the chest and ignited the fumes from the napalm.

It screamed as it was engulfed in flame. Another jar flew through the air. The jar exploded as it hit the flame. Annie had removed the lid before throwing this one.

I was worried the wolf would get closer to the barn where the gas fumes from the tub would ignite, so I started walking forward levering my Winchester and firing into the thrashing form. Dan walked forward from the left and Dennis from the right. I saw John on the other side of Dennis with his pair of 1911s firing into the wolf.

It screamed again and staggered to its feet. It bolted back away from us toward the field.

As it passed the deer it stopped and grabbed its leg intending to drag it with him.

CRUMPT!

The ground erupted and the wolf was tossed backward screaming again.

"I thought you didn't have any land mines!"

"I don't!" Dennis yelled back. "I didn't say I didn't have a claymore!"

I might have giggled. But when you're in the throes of terror, a giggle or two might be alright.

The wolf was hurt bad, but he was still alive. Both legs were gone, and one arm was mangled beyond belief.

"We need to cut its head off," Dennis said.

"Dan, get your axe," I said.

Dan had a bag strapped on his back, so he slid it off his shoulder and pulled the headsman's axe from inside.

The wolf tried to claw at him, and I stepped on its only working arm. Dan swung the axe, and the head tumbled away from the body.

The body stopped thrashing.

I stepped back as hair shed from the body and a clear looking slime dropped from it. I looked toward the head where its features seemed to melt away.

"Oh shit!" John cursed.

"Is that who I think that is?" I asked.

"Looks like we need a new sheriff," Dennis said and laughed.

"Now what are we gonna do?" John asked.

"Reckon we need to get rid of the body," I said.

"I know a place," Dennis said.

"Of course, you do," John muttered.

Annie and Milly both stepped up beside me.

"Is that the Sheriff? And is that a fork?" Milly asked.

"Yep. I duct taped that silverware John brought to that claymore."

"That's it," Annie said. "I'm going home."

"I'm with her," Milly said. "Clean up your mess."

As Milly followed Annie, she stopped in front of John, "Yes I'd love to go to the movies this weekend. Thanks for asking."

John looked like he had been hit with a club.

Milly giggled and followed Annie to the car.

I chuckled and turned back to Dennis, "So this place you know? How far is it?"

"Not too far. We need his car."

"I'll get it," Dan said. "One of you give me a ride?"

"Sure," John said. He turned to me. "Reckon we need to check out Ben Daniels? Died and came back."

I was quiet for a minute. "Dennis, what do you know about vampires?"

Behind the Trailer

By Sara Brooke

Despite popular belief, I don't hate my life.

I mean, if you were to look at what I've got, you might think this girl ended up with the short stick.

Barely finished high school, parents are raging alcoholics, had to take a job at a clothing department store waiting on assholes all day—yeah, I can see why you'd think my life really sucks.

And, yes, I live in a trailer.

It's not a nice trailer either. It creaks every time you walk, and there are cockroaches living in the walls so no matter how many times I spray them; they keep coming back.

Yep. Not exactly a golden girl's existence.

So, why do I like my life?

I guess you could say, I take things as they come. Living in South Georgia isn't like New York City or anything, but it has its perks.

It is very green and natural. Life is slower here, and people are very friendly. And, while my trailer isn't a million-dollar mansion, it *is* mine. And every penny I put into this place is worth it.

At night, my favorite thing to do is to sit on the stairs outside my front door and look up, watching the sky. I like to gaze at the stars and make little wishes.

Some nights I wish for health and peace for my parents. Other nights I wish for a handsome, rich man to find me in the sweater aisle and whisk me away from the clearance racks and wire hangers. I'm not bad looking—I'm pretty thin, with wavy brown hair, straight teeth and green eyes. A pointy chin and a decent-sized chest. The guys don't come knocking regularly, but I've kissed a boy or two. Some people tell me I look average, but a bit of make-up always helps.

Anyway, back to my nightly wishes.

Wishing isn't a delusional thing. It's just what I like doing. So, don't judge. And, if I didn't like wishing so much and watching the skies, I wouldn't have seen what I did that night.

What was it? Why did it happen? I have no freaking idea. It definitely wasn't a regular evening for sure. And I won't forget it. It changed my life forever.

The day started like any other normal Monday. Dragging myself out of bed at six thirty in the morning, hitting the alarm and trying to get ready as quickly as possible.

My car is an old Dodge Charger. It is always on its last leg. And each morning, I say a little prayer before inserting the key and turning the ignition. Somehow, the Lord has seen to it that this old hunk of junk keeps running, but each morning it's kind of a crapshoot as to whether or not I will be able to get to my job on time.

On this particular morning, my car grunted loudly, then the motor roared to life, which doesn't happen very often (it's more of a sputtering type).

Once at work, the day went pretty much the way it always goes. The mornings are a bit quieter, with the older crowd shuffling through. I waited on an ancient woman who asked too many questions about green sweaters.

I mean, how many things can you ask about a fucking green sweater? Just buy one and if the color is too bright, run it through the washing machine a few times. For the love of Christ.

Then, I had a man who was buying his wife a pair of pants and wanted my advice. I found this to be oddly endearing, so half the morning was spent pulling out pairs of the ugliest, most old-fashioned pants you could possibly imagine.

He finally decided on a pair of brown pleated slacks. And it was on sale.

By lunchtime, I was tired and dug into my tuna fish sandwich with a vengeance.

No one bothered me.

I'm kind of a loner at work. Most of the other women are older than me, and they like to talk about things that don't interest me at all. Like gardening and church and their grandkids.

Don't get me wrong. I am absolutely right with the Lord. And I do go to church on Sundays to pray for myself, my parents, and anyone else who I think could use a little divine intervention.

It's just that religion isn't what I want to spend my time talking about. My interests are in nature, astrology and things that can't always be explained, like ghosts.

I've always been interested in the paranormal and UFO's. I think it's because in science, my teachers never covered things that were really cool and not entirely explainable. We had our frog dissections and learned about cells and all that. But we never learned about why sometimes we hear sounds, and nothing is there. Or why we think about a song and then you hear it on the radio. Or why some people disappear into thin air, never to be found again.

Some people might say those missing people are murdered, but what if they're not? What if they're carried away by some indescribable force? What if there is more out there than what we're able to see with our own eyes?

The women at Shopsouth where I work every day do not want to talk about these things, and whenever I try to join their discussions, it always feels like a colossal waste of time.

So, instead, I eat lunch alone, and that's just fine with me.

After lunch, I helped out a handful of other customers who were thankfully pretty easy to assist, then it was time to call it a day.

Driving home in the dark always depresses me, and winters in Georgia can give you the blues, especially if you work indoors all day.

The temperature outside was in the high forties, which is just enough to give the winds a bit of a sharp feeling, but nice enough where you can still sit outside and enjoy the smell of the fresh air.

As soon as I got back to my trailer, I turned the lights on and took off my work clothes, opting instead for a sweatshirt and a super comfortable pair of sweatpants.

I'm not the world's greatest cook, and it's just so much easier to pop a meal into the microwave for five minutes than slaving over a small stove.

So, that's exactly what I did.

The steaming macaroni and cheese dinner looked amazing, so I decided to take it out on the steps and eat while watching the sky.

One of the things I really enjoy about my neighborhood is that the trailers are pretty spaced out and each have their own nice little stretch of land. I'm not sure how I was so lucky to snag a place out here, but it's perfect for me. Even with the pesky roaches.

The brisk outside air felt refreshing against my face and in sharp contrast to the warm, cheese-scented steam floating up from my microwaved tray.

I took a bite.

Delicious.

Chewing and looking up at the sky, I felt perfectly at ease. And I had no idea that my relaxing evening was about to change.

Bodo

I heard the sound in the distance, like a moan that was half whispered, half moaned.

Putting down my fork, I looked around for anything out of place.

The nearby trailers seemed in order, but dark windows gave me the impression that no one was home. Or everyone was sleeping.

It wasn't an unusual sight as the trailer park tended to be more laid back than other rowdier spots in the area. Still, I didn't like sitting out in the dark alone when something or someone was making strange noises.

Trying to ignore the odd sound, I stabbed at some macaroni and brought it to my lips, when I heard it again.

Bodo

Bodo

BODO

The last sound made my entire body tense up. The pitch was higher, despite its mournful undertone.

"Hello?" I called out.

It Came from the Trailer Park

There were only two options that lay before me. The first, and most logical, would be to go back inside, lock the door and finish my macaroni and cheese in front of the television where the only sounds would be coming from a movie or TV show.

The other option was to figure out what was making the sound.

Sighing heavily, I put my still-warm TV dinner on the top step and then stood up carefully.

The night air was getting colder, and I could feel my ears begin to burn from the chill. So, I pulled my sweatshirt hoodie over the top of my head and descended the stairs.

"Hello?" I called out again.

What am I doing out here? There could be some crazy person howling at the sky, ready to attack me, and I'm out here putting my life at risk.

Just then, I heard a shuffling to my right.

There is another trailer near mine, and its driveway was empty that evening, indicating that my neighbors weren't home.

They were a heavyset couple that rarely did anything but drink and sleep, so that suited me just fine.

But the shuffling seemed to be coming from somewhere near their home.

"Is someone there?"

More shuffling and then . . .

Bodoooo

This time, the word was spoken softly and had more of a whispery fashion to it. As if it was trying to lure me out of my comfort zone and into its clutches.

Feeling more than a little nervous, I walked toward the trailer and looked around.

The windows were dark, and a little plastic pinwheel that rested on the ledge by the front door was spinning slowly.

I walked up to the front door and peered inside the windows.

It was difficult to see inside the trailer, but from what I could make out, everything looked normal. No strange person lurking inside.

As I turned away from the windows, I nearly peed my pants.

There was a thing standing at the foot of the stairs looking up at me.

I call it a "thing" because while it had human-like features, it definitely didn't look like any person I'd ever seen before.

The thing was extremely slender, with long, thin legs and spindly arms. Its bald head was shaped like a droplet, held up by a thin, small neck.

At first glance, the word that popped into my head was . . .

Alien

Not sure what to say, I stood as still as possible, and looked at the thing as it stood and watched me.

Feeling like a complete idiot and terrified at the same time, I decided to try something I'd always seen in the movies when a person came face-to-face with an unknown creature.

Raising my hand, I waved at the thing and waited to see what it would do.

The thing stood still for a moment longer, then turned, slowly walking to the other side of the trailer.

I watched it move, fascinated by its fluidity.

The creature walked by slowly lifting a leg that would impossibly curl up then slowly shoot back up in mid-air, then lowering to the ground a few inches away. It didn't really walk, but rather stretched out and glided forward.

When it was out of sight, I stood for a moment longer, thoughts racing through my mind.

What was that? Was it a UFO? Or something entirely different? Why did I let it get away?

"Wait! Come back!"

Willing my legs to move, I ran down the stairs and quickly crept to the side of my next-door neighbor's trailer.

The thing was gone.

Damn. Did I just imagine it? There was something there. I need to keep looking.

After inspecting the entire perimeter of my neighbors' trailer and not finding anything, I returned to my stoop and now cold macaroni and cheese.

But I wasn't hungry. My appetite had evaporated the minute I'd seen the thing standing at the bottom of the steps, with its long body and oblong head.

It's still out here.

For some reason, I knew it hadn't disappeared and was somewhere in the darkness, waiting.

So, I would wait too.

Leaning up against the front door, I closed my eyes and listened.

The cold air felt oddly pleasant against my face, and I dozed off.

My neighbors across the street have never spent the time or money to fix their front door, so I've become accustomed to the whiny screeching sound it makes every time someone goes in or out.

The telltale screeching sound woke me up, however, because it sounded more aggravated than normal.

That's because the front door had been thrown open and was now slowly returning back to its original position.

What time is it? Shit it's one o'clock already. I've been sleeping for hours!

My butt felt numb from sitting on the concrete for so long, and my back hurt from propping it up against the door.

Standing up, I stretched and moaned, feeling my bones ache.

Then, I remembered what had woken me up.

The front door to my neighbor's trailer was open.

Shit. What the hell is going on?

The lights were off inside, and I vaguely remembered that the folks living there had taken a vacation and were in Florida for the week. They were supposed to come back in a few days.

That's probably a good thing. Wonder if that creature got into their house?

Shivering, I pulled my sweatshirt down and walked toward the trailer. I considered calling the cops but realized that I'd left my cell phone in my trailer. If I went all the way back for it, I might miss what was going on.

This really isn't smart. But I kinda want to see that creature again. What if it's some kind of extra-terrestrial from another planet that got stranded here on earth? Like E.T.? Damn, I wish

I had some peanut M&M's or something like that kid had in the movie.

I was now standing in the trailer's doorway, and I could hear shuffling inside, like someone was rummaging through my neighbors' stuff.

Suddenly, a cat darted past me and into the trailer. I wasn't sure if it was my neighbor's cat or a stray, but it scared the shit out of me. It was an orange cat, and it looked scared.

"Holy fuck," I whispered under my breath, feeling my heart pounding in my chest.

The shuffling stopped for a moment, then the cat shrieked loudly—a scream that reverberated through the trailer.

The shrieking stopped as quickly as it started and was replaced by loud slurping and chewing sounds.

Terrified now, and realizing that I'd made a mistake, I backed away from the trailer.

But it was too late—the shuffling began again and this time, it came closer and closer.

My legs refused to move . . . it was as if I was frozen in the same spot.

As it drew near, I could see an outline of the thing as it glided forward.

Then, it stopped.

The darkness made it difficult, but I could make out its shape . . . the oblong head, long legs, long arms . . . it seemed almost to sway back and forth as it stared at me.

For some crazy reason, I wanted to touch it. I knew that it was foolish and that the creature had probably just eaten a damned cat—would it make me its next meal?

But I didn't care. My life had always been predictably difficult. Work and meals. Parents who drank way too much and loved too little. Old ladies at the store, a cockroach infested trailer that I tried to clean, tried to take pride in. My life was ok for me, because I allowed it to be ok. I was thankful for all the difficulties and owned each and every one.

Then it dawned on me.

What the fuck do I have to lose? Bring it on.

Just as the thought entered my mind, I reached my arm out, fingers straining to touch the creature.

At the same moment, the thing reached out for me.

And then, we connected.

Its fingers—if you could call them that, because there were only three that emerged from the glistening arm—felt cool, wet and incredibly soft.

As soon as the thing touched me, I grew hazy . . . like my mind was disconnecting from my body.

It wasn't an entirely unpleasant sensation.

I was transported back in time to a childhood memory . . .

It was right after my ninth birthday, and my mother decided to put down the bottle long enough to take me out for ice cream. This was a special occasion because my parents had already started drinking heavily, and outings were becoming a rare occurrence.

We got into her car, and she sat at the wheel for a moment, rubbing her lips with the back of her hand as if her mouth was begging for another bottle of Wild Turkey.

I waited and watched her anxiously, hoping that she wouldn't back out and force us to return to the house.

Sighing loudly, she cast a glance in my direction and declared, "Well, alright. That place ain't gonna be open all day. We'd better get rolling."

She sang all the way to the creamery, smiling and glancing down at me periodically.

"It's just us girls. That's what I like. Just us girls."

Smiling at my Ma, it was one of the first and only times I truly felt connected to her.

Suddenly, the memory was interrupted by the sound of my television.

"Now, for only $399 you can own this brand-new stovetop oven during our winter weekend sale!"

The voice of a super-hyped-up-on-diet-soda-or-worse announcer interrupted my pleasant memory.

I realized that I was somehow back in my trailer, sitting on the couch in front of the television.

Hold on. How the hell did I get here?

The lights inside were on, and my ancient digital clock on the kitchen counter registered that it was very late . . .

3:15 am

Feeling disoriented, I looked around slowly, wondering if the creature was inside my trailer somewhere.

"Hello?" I called out tentatively.

A shuffling sound from my bedroom made my blood run cold.

Shit. It's still here. Maybe it carried me back somehow. Well, if it was gonna kill me it would've done it already. But now it's somewhere in here making a mess. Hopefully it will eat some of my roaches.

Feeling like a crazy person, I giggled. Yes, it was late, and there was some ridiculous creature in my trailer. But somehow, I was feeling the humor in the situation and wondered why in the hell I'd remembered a happy time in my past when I'd connected with the strange looking thing.

Another series of sounds came from my bedroom, so I decided that it was time to face the music.

There was a knife lying on a cutting board near my small kitchen table, so I considered picking it up as I walked toward the bedroom. Then, I decided against it. Whatever this thing was, it probably wouldn't be afraid of a small knife. And part of me didn't want to scare it. Whatever was happening was incredible, and I didn't want to somehow screw it up.

"Come on out. And stop making a mess."

I was now standing in the doorway of my trashed bedroom. The thing had torn the blankets off the bed, knocked my lamp off the nightstand and was now near my vanity table.

All the lights were on in the bedroom—I'd left them on when I had come home earlier—so now, hours later, I could fully see the creature for the first time.

It was a strange sight.

Its body was entirely gray, like a large slug. It had two black holes that seemed like eyes and another black hole underneath its eyes, which I assumed was its mouth.

Those were its only facial features, the rest of it was gray and slick—the light reflecting off of its body.

The creature looked at me, and its mouth opened wider.

"Bodo!" It moaned at me.

Not sure what to say or what to do, I figured it would be best to try to communicate in the only way possible.

"Bodo."

The words sounded absolutely ridiculous coming out of my mouth. And I wasn't sure if I was threatening the creature or just saying hello. Strange times called for strange actions.

The creature looked at me then moved closer. It glided as it curled its legs forward, one at a time.

Now, it was standing very close to me and swayed as it stood there.

"Bodo?" I asked, feeling fear well up inside me.

The creature reached out and touched my arm.

As soon as it connected with my body, the world faded away, and I was transported to another memory.

I was fifteen and had been crushing on a boy in my class. His name was Dean Carlton, and he was as handsome as his name inferred. Strong cheekbones and deep brown eyes helped to make up an attractive face that I liked to stare at continuously.

By some immense luck, Dean and I were both invited to a small party. The girl having the get-together was named Celina, but that's all I can remember about her.

Dean and I were participating in a Spin the Bottle game. There were about six of us, some were drinking, and I was just hoping to not make a complete ass of myself because I was now on my second beer and felt loopy as hell.

It was Dean's turn.

He spun the bottle so fast that it turned quickly at first. And when the bottle stopped, my heart nearly stopped as well. It was pointing straight at me.

Giving me a sly smile, Dean stood up and pointed to the closet. "Let's do this the right way," he said. "I want you in the dark."

The group hooped and hollered at us, but I found that my legs had turned to jelly, and it was difficult to stand up.

"Come on, girl. Let's get it going," Dean muttered, frustrated by my ridiculousness.

I was finally able to get my legs and feet to listen to me and after a bit of wobbling, stood up. Dean then grabbed my hand

The voice cut through the cold air and resonated throughout my stiff body. Everything hurt.

I was lying flat on my back in the clearing behind my house. My arms and legs were extremely stiff, and when I opened my crusty eyes, the sunlight made me squint.

"What? What time is it?" I asked, even though the stranger who had just woken up, had told me the time.

"It's eight o'clock or shortly thereafter. Did you sleep out here all night?"

Groaning, I propped myself up on my elbows, "I must have. Thanks for waking me up. Gonna be late for work."

"No problem, honey. You take care," she gave me a look, like she felt sorry for me, then she walked away.

Standing up slowly, the memories of the prior evening flooded through my mind . . .

The creature

Floating through space

The celestial wonderment in its eyes

Was it all just a dream? Or had it really happened? If it hadn't happened, then how had I ended up in the clearing in my backyard?

Yawning, I rubbed my head and walked back to the trailer. Then, I stopped.

Sitting calmly at the top of my stoop, with its back against the door was a cat.

It was the same cat that I'd assumed had been eaten by the creature. Only now, it was sitting there—calmly staring at me—almost challenging me to say something.

"Well, well, well. Look at you. I guess you didn't become alien food after all. Do you belong to anyone?"

I knelt down to get a look at my new feline friend. A close examination revealed that it was a boy, and it had no ID tag.

Worried that it might be feral, I picked it up slowly. But it had no problem at all and acted as if it belonged to me, rubbing itself against my cheek when I looked closely at its furry face.

My boss wasn't happy about how late I arrived at work, but she forgave me after a "if you're going to be late, just call" kind of talk.

I was almost always on time, and the other women came in late regularly, so I didn't feel too bad about it.

The rest of the morning was spent helping seniors with their clothing selections. It was easy work, and everyone was relatively decent to deal with.

At lunchtime, I drove over to the Burger Stop to grab a hamburger since I'd given all of my tuna to the cat before I'd left.

I ate lunch in my car, and after I'd finished my burger and fries and sucked down half of a soda, I thought about the prior evening.

According to the voice that had spoken to me when I'd connected with the thing, I was the only human who had ever seen it. Apparently, it had been visiting Earth for a while—or did these creatures just like to come to our trailer park in Southern Georgia? Somehow, I had a difficult time believing that UFOs were only visiting my state. Maybe they had been traveling throughout the continent all along, and I was the only one who took the time to really watch the stars, and I was just in the right place at the right time.

Maybe I was special.

In truth, I was feeling kinda important. After all, it's not every day that you discover an alien—unless you believe all of those tabloid magazines in the grocery store.

And those aren't real credible, so I have to wonder if I'm the only one who has ever experienced a UFO encounter.

It had been a very long, exhausting day at work.

My cat, Bodo—I named him the day I found him—was patiently waiting for me.

The interesting thing about Bodo is that no one ever came looking for a stray cat, and he acted like he'd always lived with me in the trailer. He was a very calm animal and never displayed any of the panic that he'd shown the night he'd raced past me. The night I met the creature.

When I came home that day, he was waiting for me by the front door, his long tail curled around his little orange body.

As soon as I opened the door, he let out a loud *meow* and began winding around my legs, rubbing his head against me as he wove back and forth, almost making me trip over his long limbs.

"Bodo! Stop that." But I was smiling and scratched him under his chin as he purred happily.

We ate dinner outside that night, both of us sitting on the stoop. For some reason, I decided to have macaroni and cheese, which reminded me of our strange, fateful night.

It wasn't quite as cold as earlier in the week, but the skies were just as beautiful—stars speckling the blackness overhead.

There was more activity around me too. Lights and sounds came from the different trailers in my neighborhood.

I sat outside for a while with Bodo, and after finishing my dinner, he waited for me to put the tray down on the ground before jumping into my lap.

We stared at the stars, and instead of wishing for things—I wondered about the strange creature who reminded me of all the good things I'd experienced in life.

The surreal experience of floating amongst stars and feeling nothing but peace continued to drive me forward, because there was nothing more I wanted than to feel that way again. My day-to-day seemed so mundane now, and like a drug addict, I wanted to feel that weightlessness again.

But no matter how many times I would sit on the stoop, the creature didn't return.

And so, on this particular evening, after relaxing and sitting with Bodo, I decided to go back inside and call it an early night.

My bed felt nice and cool when I slid in between the sheets. Bodo followed me—and as was becoming customary—positioned himself on my legs for his bed.

Normally, however, he snuggled in and went straight to sleep.

This evening, however, he sat on my legs and stared up at me, his green eyes wide and unreadable.

I wondered what was going on in his little head, "What are you thinking about?" I asked him. "Are you wondering if we will ever see our slimy friend again? He was so interesting. You know, you're the only one who knows about him."

After my experience, I had considered telling my parents or friends about what had happened. But then I decided against it. Everyone would think I was crazy, and it would somehow cheapen what had occurred, making it seem like just a momentary lapse of sanity.

It wasn't worth it to me. I decided to keep my special night a secret and only shared my thoughts with Bodo when we were alone.

Bodo didn't answer my questions, but instead, did something very odd.

He reached out and put his paw on my cheek.

We laid that way for a few minutes. Me—lying on my pillow staring at the small orange cat---and Bodo, resting his paw on my cheek, staring into my eyes.

After a moment or so, Bodo pulled his paw back and curled up, closing his eyes and making a low purring sound that he emitted every night before falling asleep.

I watched him for a moment, then closed my eyes.

It was definitely a dream. Everything about it felt dream-like, even though I was doing something that was pretty normal.

I was sitting on the stoop outside my front door, looking up at the sky.

But I could tell it was a dream because everything felt hazy; the edges blurred and out of focus.

I sat still and waited, because I knew that the creature was coming to speak with me. It was a certainty that flooded my thoughts—an absolute that felt as natural as my regular act of sitting on the stoop.

"It is time," the creature said as it approached and stood at the base of the stoop.

It looked the same as the last time I'd seen it, gray and slimy—with three holes in its face. Only now, I could fully understand the words that were formed by the third hole.

"What do you mean?" I asked, wondering if it would finally take me away to the Bodo place, where I could float for eternity.

"You know what time it is. It is time for you to really live. To have faith in what will be."

I shook my head, "You know what I've lived. It's a decent life. You've seen all the good memories I've had."

The creature looked up at the sky, its skin glistening as the moonlight reflected off its wet surface.

"Yes, I have reminded you of the good times in your life. And that is because I know that the best memories of your life are still ahead of you, planet dweller."

The best memories of your life are still ahead of you

The words made my heart soar and fill with happiness. Because I realized that the creature had not only seen the beautiful memories of my past . . . it could also see my future and all of its promise.

It was the one thing I had never considered—the jewels of future memories.

"Now, release the chains that bind you and make your new memories. We will always watch you. We will always be with you. It is time."

The dream began to fade, and I was becoming aware of waking up. But this time, I wasn't full of regret having to say goodbye to the creature—I was ready for what lay ahead.

When I woke up, Bodo was gone. I searched everywhere for him.

He disappeared that night, and although I miss his sweet furry face, I have an innate feeling that he is doing just fine.

What was it? Why did it happen? I have no freaking idea. It definitely wasn't a regular evening for sure. And I won't ever forget it. It changed my life forever.

For starters, I live in a trailer, but not for much longer. Because after Bodo disappeared, and I realized it was time to start making memories, I enrolled in Junior College and got my AA Degree. While at school, I met a really nice guy named Glenn in my Economics class. He asked me out on a date, and the rest is history. The best part is that he treats me like a princess, always taking me out on dates and buying me nice things to show me how much he cares.

Frankly, it's his personality that I like best. He's funny and smart, and all the things that I value in a person.

The crazy thing is that we had been dating for six months when I realized that Glenn is the son of the local oil tycoon in town. Rich, handsome and nice? I think I'm very lucky, though Glenn always says *he* is the lucky one.

I got a job at a local business as a marketing specialist and even though I am still working on my bachelor's degree, the job is great, and I make decent money. And I thoroughly enjoyed turning in my resignation at Shopsouth. Don't miss that place at all.

When Glenn asked me to marry him, I had to think about it. I wondered what the creature would say. Was this one of the wonderful memories I'd make in my future? Would I wake up one day and see my orange cat, Bodo standing in the yard?

I guess the only way to know all of that . . . is to live it.

And that's exactly what I intend to do.

Sitting on the stoop outside of my trailer for the last time, bags packed inside and everything ready to go, I looked up at the stars and realized that I've got nothing to wish for.

"I guess it's time to make some memories, isn't it?"

I wasn't expecting a response. In fact, after my dream months and months ago, it had been as quiet as could be.

But on this last night, from somewhere behind the trailer, I could hear it.

Bodo . . . Bodo . . .

THE END

Made in the USA
Middletown, DE
02 February 2023

23773467R00347